To Elaine —
with great
affection —

A Novel

DENIAL

BONNIE COMFORT

SIMON & SCHUSTER
New York • London • Toronto • Sydney • Tokyo • Singapore

SIMON & SCHUSTER
Rockefeller Center
1230 Avenue of the Americas
New York, NY 10020

This book is a work of fiction. Names, characters, places, and incidents either are products of the author's imagination or are used fictitiously. Any resemblance to actual events or locales or persons, living or dead, is entirely coincidental.

Designed by Carla Weise/Levavi & Levavi
Manufactured in the United States of America

1 3 5 7 9 10 8 6 4 2

Library of Congress Cataloging-in-Publication Data is available.

ISBN 0-671-89696-2

I once was lost, but now am found,
Was blind, but now I see.

"Amazing Grace"
John Newton, 1779

PROLOGUE

In the Los Angeles Superior Courthouse, at two minutes past twelve, I forced my way through a jostling, chattering throng of onlookers and rushed to the bathroom, having postponed this necessity throughout the morning's testimony.

Nick was finally on the stand. My accuser.

Grateful that the women ahead of me stepped aside, I took the next available stall, locked myself in, and sat down for a few moments of respite. Everything I had worked so hard for—my psychology practice, my good name, my financial security and independence—was being dashed like a trailer home in a hurricane.

I leaned over and cradled my face in my hands, bitter tears stinging my eyes. What was this if not a public hanging? Outside my stall the line of women spectators who had been too mesmerized to leave my trial until the lunch break stretched around the corner and into the hallway.

I wiped my face with a big wad of tissue and watched a black ant drag a crumb across the marble tile floor. Just focus on getting through one day at a time, I told myself. The cubicle next to me changed occupants and I shifted around reluctantly to flush the toilet. As I pulled up my pantyhose, a manicured hand holding a microphone appeared under my stall wall, and the voice on the other side said quickly, "Dr. Rinsley, your patient looked very convincing on the stand this morning. How do you plan to defend yourself against these serious charges?"

Livid, I stooped down, grabbed the microphone away from the hand, and yelled "Can't you people leave me alone for one minute??!!" The woman bolted out of her stall, pounded on my door and demanded her microphone back. I dropped it in the toilet, flushed, straightened my clothes, and opened the door to say "It's in the sewer system where it belongs." Calling me a bitch, she shoved past me still thinking she could rescue her lost equipment. I already knew tomorrow's headlines would read "Radio Psychologist Accosts Reporter."

The group of stunned-silent women parted to let me pass and I hurried out to the hallway. Underbruck, my lawyer, stood in the midst of the milling crowd, fending off reporters from *Real Life* and *Street Brawls*. Behind him, a man from the American Society of Mental Patients waved a placard in front of the network news-cams proclaiming "Shrinks Are the Sick Ones." Nearby, a religious group held up a banner, "Sever the wicked from among the just. Matthew 13:49."

Underbruck muscled his way to me, seized my arm, and steered me into a private conference room where he left me to bring back some coffee. Trembling, I rummaged through my purse for lipstick and a mirror. Just keep calm, I told myself. Those people out there don't know what really happened.

My mother, staying with me to offer "moral support" during the trial, didn't help. "This'll blow over, dear," she kept saying. "You can find another line of work. Teaching. That's a nice, solid job. You could go back to school later and get your credential."

How had it come to this? I had been so proud of my professional skills, so confident and cool under fire, and now I could barely keep from screaming. I cared about my patients, and had been conscientious in my work, convinced I could never have the kind of treatment disasters that happened to other therapists.

I was wrong. My analyst tells me this kind of disaster can happen to any therapist, even the best of us. She says, "One particular patient can creep into your mind, find a soft spot you've hidden even from yourself, and lean on that spot until it drives you mad."

She is right. Nick nearly pushed me to the brink, and now I need to go back and sift through the details of what happened to make sense out of it.

Part I

My first appointment with Nick was on a Friday night at six o'clock. Before his arrival, I turned my inner office lights down to half power so the room would seem restful, as much for me as my new patient. It was the end of a ten-hour day.

I unlatched and left open the French windows for a few minutes, to let some cool air waft through. The sounds of Westwood gearing up for date night drifted in—the horn-honking and idling of car engines, the occasional blare of a radio, the excited shouts of UCLA students moving by. It was March, and although it had been eighty-one degrees in Los Angeles that afternoon, the sun had already set and it was growing dark.

In my private bathroom I bent over and brushed my honey-blond hair forward to give it more volume. I reapplied eyeshadow to emphasize the green in my eyes, livened my cheeks with a little more blusher, and tried to reposition my pink silk blouse so that the grease spot from lunch wouldn't show. I was only thirty-three, but the stress of working so many hours was taking its toll.

I had been up until one o'clock the previous night completing dictation, afraid of falling behind in this tedious task because I administered at least five psychological test batteries a week, and my long reports would be impossible to complete if more piled up.

Nick finally arrived fifteen minutes late. When I opened the waiting room door, he was standing in the middle of the room, holding a coffee cup and a sandwich bag, and studying the large oil painting on my wall.

He was impeccably dressed in an expensive navy suit, white shirt, and polka-dot tie. His thick black hair was perfectly cut so that it tapered gently at the neck. And even standing absolutely still, he looked lithe and graceful.

"Let me guess," he said, turning to me. "You don't like realism because it leaves too little to the imagination. You buy original abstracts, which you pay too much for. Pastels for the office, bolder colors at home. And you like tension and motion between the figures because you think that symbolizes human relationships."

He was sarcastic in his observations, but I was surprised by their accuracy. "Do you always jump to conclusions about people prior to meeting them?"

He grinned, exuding the confidence of a man accustomed to attracting women. "I do my best. That's my job. I'm sure you've already formed an opinion about me."

Right again. Morry Helman was the internist who had referred Nick. "I've got a tough one," Morry had warned. "A thirty-five-year-old single attorney who collapsed in court from a bleeding ulcer. Chronic headaches, stomach problems, trouble sleeping. He claims his life is going well, but all his symptoms are stress-related, so I told him to call you." I had already concluded Nick wouldn't stay in psychotherapy more than three weeks.

Once in my office, Nick sat down in what was obviously my chair. "Mr. Arnholt," I said pleasantly, "please take any other seat you'd like."

Clutching his paper bag, he resettled into the chair facing mine. Through his smallest movements—a slight swagger, a vague smirk on his lips—I felt he was mocking me. "Hope you don't mind if I eat," he said. He blew on his coffee to cool it.

"Feel free." Although I disapproved of patients eating during sessions, at that moment I wished I could munch on something too. I was hungry, and the likelihood of him being a suitable candidate for psychotherapy was slim. "What brings you here?" I asked.

His even features crinkled into a defiant little smile. "Curiosity. I wanted to see who Morry admired so much. And I've heard you on the radio."

I thought Nick's elaborately casual manner masked anxiety. "That's all? There aren't any concerns or problems that also bring you here?"

No longer looking amused, he brushed a speck of lint off his spotless pants. "I'm not much interested in therapy. I'm a maverick. I like to do things my own way. Just like you."

"Why is that like me?"

"Hey, relax, Doc. Just a joke. You have your little routines and you like your patients to follow them. I understand."

"And a maverick doesn't like having to follow someone else's routines?"

"Right."

I wondered whether he knew the term maverick also meant motherless calf. "Have you found your own way of doing things effective?"

"Pretty much." He opened his bag, pulled out a chocolate chip cookie, and peeled off the plastic wrap. After pausing to examine it, he took a bite, chewed quietly, and swallowed before he resumed talking. "I managed to bend a lot of rules in the Army. And even though I quit some heavy-duty law firms, I've got a great position now."

"So you don't like being a good boy?"

"Exactly right." He smiled.

"Is seeing me being a good boy?"

"Yes—and discussing my feelings," he said, finishing off his cookie. He folded the bag into a neat square and stuffed it into his empty coffee cup. His nails were immaculate, and his fingers evenly shaped. "The peculiar thing is I really don't feel much of anything."

In response to my direct questions, he briefly summed up his current life. He was putting in over eighty hours a week at McCutcheon and Oberdorf, a prestigious law firm in downtown Los Angeles. He jogged five miles a day, smoked marijuana in the evenings, and sometimes snorted cocaine between mouthfuls of gin on the weekends. He was a veteran, but he hadn't seen combat, and the benefits had helped put him through law school. His main problems, he said, were his physical health and women. The ulcer was under better control with medication, but sometimes an attack of diarrhea forced him to leave court and rush to the bathroom, which was very embarrassing. He had trouble sleeping without marijuana, and in the middle of the night he often woke up with his heart pounding. He'd never had an exclusive love relationship longer than three months.

"Have you ever been so down you thought about killing yourself?" This was one of the standard questions I had to work in during any first interview.

"No. But sometimes I hit a hundred and twenty on the coast highway in my Ferrari. It's like that first snort of coke—"

Death-defying behavior. A way of counteracting inner deadness. "Have you ever made a suicide attempt?"

"No," he replied. "Suicide is for cowards."

My screening questions revealed no signs of psychosis, violent acting-out, or acute emotional distress. I returned to his "presenting complaint," the conscious problem that brings the patient into the office. "Tell me about your relationships with women."

"I get tired of women quickly. They always want me to tell them how I'm feeling." He paused to read my framed degrees on the wall. "Sex with a new woman is the only thing that makes me feel, but even that doesn't last. I can usually seduce a woman within two to four dates. Sometimes I hold back until she thinks she's too fat or I'm in love with someone else, then I stumble over my words when I tell her I'm falling in love with her so she believes the feelings are real."

What a manipulative son of a bitch, I thought.

He paused and flashed a charming smile with a hint of amusement. "I love to be in the catcher's mitt."

It took me a moment to realize he was referring to oral sex. I smiled politely and said nothing, but I already knew why women would toss him the ball. His face was tanned and angular. His eyes were a startling blue, translucent as stained glass. And he had that disregard for rules that some women find so enticing in a man.

"After a while, the sex gets dull, like everything else," he finished. "I just split up with my latest. She wanted to discuss everything ad nauseam. It wasn't enough to argue: she wanted an eight-hour rehash of every line."

He fell silent for a minute and looked around the room. "Your office is so neat and orderly. I bet you keep your house and your car and your clothes like that too."

The image of my dresser drawers flitted through my mind, the bras and panties carefully lined up, and my good sweaters wrapped in tissue paper. "You're very observant," I said. "I do pay attention to details. Perhaps you think our relationship would be like the one with your last girlfriend. I would want you to discuss every detail of your feelings ad nauseam."

"Of course you would. That's what shrinks do."

"Are there other things in your life that bother you?"

"I have nightmares. And I get headaches."

"Perhaps you are more tense than you realize."

"I guess."

It sounded to me like he might have a personality disorder—a pathological exaggeration of normal personality traits—but it was too soon to make a diagnosis. At this point I only knew he was denying anxiety, which was expressing itself physically, and he had no contact with his own depression, which was causing self-destructive behavior. His arrogant manner was the tip-off of a possible personality disorder, but I needed more time with him to explore that. Some people just act that way when they feel threatened. For others, arrogance is a lifestyle.

"Do you think therapy can help me?" he asked. He looked serious, but before I had a chance to respond, his unguarded look was replaced by a sneer. "What am I saying? You think therapy's the solution to everything."

I suppressed a retort and instead suggested a three-session evaluation, which would give us both a chance to test the water and back out if we wanted. "If you have any dreams you remember during this time, please write them down so we can discuss them," I said.

I explained my policy of being paid at each session and had him complete my intake forms. "One more thing," I added. "In the future I'd prefer you not bring food to our sessions. I didn't want to deprive you today, but in general I find it distracting."

He stood too close to me as he gave me his check, staring down at me like a dominant wolf.

After he left, I dusted off the fronds of the palm tree, sprayed and wiped the beveled glass windows, and cleaned the coffee table. When I realized this restless activity was an attempt to restore my inner peace, I put the glass cleaner on my desk and sat down.

What was it about him? His restrained sexual energy? His intrusive guesses about me? Whatever it is, I'll handle it, I decided. I've had plenty of haughty, self-centered patients before.

I got up again, sprayed the top of my gray Formica desk, and rubbed it until it shone.

2

That evening, my last stop on the way home was an in-patient ward at Westwood Hospital where I was treating an anorexic teenager. Before beginning my session with her, I spent a few minutes gossiping with Linda Morrison, the head nurse. We had become personal friends over the last year, and we agreed to get together for dinner soon.

I worked with the teenager for forty-five minutes. Just as we finished up, a loud battle of shouting and scuffling disturbed us, and I stepped out of the room to investigate.

At the end of the hallway, a group of patients was huddled around two orderlies, wrestling on the floor with a huge, gangly teenager. They had his arms mashed to the floor over his head, while he tried to kick and buck them off. "Fuck you!" he bellowed.

Linda was in the midst of the crowd, calling security on a mobile phone. I walked quickly over to her to ask what had happened.

"He's got a scissors and he's threatened to stab his roommate in the eye if we don't let him go home. We're going to put him in four-point restraints and medicate him as soon as security gets here."

"Have you called Glazer?" Glazer was the boy's psychiatrist, and from the history of this patient he had presented at staff meeting, I knew the boy was frightened.

"I've paged him three times already."

I had tremendous respect for psychiatric nurses, who are usually the backbone of any in-patient unit, but Linda had witnessed a patient attacking another nurse two months earlier, and she was still feeling intimidated. I said, "Let's see if we can defuse the situation ourselves. Help me get everyone else away from here."

Linda nodded, stepped into the midst of the patients, and said loudly, "Okay! Show's over! Everybody back to your rooms! Now!"

I backed her up with "TV room, your bedroom, just leave us alone here, please!"

The patients reluctantly shuffled off, turning to watch as they dispersed. Then I moved closer to the struggling men and said, "Let him up."

One orderly grunted, "Bad idea, Doctor!"

"Let him up," I said firmly.

Two burly security guards burst through the door at that moment and rushed over. I was relieved to see them, but I said, "I want to talk to this boy before you restrain him." I was convinced that strong-arm tactics usually escalated these situations unnecessarily.

The orderlies let go of the boy and rose slowly, leaving him on the floor, red-faced and frothy at the mouth, the scissors clutched in his right hand.

Without moving any closer, I said to the kid, "I'm Dr. Rinsley and I want to find out what's going on. Are you willing to talk to me calmly in a private room?"

He glared at me and stood up. He was at least six foot four and very stocky, and the security guys moved in closer.

I held out my hand. "Give me the scissors."

He shook his head.

"You're scaring people with the scissors. You'll never get what you want like that here. Let me have it." I continued holding out my hand.

After an agonizing moment of my staring at him hard, my arm beginning to ache from being held out, images of a punctured palm making me sweat, he raised his hand and dropped the scissors in mine. I turned and handed it to Linda, who accepted it with an open look of admiration.

Then she and I sat down in a private conference room with the boy and listened briefly to his story. His roommate was trying to poison him, he said. His orange juice tasted funny, and there was ground glass mixed in with the ice. He had to get home and lock himself in his attic where he knew he'd be safe.

Linda said, "You can sleep tonight in a separate room, and I'll have your food tray brought directly to the room in the morning."

The boy hung his head and started to cry. "I hate this place. Locked up with a bunch of crazy people."

"Do you understand that you scare them too?" I asked.

"But I just want them to leave me alone," he said, crying.

I said, "The best way to make sure they leave you alone is to leave them alone. When we reach Dr. Glazer, we'll ask him to prescribe some medicine for you tonight to help you sleep, and in the morning you need to talk all of this over with him."

"Okay," he sniffed, calming some. "And they won't pin me down?"

Linda said, "As long as you don't try to attack anybody, we won't pin you down. As soon as you start acting out we'll have to restrain you for your own protection and to protect others. You understand?"

He nodded, and I rose to go, my legs still shaky from the confrontation. As I opened the door, he said, "Thanks, Doctor. Thanks a lot." I closed the door, made some notes in my patient's chart, and said good-bye to her before I left.

On the way home, I called Morry Helman on my car phone. He was a fine physician, one of the few who understood physical symptoms as a signal of emotional distress, and I wanted to let him know Nick had shown up.

"I'll do my best with Nick if he continues to come," I said. "And thanks for thinking of me."

"You know I think about you a lot." The year before last I had broken off a brief romance with Morry.

"How about lunch?" Although I had never grown to love him, I respected his work and appreciated his referrals.

"Paradise restaurant, Wednesday after next, one o'clock?"

I pulled up to a traffic light and checked my book. "Perfect. See you then."

I arrived home relieved that the day was over. The temperature had dropped considerably, and a brisk, cold wind whipped through the sycamores. My little one-story house in Brentwood looked particularly inviting with the spectacular pink and red roses stark against the white siding. Working as hard as I did to make the payments was worth it.

Inside, I dumped my mail on the hall table and romped with my basset hound, Frank, before changing into my shorts and riding the stationary bike for half an hour. Then feeling revived, I fed him, ate a bowl of vegetable soup, made myself a cup of peppermint tea, and punched playback on my answering machine.

My service had left four messages: a psychiatrist was requesting a test battery, the KPXQ station manager wanted to know if I could stay for a meeting after my show next Tuesday, my three o'clock Monday had canceled, and one of my depressed patients said it was urgent.

The last message after those was from Valerie Meldon, another psychologist in private practice who had been my dearest friend since graduate school: "Hi. I need your advice. Call me tonight, I don't care how late. Love you, 'bye."

I smiled. Through long relationships with boyfriends, and stints of single time like the present, we were there for each other, thinking through professional dilemmas, gossiping, confessing fears and hurts, and cheering each other on. A thousand times a day I had to choose my words carefully and measure my behavior. It was always a relief to let down my hair with Val and say whatever I felt.

While I scratched Frank's belly, I talked at length with my depressed patient first. Whenever I concentrated on my patients, any fatigue I felt evaporated. I loved to find exactly the right words to illuminate the problem, I was fascinated by the complexity of the human mind, and, truth be known, I loved being so important to people.

Afterward, I called Val. She said, "You know what I ate today? Two

Oreo cookies and half a bag of popcorn. And tonight I didn't even have the energy to order in. I had a Diet Coke and a package of turkey salami."

"Hey—you've got the four food groups—fat, sugar, preservatives, and artificial sweeteners. I splattered Thai dressing on my blouse today at a horrible buffet."

"Listen, I need your advice. I've been seeing this couple together to work on marital problems. Then the husband asked if I would see each of them alone a few times, since they have so much trouble expressing themselves in front of each other."

"Uh-oh."

"Uh-oh is right. Can you guess? He got me alone and told me he's been having an affair for the last two years, but he doesn't want me to say anything to the wife."

"You didn't lay the information ground rules before you saw them individually?"

"I only thought of it later. Do you think I'll ever forget to do that again?"

"Not likely."

"So what do I do?"

"You can't tell her. All you can do is focus on the problems in the marriage, which is probably the reason for the affair in the first place. But you should see him alone again and tell him as long as he's siphoning off his feelings into an affair, his marital problems will never be resolved."

"Okay, thanks, that's good." Val paused for a moment. "You know, Sare, half the time when I'm doing therapy I feel like I'm just making it up as I go."

"You're a solid therapist, Val. I know. I've seen you work. So stop beating yourself up."

"Okay, okay. Now to more important topics. I have a meeting with a neurologist tomorrow and I think he's really attractive. Should I wear my navy suit with the pink shell or a long flowy thing with a tailored jacket?"

"Definitely the suit. And leave your hair down. And what do you know about him?"

"Married."

"Shit." Val seemed to have a talent for finding unavailable men she was crazy about. "What happened with that computer guy?"

"Too young. And I've got a story about too young, but first tell me if you've heard from Pallen."

"Twice. And both times it turned into one of those marathon discussions about why things would be different now." I had dated Pallen for eight months before I found out he was cheating on me. "The annoying thing is I miss him. Do you think I should see him once in a while?"

"No. He wants to cozy up to you again as if nothing happened and you'll get sucked in."

"You're right. You're absolutely right. What's your story about young?"

"I've got this patient—a forty-eight-year-old actress passing as thirty-five, who's dating a guy of twenty-three. He doesn't know it, but she's already gone through menopause. So every morning she takes her estrogen and he thinks it's her birth control pill. Last month he told her he wanted to marry her and have a baby, so she asked her gynecologist if they could do in vitro fertilization with a donor egg and not tell the guy. He refused, so she's been calling places in Mexico and France. Then last weekend, her guy invited a bunch of buddies over for a pool party, and by some bizarre coincidence, one of the guys was the stepson of her second husband."

"Oh my God. What happened?"

"Instantly over. Lover boy moved out the same day, and she's scheduled for a face peel next week."

"Oh, Val, that's so sad. Are we going to end up like that? Promise me if I'm still shopping in the Juniors department at the age of fifty you'll tell me to stop."

"Ha! When you get to fifty you'll probably still look good in skimpy clothes, and I'll be trying to convince everyone that large is lovely and dinner at six is chic."

We laughed and said good night.

In the bathroom, I lit a few votive candles, filled the tub with hot water, and eased into it, with a glass of ice water set in one corner. Frank lay down on the bathmat next to the tub and dozed off, occasionally making high-pitched whimpers in his sleep.

The heat of the water melted the tension in my body, and I relaxed completely while I mulled over my personal life. Morry had been kind and reliable, but his affection was cloying, like my mother's. Pallen had been captivating with his quirky sense of humor and athletic build, but my trust in him had been too badly damaged.

I still missed the laughs and the sex with Pallen, but after my father's behavior, infidelity was a sore point with me. Eventually someone will come along, I thought. As I watched the drops of condensation wiggle down the side of the glass, I let go of all thoughts. My body felt heavy and warm when I drained the tub and stepped out.

I shut all the lights, took a box of brown sugar to bed, and watched TV while I ate little clumps of sugar with a spoon. Tomorrow was Saturday, the day for hospital rounds and test batteries too long to squeeze in during the week.

3

Nick arrived promptly for his second session, wearing a gray suit and a beautiful blue silk tie. "I was out of court by two," he said grinning, "so I ate lunch before coming here." He sat down in the chair opposite me, spread his knees so his crotch jutted out, and gazed steadily at me. "Shoot," he said.

"Tell me about your family," I replied.

He was an only child, born and raised in Inglewood, California, where family talk was dampened by the whine of planes from the airport. His mother committed suicide when Nick was three, and he understood little about the reason. His father was an auto mechanic: a stern, demanding tyrant who lapsed into petulance when he wanted attention.

Shortly after his first wife's death, Nicholas Senior married Candy, a nightclub hostess with shiny black hair, a quick temper, and a closet full of sling-back high heels.

"My father was crazy about Candy, and insanely jealous. Sometimes he'd show up unannounced at the club to spy on her, and if he found her having a drink with a customer he'd beat her up in front of everybody."

"How did she treat you?"

"She was okay. I hated her because she tried to take my mother's place. She'd buy me stuff and bake for me, but I wanted my mother back."

"And their marriage?"

"Awful. She tried to please him and it was never good enough. She drank, and they fought over that. Their worst fights were over her wanting to have a child with him. She begged him. She threw dishes at him. And whenever she was mean to me, I was sure it was because I wasn't hers. She disappeared for good when I was ten."

"You never saw her after she left?"

"No. I'm sure she thought my father would kill her."

"What is your relationship with your father like now?"

"He's gone. Had a heart attack four years ago."

There were a few relatives on his father's side back in Ohio, but Nick had never kept in contact with them. He was strikingly alone, and I felt sad for him because his lack of trust prevented him from drawing new people close to him.

"I don't see what good this is doing me," he said. "So now you know about my childhood. So what."

I steeled myself. He would come to therapy and fight me every step of the way, and I would have to understand the fear behind each ploy and address it directly. "Perhaps you wish to separate yourself from the past because it holds painful memories?"

He cocked his head to one side. "Maybe. So how old are you? Twenty-eight? Thirty?"

Patients are justifiably concerned with whether their therapist is competent. I thought the issue of age was Nick's way of communicating this, and the subject had to be discussed directly. "I'll be happy to tell you my age, but first let's explore what it means to you," I replied.

"Hey—you talk a great game on the radio, but I'd like to know just how much experience you have at real therapy." He retrieved a small bottle of antacid from his briefcase and took a swig.

"Perhaps you're afraid I won't be able to help you."

"You look—well, why don't you give me a rundown on your credentials?" He returned the bottle to his briefcase.

"My guess is that you've already researched my credentials."

He shot me another full-voltage smile. "Born and raised in Bandon, Oregon, graduated from UCLA, youngest training analyst at the Southern California Institute, Associate Professor at NPI, co-author of two books and a bunch of journal articles."

He had done more than study my credentials. "You started to say something about the way I look?"

He hesitated. "You've got great legs and a nice face, but you look like you need a good fuck. If I can be so bold."

I was used to patients occasionally being rude or raising their voices to me, but this was unusually provocative. "Perhaps you feel one down in this situation and you'd like to even the score."

His face lost some of its defiance. "I hate airing my dirty laundry. Especially to a woman."

"Why is it worse with a woman?"

"Once you give up control to a woman, you're fucked."

"So it's either you or me? Either I need a good fuck or else you're fucked?"

He laughed, then immediately grew serious. The muscles of his jaw bunched as he clenched his teeth. "Actually, now that I think about it, I would trust a man even less."

"Perhaps you can demote a woman in your mind more easily than you can a man. Then if she knows your secrets it doesn't matter so much because she's only a woman."

He raised his eyebrows and looked at me. "You're pretty sharp, aren't you?"

I smiled benignly. "Any dreams you remember since last week?"

"Two. I wrote them down." He pulled a neatly folded piece of paper from his pants pocket. "I'm in an armored tank on some street in the Middle East. I'm hot and sweaty and feel like I'm suffocating. Then some American men and women yell at me to let them in, they'll help me, but I don't know if it's a trick or not. They're banging on the hatch, I'm terrified, and I wake up." He looked up from his paper for a moment, and then resumed.

"In the next dream, I'm in the park overlooking Santa Monica Bay, and a man in a gray three-piece suit walks up to me and offers me food out of a paper bag. I'm hungry but I don't know if I should reach into the bag. I look down and see the man is wearing pink high-heeled shoes. That's all."

"What comes to your mind?"

He looked puzzled.

"Tell me everything the images in the dream make you think of—memories, ideas, people—anything at all."

He shook his head, but after a pause, began. "People have always been at war with each other. Armored tanks are my favorite fighting weapon—they're really well protected and you can move in them. And I often dream of being in small enclosed spaces, hot and scared."

"How about the feeling that the help offered might be a trick?"

"People lie all the time to get what they want. Sometimes women have the best tricks of all."

"What thoughts do you associate with the second dream?"

"The only thing I can think of is that old C & R Clothiers TV ad. It shows a guy looking ragged and sweaty in his tennis clothes and then they play the song 'What a Difference a Day Makes,' and they show the same guy in this great three-piece, looking groomed and perfect."

I knew I'd been wearing pink high-heeled shoes the previous week when I saw Nick, but only his unconscious had remembered. I said, "The first dream suggests you feel life's a war. You've protected yourself by building a kind of psychological armored truck around yourself to survive. Now you're frightened and alone and suffocating inside this armor, but you still feel you need it. And women are no more trustworthy than men, maybe even more dangerous.

"The second dream may be about your dilemma over whether to begin therapy. I think I'm the man in the park with the bag lunch."

"But it was a man!"

"A trickster man, a man who's really a woman disguising herself as a man, or a man disguising himself as a woman. He/she offers you food in a container, the way I offer you something only in a contained time and place. Perhaps you anticipate it will be so little you need to bring your own food to eat with me, as you did last week.

"And the three-piece suit and the song 'What a Difference a Day Makes' may express your hope about therapy—that in just one day of meeting me, your life might change, and if so, what a difference a day made."

He considered this in silence a few minutes before responding. "Maybe it was about you. But aren't you being awfully presumptuous about yourself?"

"I don't mean the dream is about me personally; I think it represents your hope to have a different life."

"Yes," he said, and for the first time there was a hint of sadness in his eyes. "I would like a different life."

After he left, I wanted to make a few quick notes in his chart, but became sidetracked when I couldn't find my Mont Blanc pen. I cared about it because it was a gift from Pallen, and I hunted unsuccessfully for it until the Romaine sisters arrived.

When they were two, May and Joy's father had been killed in military action, and Mrs. Romaine had never recovered from the loss. She made her identical daughters her entire world and often painted on them a heart-shaped beauty mark near the left eyebrow to symbolize their devotion to each other. She insisted both girls play Mary in the school Christmas pageant.

As they grew older, Mrs. Romaine frightened May and Joy with stories of treacherous and unfaithful men. Her obsession was abandonment. "You have each other," she would say. "Don't squander your gift."

The one thing Mrs. Romaine hadn't considered was the possibility her baby daughters would grow to hate each other. May and Joy had tried to kill each other on several occasions. Of course neither of them ever succeeded, because each always knew exactly what the other was thinking.

By the age of forty-two, the girls were still living with Mrs. Romaine in their big house in Hollywood. She died of a sudden brain hemorrhage that year, and they found a hundred thousand dollars in a cash box under her bed, but each bill was torn in half, and there was an accompanying note: "My darlings May and Joy: Never forget that your riches lie in your togetherness. All my love, Mother." It took them months to sort and tape together all the bills so they could deposit the money in their joint bank account.

The twins arrived at my office on this particular day wearing loose, faded housecoats, oxford shoes, and sagging stockings. They carried square black purses, wore no makeup, and kept their hair in place with large, lavender hairnets.

The most remarkable thing about them was their speech. May and Joy spit their words out like they'd just been asked to chew on shit. And they couldn't get it out fast enough.

"You-bitch. I-know-you-were-talking-to-that-man-on-the-phone-while-I-was-washing-clothes! Just-what-the-hell-are-you-*doing*-May-are-you-trying-to-*kill*-me-again? You-cunt!"

"So-what-if-I-was-talking-to-him-So-*what!* Can't-you-*mind*-your-own-fucking-business-for-two-minutes?!"

Somehow, one day, May had noticed another human being. A man. It had upset the balance, and now Joy was terrified, and May was sneaking around like an escaped convict.

"I want to talk to you about a new plan," I said. I'd been treating them together for six months. "Starting next week, I'd like to divide the therapy sessions into three fifteen-minute segments, and spend fifteen minutes with each of you alone, and the last fifteen minutes together."

May-and-Joy panicked. They spit their words at me for a half hour, calling me a "scheming-bitch." "Don't-you-know-we-can't-be-separated? We-have-nothing-to-say-that-the-other-one-doesn't-know-so-what's-the-point? Do-you-just-want-to-torment-us-like-the-others?"

I let them go on.

"Five-minutes-is-all," they said. "Five-minutes-is-all," echoed again from each of them. I smiled. I was winning the battle.

The hairnetted sisters shuffled out of my office and I punched the air in victory. In the sea of insanity, even a tiny move toward shore is a triumph.

That evening as I walked down the street to keep a dinner date, I saw Nick browsing in the video store near my office. When he caught sight of me, he waved, and I waved back, wondering what kind of movies he would rent.

I hurried on to meet Kevin Utley, chief psychologist of a Santa Monica clinic, who wanted my help in setting up an eating disorders program. He was married, serious and conscientious, and we often consulted each other on difficult cases.

Over sourdough bread and wine, I said, "You've got to invest in video equipment. I can't tell you how valuable it is in breaking down a patient's distorted body image."

He was worried about his budget, and how much a video room would cost.

I said, "Something about a girl seeing herself on videotape is different from seeing herself in the mirror. You know how we all have a certain way of looking at ourselves in the mirror? A certain expression we assume and certain angles we always choose? The videotape breaks that relationship with the mirror. And these girls are shocked when they actually see themselves as we do."

We talked through salad and pasta and several cups of cappuccino, and I didn't get home until ten. As I put the key in the door I heard Frank sniffing at the seam, and the moment I opened the door he hurled himself at me. I dropped to the floor and wrestled with him, scratching his belly and grabbing at his ears.

"Poor starving baby!"

"Brooo!" he insisted, scrambling away from me and running to the kitchen. Even though he always had dry kibble available, canned food was his favorite, and he shuffled his feet restlessly, making his toenails click on the linoleum until I placed the Steak'n'Cheese in front of him. Food was of the utmost importance to Frank.

Before I took off my business clothes, I examined myself in the full-length mirror. Did I look like I needed a good fuck? I hadn't dated anyone regularly in the four months since Pallen and I had split up, but I certainly didn't think it was written all over me.

Maybe it was my outfit? I tried putting the collar of my blouse up so the points in the front stuck forward. Maybe the pleats in the skirt made me look prissy? I turned sideways to see it from that angle. The skirt was definitely too long. Or maybe it wasn't my clothes. Maybe it was just something he could sense.

Again I missed Pallen, but I had resolved not to see him. I turned away from the mirror and undressed. Perhaps I would go out with that psychologist who had been calling, or the lawyer who had referred a testing case last week.

I searched the house unsuccessfully for my Mont Blanc, then thinking it would eventually turn up, I forgot about it, did twenty push-ups, and rode my stationary bike a half hour. Rosy-cheeked and refreshed, I chided myself for letting a patient get to me.

My lunch date with Morry was at the Paradise restaurant, a long one-story brick building with wide brass doors and small windows facing the street.

The last time I was there I'd been with Val, downing tequila in the Tapas room, where power players without a dinner reservation crowded together to drink. This time I entered the restaurant amid a group of middle-aged women wearing hats and heavy makeup.

The main hallway of the restaurant separated the Tapas bar from the formal dining room and led to the outside Paradise garden. The maître d', wearing the restaurant's trademark emerald-and-black colors, escorted me to the latticed patio, landscaped with tropical plants, flagstone, and small pools. There were a dozen tables, shaded by bright green-and-black striped umbrellas. A brilliant macaw held court from his perch in the center.

"Would you like a drink?" Morry asked, standing to greet me. He looked distinguished with his salt-and-pepper hair, and a Movado watch peeking from his starched cuff. He'd already finished half his brandy and soda.

It was so pleasant and tropical I kissed him on the cheek. "I can't drink at lunch."

Morry ordered me a Pellegrino water with lime, and said to the waiter, "Please tell Humberto that Dr. Helman is here."

The macaw on the perch behind me let out an ear-piercing shriek, and I turned to examine him. He was two and a half feet long from head to tip of tail, and crimson red, with bright yellow-and-blue streaks on his wings.

"He is a magnificent bird, isn't he?" an unfamiliar voice said.

I turned back to see a tall, olive-skinned man standing next to our table. "Spectacular!" I said, realizing who the stranger was. "Morry," he said warmly, as he held out his hand and bowed slightly, "please. Don't get up."

"Sarah Rinsley, I want you to meet Humberto Cortazar," Morry said. To Humberto, he said, "Dr. Rinsley is a psychologist. You might know her from her radio show."

Humberto's face opened in a smile of recognition, and he reached out to grasp my hand in both of his. "Tuesday and Thursday afternoons! KPXQ! I listen every chance I get." He spoke with a very slight accent.

I laughed with pleasure. "I wouldn't think the owner of such a lovely restaurant would be interested in eating disorders."

"Many of my customers have eating problems, or must stay very thin for their careers, so I'm working on an alternate menu of spa food. Perhaps I can show it to you."

"Tell us about your bird," Morry countered. He tore into a crusty roll so forcefully a piece of it snapped off and shot across the table.

Humberto deferred to Morry. "Rojo is a domestically bred Scarlet Macaw. He doesn't talk much—" The bird interrupted him with another shrill squawk. "—at least not in a language we can understand." His face relaxed into an apologetic smile. "I hope his beauty will make up for his noise. Please, enjoy your lunch."

On his way out Humberto stepped over to the bird and stroked his feathers. "Shhh, Rojo, you'll give these people indigestion," he soothed, and then pulled from his pocket a Brazil nut, which he gave to the bird before disappearing.

"Every dish is a masterpiece in this restaurant," Morry said, pleased again now that he had my undivided attention. "Humberto told me he hired a graphic designer to plan the layout of the food and the sauces." He paused and looked at me quizzically. "You were drawn to him, weren't you?"

"It's always fun for me to meet someone who likes my show. What do you know about him?"

"He's thirty-seven. From Nicaragua. Left with his family when he was young. Rumor is he was engaged once and broke it off over some weird thing he won't talk about. But his restaurant is making him an international celebrity."

Humberto sent a bottle of dry champagne to accompany our meal, and while Morry and I discussed our mutual patients, I took a few sips. Morry was sure Nick's physical symptoms were related to emotional distress, and said he had prescribed tranquilizers and sleeping pills for him on several occasions. I asked him to refer Nick for a psychiatric medication consult if Nick asked for refills.

Dessert was a variety of small iced cakes, miniature pies, and tiny scoops of fresh fruit sorbets. Morry and I fought over the bill and he finally let me pay before we stood up and kissed good-bye at the table. On my way out I made a quick trip to the ladies' room, down a corridor that led to the kitchen and an office.

When I emerged from the bathroom, I almost collided with Humberto. His face lit up again. "How was your lunch?" he asked.

I smiled my true appreciation. "The best I can ever remember. And the champagne was so good I was tempted to drink the rest after Morry left." Immediately realizing how transparent that sounded, I covered by adding, "Thanks again. I'd better get back to work too."

"Wait, wait," he said, placing a hand on my upper arm. "Let me show you something before you go."

I thought perhaps he wanted to discuss eating problems, but the laugh lines around his eyes and the way he had talked to his bird promised something more. I followed him with pleasure.

His office was a messy jumble of things scattered everywhere. The whole top of his broad cherry-wood desk was covered with papers and menus. The wall opposite his desk was lined with shelves of books at all angles, interspersed with souvenirs and antique cookware. In the far corner stood a hatrack holding a mound of full-length aprons.

"How can you work like this?" I blurted out in amazement.

He laughed. "It feels lived-in and homey to me. A work in progress." He pointed to the loveseat across from his desk. "Please, sit down."

As I turned and seated myself I saw the reason he had brought me into the office. To the left of his desk was a large birdcage, with another parrot inside. "Leave a big tip!" demanded the parrot abruptly.

It was my turn to laugh. "What kind of parrot is he?"

"She. An Orange Winged Amazon—not an endangered species—and a brilliant talker. Her name is Esperanza. Would you like to pet her?"

"I would love to."

I studied Humberto as he moved behind his desk and reached into the cage. At first glance he looked polished and elegant with his black hair trained back and his finely tailored suit, but his bouncy step and the way his hands moved gave the impression he might break into a run at any moment. He had a long, straight nose that came to a sharp tip as if a sculptor had fashioned it, and his small brown eyes were deep-set and lively. I could picture him whipping up cake batters, stirring giant pans of julienne vegetables, and grilling fish simultaneously, making a complete mess as he worked. The sides of his soft leather loafers were slightly misshapen along the outside edges, where he rolled his feet as he walked.

Gently he placed the bird on his wrist and stepped over to present her to me. She was lime green, with soft gray feathers on her chest and layers of orange, white, and green underneath. "Ooo-la-la," the bird said, when I scratched her head. "Ooo-la-la."

I laughed again, conscious of Humberto's sleeve grazing my arm and the heat of my own interest in him. "She's wonderful," I said.

He smiled proudly, showing his best feature—white, even teeth. "She's the love of my life."

"I understand. I have a basset hound I adore."

Esperanza bobbed her head, and Humberto fumbled around in his jacket pocket and produced a few sunflower seeds for her. I liked the idea of a three-thousand-dollar suit stuffed with seeds and nuts. As he returned her to the cage, I glanced briefly at his shelves. There were books on photography, birds, politics, Nicaragua, physics.

"I must get back," I said, standing to leave.

"Do you—would you be free some evening?"

I was so pleased by this invitation it took me a moment to find my voice. "Sure. You'd like to discuss how to handle your weight-obsessed customers?"

He shoved his hands in his pockets. "Among other things. I mean if you're—not seriously involved with someone." The way he pronounced his words so precisely was very appealing.

I smiled. "How about next Thursday? I usually finish by seven."

"Why don't you meet me here? I'll order something special for you."

"It's a deal. Let me give you my phone number in case you need to cancel."

He took my hand between both of his. "I'm happy to have your number, but I promise you I won't cancel."

His hands were warm and dry and I did not want to let go of them. Humberto was by far the most interesting man I had met in a long time.

That evening, I called my parents.

"Honey," my mother said, "I'm so glad to hear from you. I thought maybe you were mad at me." In spite of the warmth between us, there was always a taut band of tension.

"Why would I be mad? I'm just atrociously busy. But I found that fabric you wanted. Should I Fed Ex it to you tomorrow or can it wait till the weekend?"

"Tomorrow would be perfect. And tell me all about your week. I like to hear about life in the big city."

"My schedule is jammed. I've just been asked to supervise a new group of interns at the V.A. Hospital, and the radio show is a kick. What about you? How's your hip?"

"A little worse. The cold, wet weather, you know. And you, dear? Did you get to the dermatologist?"

"Last week," I lied. "My skin's much better." That worried tone of hers always made me feel like a bug under a microscope, and I didn't think an occasional allergic rash was worth worrying about.

"Do you think you might make it up here in August for Abby's wedding?" Abby was my cousin, and still lived near my parents in Bandon, a small town on the Oregon coast.

"I can't promise, but I'll try." I missed their spectacular beach where I was raised, with its broad stretch of sand and its gigantic tidal rocks. "You know how hard it is for me to get away."

"They won't be surprised if you don't come. You've never made much time for family."

I sighed. "I'll do my best, Mom. How's your business going?" She owned a dressmaking shop.

"I have orders for three full wedding parties—bridal gowns and all bridesmaids."

I let her tell me the details—the colors, the fabrics, the wedding party, and who else in town was getting married, was pregnant, or had developed cancer or diabetes. It grounded me, having this history in common with her. My life now was so distant and different from hers.

I debated telling her about Humberto. She would be intensely interested, but it was too soon, and I was still smarting from the last conversation about my personal life. When I had told her my decision about Pallen, she had said, "I hope you know what you're doing."

"I'm doing the only thing I could," I had replied, and then ended the conversation.

Later that week I had called to apologize for cutting her off. She wasn't home. My father, trying to smooth things between us, had said, "Don't worry about it. I told her every woman's got a sweet spot. You just haven't met the guy yet who's found yours."

Of course he wouldn't think Pallen's behavior too reprehensible, but I had appreciated the support at the time, and decided to be cautious about what I shared with my mother in the future.

I said, "How's Dad? Is he there?"

"I'll go get him. I love you, dear."

"Me too." I wasn't sure if she heard me.

"Hey, sport!" Dad's voice crackled. "How's it going in the big city?"

"Hectic, Dad. You'd hate it. How's business?"

"You know how it is this time of year."

I felt bad for him. Owning a sporting goods store was a far cry from what he had always wanted—to play major league baseball.

"Yeah, but it's the right time of year for steelhead," I said, switching to his second love. "Caught any big ones lately?"

"Nah, I'm getting soft in my old age. I just feel 'em wiggle in my hand and then let 'em go."

"That's nice, Dad. I like it."

"Baloney. You like that I'm getting soft in my old age."

"A little softening wouldn't hurt."

Ruefully I thought how true that was. He could identify the creeping butterfly and golden-eyed grass that clung to the shoreline near our home, he could recite the statistics of fifty baseball greats, with their batting averages and ERAs, but my father still didn't know how to say he loved me.

We joked, skimming the surface as usual.

When we said good-bye, he added, "Thanks for checking on us, kid. Keep your powder dry."

I blew him a kiss, and said, "Tell Mom I love her."

After I hung up, I forced away the sadness that always surfaced when I talked to my parents. I could not repair what had gone wrong in their lives.

They were still together after thirty-six years, perhaps because neither of them had the courage to leave, but the resentments and betrayals had piled up. My mother stuffed everything down with food; my father stayed out very late and sometimes didn't come home at all.

When I was young, I used to peek around the aisles in my father's sporting goods store and watch ladies sidle up to him. I wondered why they always giggled so much. Years later I started sneaking out of my bedroom window at night to run to the beach. One night, I saw a man and a woman rolled up in a blanket, five feet above me on the edge of the bluffs. I divided my attention between the moon and the couple, until I heard the man laugh. There was no one else's laugh like my dad's.

5

Nick began his third session with a joke. "Did you hear the one about Little Red Riding Hood?" He looked more relaxed that day with his blue cotton shirt open at the collar and his hands less restless. "She was in the woods on the way to her Grandma's house when she was accosted by the big bad wolf."

I smiled politely. Even though he appeared to be telling an innocuous joke, I was listening for other possible meanings of the material. Often the first statement of the day holds in cryptic form the patient's unconscious conflict of the moment.

"The wolf growled at her and said 'Lay down, I'm gonna rape you.' So Little Red Riding Hood put her hand in her basket, pulled out a gun, and said, 'No you're not, you're gonna eat me, just like it says in the book.' " He chuckled expectantly and I gave an obligatory grin, but said nothing because I wanted to see what else would emerge in the hour.

I learned that Nick rose at five in the morning to allow time to weight-train, jog, style his hair, iron his shirts, and polish his shoes. He lived in a pricey Marina apartment, with an expansive view of the harbor and the bay beyond. The amount of time he took in the hour to describe his possessions highlighted the lack of people close to him.

"Tell me about your career," I said.

He snorted. "It's going great. If I keep racking up this many hours I might make partner in two years."

The pattern of his job history suggested otherwise. He had an easy time getting into schools, and after graduation, getting jobs, because he made an initial good impression, but he had moved through five firms in the eight years since he'd passed the bar. As in his relationships with women, when conflicts arose, he left.

"Can you tell me more about your father?"

"He beat me with a metal-studded belt if I got in trouble. One time, I had this pet hamster named Spike. Used to run around in his cage every night. I really liked him, but Spike's squeaky wheel kept my father up at night. My ma took me to the hardware store and bought some oil to quiet the wheel, but it didn't work that well. One night my father came in, grabbed Spike out of his cage, threw him against the wall, and killed him."

"How old were you?"

"Six."

I wanted to say, "What an awful thing your father did," but Nick was likely to be intensely ambivalent about his father, and if I expressed only one side of his ambivalence it might interfere with later expression of the other side. Instead I asked, "How did that affect you?"

"I couldn't eat meat for months." He crossed his arms over his chest and stared at me. "What else do you want to know?"

"More about how your stepmother treated you."

"We fought at first, but after a few years she got to like me. She tried to protect me from my father sometimes. Other times she teased me and made me feel like shit."

"You have no desire to reconnect with her now?"

He looked out the window as if she were standing there on the street. "She tried to get in touch with me after my dad died. Saw his obit in the paper. But I thought, fuck her. She abandoned us. Why bother now? As far as I'm concerned she's dead."

"How do you think she affected your relationships with women?"

He pulled out his Mylanta, took a few sips, and returned it to his pocket. "Ma gave me a taste for tight, short skirts and low-cut sweaters. But I like a woman who's different from her—a woman who'll do anything I want. And when she does, I'll do anything she wants in return." He moved his head from side to side like a plastic dog in a rear car window. "You know what I mean? A love slave. Like that old Rod Stewart song, 'Tonight I'm Yours.' Do anything, do anything. That's how the song goes. No limits. I can take on the world after a night like that."

I stared at him in silence, imagining such a night.

He narrowed his eyelashes. "I know what you're thinking. I'm an asshole. Well, maybe you're right, but some women don't think so. They do me like I want to be done and they like it."

"Do you see any connection between losing both of your mothers and seeking women you can control?"

He cocked his head to one side. "You don't get it. It's a mutual control thing—a sexual trip."

Why had I risked a premature interpretation? He was not ready to examine his unconscious motivations and my rushing him was a stupid mistake. I nodded in silence.

He was angry. "I'm not a complete idiot, you know. I think about that stuff. I know sometimes I picked fights with my last girlfriend on purpose."

"Then you sense there are forces in you operating out of your awareness?"

"Of course." He stood up abruptly and walked over to the window. After a moment's silence, he said, "I don't see what good this is doing me." He flicked his index finger at the wooden shutter slats. "I have to go to the bathroom, I'll be back in a few minutes."

He walked past me and left my inner office door open behind him. I expected him to reek of some expensive cologne, but the fragrance that wafted by was a mixture of polished leather and soap, fresh as a seventh-grade student on his first day of school. He was gone ten minutes and when he returned he said, "Sorry."

"Perhaps what we're discussing was upsetting."

"Or maybe I had a bad hamburger for lunch."

I stared at him. Surely he realized there might be a connection between his feelings and his upset stomach.

His face turned an angry red. "Don't patronize me," he said. "I know there's something wrong with me; I just can't get a handle on it."

"I hope we'll be able to do that together," I replied.

He remained sullen and silent, and then left for the bathroom again. When he returned I began the last phase of the session. "The joke you told me at the beginning of the hour is similar to your dreams of last week. I wonder if you anticipate this therapy to be a battle of wills, and you're unsure if you want to risk it. Last week you said I was pretty sharp. Today I have a gun and I'm going to force you to do things my way. Maybe you worry that I'm going to use you, instead of you using me."

He shook his head disdainfully. "It was just a joke, for Pete's sake. Do you have to analyze everything?"

"Everything you say here has meaning, and it's my job to point out meanings you might miss. I think it's hard for you to imagine a relationship between a man and woman who collaborate rather than control and use each other."

By noting his difficulty in imagining a collaborative relationship, I was implying not only that it existed, but that we could develop it together. This acknowledged his views and, without criticism, presented the possibility of another way.

The answering machine on my desk clicked on quietly. He stopped and looked at it. "Aren't you going to answer? Maybe it's an emergency."

"No. During the time we set aside for each other, I devote my full attention to you. This is your hour."

"What a good mother."

"Perhaps you wonder how long it would take me to respond if you called with an emergency."

"I don't have emergencies. Anyway when I need something, I know I can count on only one person. Number one."

"You've been disappointed many times by others?"

"You might say that."

I felt frustrated by his unwillingness to explain. It was so locked away beneath this defense of flippant comebacks. Depleted now of energy, empty from his trips to the bathroom, he looked crumpled and sad. "Nick, you've had some tough times in your life, and to survive you've built internal walls. Now you're stuck inside your walls and you're lonely."

I thought for a moment he was going to cry, but I continued. "You have to knock a hole in the wall. It's going to take courage, because it involves the very things you fear the most—feeling your feelings and letting yourself trust someone. I'm willing to work very hard with you, if you want to try. It won't be easy."

He stared at me intently, his eyes as brilliant and immeasurable as the sky. "I'll see you next week," he said and departed without another word.

Later, I straightened the pillows in my office, combed my hair, and pulled a few wilted petals off a bouquet of irises. When I went out to the waiting room to lock up, I couldn't believe my eyes. Someone had taken a razor blade and cut out a thin horizontal strip of wallpaper across one whole wall. The missing strip extended up to the middle of a painting, down around the painting and up to the door frame.

"Damn!" I said aloud. "I'll have to have the whole wall redone now. Who would do this?"

I considered Nick. Was this what he had been doing on his trips to the bathroom? No, I thought, this sort of indirect destructiveness was a woman's work, and I ran back through the list of patients that day and singled out a few possibilities. Besides, I thought, anyone walking down the hall could open my waiting room door and steal something or slash my wallpaper. A radio-show listener could have found my office, and there were any number of vagrants wandering the streets outside.

I notified the building management of the vandalism, resigned myself to fixing it as quickly as possible, and locked up. Before leaving Westwood, I walked over to Tower Records and bought Rod Stewart's tape, "Tonight I'm Yours." I wanted to hear what a love slave sounded like.

6

"This is Dr. Sarah Rinsley, and you're listening to 'What's Eating You?' on KPXQ. Hello, Alycia from Glendale."

"Hi, Dr. Rinsley. I think your show is great and I listen to it all the time. I'm twenty-six and my fiancé loves me, but he complains about my thighs and says I should have liposuction. I'm five foot five and weigh a hundred and thirty pounds, so I'm not gross, but I probably would look better if I had the surgery. Do you think I should?"

"I think your fiancé wants to make you fit some perfect image of a woman."

"But he says it's for my own good because my thighs bother me and I would enjoy looking better."

"First he criticizes your thighs, then he tells you if you changed them you'd feel better. Of course you'd feel better, because he'd quit complaining about your body!"

"He's embarrassed to be seen with me on the beach."

"I'm sorry, that's not the voice of someone who loves you. That's the voice of an insecure man who wants to feel better about himself by showing off a perfect-looking woman.

"And Alycia, most of us are never going to look like those gorgeous girls in the magazines who starve themselves to stay so thin. So until we start loving ourselves more, as we are, and start focusing attention on our character and our work and our capacity to love, we'll be easy prey for someone else's criticism.

"Now I have nothing against plastic surgery, but you have to think long and hard about a guy who is focusing so much attention on improving your body and so little on appreciating who you are. I'm Dr. Sarah Rinsley and you're listening to KPXQ talk radio."

I sat back in my chair and sipped Pellegrino while the commercials played. Tonight was my dinner date with Humberto and I was a little preoccupied with my own appearance. I was wearing a fitted black suit, an embroidered silk blouse, and an elegant pair of black suede heels. Knowing I was going to see him was a delicious secret I had savored all day.

I punched line four. "Go ahead, George from Van Nuys."

George was a depressed college student who couldn't stop eating while he studied. He was desperate to get into pharmacy school, and in the process of trying, had gained over fifty pounds.

"What would happen if you didn't get into pharmacy?"

"My parents would be wiped out. I couldn't face them."

"George, your goal is admirable and I respect your working as hard as you can to achieve it, but you're piling more pressure on yourself than you can handle. The fear of failure is actually interfering with your success."

"Right! Worrying totally screws up my concentration."

"Talk to your parents. Tell them how you're feeling."

"No way. They wouldn't understand."

"Then you have to help them understand. Say 'Mom, Dad, I'm working very hard, and I'm afraid if I don't get into pharmacy you'll be very disappointed and maybe you won't even love me or accept me as much.' "

"They'd pretend it wasn't true."

"Then you have to confront them. Be blunt."

"That freaks me out. I don't know if I can do it."

"George, it doesn't take courage to do something easy! It takes courage to do the things you're afraid of. But you'll feel more self-respecting if you say the truth, even if you're risking anger or rejection. And when you do that, you'll feel less depressed. I'm Dr. Sarah Rinsley on KPXQ."

After my two-hour stint was up, Mike, the station manager, pulled me into his office. He was a heavy man who wore white shirts and wildly patterned suspenders, and his insatiable ambition had already prompted several fights between us. For ten minutes he buttered me up with flattery about how popular I was and how much respect he had for me.

"But what," I interrupted.

He stuck his thumbs through his suspenders. "Okay, your ratings are good, I grant you that. But they'd go through the roof if you had specialty days—like wives of cross-dressers, siblings in love, women who marry guys on death row—that sort of thing."

I shook my head and stood up immediately. "Not me. If you want that, get somebody else."

"Now, c'mon, siddown a minute. I've just finished telling you how much people out there like you. But that's why it would work! You're quality! Not some schlock doc! So if you talked to these people it would be different than the other shows."

"No. No, no, no. For every wife of a cross-dresser, there are twenty wives so depressed they can't get out of bed in the morning. For every incestuous marriage there are fifty straight marriages that aren't working! I put people on the air because others can *learn* from them, not to display them like freaks in a circus!

"And you know *why* my ratings are good? Because most people need to hear the basics—how to love, how to take risks, how to stop blaming others for what's wrong!

"Damn it, I feel good about this show the way it is! People send me letters telling me how I've changed their lives. And thousands more are thinking about how it applies to them. Why narrow it down to a parade of freaks? Forget it, Mike. Not me. Besides, I think ratings would drop."

He pulled a toothpick from his drawer and started working on his teeth. "You could use any of those freaks to demonstrate what you want to say to the rest of us."

"That's just it. I don't want to use people. And that's what I'd be doing. For ratings."

"Okay, okay. We'll leave it for now." He rolled his eyes and gave me an affectionate grin.

Humberto ushered me into the Paradise dining room, a quiet, dimly lit space overflowing with fresh flowers, cut-glass, and linen. Iced champagne was ready at our table and after clinking glasses, I drained mine immediately.

His eyes were bright with interest, his smile warm. "I've been listening to your radio show," he said. "I thought you said exactly the right thing to the girl calling about plastic surgery. Some women around here have been pulled up so many times they can barely close their mouths."

"Yes, but it's hard to accept aging when you think all you've got going for you is your good looks."

"I didn't think about that. It's sad, really."

How quickly he understands, I thought. How quickly he cares. A lovely quality in a man.

"Now here's something else I wonder when I hear you talk to bulimics. How can they be so hungry for food and hate it at the same time?"

"Splitting—the tendency to think of things as all good or all bad. Food in front of a bulimic is good. As soon as it's inside the body it feels dreadful, as if she's just eaten poison. That's the basis of the binge/purge cycle."

"How fascinating. Would this idea of splitting explain why people rush to a new restaurant and then shun it after a few months?"

"Sure. The new is all good—glamorous and high-status; the old is used up and passé."

"Maybe I should open a place called the All-Good Cafe?"

"Open it and close it within three months, so it will always be remembered as perfect."

We chuckled at this lame humor. It was that awkward moment of beginnings, when two people search for common ground and are most forgiving. It wouldn't really have mattered if he had read me the phone book. I was already falling in love with him.

When he refilled my glass, I noticed a one-inch scar across the back of his hand, and after he replaced the bottle in the ice bucket, I reached over and ran my finger lightly over his scar. "How did you get that?"

He stretched out both hands to me and after showing the backs, turned his palms up. They were splattered with scars. "Cooking. This long one's from the grill at Chaya Bistro. These two are knife cuts. This round one's from boiling grease. And I have a long one on my right shoulder from a pot of chicken stock that fell on me."

"My God, I had no idea being a chef was so hazardous."

"And hot. What about you?" He took my right hand and traced his finger over a red patch on one of my knuckles.

"Allergies. If I put on a wool sweater or jacket I break out immediately. I can only wear suits with silk linings."

"Doesn't stress make it worse?"

"It can."

"Sounds to me like you need a vacation." A smile played around his lips as if he were offering to take me away. I wanted to go.

There were many interruptions in our conversation as men shook his hand, women kissed him, and the maître d' and several waiters whispered to him. Each time he introduced me as "Dr. Rinsley, the radio psychologist." I was pleased by his obvious respect.

When interrupted, Humberto rubbed his lips with his forefinger, leaving them red and irritated. He whispered fiercely and impatiently to his waiters, then turned back to me each time, trying to resume our conversation.

"Sorry," he said. "Never a moment's peace. And you? Do you find your work disturbing?"

"Mostly not. After all, therapy is doing something about problems. I find it more disturbing to leave things silent and locked away."

He studied my face intently. "There are a lot of things I'd like to ask you."

He sees something in me he wants, I thought. This pleased me as I watched pretty women wave to him.

"For example, can you help someone who says they've never loved anyone?"

Nick flitted through my mind. "Hopefully. Why do you ask?"

"I knew someone like that."

I was exceedingly curious, but at that moment a familiar actress sat down at the table next to us and began quizzing the waiter loudly about salt content, type of fat used, and source of the fish served. "Make sure the grill is wiped clean," she added after making her choice. "And what kind of filter paper do you use for the coffee?"

"Why doesn't she stay home if she's that worried?" I whispered.

Humberto smiled and said in a low tone, "She probably eats Twinkies and french fries at home. But she's just like the rest of us—fighting for territory, showing off to attract a mate, eating, and hoping she won't die soon."

I liked his insight. "You know a lot about wildlife, don't you?" I asked.

"Some." Exotic birds were at risk, he said, and so many die before the illegal traders even get them into the U.S. He was working to lobby for domestic breeding programs and tighter import legislation.

I watched Humberto's lips for a while, barely hearing his words. Every time he smiled, I thought how beautiful his teeth were—even and white, with no sign of fillings or crowns. I sometimes wished I had such a perfect endowment.

When I tuned back in, Humberto was discussing the oil painting on the wall behind him—a seascape with a faint image of an old sailing ship. In large calligraphy over the ship was a sentence, printed diagonally from the upper left corner to the bottom right: BRAVE MEN RUN IN MY FAMILY. "Is there a particular significance to the words?" I asked.

"My father sold our ranch in Nicaragua and brought us to Miami when I was thirteen. I've never been able to decide whether staying or leaving was the courageous thing to do."

"Couldn't it have been both?"

His lips curled into a slow smile and he wagged his forefinger at me. "I like you," he said.

I smiled back, flushed with pleasure. "Did you run away from something too?"

"My family." He had left school at seventeen, hitchhiked to L.A., and worked his way up from peeling potatoes in restaurants.

"Families," I said, shaking my head. "My grandmother dangled her money in my mother's face her whole life. And she made my mother feel like two cents." I raised my champagne glass in a toast. "To leaving home."

He touched his glass to mine and smiled. "When I left Nica, I wanted to become American in every way. I practiced English in front of the mirror for hours. I even held open my mouth with a little stick between the roof of my mouth and my tongue, so I could learn to pronounce the hard R only with my lips."

I didn't tell him his accent still peeked through. "Why was it so important?"

"I didn't want to sound like Ricky Ricardo."

The maître d' approached and whispered something to Humberto. "*Yo me haré cargo,*" he said, and rose quickly. "Another problem in the kitchen. Please excuse me."

I picked at my food, thinking about my Grandma Covey. She had planned for my mother to attend school in Europe, but after Mom met my dad, it was all over. He was energetic and good-looking, with straight, sandy hair, arms sturdy as tree limbs, and big, squared-off front teeth. "He'll never amount to anything," was all Grandma ever said about him.

I did not understand until much later what my mother had sacrificed by choosing my father. When I was ten, I found her papers, neatly bound in a dress box in the attic. There were colorful drawings of women in dresses, suits, and gowns, with insets showing the details of sequins and pearls. Amid teachers' recommendations and school transcripts was a letter from Paris, accepting her to a school of design. "I'll never give up my dreams," I vowed, and carefully put the papers back.

Twenty minutes had gone by since Humberto had left the table. Out of boredom I went to the ladies' room, primped, and arranged my clothes, and emerged to see Humberto's office door ajar. Assuming his business was completed, I walked toward the open door, then stopped, transfixed.

Inside his office, his back to me, Humberto stood in an animated conversation with a woman. I watched as he banged his fist on his desk and some papers went flying. He bent over and snatched the papers up angrily and threw them back on the desk. I couldn't hear what he was saying, but the woman seemed to be on the verge of tears. She was dressed in a black sheath dress, high heels, and a diamond necklace.

When I saw her fling her arms around him, I turned and walked briskly back to the table, furious. The gall to leave me sitting alone for so long! While he was having a lover's spat! I put on my suit jacket and turned to leave, just as he hurried up behind me.

"I'm so sorry. My maître d' told me you walked by my office. Please let me explain."

"Perhaps some other time. I'm ready to leave."

He leaned in and lowered his voice. "Please come with me to my office. I can't have this conversation here."

I marched ahead of him angrily, having decided I'd hear him out before telling him good-bye. I had no desire to get involved with a man who wouldn't treat me well.

We stood in the middle of his office after he closed the door, because I refused to sit. He said, "She's an old girlfriend I haven't seen for months. She came in drunk, demanding to see me, and I thought I could take care of it quickly. But I had to have it out with her, because it's completely over, and I don't want her coming in here. The whole time I was worrying about you sitting alone."

"You kept me waiting a half hour!"

"Please forgive me," he said.

"You could at least have had the courtesy to send someone to explain."

He threw up his arms. "I know! But I kept thinking it would just take a few more minutes! I apologize. I should never have invited you here. I have to handle what comes up and people are always dropping by to say hello."

I crossed my arms and continued standing, ready to leave. "Then why didn't you suggest some other place?"

He hesitated. "Truthfully? I wanted to impress you. I probably thought I'd look good with people greeting us and asking my advice. It was a stupid mistake."

"Okay," I said, relaxing some. "Let's try it again another time. I think I've had enough for tonight."

He went over to his sofa, sat down and patted the seat next to him. "Come and sit here a minute before you go."

Somewhat reluctantly I joined him on the sofa, then looked around the office. "Where's your bird?"

"I had to take her home. She caught a cold. Why don't you come to my house next week and let me make dinner for you? You can see her too."

"All right," I said, smiling. "But you're definitely on probation."

7

When I saw Nick again, it was toward the end of a long day. Before I opened the door to him, I sat in my chair a few minutes, listening to the room.

Although I'd never told anyone, I thought I could hear my office breathing, particularly in the morning before the air filled with the sound of human sadness. Books stretched solidly from floor to ceiling along the wall next to my chair, and the authors whispered: boundary and space, psychoanalytic technique, fear of fat. Sunlight through the beveled glass windows sometimes cast brilliant little squares on the pineapple palm in the corner or smoky light on the desk. Even the walls seemed alive—thick structures insulated to hold in voices and shut out noise.

Every aspect of this space had been planned to provide an atmosphere conducive to therapy. Separate entrances and exits protected privacy. There were comfortable chairs opposite mine, and a sofa where a patient could lie facing away from me or sit at an angle and look at me. Clocks were prominently located, and a light signal let me know silently that my next patient was in the waiting room. Bouquets of fresh flowers, handy boxes of Kleenex, and recessed fixtures on dimmer switches added to the soothing mood.

After restoring myself, I opened the door.

The familiar fragrance wafted by in the wake of Nick's path: some concoction of soap, baby powder, and leather. "So hey, what do we talk about today?" he said. He adjusted his tie and smoothed the fabric over his thighs. It was astounding how someone with so much to talk about could have nothing to say.

"You don't have to come here with a prepared agenda. Just say whatever's on your mind without censoring it."

"Shit. So I'm going to waste my money if I don't spill my guts here? I just hope you don't fuck me over."

I accepted that as an offensive but small step forward, which he followed by opening up a little. He said that life was a hostile competition and he was determined to be on the winning side. He said he hated one of his law firm partners, a man who prided himself on playing fair.

"Fuck playing fair," Nick said. "Play to win. State inadmissable evidence. The jury's instructed to disregard it, but if they've already heard it, it's bound to have some effect. I do it till I'm threatened with contempt. Then I back off."

His practice was mostly personal injury and divorce work, a choice I found ironic. "I usually represent the women," he said. "They pass my name along to the next one and my reputation grows." He raised one eyebrow and winked at me, making me wonder just what it was the women said. "It can be a dangerous job, though," he added.

"What do you mean?"

"I never know when an irate husband might come after me. Or some disgruntled defendant. So I keep a loaded pistol in the console of my car. Any carjacker tries to mess with me, he'll get a sorry surprise."

Many people owned guns, particularly men like him who had been trained in the military, but I hated the idea of him driving around L.A., armed and stoned. I paused to consider the possibility that he was more dangerous than I had assumed.

My concern must have shown on my face, because he looked at me and laughed. "Relax, Doc! This is purely for self-defense. With the kind of work I do, someone could always come after me."

When the session was almost over, I said, "Any dreams?"

He looked suddenly tired. "I dreamed I was at the bottom of a dry well and there were people coming to get me. I've had this dream for years. I'm always in a small space, scared, and I wake up frightened and sweating."

"Have you noticed any pattern as to when you have this dream?"

He shook his head.

"From now on, let's search for a pattern. This time you've had this dream shortly after meeting me. Perhaps I'm the one who's coming in, and you're scared."

He shrugged. "Maybe."

Even though he didn't appear to accept my observation, I knew he'd heard it and on some level would continue to consider it. Therapy takes place gradually, with ideas introduced on one day being accepted sometimes six months or even three years later.

Nick opened his briefcase, removed a pair of sunglasses and a small cloth, and began polishing the lenses. When he was finished, he said, "My father used to lock me in my closet sometimes."

If his dreams were any indication, being locked up had been a terrifying experience, and I felt a rush of sympathy. "What do you remember about it?"

"Being alone and scared."

I waited for him to elaborate, but he simply clamped his lips together, folded the glasses, and returned them to his briefcase.

"How old were you?"

"Four or five."

"Why was it done?"

"To punish me."

"How many times did this happen?"

"Don't remember. A lot." After a few minutes he said, "I don't want to talk about it anymore. I don't see what good it's doing me."

This was resistance, the conscious and unconscious efforts to avoid engaging in the process of treatment.

"It sounds like being locked up still haunts you."

"It was thirty years ago. It's over and buried and I hope therapy isn't just raking over dead leaves like this."

It was time to stop, and not the right moment to push him. "We'll cover everything when you're ready to talk about it. If you need to speak with me for any reason, I'm available by phone twenty-four hours a day."

He hauled out his antacid again and gulped it down. After a few minutes, he raised his hands in surrender and said, "Okay, okay. I need something. Maybe this is it."

When he stood to leave, he took a few extra minutes to repack his briefcase, put on his suit jacket, and adjust his shirt cuffs. At the door he paused to say, "See you Monday," and I thought perhaps he wished his next appointment was sooner.

After he left, I thought about his father locking him in a closet, and understood a little about his mistrust. It also prompted a closet memory of my own.

In the house where I grew up, there was a hiding place under the stairs to the second floor. It was intended as a storage closet, but its half door was poorly constructed and from inside I could see the dining room through small vertical slits. The saddest thing I ever saw was my mother crying at the table.

I was eleven, and she had entered us in a mother-daughter fashion show without asking me. When she told me her plans, I said, "I don't want to get dressed up with a bunch of prissy girls and parade around. I'll look stupid in a fancy dress. I won't do it!"

My mother pressured and wheedled until I finally consented, but as the Saturday afternoon of the fashion show grew closer, I became more anxious. I had small mounds developing on my chest, and I was embarrassed by them. I didn't want my mother looking at my body anymore, and I hated enduring the fittings for the dress.

When finished, my mother's dress was lovely—a pink confection of imported French lace and organdy, with a wide silk waistband and tiny hand-sewn pearls across the front of the low-cut bodice. For three months my mother had been preparing for this show by starving herself down to a size fourteen. She looked as pretty as I'd seen her in years.

I thought my matching dress looked ridiculously childish. In place of the elegant waistband were long pink satin ribbons, and the neckline went all the way up to my neck, with an organdy Peter Pan collar. Mom had also sewn the tiny pearls across the front of my bodice, but those small mounds on my chest made the pearls form a swirling pattern around the center and I was acutely self-conscious.

The night before the fashion show, when we tried on our dresses, my father said, "Mmmm. You both look delicious. And I do believe our little girl is turning into a woman."

That was all I had to hear. I raced upstairs, unzipped the dress, piled it into a heap on the floor, and threw myself on the bed in tears. He was mocking me, I was sure. And for some reason my nipples hurt and my belly ached. Two hours later I got my first period.

"Please, Mommy," I begged the next morning, "don't make me wear it. Please go without me!"

"I understand how you feel, angel, but do this for me one last time. I've worked so hard on these dresses and I'm sure we'll get first prize!"

I cried until my face looked so bad it was impossible for me to go. My mother finally left without me.

That Sunday night from my hiding place under the stairs, I watched my mother tenderly pack her pink organdy dress into a shipping box for San Francisco where she hoped to sell it on consignment. When she finished addressing the box, she sat down at the table and wept. Watching her, I let tears fall without a sniff so she wouldn't hear me.

I left my dress hanging in the closet that whole year. The following summer, when Mom asked me to weed out old clothes, I couldn't bear to remind her of how much I'd hurt her, and I stuffed the dress into my sleeping bag and shoved it to the back of my closet. It stayed hidden in there for years, until I quietly packed it among my books and mementos and shipped it off to college with me.

8

The next day was crammed with therapy sessions from seven in the morning to six at night. At midday I received a package by messenger, and inside I found a small cut-glass elephant from Humberto. "Don't forget," it said. "Dinner with me at the All-Good Cafe."

I smiled and held the little ornament up to the light. How sweet, I thought, and I placed it on the coffee table next to the sofa.

My afternoon sessions were taxing. One woman confessed a bizarre habit of chewing her food and spitting it into a glass so she could eat it again. She'd been in treatment with me six months and was only now revealing this nauseating little problem.

Humberto called late that evening. "Thank you so much for the elephant. It's lovely," I said.

His warmth came through the phone like a caress. "I picked it out myself at Geary's. And I'm happy you're coming for dinner. You won't be sorry. You'll see."

We talked for half an hour. He said his work on the spa food was going well and he had thought of asking me to add a few lines of explanation to the menu. "Something psychological," he said. "To make my customers feel I really understand their needs."

"I could do that," I offered.

Since my weekend was already booked, we chose the middle of the following week for dinner, and said good-bye.

I sat down at the kitchen table and ate a few teaspoons of brown sugar out of the box. I liked him. I hoped I wouldn't be sorry I agreed to see him again.

Seized with a sudden desire to clean house, I dusted and polished the wood tables and cabinets, damp-mopped the floors, and did a load of laundry. By midnight I began reorganizing my closet, thinking it was as good a time as any since the next day was Saturday.

In the morning I woke early, glad that I had a few hours before my first appointment at the hospital. I put on a sweatshirt and shorts, examined the condition of my garden, and watered and pruned the roses. The most fragrant ones were a deep red, although my favorites were the orange ones with the yellow centers. I clipped off a few stems for my living room, then leashed up Frank and took him for a walk.

Mr. Slewicki, my neighbor across the street, was already raking and weeding his lawn. He wore a large fur hat, red houseslippers, and a woman's bathrobe, the sleeves of which only reached his forearms. I waved and headed for the main thoroughfare, wondering what prompted him to dress that way. Everyone has a story, I thought.

Even at that early hour, a surprising number of people were walking, jogging, or strolling to the newspaper stands and breakfast. I chose the center island of San Vicente Boulevard, where hundreds of joggers had grooved paths in the soft grass. The salty ocean air smelled good as I reached the western end of the boulevard, and Frank's jaunty presence amused me.

"Hey, Doc, how you doing?" a familiar voice sounded behind me.

I whirled around. It was Nick, in black silky shorts and a tank top. Did he know where I lived?

I stammered a greeting, trying to cover my discomfort as best I could. He chuckled and knelt down to pat Frank. The soft tuft of hair sticking out from Nick's armpit looked oddly appealing, and I became acutely conscious of my own brief shorts, unmade face, and tousled hair.

"You're far from home," I said lamely.

He winked. "Spent the night with a friend."

"See you next week," I said awkwardly, and gathered Frank up to proceed in the opposite direction.

I didn't like encountering any patients outside the office, because it fanned their curiosity about me, and made it more difficult to separate the reality of who I was from their transference reactions to me. Nick stuck in my mind like a thorn all day long, and that night I fell into a restless sleep.

I was on a train in Brazil, and my sleeping car rocked back and forth rhythmically, clattering noisily as it passed small villages. It was late, and lights from the street lamps flashed on and off in the darkness of my compartment. Then a man was standing over me, legs planted firmly apart. He was wearing a white shirt and pressed navy pants, but he had the head of a tiger, with huge blue eyes. I froze as he unzipped his fly and pulled out his penis. It was erect, veins bulging. "Suck it," he said.

I took him into my mouth and felt his surge of excitement. My own arousal mingled with fear. When he withdrew and pulled me to a standing position, I was his.

He opened my blouse, and bent to cover me with his mouth. Then he pointed to the narrow berth. "Spread your legs," he growled. I became swollen and hot, and stretched out my arms to him. Then he was on top of me, crushing me.

The aroma of baby powder and soap enveloped me as he entered me. I thought he might kill me, but I didn't care as I held myself out to him, pushing back. He moved quickly, pounding at me until he gritted his teeth and dug his hands into my shoulders. His final thrust forced my own orgasm.

I felt myself falling through space until I jolted wide awake in bed, stunned by the dream and the real climax that had roused me from sleep.

Nick. It was unmistakably him. The eyes, the clothes, the fragrance. I sat up in bed, heart thumping, startled and disturbed. The digital clock radio said 4:23 A.M., but I groped for the light and turned it on to collect myself.

Having a sexual dream about any patient was unnerving, but a dream about Nick was particularly disturbing. And wouldn't he just gloat, I thought. Mr. Don Juan. I'll have to keep an eye on my feelings for him and get a consult if necessary. I shut off the light, but when I closed my eyes the memory of the dream was so strong that I felt him inside me again.

• • •

When I saw him on Monday, Nick said it was nice to meet me out of the office. "Your dog is dynamite. But someone should tell him to pull his socks up," he said, referring to the folds of skin that cluster at Frank's ankles.

I laughed at this perfect description of Frank, and the session went on like that, with Nick chatty and charming. It reminded me of fishing trips I'd taken with my dad, where the pleasure I felt from his company was more from the tone of his voice than anything specific he said.

I allowed Nick's small talk, because I didn't trust myself so soon after that dream. I thought it safer to waste a therapy hour than take the chance that something about me might betray the experience. I also thought it unwise to confront him incessantly with his avoidance of deeper issues. Some of our work had to be pleasant, and I thought whatever wasn't going well in the therapy would gradually change.

In contrast to Nick, therapy with my other patients was progressing much faster.

The Romaine sisters had each allowed me ten minutes alone, during which I had uncovered one thing: since age fourteen, May and Joy had been having sex with each other at least once a week. Because they were psychologically one person, I considered it masturbation.

Another patient, Luness Montague, had come to treatment the year before complaining of a constant binge-eating and purging cycle. Now she was beginning to recognize the emotional triggers that prompted her symptoms.

Even my oldest patient was slowly improving. William Swan was a retired history professor who at seventy-two was still struggling to break free from the memory of his oppressive and demanding father. In spite of his constant struggle with hopelessness, he was forcing himself to exercise and keep a daily journal.

In between sessions later in the week, I picked up a call from Nick, who said he had to cancel his next appointment. When I offered him an alternate hour, he replied, "Can't do it. Got a depo." I wondered if he would start canceling often, and I was reminded that he was the kind of patient who required constant vigilance.

Later I found a greeting card in the mail—a cartoon of a man dancing wildly and holding a little clump of daisies. "Happy I met you!" it said. Inside it was signed, "A secret admirer." Assuming it was from Humberto, I was touched, and put it upright on my desk.

Wednesday evening before my date with Humberto, I tried on several different skirts, sweaters, and dresses, until I chose one I thought was just right.

As I slipped into my shoes, Frank appeared at the bedroom door, his long, velvety ears soaking wet. "Don't come near me," I warned. He lowered his head and cautiously crossed the bleached hardwood floor to lie down near the window. "Good Frank," I cooed. "You're my best short guy."

When the doorbell rang, Frank ran to the front hallway, barking loudly, and I had to lure him out the back door with a beef bone.

"Dissension in the ranks?" Humberto asked after I finally opened the front door.

I smiled. "I thought I'd spare your clothes."

"You look very pretty." He bent and touched his lips to my cheek, and I was glad I had settled on the peach dress with the black braid trim.

"Thanks for the card," I said.

He looked puzzled. "Card?"

"Someone sent me a card. I assumed it was you."

"Nope. Put that thing in the garbage!"

We laughed, but I wondered who might have sent it, and I had to brush away an uneasy feeling.

Humberto wore a white turtle-neck jersey, jeans, white socks, and black leather loafers. It was the first time I had seen him out of formal clothes and I had not realized how slender and fit he was. As we drove to Pacific Palisades where he lived, we talked and joked, and whatever remnants of anger I felt melted away.

He owned a large two-story Spanish house overlooking the ocean: an inviting home of white plaster walls, open stud beams, and white-washed pine furniture. Newspapers and magazines were piled everywhere, the mantel was cluttered with framed photographs, and the centerpiece of the living room was a massive, navy-blue sofa that formed an L shape. The fireplace was bracketed by sleek stereo speakers and a stack of electronic equipment on the adjoining shelf system. Rows of CDs and tapes lined the shelves.

Humberto asked, "Vivaldi or Gato Barbieri?"

"Vivaldi."

After the sweet flute sounds began, he disappeared into the kitchen, and I sank into the sofa. Something sharp dug into my hip and I reached down and discovered a screwdriver, which I put on the sidetable next to a pile of collar stays, two credit card receipts, and a mug half-filled with cold coffee and stale cream.

In the house where I grew up everything was always in place, and as a toddler I had learned to pick up my things and put them in order before leaving a room. This house was different, and with the sunlight of early evening shining through its tall, curved windows, the stereo playing, and little piles of mess here and there, it seemed more comforting and cozy than any home I had ever lived in.

Humberto returned with drinks in heavy cut-glass tumblers, and suggested we walk out back to the end of the garden to watch the sun set. The path was bordered by flowering oleander, and there were six bird-feeders scattered over his property. We passed a long, rectangular swimming pool gleaming turquoise in the waning sun.

"Why do you like birds so much?" I asked.

He stopped and turned a palm skyward. "Because birds give the world so much beauty and they do so little damage!" I was reminded of how focused I was on inner life.

We sat down on a bench and sipped our drinks, facing the ocean until the sky was a soft rose and there was barely enough light to see the tiny white sails on the horizon.

There was a foot and a half of space between us, and Humberto placed his arm along the back of the bench so that his hand rested at the base of my shoulder blades. He said, "Do you realize this very minute there are millions of neutrinos passing right through our bodies?"

As he traced a gentle circle at the base of my neck, he explained that neutrinos were the tiniest and most abundant particles of matter and about ten percent of the sun's power came from them.

I was aroused by his casual touch. "How can they pass right through our bodies?"

"They're so small that the cells of our bodies are like a big tennis racket, and they go through the holes between the strings."

"How do you know this?"

He moved up to my hairline. "I love astronomy. It gives me a sense of some great order out there. I think of it as being how God works."

"So you believe in God?"

There must have been a hard edge to my voice because he pulled his arm away and twisted around to look at me. "I have to. Otherwise life is too depressing."

I felt again the sadness of having lost the ability to believe in God. "What was it like growing up in Nicaragua?"

He sat back and looked out to sea. "Different. My family had a big coffee plantation near Matagalpa—three thousand *manzanas,* which is nearly six thousand acres—and two thousand head of cattle besides. We lived in a beautiful house with many servants."

"Do you still have relatives there?"

He nodded slowly. "I come from a big Catholic family and many of the people I loved are buried there." He looked pensive, glanced away again, and sipped his drink.

"I'm sorry," I said softly.

He flashed a quick smile and let it fade. "It's okay. I used to sponsor fund-raisers for humanitarian aid, but I couldn't reconcile it with my life here—my business, my money, my family. I had to turn away and bury the guilt. But you see—because you would see—it's still there."

I felt great empathy for him, and a strange sense of alienation. This was not a man who grew up in Little League like I had; he had different holidays, a different religion, a different language.

"What about you?" he asked. "Am I to be naked all alone?"

"I grew up in the midst of a small civil war," I said. "I was an only child and my parents fought a lot."

"Why did they have only one child?"

"My mother had two miscarriages and then had to have a hysterectomy. I wish I had had a younger sister or brother. It would have taken a lot of pressure off me."

"I don't know. I'm the youngest of five, and that's plenty of pressure as well. I'm the only one who didn't go to college. My oldest sister and brother are lawyers, the third brother is a dentist, and the one just a year older than me is an optician."

I smiled. "I love a black sheep. They're usually the most interesting family member by far."

"Sure. Who do you think handles my mother's business? Who has to be by her bedside when she's ill? I'm the only one not in Miami and the only one she wants."

Oh no, I thought. She'd probably be a nightmare of a mother-in-law. Call in the middle of the night. Ask him to fly home for some minor reason. Hate me for taking her precious one away. "Is your father still alive?"

He shook his head. "Died five years ago of a stroke. My mother is eighty-one now and has full-time live-in servants, but she's pretty strong."

Strong and strong-headed, I thought.

He turned to me. "Well, Doctor, am I failing your tests?"

I blushed and laughed, and then he took my face in his hands and kissed me on the mouth.

Time slowed down. I closed my eyes and felt my bones turn to jelly. When he pulled away, I tossed back the rest of my drink and smiled inanely, but the world had already changed.

Before dinner, I used the guest bathroom on the main floor. On the counter was an open heart-shaped box of potpourri, a pair of nail clippers, a bottle of Windex, and a cluster of family photos in oval, silver frames.

I recognized Humberto as a teenager, dressed in a tuxedo. There was a photo of an old woman in a wheelchair with a black mantilla around her head and shoulders. One picture showed Humberto holding the hand of a very small boy. I decided I would ask him later to tell me about the people in the photos, and I joined him in the kitchen.

He had put a Natalie Cole CD on his sound system, which also played in the kitchen. As he worked, he sang along, but only the last few words of each line.

"—in every way—" he crooned. "—you'll stay—" Unfortunately, although he obviously loved music, he was painfully off-key. "—unforgettable too—"

I smiled.

Esperanza sat on the kitchen counter in a specially heated intensive-care unit that dispensed a warm mist of antibiotics. She had developed an upper respiratory infection, and Humberto explained that this was the best way to treat it. She looked a little forlorn inside her plastic box, but he reassured me she had been through this before and would come out of it. He was going to keep her at home from now on.

"I wish it would rain," he said, glancing out the window at the clear sky just beginning to show stars. "That's one thing I miss about Nica. Some months it rained every afternoon."

"To me the best thing about rain is listening to it when you're lying in bed and you don't have to get up. But I can't remember the last time I didn't have to get up."

"See? I knew you needed a vacation! I love rain. The smell of it, the sound. I imagine every blade of grass, every tree, every thirsty creature, saying 'aahhhhhh.' "

I laughed and watched him cook.

I was right about him in the kitchen. He practically danced from one dish to the next, testing the seasoning in one, shaking the pan of another. He pointed out that the kitchen was the only place where he followed the rule "Clean as you go." From the looks of his house it was clear he didn't follow that rule elsewhere.

The meal was simple—Chilean sea bass, mashed potatoes, and chopped salad—except everything was perfect. I had never eaten sea bass so soft and sweet, never remembered mashed potatoes so creamy, or a chopped salad with such a perfect blend of vegetables.

It wasn't until we had finished dinner and a full bottle of wine that I decided to ask him something I had been curious about since our first date. "Tell me about the person you mentioned. The one who's never loved." Please, don't let it be him, I prayed.

He picked up his wine glass, drained the last few mouthfuls, set it back down, and then twisted it slowly for a few moments. "I never talk about her."

"Sorry."

"No, I'll tell you. She was very beautiful. From a wealthy Nicaraguan family who lost their money. I met her in Miami eight years ago. As I got to know her I became consumed with her. She had a reputation for being remote. La Reina de Hielo, they called her. Ice Queen.

"She was in medical school, and she transferred her training here to be with me. Our lovemaking was difficult and required a great deal of patience on my part, but I viewed that as one more hurdle to reaching her.

"When she finished her internship, she left me. Yes, of course this pain is here, I said to myself. You always knew it would come.

"For three years I had no contact with her, and during that time I devoted myself ceaselessly to establishing Paradise. The restaurant kept me going. I enjoyed the praise and recognition I earned for my cuisine, and the attention of other women helped restore my wounded pride.

"One day she walked into the restaurant unannounced and I ushered her into my office. 'I'll make it brief,' she said. 'I made a mistake. I shouldn't have left you.'

"I embraced her and told her I'd never stopped loving her. Then I asked 'Why have you come to me now?'

" 'Because,' she said, 'when I was with you, I felt as content as it is possible for me to feel. I have never loved anyone. I've tried and I can't. But I'm willing to offer myself to you as long as you know that.'

"Can you imagine that? The only woman I had ever wanted to marry and she was like a stone! It took all my will to tell her I could not possibly marry her under those circumstances, because there were many hopeful voices in me begging otherwise. But what I had known and denied to myself before, I forced myself to accept then." The sadness in his eyes and his formal way of speaking heightened the poignancy of his story.

I wanted to know that woman's name. Maybe later I would imagine Humberto lying in his bed repeating the name like a mantra and the picture wouldn't be complete without the sound of it.

"Carmina Angelica Marisombra de Alejandro." The syllables rolled off his tongue like a recitation of poetry.

"Does she still live here?"

He shook his head. "Miami. She's a cardiologist now."

"Your mother's cardiologist?"

"How did you guess? It's exceedingly awkward for me."

I'll cross that bridge if I come to it, I thought. I got up from my side of the dining table and walked over to his chair to hold out my hand to him.

After he rose, I wrapped my arms around his neck and rested my forehead against his cheek, where a faint smell of shaving cream lingered. We stood in a full body hug, and I felt his heart thudding heavily, but he did not move his hands from the back of my waist or attempt to kiss me.

He led me by the hand to the living-room sofa. "You might be surprised to hear this—" He paused, pulled me close to him, and rubbed the back of my hand. "I am lonely. I meet people all the time, but rarely someone who interests me. That's why I was so intent on seeing you again. You're such an intriguing mixture of things. In spite of all your professional accomplishments, you still look like you need to be taken into someone's arms and soothed to sleep."

"You're right," I said. If Humberto was seeing the same thing in me as Nick had, he was certainly much kinder about it. I leaned into the curve of his body.

We sat together a long time, saying nothing, holding hands. I was glad he didn't try to rush into sex. Later, after he had taken me home and kissed me good night at the door, I mulled over every detail of the evening.

During our work over the ensuing weeks, Nick resumed acting ill at ease, and I wondered if he was the one who had sent me that card to communicate feelings he couldn't express directly. I had stopped considering him a suspect in the wallpaper slashing. The Romaine sisters were the likely ones, because they had been so angry with me, and this was a typical example of their style of revenge.

I suggested Nick see me twice a week to speed up his therapy, and he agreed, but his eye contact remained poor, and he fidgeted on the sofa, or paced around the room.

"Perhaps you don't feel comfortable discussing your problems here," I would say, or "Perhaps you don't think I'd understand."

To these empathic overtures he would reply, "I don't really know what my problems are," or "I don't understand myself." Yet he kept coming back, which told me that in spite of his wish to deny his difficulties, there was a stronger force wanting help.

He said his stomach was better. He told me jokes, made bathroom visits, or indulged in impersonal chatter. To his irrelevant questions I gave brief responses and lapsed into silence. Although I explained I wouldn't discuss my personal views on such things, I allowed him to continue, while I searched for themes in his thoughts that might reveal something important. Nothing said in a therapy session can be considered meaningless or haphazard, and even seemingly irrelevant subject matter may hold clues to a patient's deeper experience.

He greeted my silence with resentment and increasing hostility. He felt if we weren't talking all the time, it was wasted money. And he focused his hostility on my physical appearance. "You're showing too much thigh today," he'd say, if my skirt fell just above my knee, or "I think you need a more subtle shade of blusher." Once, he said "I think you should wear smaller earrings. You look like a news anchorwoman."

I had long ago mastered a strange trick therapists learn: how to consider another person's perception of me dispassionately. A patient could say he hated me, loved me, envied me; he could criticize me, praise me, or be oversolicitous, and I could separate myself from his comments enough to evaluate what those expressions said about him, without reacting as if the statements were true.

I therefore dutifully responded to Nick's attacks by focusing on the anger or wishes behind them. I knew no matter how I looked he would continue his comments, because challenging me served to keep distance between us, and that's how he maintained control.

Yet in spite of my training, his remarks stirred up my self-consciousness, and I began examining myself carefully in the mirror on the mornings of his appointments.

By the end of May, I'd been seeing Nick twice a week for almost two months. "I have nothing to talk about today," he began again. "I feel fine."

"Tell me more about the ways you're feeling fine." I tried to control my frustration by counting the number of squares in the leaded glass windows. Eighteen.

He shrugged his shoulders. "Nothing's bothering me. I got a great blow job under my desk today, and I'm looking forward to watching the game tonight."

I was struck by the poverty of his inner dialogue. He filled his mind with political facts, legal information, sports trivia, and car performance statistics; he spent his time in constant activity, cramming in too many clients, driving to courthouses, drinking with buddies, playing racquetball, and listening to music. It all served the purpose of limiting contact with his inner self.

"I went out with a new woman last night," he said. "She was lousy in bed. Must be frigid."

Naturally he attributed the problem to his partner. "Have you encountered that before?" I asked.

"Not often. Women like me. I even help them with their clothes and hair. Take you, for example. No offense, but I think if you did some highlighting in your hair, lightened individual strands, it would give your face a lift, and the color would look better. Less mousy."

What a hostile son of a bitch. I was getting sick of this, but I forced my face to remain immobile. "Your interest in improving my physical appearance is quite remarkable."

"I know it bugs you, but I'm doing you a favor. I have an eye for what looks good on women. My ma taught me all that stuff. I give a great pedicure. I've even got the little foam rubber thing that holds your toes in place."

I held back a smile at the image of Nick bent over some woman's foam-spread toes. "So this is one way you show your affection?"

"Yes."

"It might also be a way of pushing women away."

He loosened his tie and then yanked it off. An ugly smirk distorted his mouth, and he leaned over to the coffee table and dusted the edge with his fingers. "You would think that."

"Why's that?"

"I guess you're pretty insecure about your appearance."

I was wearing a buttoned suit with no blouse, and because I hadn't been able to take off the jacket, I was now sweating. Ironically, I'd picked this suit because I thought the crisp French fitted waist and soft blue color looked particularly attractive on me, and part of my defense against Nick's attacks had been to take extra care with my appearance on the days of his appointments.

As evenly as I could, I said, "Perhaps you're attacking me where you sense I'm vulnerable." My leather chair felt hot and sticky, and I wished I had an upholstered one.

He raised his hands, palms upward in a gesture of innocence. "Why do you see it as an attack instead of friendly advice from someone who's got the nerve to be honest with you?"

"You know you're insulting me. I'd say being close to me frightens you, and if you feel one up, you feel safer. Your friendly advice is designed to put me down and stay in control."

"You're wrong. But never mind." He turned his head to the side and looked away, then crossed his right leg over the left and jiggled the dangling foot. "Let's talk about something else. I have a new heavy-duty divorce case. The husband had an affair, got the woman pregnant; now he's leaving my client for the woman. We're going to take him to the laundry and hang his ass out to dry."

"Perhaps you'd like to divorce yourself from this therapy."

He laughed. "You're probably right about that. I don't seem to be getting much out of it."

"I think you're angry at me right now."

"Me? No." He reached over to the palm leaf next to him and crushed a frond.

I'd broken my own rule and sounded defensive; worse, I'd used psychological knowledge in the service of anger. I could have lost him.

He opened his briefcase for his checkbook and pulled from his breastpocket a Mont Blanc pen exactly like mine.

Startled, I said, "Your pen—"

He looked directly at me. "I just bought it. They're great pens, aren't they?"

My face flushed. Was that really his pen or had he stolen mine and was he now taunting me? "Yes. Great pens."

He left immediately, before I even had a chance to get up and see him to the door. I didn't know what was upsetting me more—suspecting he had stolen my pen or thinking about how I had mismanaged the session. I wondered whether he would ever come back, and if he didn't, if I would care. The whole case was becoming a headache.

Between sessions, I pulled a brush through my hair while I listened to messages: two cancellations, my mother calling to give me my cousin's wedding date, a quick question from Kevin Utley about video equipment, and a reminder from Valerie to meet her at our aerobics class.

I examined my skin, powdered my face, and reapplied my lipstick. My glasses were making a dent on the left side of my nose, so I fiddled with the frame to take some pressure off. I didn't have time to run to the optician, and I needed to see the dermatologist, but I thought I'd postpone that too.

Before I left the office I phoned my mother and told her I didn't think I could come home for the wedding. She clucked her tongue and said, "That's the price I pay for having a high-powered daughter."

"But you want that for me, don't you?" We both knew the more independent and financially secure I was, the less likely I would have to endure what she'd been through.

"Of course, honey. I boast about you all the time."

This pleased me. "Thanks, Mom. Love you."

Our conversation made me late, and I raced through yellow traffic lights to get to the Sports Club. In the women's spa, I found Val in a corner, struggling into her spandex leotard. "It's hell when you're over thirty," she grunted, and left her strap dangling to hug me hello. Val's mass of curly brown hair swept into my face.

"Will you look at these women?" I asked in a low voice, as I disentangled myself. The room was full of Westside beauties, dressed in thong-strap leotards and contrasting tights. After sitting down, we were eye-level with brightly colored, completely exposed butts, and all I could think of was baboons in heat, with their swollen red behinds bobbing in the faces of their mates.

After aerobics class, a quick swim, and a shower, we sat at the juice bar and savored twenty minutes together.

"I'm exhausted," Val said. Her unruly hair was now caught in a scrunch at the nape of her neck. "There's never enough time for everything, and I've been getting about five hours sleep a night." She traced a path of parallel lines through the water drops on the table, as if making orderly motions could organize her life.

"I'm always starved for time, too. But what can you eliminate?"

"Driving crosstown two nights a week to meet Richard in a motel." It was another affair with a married man, this time a nationally known psychiatrist. "He's brilliant. It's worth it," she added.

"You know what I think."

"Yeah, yeah. And what's going on with Humberto?"

I smiled. "I've been seeing him at least twice a week, and he's started calling me every night at eleven. But I haven't forgotten that woman he was with at the restaurant. And his old girlfriend is still around."

"Why don't you just wait and see how things develop?"

"I will. Now let me ask you this. I think one of my patients stole something from me. And he may be trying to worm his way into my life."

When I told Val the details, she reassured me. "Anyone could have bought a Mont Blanc pen. And you've only bumped into him two times, one of which was near your office. I see patients near my office all the time. They shop after their sessions. Ha! Probably because they feel I'm a withholding bitch and they have to treat themselves to something."

We laughed, and when we hugged good-bye, I felt the way I always felt after being with Val: that the rough edges of my life were smooth again, and I could take my problems home in my pocket like worn stones from the beach.

11

Although I had begun dating Humberto regularly, between his commitments at the restaurant and my own schedule, we were not able to see each other often enough.

On weeknights, we went to prestigious restaurants where the menus had brand-name meats and vegetables: free-range Chatanille chicken, Botsas radicchio. Weekends we went to hidden restaurants: a tiny Vietnamese diner in Huntington Park, a Cuban bistro in East Hollywood, a Chinese-French cafe in Redondo Beach. At these places he examined the ingredients of the food, talked with the cooks and owners, and explained to me why certain flavors blended so well. Sometimes when he bent down to look closely at his plate, or gently picked apart the layers of a dessert, images of my mother sprang to mind, of evenings in front of the fireplace, holiday recipe books in hand, a look of intense concentration on her face.

One night on the way home we stopped at Paradise so Humberto could check for any problems. I waited in the Tapas room and watched people while I sipped a vodka tonic. An attractive silver-haired woman walked by wearing velvet slippers and a tailored black tuxedo with no shirt underneath. Two white bow ties were glued to her bare chest, with a third tied around her neck. A bearded man stood near me holding a drink and laughing loudly. His tie was a rectangular flat plastic box, containing water and a live goldfish. The woman next to me had her hair in a dyed black-and-white mohawk.

When my beeper sounded, I retreated to Humberto's office to call the service. He was in there, completing some paperwork, and he shook his head while I mollified a panicky patient. Afterward he said "I don't know how you stand all that insanity."

I looked at him in amazement. "This place has every bit as much insanity as my office. Believe me."

He laughed. "I'm sure you're right."

We sat on his loveseat and kissed. It was so sweet, so exciting, that the urge to continue was almost irresistible. Yet I did stop, and when he respectfully drew away, his flushed face and obvious erection made me feel like a tease. "I just need a little more time," I explained.

"Listen to this new CD," he said, springing up to turn on his stereo. "The tenor sax is absolutely heart-wrenching." He shut off all the lights except the one over his desk, pulled me to my feet, and began a slow dance. I loved the feel of the length of his body against mine. As we navigated slowly around the small floor space, I felt swept up in his energy and enthusiasm for life. "You make me glad to be alive," I said into his ear.

He held me tighter and I felt a surge of arousal.

Little things I never noticed before reminded me of Humberto—birds, news stories on Nicaragua, restaurant reviews. I tried to be even more interesting and insightful than usual on the radio, knowing he was listening.

One soft June evening we went to a concert of Mexican mariachi music at Hollywood's ornate red-and-gold Pantages Theater. After the show started, he took my hand and held it in his lap. The way he massaged my palm with his thumb was wildly distracting, and when he whispered in my ear I was mesmerized by his talking—the soft rhythm, the timbre of his voice, the Spanish inflection. It almost didn't matter what he said, it sounded like music to me.

I fixed my eyes on the women whirling around the stage in white three-quarter-length dresses and sturdy dancing shoes. Each one had black hair, shiny as patent leather, tightened into a chignon at the base of the neck and crowned with red hibiscus. They danced with arms held up, noses high, and faces turned to the side.

Not since high school had I let myself get close to a man who excited me so much. Even though I had begged for time, whenever he pushed his tongue into my mouth or tightly grasped the hair at the back of my head, so great was my desire for him that I had to wrench myself away.

It was his enthusiasm for life I found so sexy—his curiosity and spontaneity. I had been with educated men before, dutiful men who had endured the rigors of medical school or architecture or law, who had planned out their lives at age twelve and had stayed the course, but here was an intelligent man bringing me the unexpected as a gift—stepping into my calendar, filled months in advance, and asking, "Did you see the partial eclipse of the moon last night?" or handing me long stems of pampas grass he had spent a half hour collecting on the hill near his home.

The stage was a village in Mexico, where the women sighed and waited, and men strutted and died. The men were older, mostly stout, mustached and wearing huge white hats that curled up in front and back. They stood facing forward, feet apart and firmly planted, with a defiant power to their carriage that was convincing. They played guitars, horns, and violins with such energy that the instruments themselves seemed alive.

"For a love, I can't sleep and I live full of passion," Humberto translated. His warm breath and the motion of his lips against my ear caused me to shudder.

The men formed a semicircle around the lead songstress, a woman whose voice soared over the audience and broke into a high falsetto, then back down to a rich contralto. *"Ayeeeee, mi corazon enredado con el tuyo . . ."*

The backdrop on the stage was black velvet, covered with red and green sequins and little bits of mirror. Probably in the daylight it would have looked tacky, but in the darkened theater with the stage lights on, it looked like a sea of precious stones.

I wanted my relationship with Humberto to hold up in the daylight, but I had seen glimpses of things I didn't like—a reckless competitiveness with other cars on the road, the impulsive firing of a waiter who embarrassed him in front of a customer, an occasional glance past me at a beautiful woman.

Later, in my darkened living room, he stroked my hair as we sat in silence on the couch. "I'd like to tell you something I've been thinking," he said.

"What?" I turned to face him. The only light came from the street lamp outside, and all I could see was the dark outline of his features.

"I want to make love to you slowly, so you can feel every moment of it."

I drank the words in like a woman dying of thirst. Sensing it, he was on his feet in a moment, pulling me up to him. His mouth closed over mine. I couldn't open my eyes and I couldn't let go of him.

He insisted that Frank be locked in the kitchen, and to the sound of Frank's muffled howling, he led me into the bedroom. I stood in the middle of the room, tense with excitement, while Humberto turned on the bathroom switch and left the door slightly ajar so there was just enough light in the bedroom to see each other clearly.

I was wearing a red wool jersey dress that buttoned down the front to the navel, and except for his jacket and tie, he was still fully clothed in his dress shirt, slacks, and leather belt.

I wanted to tumble into bed and get lost in the physical sensations, but Humberto was slow and deliberate in his movements. He took my head between his hands and kissed me deeply as he had in the living room, then he pulled back and undid only the top two buttons of my dress.

Ordinarily I would have taken the lead, finished undressing, and undressed him. That's the way it had been with Pallen the first time, but now I felt hypnotized, and compelled to let him set the pace.

He took me by the shoulders, and traced his tongue around the base of my right ear. Then slowly, he worked his way down my neck to the hollow between my breasts.

"I can feel your heart pounding," he whispered.

I pulled off my dress, let it drop to the floor, and pressed myself against him. He was erect, and I put my arms around his neck and hugged him to me so tightly I could feel his hardness digging into my belly.

He pulled my arms from his neck, placed them at my sides, and carefully took off my bra. When he gently cupped one of my breasts in his hand and enclosed it in his mouth, I went weak, and murmured, "Let's lie down."

"Not yet," he said, returning to my mouth. "I want you to see us together in the mirror." He embraced me again and stroked my hair. "You're so lovely."

He removed his own clothes and let them drop to the floor. His chest and back were hairless, and his nipples were dark and small. He had long, slender legs and a high, round butt, and his full erection reached almost up to his belly button. There was a mole over his left shoulder blade, and several more scattered across his back; his feet faced outward like a duck's, and his toes were too long, and overlapping. Still, I thought his body was beautiful.

He encircled me from behind and pressed the full length of his front against my back. The heat of his chest against me startled me.

In front of the full-length mirror, I watched him work his way down my front with his hands, then kneel and lick the back of my knees. When for a moment, he reached his hand around and dragged his fingers through the moist spot between my legs, I gasped, and he led me to the bed.

After stretching out beside me, he asked so many questions, it surprised me. His hands roamed over my body, and he stopped in places and asked, "Do you like it when I touch you like this?" I answered quietly, yes here, no there, softer on my inner thigh, harder on my nipples. When his fingers dipped between my legs, he asked, "And here?" and I placed my hand over his fingers, and showed him how I liked it. It had taken Pallen eight months to learn what Humberto knew in a half hour.

But as deft as he was with his tongue and his hands, orgasm eluded me, and I stayed poised in a heightened state of excitement, breathing rapidly, and aching for release.

After some time he stopped, and crawled up on his hands and knees until he was directly over me. His erection was gone, and in the dim light I could see he was flushed, and his muscles trembled, not from excitement but from overuse. "Don't feel any pressure," he said.

"Whatever happens tonight is fine. Relax. Enjoy the sensations. I'll do anything you like for as long as you want."

Apologetic tears brimmed onto my cheeks, and he covered them with his mouth, warm and tart from my own juice. He continued kissing me, again working from my face down my neck to my stomach. Gradually I relaxed.

By the time his tongue darted quickly around my inner folds again, it took only a few minutes before I thrashed my head around side to side from the intensity of the orgasm.

Then he was on top of me, and I wrapped my legs around him to take him inside me. He moved slowly, making me feel, as he had promised, every moment of it. Tears spilled from my eyes. My hands kneaded his back. I whimpered and sucked on his lips. It was the sweetest torment.

He stroked inside me harder and faster, and this time I came easily and laughed with pleasure that it had happened so fast. When he finally released himself into me, I felt we were one being, and I moaned along with him as if his orgasm were mine.

Later, after we had downed several glasses of water, sprung Frank from his prison, and turned out the bathroom light, we lay on our sides in bed, he curled around my back, arm tucked around my waist, and me facing the window, able to see the outline of Frank's sturdy body settled on the floor next to my bedside table.

Humberto pulled a strand of hair away from my face, and kissed my ear lightly. "Good night," he said.

"It was the best," I whispered. And how well you know women, I thought.

Long after the reassuring sound of his deep breathing began, I lay wide awake.

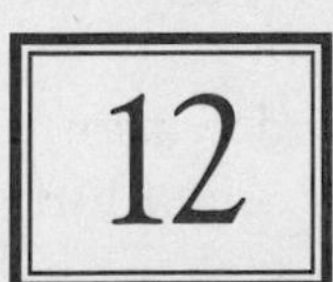

12

Like a schoolgirl, I told Valerie the details of our lovemaking, and I started shaving my legs every single morning in case Humberto spent the night. Even in the middle of a therapy session, I sometimes had a sudden memory of the way his body felt against mine.

I confessed to Humberto that I worried all the time about making mistakes with my patients. He told me his restaurant had a terrible cockroach problem. I began adjusting to the idea of being with someone from a different country. He tried to be more neat when he knew I was coming over. In the short time I'd known him, he had become the highlight of my day.

Nick, on the other hand, was becoming a definite problem. "I dreamed about you after our last session," he said when I saw him again. He was agitated, first crossing and uncrossing his legs, then pacing, now standing next to the wall, then rocking forward on his toes. "You were wearing only a white slip, the kind that has a top with shoulder straps. You started talking to me and then you turned into that mermaid sitting on a rock, the one that lures sailors to their death, like the Sirens. I tried to run, but I realized I was in water, and as hard as I was running I was barely moving. I panicked and started to drown and woke up yelling."

I waited.

"I think I'm getting worse. I came to see you to get rid of my nightmares and instead you're in them too now."

"I think you'd feel that way about any woman you need."

He moved to the window and picked at a tiny chip in the paint of the sill. This destructive gesture aggravated me.

"I learned a long time ago," he said to the sill, "there's no one I can trust."

"What do you associate with a woman's full slip?"

"My ma used to walk around the house in her slappy heels and a slip like that. I could see her triangle."

"What do you think about the dream?"

He returned to the sofa. "That you turn me on."

"I think the sexual element in the dream is really secondary," I said quickly. "It's just a cover, like it is between you and me. Your real fear is that you can't trust me, that I'm like a hooker doing it for money, or a Siren luring you to your death."

"I want to trust you," he said in a softer voice. "But a lot of times I have no thoughts here. Later when I'm at home I think of things I should have told you."

"Your mind is protecting you from getting close to me by emptying itself of thoughts in my presence."

He was all movement again, throwing his hands up and pacing. He reminded me of my dad: athletic-looking, muscular, white shirt-sleeves rolled up to reveal tanned skin. I noticed the outline of his thigh through his pants, and the way his top front teeth came together too close to his bottom teeth, so that the S was pronounced with his teeth in the bite position, a sound that seemed appealing for no apparent reason.

"What's the point in getting close to you?" he said angrily. "You think I can count on you? If I really need you, you won't be there. Sure I can call you or see you for an hour any time I've got the hundred and fifty bucks, but that doesn't mean I can count on you."

"Nick, the very limits of our relationship are what make this treatment work. You can say anything here, because nothing will be acted upon and we'll never spend time together socially. If we saw each other outside this office, we'd no longer be able to use our relationship to examine your assumptions about yourself and other people."

He stood up, shoved his hands in his pockets, and turned to go. "How can you talk about being close two hours a week? It's ridiculous! And frustrating. Besides, I think you like me more than that, even though you won't admit it."

He was almost right: when I was with him I sometimes had sexual thoughts about him, even though I was in love with Humberto. There was a tight, graceful energy to Nick that was exciting—and even his insolence, his defiance, had a sexual quality.

But the idea of breaking the boundaries of therapy was abhorrent to me. Most patients had sexual fantasies about their therapists, and therapists often had fleeting sexual fantasies about their patients, all of which were to be analyzed and contained. To take advantage of a patient's desires was the most reckless form of malpractice.

For his next two appointments, Nick arrived late, and then tried to stay an extra ten minutes to make up for it. I refused to extend his sessions, and over this issue we haggled most of one hour.

I said, "There's a reason why you haven't managed to get here on time."

"Traffic! Don't you understand L.A. traffic?"

"Sometimes it's more complicated than that. Perhaps some anxiety about being with me?"

The color in his face deepened and he said curtly, "What makes you so smug anyway? You have to start and stop exactly on time. You've got a response for anything I say. Your thinking is like a fundamentalist religion. Airtight."

I tried not to react to his baiting. He was certainly wrestling for control by challenging the time boundaries, but perhaps he was also afraid my responses to him were not what he needed. And I could have been acting smug. I was clinging more rigidly than usual to the formal framework of the therapy, because he so desperately wanted to violate it. Would it really have made such a difference if I had let him go over five minutes?

I brushed a hair off my cheek. "Like everyone else I certainly have my flaws, and yes, I do have theories and principles I use to do my work, but let's talk about why that makes you angry."

"You're just so high and mighty."

"And that's my way of letting you know I think you're small and weak?"

"You see? That's exactly what I'm talking about. For everything I say you've got a theory about what it means. And it's probably a textbook theory."

"So I don't do any original thinking about you? Just plug you into a book and spit out the prefab responses?"

He got up, took off his suit jacket, and flung it on the cushion seat next to him, before sitting down again. "Maybe not. But what makes you so sure your therapy's right for me? How do you know I won't be worse off?"

He was scared. I should have seen it immediately, but I was too worried about looking smug. "I can't predict the outcome," I said. "That depends on whether you can trust me and whether I can understand you. I can't guarantee you won't be worse off, although I believe a person is always better off knowing his inner thoughts. But that's part of what you call my airtight system." I smiled kindly to show I really wanted the best for him.

His shoulders relaxed and his hands came to rest by his sides. "Am I just a case to you?"

"Did I do something that made you feel that way?"

He looked like an adolescent whose mother has just found him with pornography. "I saw a brochure on a lecture you're giving at UCLA. 'Narcissistic Underpinnings of Eating Disorders.' It said case presentations."

Jesus Christ. Patients had transference reactions to everything. Unless I lived in a box I'd always have to deal with it, and I was much more visible than the average therapist. Why hadn't he just told me in the beginning? "You saw that and concluded I must think of my patients as cases, rather than real people whom I care about?"

"Yes."

"Have I done anything else that gives you that feeling?"

"Sometimes I see the patient before me leaving, and the light on your wall signaling another patient waiting. Like I'm on an assembly line."

"Meaning you couldn't be special to me?"

"Right."

"You didn't feel special in your family, either."

"No."

"Might you therefore be quick to conclude I don't think you're special?" Here was the flip side of narcissistic grandiosity: feelings of abject worthlessness and the chronic search for special treatment to counteract those feelings.

"Probably." Then he fell silent.

I hoped he'd see how much the past was guiding his reactions to the present. My anger and frustration were replaced by sympathy. After a few minutes of silence, I asked if wanting to be special was an issue in his life, and slowly, and reluctantly, he gave examples: he demanded that women date him exclusively; he fired a law clerk who'd made inquiries at another firm; he hated to wait in line; he tried to get the best seats for a show, or backstage passes, or discounts when clothes were not on sale.

I was pleased with the rush of confirmatory material. It had been an uncomfortable session, but by the end a productive one, and that's what mattered.

After one deep relaxing breath, I opened the door to my next patient, Luness. She sank down into the sofa until her shoulders rounded and her chest caved in.

"I was really good yesterday," she said. "I had a bowl of tomato soup and three pretzels."

Her world is so narrow. How sad to force all of existence through such a tiny funnel: what she ate today and how her body looks. "How many times have you vomited this week?"

"Probably nine." She jiggled her foot. "Don't be mad. Vomiting is the only sport I'm good at."

It was not uncommon for bulimics to feel that vomiting gave them a sense of mastery over their bodies, but I had never heard it put quite this way.

"If there was a contest to see who could vomit anywhere, any time, I'd be right up there."

"Why don't we explore other physical activities that you've enjoyed? Maybe we can expand your repertoire."

Luness giggled. "I started seeing someone new. Very handsome.

Smart. But he drives too fast." She fell silent and continued jiggling her foot.

"What's wrong?" I asked.

She covered her eyes. "I'm afraid to tell you." Then she crossed her arms and stared at the carpet.

"What are you afraid will happen if you tell me?"

"You'll be mad or you'll tell me not to see him."

"Why would I be mad?"

There was a tense pause. "Because he's your patient."

Instantly I knew it was Nick. The description. The fact that his session directly preceeded hers. Hadn't he just said a half hour ago that he was noticing my other patients? I said, "How did this develop?"

"Usually, after my session with you, I go to the bathroom, and when I return the key to the waiting room, he's there. We just started talking."

I'll bet. Talking about therapy and comparing notes.

"So are you mad?"

"No. But you must understand that I cannot reveal any information to you about him, just as I would not share anything about you with him."

"I'm really attracted to him. Don't you think he's gorgeous?"

I did my best to discuss Nick with Luness as if he were a complete stranger, but it was difficult. He was acting out some unconscious process with her that was intended for me, and I was afraid she was going to get hurt.

Yet I could not interfere. Gone were the days when a therapist could tell patients not to date other patients or not to make important decisions. I was going to have to sit on the sidelines and mop up the tears.

After Luness left, I decided I would get a consultation on Nick. Something about his dating her gave me a queasy feeling in the pit of my stomach.

PART II

13

Val followed my advice and broke off her relationship with the psychiatrist, but this resulted in her spending Saturday nights alone, eating candy and watching old movies.

"Why don't we have a party?" I suggested. "Invite all the single guys we know." I wanted to do something for her and I hadn't had a party in years.

Her face lit up. "Let's do it! How about the weekend after next? We could have an afternoon barbecue."

We went through our address books and made a list. Humberto offered to cater, but I told him I wanted it very casual and all he had to do was show up and meet my friends.

We sent out written invitations, and after the replies we expected about forty people. I was relieved that Morry was unable to attend, because I felt a little awkward about having met Humberto through him.

I ordered coleslaw, potato salad, baked beans, and stuffed tortillas, and Val planned to grill her specialty, turkey Southwestern style.

The day of the party began with carrots. As I hauled the grocery bags into the kitchen, Frank barked frantically because he assumed every grocery bag held carrots—his favorite treat. When I gave him his vegetable, he accepted it like a communion wafer and retreated ceremoniously to the living room to settle in a corner.

By the time our guests began arriving, Frank had downed five carrots and was excitedly greeting everyone in person. It was seventy-five degrees and sunny, with almost no breeze. I became light-headed from a few beers, and felt wonderfully relaxed.

The four interns I supervised at the V.A. Hospital came. One brought her husband—a short, round man who talked a lot about the European Economic Community. The male star of the group brought a date who kept sneezing and reapplying her lipstick. The other two worked the party for referrals.

Frank roamed happily from one guest to another, affably accepting handouts, and nosing through women's purses. We put my stereo speakers in the back windows and played a stack of CDs, and as the party went into full swing, I thought everyone was having a good time.

Kevin Utley brought his wife, whom I had never met before. He was stocky and blond, with bulging brown eyes and a huge handlebar mustache. She was petite and dark, with small, even features. The walrus and the wren, I thought, smiling. I told her how much I relied on Kevin's judgment when I needed a quick call from the bench.

Humberto busied himself as bartender, charming everyone with his easy style. One of my interns spilled a plate of beans on her lap, and let Frank eat the remains. She laughed and thanked him for the cleanup job.

Val's barbecued turkey was a big hit, and Val, several vodka-and-tonics into the afternoon, managed to become deeply embroiled in conversation with yet another married psychiatrist. I gave her a warning look and she moved on to a single, curly-haired hospital administrator, one of the ones we had decided might be a possibility for her.

By eight o'clock everyone had left except Val and Humberto, who were in the kitchen cleaning. Val was singing along with Bonnie Raitt, giddy with the secret she had told me: she and the administrator had a date for the next evening.

As I collected the glasses, I caught Frank, nose in the garbage can, gobbling a few more pieces of discarded turkey skin. "No more!" I cried and yanked the rest away from him.

The turkey skin turned out to be the final blow. By the time Val and Humberto had restored the kitchen, Frank was dragging himself restlessly from one place to another, apparently unable to get comfortable.

"Do you think I should call the vet?" I asked.

Val said, "I saw him lap up at least two beers. He's probably drunk and just needs to sleep it off."

I hadn't known about Frank's beer quaffing, and I assumed that was the problem. I helped Val pack her bowls in the car, gave her a big hug, and then Humberto and I flopped down on the sofa to watch TV.

We woke up an hour later to the sound of Frank's whimpering. Concerned, I got up and followed the sound to the dining room, where I found him stretched out motionless under the table, his breathing labored. Usually wild with affection, he barely wagged his tail when I bent down to stroke him.

I roused a sleepy Humberto, who helped me put Frank in the car and drive him to West L.A. Veterinary Hospital. I was grateful the facility was open all the time, but still surprised at that hour to find the waiting room full of pet owners and their animals.

"Weekends are big for us," the receptionist explained casually. "Barbecue burns, swallowed napkins, plastic utensils in odd places, steak bone fragments lodged in the throat, and of course, car accidents. Holidays are the worst. I can't tell you how many dogs we've x-rayed that have half-eaten Christmas ornaments in their stomachs."

"What do you do for them?" I asked, making a mental note not to decorate my tree this year.

"Surgery. It's the only way to get the stuff out. It'll be about fifteen minutes before I can put you in an examining room. Just have a seat."

The place smelled like an old YMCA because of the bleach used to keep things sanitary. There were video cameras for security, prints of animals on the walls, and a janitor continually mopping up hair and puddles. When I saw the staff roster, with specialists like canine oncologists and avian respiratory therapists, I told Humberto I felt guilty that the pets on the Westside of L.A. received better health care than a good percentage of Americans, to say nothing of children in Third-World countries.

We turned to the rows of plastic chairs. A huge woman in a red warm-up suit sat stroking a shivering Chihuahua. Two Asian girls were whispering and poking their fingers through their iguana's cage. A middle-aged woman in an evening gown was holding a Persian cat, next to a police officer reining in a drooling German shepherd. The room was filled with the sound of mewing, barking, and whining.

I walked Frank slowly toward a few empty chairs and sat down. Humberto wandered around for a while, looking at the posters and reading the bulletin board, before sitting next to me.

Frank chose the moment of Humberto's return to begin a protracted whine. Humberto looked at him huddled on the floor and said, "I hope nothing serious is wrong with him." He reached down to pat my miserable-looking pet.

While Humberto's hand still rested on him, Frank suddenly struggled to his feet, his whole body growing rigid. Humberto withdrew his hand in alarm.

My dog stood motionless, feet firmly planted on the floor, eyes staring and glazed. His tail slowly lifted until it was held straight out from his body. From deep within his belly a gurgling sound began that held Humberto and me frozen in our respective positions.

The fat lady in red picked up her Chihuahua and held him tightly to her chest. Several dogs began barking.

The gurgling turned into a low-pitched, undulating howl of intestinal gas that increased in volume and sound as Frank slowly released it from his body. Five seconds of gas was enough to surprise us, ten seconds was astonishing, and the full fifteen-second performance, though it seemed to help Frank tremendously, took all of us beyond the reach of propriety and into the common bond of helpless laughter.

With the arrival of Frank's toxic cloud, however, mirth quickly mingled with disgust, and everyone, including Humberto and me, moved away from the offending area.

"Sorry, folks!" Humberto said to the room. "That's the last time we use those prune dog biscuits!"

After we relocated, Frank let out another few short pops of noise. He looked positively perky by the time the vet came out to take him to x-ray. When she returned, she said the x-rays showed Frank hadn't swallowed a foreign object, and had simply reacted to a strange mixture of unfamiliar foods. He was as energetic and adorable as usual by then. Apparently all he needed was that monstrous fart.

I put my arms around Humberto and laughed and thanked him for helping me. I had been proud of him at the party, and he had been very kind to Frank.

14

Over the next few weeks, more things disappeared from my office waiting room. One day it was a brass cardholder with all my business cards. Another day it was the key to the men's restroom. More curious was the disappearance of toys. Since some patients brought their children to sit in the waiting room if they were unable to locate a babysitter, I had installed a shelf system along one wall, filled with Lego, dolls, puzzles, crayons, and drawing pads.

One week a Lego house vanished. Another week two troll dolls were missing and I had to run down to a toy store at noon to replace them. When I returned I noticed that the crayons looked different, and on closer examination I discovered all the red ones were gone.

The most peculiar things stolen were ordinary: a box of Kleenex, an old *Time* magazine, a light bulb. Anyone passing through my building could have opened my waiting room door and taken something, but I couldn't help thinking it was a patient, and the one patient I suspected was Nick.

These thefts made me nervous, because they were so small and personal, and I had the nagging feeling that he was toying with me. I was loathe to raise the subject directly with Nick, because I had no evidence it was him, and if I was wrong he would feel attacked. So I watched and waited, and wondered why he would do such a thing, if it was him.

For my consultation on Nick, I chose Zachary Leitwell, M.D., a robust, pink-cheeked training analyst in his early sixties, who specialized in disorders of the self. Over the years I had heard him lecture, and his expertise and humaneness always impressed me.

We met during the first week of August. Zachary's office was in the Cedars towers next to the medical center, with a lovely view of the Hollywood Hills. "I remember you," he said smiling. "I was impressed with your lecture at UCLA on psychosomatic illness."

I thanked him and sat down in a comfortable plaid chair. Briefly I summarized Nick's history, disguising the identifying information to protect his privacy. I said I'd chosen not to administer psychological tests to Nick, because he was so distrustful. I told him about the chance encounters outside the office, the thefts, and my concern about feeling aroused by Nick. I finished by emphasizing how difficult I found him.

"In fact," I added, "sometimes I hate all the practical stuff of therapy—the preparations for vacations, the haggling over money, the intrusion of my own feelings."

"But your own reactions are guideposts and you must pay attention to them. If you listen to your feelings for Nick you may discover you have a Borderline on your hands."

I was surprised. I had pegged Nick for a Narcissistic Personality with some paranoid traits—an arrogant, self-centered guy who had difficulty trusting people. I said, "But he functions well at work, and he complains of feeling nothing, which doesn't sound like a Borderline to me."

Zachary put his feet up on his footstool and I could see a hole forming on the sole of his shoe. I found this endearing in a man who could obviously afford new shoes. He said, "Listen to what you've told me. He manipulates, he undercuts, he provokes and seduces."

"That all sounds narcissistic."

"I don't have to tell you it isn't either-or. He can look narcissistic on the surface and have a borderline personality structure underneath. Some Borderlines develop a false self that looks pretty good on the surface, but underneath there's a fragile, partially formed true self that isn't exposed until the person attaches to someone."

"This might turn out to be more of a challenge than I thought." People with Borderline personalities are impulsive and self-destructive. They live in constant emotional pain and are prone to episodes of rage uncalled for by the reality of a situation. They're manipulative, needy, demanding, and disruptive. They may feel empty or confused, make suicide attempts, or get into fights. They call in the middle of the night. They don't respect other people's privacy. They hurt themselves and others as well.

I said, "I started out thinking my biggest problem was hooking him into treatment, and I was pleased because he was bringing in interesting dreams to analyze."

"Don't be fooled by that. It may just be a form of dating. You bring a woman flowers to woo her, you bring a shrink disturbing dreams. It doesn't necessarily mean he's really working at the therapy."

"No. In fact I think he's trying to seduce me instead of engaging in the therapy."

"Absolutely. His seductiveness is resistance. If he succeeds in seducing you, the purpose of the therapy is derailed and his true self remains hidden."

"He's very good at it."

"Sarah, I've had women actually take off their clothes in a session. You just have to keep interpreting it and refuse to participate."

I gave a shocked laugh. "You're kidding!"

"Not kidding. And for some reason it's always the beautiful ones. But you can handle it. Keep remembering it's not really personal."

"It sure feels personal at the time."

"Yes it does, but really it's a testament to the power of transference."

"I know he's doing it on purpose to distract me and it pisses me off that it's working."

"It's fine as long as you don't act on your feelings, and as long as you keep interpreting his behavior. Eventually you're going to break through that manipulative show and get down to a depressed, angry little boy."

"What about the other stuff—the thefts, the run-ins with me, and his dating my other patient?"

"All of it is a way to hold onto pieces of you. He's afraid to trust you and get close to you, so he does these things instead. I think confronting him about your other patient is a good place to start."

"But he hasn't mentioned a word about it! How can I bring up a relationship he's not talking about? I'd be violating the confidence of my other patient!"

"Hmm. He's clever, isn't he? But of course he knows you know, and he's watching to see what you'll do. Let him play it out. And if he gives you the opportunity to talk about it, focus specifically on the fact that the patient is a connection to you. This is a guy who can't talk about his feelings and is acting upon them instead."

"Do you think he's dangerous?"

"Every Borderline has the potential for violent acting-out, but you haven't told me anything that alarms me."

I breathed easier. I was overreacting.

Zachary ran his fingers through his hair and an unruly lock fell over his forehead. "And one more thing. You underestimate the value of practicalities."

"What do you mean?"

"Therapy is like the work of a mother and infant. Through the mundane process of changing diapers, giving breast milk, soothing to sleep, something magic happens: a self is formed. If a child doesn't get those things he suffers and sometimes goes crazy. It's the same in therapy. The practicalities are often the very music of the process."

He was right. I said, "Thanks, you've been very helpful. Can I see you again in a few weeks?"

Zachary smiled broadly. "Of course. And Sarah, don't worry too much that this man gets to you. It's important that you remain open to your patients. Otherwise, the magic is lost. They always know when they're with a therapist who's created distance; they feel the disdain and go away inside to protect themselves. Only a fool would show his jewels to a thief."

I returned to my work feeling a renewed commitment to the therapeutic process. It was the most hopeful work I could imagine, and even if things were difficult with Nick, I could take consolation in the progress of other patients.

Luness filled her next few sessions with intense rumination about Nick. Discussing him with her was a perilous course to navigate, but I was able to pick apart the meaning of the relationship for her, without commenting on Nick himself.

I did ask her whether she had discussed her therapy with him. She said, "Yes—that's how we spend most of our time together. He does a great imitation of you."

This angered me, not only because I could imagine them laughing together about me, but because I knew Nick would tire of Luness and eventually hurt her.

The next week my depressed patient, William Swan, arrived with disastrous news: his wife, Elizabeth, was leaving him. "She's fifty-five and her lover's thirty-one. You'd think she'd be embarrassed in front of the children. My heavens, he's just three years older than our son!"

"This is a complete shock to you?"

"I'm beside myself. I knew she fancied younger men, but I didn't think she'd do something like this. After all, we've been together nearly thirty years."

"You think a marriage ought to stay together regardless of how it's going?" I asked toward the end of the session.

"The motto on our family crest reads 'Let us be judged by our actions.' Propriety and honor are everything."

"No matter how you feel?"

"Yes."

In a way I was glad Luness was taking a chance on Nick, even if she might later be hurt, and I scolded myself for feeling impatient with William. I wanted my patients to take healthy risks, because I knew how easy it was to get used to a bad situation and become stuck in it. This I learned from my mother.

When I was seven, my grandmother had several small strokes and began requiring daily care. My mother's brother lived in Milwaukee, Grandpa was dead, and Mom didn't have the heart to put Grandma in a nursing home. So every day from ten until three, Mom shopped, cooked, and cleaned for her mother, trying to ignore the steady rain of insults.

By my early teens, my talented and beautiful mother had allowed herself to be defeated, and I hated her for letting it happen. It made me furious to hear the sound of Mom's footsteps clumping up the wooden stairs to our back door at the end of the day. I knew her shoulders would be slumped forward so her breasts almost touched her waist; I knew the way her sigh would sound as she fumbled for her key; I knew she had eaten too much yet again that day to soothe herself through the aggravation. Sometimes I would listen in a rage to the sound of her grocery bags rustling, but I would not get up and let her in.

I often thought the first blood clot in Grandma's brain landed on her small kind spot and eradicated it completely. I hated my mother for taking the abuse and sacrificing her life, and I dreaded the possibility that she might get sick and face me with the same dilemma. She wanted me to anticipate her needs and try to fulfill them—to make her hot chocolate at night, and watch TV with her and take her side against my father. I failed her again and again.

I realized much later that my searching to understand the most subtle nuances of my patients' experience was the obverse of my determination to ignore my mother's. I had been unable to bear her suffering; I tried to relieve everyone else's instead.

The summer weather was typical—afternoons so hot and dry that when I sat down in my car the air inside burned my skin. I wore sleeveless dresses and put my hair up, and I noticed that even my neighbor, Mr. Slewicki, had exchanged his fur hat and bathrobe for a cool ensemble in pastels.

Not surprisingly, Luness announced tearfully one day that Nick had stopped seeing her. "He said we weren't right for each other, but I'm sure the real reason is my fat. My body is so repulsive. I just hate myself."

"I think you hate having the decision taken out of your hands. But let me remind you that you had your own misgivings about him." And, I thought, you're better off without him.

When I saw him again, Nick continued to be completely silent about Luness, so I questioned him about his family.

"My father believed in absolute obedience," he said. "My ma and me both had to listen sharp. You could feel the tension rise as soon as his car sounded in the driveway. She had his supper waiting. I had my homework done. If he hadn't been drinking, we figured we might get through the evening without a quarrel, but you could never be sure when he'd explode. And then there was my ma—"

Nick abruptly fell silent, and the change in his tone caused me to ask, "What about her?"

"We were too close sometimes—"

I waited, but he didn't continue, and the possibilities fanned out in my mind like exploding fireworks. After a few minutes of silence, I asked, "What do you mean too close?"

He pulled a piece of Kleenex from the box on the coffee table and wiped his forehead. "Some other time," he said.

Trust develops slowly, I told myself after he left. Be patient and prove yourself trustworthy.

15

One late August night when I arrived at Humberto's house, he said, "I'm going to an international chef's conference in Paris the week after next. Can you come?"

"I'd love to go, but I can't go on such short notice!"

"Why not?"

"I'm booked up months ahead and I have to prepare my patients for my absence. I need to know not less than four weeks in advance. How long will you be gone?"

"A week or ten days. I might stop in Miami on the way back and see my family."

And Marisombra? I wondered. I felt a pang of loss, even though I was used to being alone and wasn't willing to change my schedule to suit him. "I'll miss you," I said.

"I'll call every day. And you'll be glad when I'm gone. You'll have more time to study your books in the evening."

"I wish my studying was paying off better," I said. Several times I had shut myself in a separate room from Humberto to read about Borderlines.

"What do you mean?"

"I have a patient I'm not handling as well as I'd like."

"If it's so tough, why don't you get rid of him?"

"Why would I do that? He wouldn't have an easier time with a different therapist."

"Yes, but you'd have an easier time."

"I don't give up just because something is difficult."

Humberto hugged me. "Of course you don't. That's why you're good. But I wish you could come to Paris."

"So do I. Next time, let me know far in advance."

I asked Humberto to give me a tour of his photographs and explain them. When we came to the guest bathroom and I pointed to the picture of him holding the hand of a little boy, he said "That was my brother. He died in a swimming accident."

There was something odd about the way he said it, and I looked at him sharply.

"I suppose you want to hear the story."

"If you want to tell me."

He brought the photo back into the living room and traced his finger around the frame as he talked.

"I was ten years old and he was six. We were diving off rocks into the river that ran through our plantation. I was showing off by diving from the highest rocks, and he wanted to prove he was as good as me. I yelled to stop him, but he climbed to the top anyway. Just before he was about to dive, he slipped, and as he fell into the river he hit his head on a sharp boulder near the water's edge. I swam to him as fast as I could and pulled him onto the riverbank, but he was already dead."

"I'm so sorry."

"I cried and cried over his body until we buried him. And of course I went over the incident a thousand times. I could have been more insistent that he not climb up there; I could have not teased him or boasted about being a better diver. I used to think God had punished me for my pride, because I was very proud of the way I could swim and ride and play soccer."

"But at some point you were able to stop blaming yourself?"

"Gradually. It didn't help that he was my mother's last baby. Maybe that's why I feel more obligated to her than the rest of my family does.

"My father helped. He took me to Argentina to watch his thoroughbreds race. But after Carlos died, I took his place as the baby, and I felt guilty about that too—I thought I was getting love intended for Carlos and I didn't feel I deserved it. Maybe that's why I had to run away."

"You know running away isn't really leaving."

"No, I suppose not. Still, if I have a son, I'd like to name him after Carlos."

I took Humberto's hand and held it, but I couldn't help thinking about my family therapy training, where they demonstrated that a child who is given the name of a relative, or inherits his physical characteristics, is often perceived to be like that person and not allowed to develop his own full individuality.

I started my radio show that week feeling a bit low about Humberto leaving. My first caller was a woman who had gained over a hundred pounds after having her first child, and I spoke briefly about the adjustment to being a parent.

During commercial break I checked with Westwood Hospital to see how a new anorexic patient was doing, and the desk clerk told me Linda Morrison was out sick. I called her at home and she sounded terrible, her voice practically gone, her chest congested.

"Do you need anything?" I asked.

"No, no," she said, erupting into a fit of coughing.

"Who's looking after Jeremy?" Linda was divorced, and supporting herself and her four-year-old son alone.

"Me. And I haven't had the strength to run after him. It's his third day without a bath."

"I'm coming over. Anything else you need besides soup and juice?"

"Are you sure you want to do this? I know how busy you are. And you don't want to get sick too."

"I never get sick. Just tell me what you need."

"I need a humidifier."

"I'll be there around seven-thirty."

I called Humberto and canceled our plans for the evening, loaded up on supplies at the market, and stopped at Thrifty's for a humidifier. Maybe if I hadn't felt disappointed about Paris I wouldn't have changed my evening plans, but I owed Linda. She had picked out my new sofa with me, and painted the red-and-blue floral pattern on my bedroom floor to match the curtains and comforter. She could have easily been a decorator instead of a nurse, and since I had little sense of color or design myself, I relied on her for such things.

By eight o'clock I arrived at Linda's house, on one of the canals in Venice. "Hi, sweetie," she said when she opened the door. Her lovely skin was flushed with fever, and her straight blond hair was matted and flat. Jeremy clung to her pajama leg, hiding his face in the fabric.

I bent down and put my arms out to him. "C'mon, Jer. One little hug."

Shyly he put out his hand and I shook it. It was sticky and dirty and a little cold.

"Lin, get right back into bed. I'll set up the humidifier in your room and then give him a bath."

Too sick to argue, she went obediently back to bed. Her wastebasket was full of used tissues, and her bedside table covered with half-filled glasses of various liquids.

I collected all the glasses, dumped out the trash, heated up some chicken soup for her, and then sat in her room a while, gossiping about people at the hospital.

"Mom," Jeremy yelled, trotting in from the next room. "My samich broke. Can you fix it?" He held up two halves of a melting ice-cream bar, his face and hair splotched with chocolate.

"Oh, Jeremy," Linda moaned. "Go put it in a bowl."

"I'll help him," I said, springing up.

I sponged off his sticky fingers and face, put his treat in a bowl, and sat him at the kitchen table with a spoon. "When you're done, I'll give you a bath," I said.

He was so cute playing in the tub. Water pistols, rubber soldiers, motorboat games. He already knew how to wash his hair and rinse it. We played army battles until I was covered in water, and then I toweled him off and dried his hair. All clean, he put on his pajamas, little sleepers covered in teddy bears, and we returned to Linda's room to show her his shiny face.

"If I could have one just like him, I would have a child for sure," I remarked.

Linda sneezed. "With all the guys after you? You will. Whenever you want to."

Linda hugged Jeremy and told him how proud she was of him. "Say good night to Auntie Sarah."

I bent down to kiss him. "Good night, sweetie. I wish I had pajamas like yours."

"Mommy will buy you some."

"I hope they'll have feet in them too."

Linda laughed. "Here you are healer of people's souls and you want pajamas with feet?"

"Just one pair," I said, and got up to leave.

"Sare, you're an angel. Thanks a million."

I squeezed her hand. "You're welcome. Keep drinking fluids and sleep, sleep, sleep. I'll call you soon."

• • •

At my house there was a brown box from UPS on the doorstep, and in it I found a present from my mother: a twelve-inch, triangular sculpture. The southern Oregon wildflowers I'd loved to collect as a child were pressed between rippled, clear bubble-glass, which reflected and magnified their colors. The panels were held together with lacy veins of solder, polished to shine like silver.

I called her to thank her. "It's beautiful, Mom. What a nice surprise."

"I thought you'd enjoy it. Something to remind you of home, you know." Even in her most innocuous phrases I heard her yearning for my return. "How are you?" she added.

"Fine. Great." I took the plunge and told her about Humberto.

"He sounds very successful," she said with pleasure.

"His restaurant was named one of the top five in the city, and you know how many there are."

"Maybe the two of you could come up for Thanksgiving or Christmas?"

"I don't know if I'm ready for that yet."

"Are you embarrassed to bring him here?"

"Of course not! Why would I be embarrassed?"

"Oh, with his family being rich and all."

"Please! He's not like that. Why would I be with someone like that?"

We were back to our usual, and I was glad when I could hang up. Visiting them would be a mixed blessing.

My head hurt. I stretched out on top of my bed and gazed around the room. A fat bouquet of pink roses sat on my dresser, a weekly gift from Humberto. Several baseball caps from my father's collection were hooked on the back of the door. Val smiled at me from a silver-framed photograph, taken on our trip to Maui the previous year. I wondered if I would ever have a child.

That night I dreamed of carrying a baby around in my arms. I was shopping in a peculiar store filled with groceries, none of which were edible: plastic meat, metal carrots, frozen milk. I was in tears, my baby crying, starving, and I couldn't feed it. When I came out of the store, I strapped the baby into a car and drove away, determined to hold on to her, but unsure of how to keep her alive and well.

16

When I took Humberto to the airport, he asked, "Are you sad?" and I nodded.

He held me and whispered "I love you," for the first time. I said, "I love you too," and it made saying good-bye easier. I squeezed him very tightly and watched him walk down the jetway before turning back to my own life.

I continued trying to elicit from Nick any feeling he had for me. He in turn suggested I might be hiding from him thoughts I wasn't supposed to have. Without pausing, he launched into a description of an afternoon's tryst with the wife of one of his firm's partners. He left out no detail of their lovemaking, and described his sexual techniques so explicitly I could not help feeling aroused.

When Nick finished, I said, "Perhaps in telling me about your afternoon you were hoping I would share some feelings with you I'm not supposed to have?"

His features darkened with irritation. "Maybe. I probably get some sadistic pleasure out of exciting you when you can't do anything about it."

"What thoughts come to your mind about having to hide excitement?" And how sadistic are you?

Nick was silent for a long time. The shadows in the room grew long and I heard the sigh of the vent system turning off for the night.

"I was only five when Ma came to live with us—" His voice was strange now, distant and quiet. "She wasn't real pretty, but she had this beautiful, long hair. And she always wore low-cut tops, so I could see the line where her tits met. Sometimes when she wasn't home, I'd open her lingerie drawer and touch her panties to my cheeks."

I said a silent thank you for the glimmer of understanding. "So you'd like to turn the tables with me: excite me, knowing I'm not supposed to feel excited by you?"

"Yes."

"You must have felt victimized by your feelings."

"I guess so. When I was older she turned me on and I was embarrassed by it. It made me hate the idea of wanting a woman too much."

That was it. A huge accomplishment for one session. He glanced at the clock, pulled himself to a standing position, and gave me the look in the eyes. At least this time he didn't lick his lips before he left.

I locked the office and then, feeling suddenly tired, decided to lie down for a few minutes before driving home. I shut all the lights, closed the shutters, and unplugged the phone, leaving only the red light of the answering machine glowing in the dark.

After sitting down on the couch, I removed my shoes and stretched out on the spot where Nick had been not five minutes before. I could smell that fresh fragrance of soap against the fabric. Maybe he washed his hands very often.

I closed my eyes and relaxed, intending to float away and let go of all the words I'd heard that day. I missed Humberto already.

I rolled onto my side and felt the curves of the sofa that had touched Nick only minutes before. I buried my face in the sofa-back and inhaled his aroma.

I woke up two hours later, disoriented. My office was dark and the luminescent clock said it was after nine. When I sat up I felt dizzy, and I turned on a light to clear my mind. My throat ached and my face felt hot.

By the time I arrived home I knew I was getting very sick. I made it to the bathroom just in time to throw up. Every joint in my body ached. I walked shakily to the kitchen to feed Frank and had to rush back to the toilet. I felt too ill to move after that, and lay down on the bathmat. Frank appeared after some time had passed, sniffed at me, and whined. I was shivering uncontrollably.

I wrapped myself in a bathtowel and got into bed with my clothes on, not only feeling miserable, but depressed. When I thought back on it, I had already had a mild sore throat the day before and had brushed it off with vitamins and apple juice. Work tomorrow was out of the question, and I had to drag myself out of bed and find my appointment book so I could call everyone and cancel.

After that I called Val. She said, "You sound awful. What do you need?"

"I've got lots of juice in the house, and I don't want you to come over and catch what I've got, but would you cover my emergencies for me? I can't think straight."

"Of course. I'll call your service and tell them. And what about antibiotics?"

"No, it's a virus. I caught it from looking after Linda Morrison. Nothing to do but rest and fluids."

"But if you can't keep fluids in you, you might need to go to the hospital and get an I.V."

"I'll be *fine.* Just call me tomorrow." I hated being sick, and the idea of going to the hospital sounded extreme.

"If you get worse because you're not looking after yourself properly, I'll really be mad at you."

"I promise I'll flood myself with chicken soup."

We said good night, and I tried sipping juice and 7UP, but no sooner was it down my throat than I was back in the bathroom. My temperature was one hundred and three, and I had terrible stomach cramps.

At eleven o'clock, the phone rang and from the bathroom I heard Humberto's voice on my machine. "Are you out enchanting some lucky guy? Or are you in the bathtub reading your books? I learned some funny French expressions today. *Quelle salade!* means 'What a pack of lies!' and a lisp is called *un cheveu sur la langue*—a hair on the tongue. Call you later, love." I was unable to rush to the phone, and I didn't want him to know I was that sick anyway.

I hated needing to be looked after. I still remembered being laid up in bed as a child, my mother giving me alcohol rubs, reading to me and brushing my hair. Even then I sensed in her some satisfaction in having me captive, and I would deny feeling ill until it was too obvious to ignore.

I fell into a feverish sleep and woke at seven in the morning, my throat extremely painful, my nose congested, my stomach still hurting. After I had my pharmacy deliver some Tylenol and a decongestant, I took the medications, drank a quart of fluid, and then unplugged the phones to sleep uninterrupted. The following morning, my stomach felt better, but the congestion had spread to my lungs. Afraid Humberto would worry about me, I tried to call him, but I didn't speak French and I had trouble leaving a message. When he phoned again that night, I answered.

"Where have you been?" he said, angrily. "I've been calling you for days!"

"I'm sorry, I've been sick. I had the phone turned off."

When he heard the way I sounded, his anger immediately dissolved. "Should I come home and look after you?"

"No! Stay at your convention. I'll be fine."

"I can't believe it. The first time you really need me and I'm halfway around the world."

"I'll be *fine.* I just need to stay in bed."

"I'll call you tonight, love. I miss you."

Val ran a few errands for me—picked up my office mail, some groceries, and more Kleenex—and I canceled the rest of my following week's appointments.

As soon as I heard Val's car pull out of the driveway I felt lonely. Suddenly and surprisingly, I wanted my mother to kiss my forehead and bring me dinner on her tray, the vegetable soup in bone china, with a silver spoon and a miniature vase of blossoms from her garden. I thought of calling Humberto back, but if I was going to be loved for my needfulness, why not get it from the original?

"Dear, you sound terrible!" she said, her voice at first heavy with concern, then angry. "You don't look after yourself properly! You have to work too hard to keep up that fancy lifestyle of yours!"

My eyes filled with tears. Why was her love always mixed with animosity? "It's just a cold," I said.

"I wish I was there to look after you."

"So do I," I said, but it wasn't true anymore. "Really, Mom, I'm fine. It's just a little bug."

She said the shop was doing well, the neighbor's cat had been killed by a car, and my dad was getting physical therapy for his arthritic shoulder. I took comfort from the sound of her voice and from knowing that in spite of her shortcomings, she loved me, and she was there.

Afterward, I heated up a can of soup and ate it out of the pot at the kitchen table. Through my thin nightie I could see my stomach stretched flatly from one hip bone to the other. A small consolation.

Sitting in the kitchen, I studied my mother's china, protected by the bleached wood and leaded-glass panes of my cupboards. The week after I had moved into my house, a large parcel had arrived from Bandon. I had torn through it quickly, imagining it to be a set of fireplace tools or gardening equipment, things I'd said I needed. When I encountered the first bowl carefully wrapped in bubble plastic and tape, I had collapsed into a kitchen chair and stared at it for a long time.

It was from England, fine white bone china with small red flowers scattered across the surface and the edge rimmed in gold. My mother had collected it piece by piece out of her household allowance. On birthdays, Christmas, Easter, and Thanksgiving, my mother had set the table with her beloved china, handwashing it herself afterward.

It was a beautiful gift and I was deeply touched by it. Yet I felt guilty accepting the most valuable thing she owned, and such gifts never came from my mother without strings attached. She expected to be invited to stay with me; she wanted me to hold a dinner party in her honor and serve on the china plates.

Now, I dragged a chair over to one cupboard, stood on it and retrieved a dinner plate. I sat down on the chair and held the plate. It felt warm as I ran my fingertips lightly over the surface. It ought to feel cold, but it doesn't, I thought. Bone china. Made from ash of bones. But whose bones? Animals'? People's? It's pretty, this china, my mother's china. I stood up abruptly and put the plate back in place. In the two years since I had received it, I had never once used it.

Resting in bed, I kept mulling over my last session with Nick and the way he had described his stepmother. Why had she abandoned them and never kept in touch? What wasn't he telling me about her? Or his father and birth mother, for that matter? Why had she killed herself?

The following afternoon my doorbell rang, and a delivery man handed me a cobalt blue vase filled with glorious red chrysanthemums. Assuming it was from Humberto, I signed for it happily, and placed it on the dining table to open the card. It said, "I hope it wasn't something I said. Get well soon, Nick."

Surprised and disturbed, I threw the note on the table. He knew where I lived. He had just spent a hundred dollars on me. How was I going to handle this? After pacing from room to room, I retrieved a few articles I had saved on managing the boundaries of therapy, returned to bed, and phoned Zachary.

"I'm getting worried," I said. "I don't want to alienate him, but I think I should call him and tell him I don't accept expensive gifts from patients."

Zachary agreed. "I would also emphasize that he should not contact you at home. If he wishes to speak to you he should always call your service."

"You think he has my phone number too?"

"If he has your address, chances are he has your phone number, and probably has had it all along, but it doesn't necessarily mean he's going to abuse it. Lots of patients have had my home address and phone number over the years. The important thing is to confront him directly about his intrusiveness, and now you have the perfect opportunity."

"Thanks." I made an appointment with him in two weeks.

When I called Nick, he was pleased to hear from me until he heard what I had to say. Then he countered with, "I do something nice for you and you're complaining?"

"I want you to respect the limits of our relationship."

"Hey, Doc. You're sick. I was just trying to cheer you up." He hung up the phone abruptly, and I worried that even though I had done the right thing, it had upset the fragile balance between us.

That evening, I was awakened out of a drugged sleep to the sound of Frank's barking at the front door. I bolted up in bed, heart pounding, until I heard Humberto say, "Down! Get off me!" A moment later, he walked into the bedroom.

"What are you doing here?" I croaked.

"I left the conference. I wanted to look after you."

"Oh, hon, that was so sweet of you."

"Have you eaten anything today?"

"A quart of apple juice and two pieces of toast."

He moved into action immediately. An hour later I was eating a perfect mushroom omelet on a bed of wilted spinach. He said, "Who's my competition?"

"You have no competition."

"Who's Nick?"

I waved my hand. "An annoying patient who's trying to break the rules. Believe me, it's nothing personal."

"Fine. Let's throw the flowers out."

"I don't see any reason to throw them out. They're beautiful and I've already told him not to do it again."

"I don't like them. Okay?"

"Fine. Throw them out." I already wished he hadn't come home.

While Humberto cleaned the kitchen, I lay in bed clicking idly through the TV channels. I imagined marrying him and having jealousy fights with him, or having children and fighting with him over their religious upbringing. That's a serious one, I thought.

I had been raised in the Unitarian church, my father having prevailed over my mother, who was Episcopalian. He made fun of my mother's ministers with their "shirts on backward," and warned me not to marry a man whose religious views were far different from mine. I was angry at my father for hurting my mother's feelings, but as I grew older I came to appreciate his point of view. I had seen a number of marriages disintegrate over religious differences.

That night I couldn't sleep lying down because I was having difficulty breathing. I blamed myself for not starting on antibiotics as soon as I had become ill. My lungs had remained weak from a childhood bout with pneumonia and any virus usually settled there.

In the morning my doctor had the pharmacy send over a prescription, and when I threw the bag away, I saw a few red blossoms still vibrant at the bottom of the garbage can. I felt a momentary tug of sadness. Poor Nick. He was so afraid to reach out, he could only do it on his own terms.

I gave in to Humberto's caretaking. He cooked, brought videos to watch, changed my bed, and massaged my feet. It felt wonderful to be so babied, but I didn't like being helpless, and I was eager to resume my usual routine.

Humberto said he loved having me to himself without my being able to run out the door. When I recovered enough to return to work, I was not only glad to feel well again, but happy to regain my freedom.

Nick greeted me politely, but after some preliminary conversation said, "I'm thinking about quitting therapy. No offense, but I don't think it's doing much for me."

"Is this because I told you not to give me gifts or contact me at home?"

"That's part of it. You made me feel like a boy getting his hand slapped while I was trying to be nice."

"How did you get my address?"

"Oh, I've had it since the beginning. Our firm subscribes to commercial databanks. Information America, Assets, Skip Tracer. We can find anyone in this country in a few hours, and anything we want to know about the person."

How awful, I thought. "Anything?"

"Just about. Bank records, property holdings, previous lawsuits, liens, marriage records." He laughed. "Don't look so shocked! Don't you know there are surveillance cameras on you in almost every public place? That there's a databank somewhere with your weight and height and income and how many children you've had?"

"So you know all this about me?" I was appalled to think that not only Nick knew so much about me without my permission, but that my other private patients, my radio listeners, and my hospital patients could all obtain this information. How vulnerable I was!

He said, "The privacy laws in this country are totally lame. I run profiles on people all the time."

"And you ran one on me without my permission." I was outraged by his violation of my privacy, and shocked to learn this was routine practice in law firms.

"I assumed you knew! C'mon! Didn't I list off your birthplace and schools when we first met?"

"Yes, but I didn't think you had researched my life in such depth. Didn't you think I might find that intrusive?"

"Why wouldn't I run a check on you? Someone I'm going to trust with everything about me!"

"But you have not trusted me with everything."

He looked caught off guard for a moment and then his face relaxed. "Oh, you mean Luness. I figured she'd tell you everything herself."

"It's not just Luness. There is a great deal about yourself you hold back."

He leapt up from the sofa and began pacing back and forth in front of me. "This is all irrelevant. I apologize for getting a profile on you, but I'm going to quit therapy, so you don't have to worry about it."

At this point I wouldn't have minded his quitting. "Why have you decided to leave?"

He stopped in front of me, and enumerated the reasons on his fingers. "One, your fee's taking a big chunk out of my bank account. Two, it's hard for me to interrupt my work schedule to get here. And three, I've told you my problems and nothing's changed, so why spend the money and time?"

It's not unusual for patients to respond to a therapist's absence by deciding to terminate therapy, and although the expenditure of money and time are legitimate concerns, they often camouflage deeper reasons to stop treatment. I searched for the hidden agenda. "What was last week like without me?"

He retreated to the sofa and sank back into the cushions, losing some of his defensive posture. "The first few days were wasted, especially after you ragged on me about the flowers. But then I got totally into work. I finished four depos. I've been weight-training, running, playing basketball. I feel great."

The manic defense, I thought. In the face of loss he'd thrown himself into a flurry of activity that numbed him.

"And I'm thinking about getting a Great Dane."

Another defense. If he couldn't count on me, he wanted something completely in his control.

"Maybe this isn't the right kind of therapy for me. Maybe I need hypnosis. Or something stronger or more direct. You sit there in silence half the time. To me that's just wasted money."

He wanted me to crash through his defenses and rip away control from him, the very thing that would confirm his deepest fears.

"You look angry," he replied to my silence.

"You're angry with me for being gone. And although the flowers were a generous gift, I think you sent them so I'd be angry at you, and then you could leave therapy and not regret it."

"Well, no matter what criticism I had of the therapy you'd say that! There can't ever be anything wrong with the therapy, it must be the patient!"

"Of course things can be wrong with the therapy or the therapist, but if there's something wrong between us, why is your automatic solution to dissolve the relationship?"

"Maybe the reason you don't think of dissolving it is because you need the money."

"This is how I make my living, but if you gave up this hour, there'd be someone else to fill it. You might consider other reasons why I would want to keep trying."

He looked sullen, and picked up my glass elephant from the coffee table. "Sorry." He placed the little ornament in his hand and held it up to the light.

"Can you tell me more about how the first few days after I was gone were wasted?"

He put the elephant back, examined the stitching around his shirt cuff, and then folded up both sleeves. "I felt aimless and lost. I couldn't concentrate because of my headaches. I started jogging at three in the morning because I couldn't sleep."

"I think you missed me and it made you anxious."

He stood up abruptly and walked over to the window, where he rotated the plastic rod that controlled the shutter slats. Sunlight poured into the room and he stared out at the cars moving by. "I did miss you. How stupid. Missing someone you see two hours a week. I guess the flowers were my way of keeping contact with you."

"But it seems you would rather have contact with me outside of our sessions than when you're with me."

He turned around to look at me. "Are you telling me I sent you the flowers instead of trusting you?"

"Yes. You want to hide yourself in my presence and you want to know everything about me instead."

"Well, I'll be goddamned. I'll be just fucking goddamned."

After Nick left, I turned with relief to my other patients, who seemed to have no need to overstep the boundaries of therapy the way he had.

Even the Romaine sisters, who brought me a modest present, did so in a discreet and thoughtful way that gave their gift an entirely different meaning than the one Nick had sent.

When I held open the waiting room door for them, they rustled past me in green taffeta skirts, and then presented me with a white wicker basket. The contents had been carefully assembled by them personally: a book titled *The Art of Self-Healing*, a packet of multi-vitamins, a bottle of Milk of Magnesia ("it's-important-to-keep-regular-when-you're-laid-up"), cellophane-wrapped potpourri tied with a pink ribbon, and a tin of shortbread cookies from Scotland.

The consideration and the amount of time they'd taken to shop for me surprised me. I saw it as great progress in a therapy from which I had only expected limited results. The twins, so cut off from normal social contact, had formed an attachment to me. I said with genuine enthusiasm, "How thoughtful!"

They smiled and pinched each other's forearms in pleasure, and I saw that, although it was unlikely I could ever pry these two apart, a great deal could be accomplished if I treated them as one person. I even forgave them for the wallpaper.

Luness was still struggling to recover from the rejection by Nick, and I complied with her request to change her appointment so it didn't coincide with his. I felt it allowable to tell her that from the way he had treated her, she was better off without him.

She said that rice had some curative power for her, and she cooked pots full of it and stuffed it in her mouth by hand. I told her rice was like a gentle blanket of snow that covered and muted everything.

The impending upheaval in William's life created by his wife's desertion was provoking change in him too. He sighed audibly as he stretched out on my office couch. "We'll have to sell the house," he lamented. "Fifteen years we've lived there and I'm fond of every crack and squeak."

Like my mother, William's need for a predictable life was so great that he had often swallowed his anger both at work and at home. Now he said bitterly, "I hate her. This might kill me."

When I pointed out that the reality of the future was not necessarily as bleak as he anticipated, he said, "That's not surprising. I always expect the worst."

"But expecting the worst makes you miserable before anything has even happened."

He said, "The advantage of pessimism is that you're never caught embarrassed by the stupidity of your fantasies. You're never disillusioned. Just surprised sometimes when things go well and you back into happiness rear-end first."

"I'm glad to know there's some advantage to pessimism, considering how much needless suffering it's caused you."

"I'll have to think about that," he said, and I felt the satisfaction of having chipped away a tiny piece of his melancholy.

I'm a good therapist, I thought. I have one case that's proving troublesome, but considering how many patients I have, that's a pretty good track record.

When I saw Nick again, it seemed at first that he had resolved to participate more in the therapy. He said, "I dreamed I met Death last night. I was in a horse-drawn carriage and she boarded, wearing a black velvet gown and beautiful black satin ribbons in her hair. She smiled and I thought I had to go with her, but at the next stop she got up and left without me." He closed his eyes and leaned back his head. "I used to imagine Death was a beautiful lady who'd come during the night on a horse, sweep me up in her arms, and carry me away."

"Perhaps it's a fantasy about being reunited with your birth mother?"

He opened his eyes. "I do believe I'll be reunited with her when I die. She's the only one who ever loved me."

"Yet you live with the pain of knowing she wouldn't stay alive for you."

"I heard she was a sensitive person. Couldn't take my father's abuse."

"Perhaps she was unable to see any other way out of her situation."

"I guess."

"And your stepmother?"

"She dumped us too—a bunch of times before she left for good. Sometimes I'd come home and there would be a note saying she was gone, but she usually came back within a week or two. She would tell me she missed me but I didn't believe her. She drank too much to look after me." His hands slipped down so they covered his crotch.

Toward the end of the session I said, "You mentioned how aimless you felt the first few days after I was gone. Perhaps you experience me as being like your stepmother?"

"You have a long way to go to loosen up to her level."

"What do you mean?"

"She fooled around on my dad. I saw her with a guy in a cafe once. A few days later she was gone for good."

"Do you remember a while ago, we talked about how you found it disturbing to see a patient leaving here before you, and another one coming in after you?"

He burst out laughing. "Son of a bitch! You're right! I must think you're like her." The smile faded. "What a thought."

"Why?"

He straightened his already perfect tie, stood and adjusted the waist of his pants, then turned away from me and stepped to the window. "Let's just say she left an impression on me." He had timed his comment for the end of the hour, and without another word he gathered his things and left.

I was disappointed again.

18

Since Valerie had started dating the hospital administrator from our party, I had heard from her much less, and I missed her. I left her a message: "One of my patients showed up today wearing all her clothes inside out. Great labels. She must shop at Saks. Can you have lunch soon? Love you, 'bye."

Later that night, she called while Humberto and I were watching the news. She said, "I've got so much to tell you. How about Stratton's Grill at noon on Friday?"

"Perfect."

"We should have dinner with them some time," Humberto said after we hung up.

"If they last."

Valerie and I crammed in our stories as quickly as possible on Friday. She said, "Gordon could be it. He's too short, but very sensitive and smart. Sex is incredible. We've done it in his office three times this week."

I laughed. If people only knew what went on in hospitals and doctors' offices. "What else is happening?"

"We admitted a guy to the psych ward yesterday because he showed up at medical emergency complaining someone had stolen his rectum. He said it wasn't the first time it had happened either, so he knew he needed a size thirty-six and he was sure they kept them in the stock room and couldn't the nurse go back and get him a replacement?"

"He was absolutely serious?"

"Completely serious. The most bizarre delusion I've ever heard, and other than that, the man sounded perfectly normal. Polite, good eye contact, not disoriented, no hallucinations. They snowed him with Thorazine and are waiting to see the result."

"The human mind never ceases to amaze me." I paused. "But I've got a much more mundane story."

"From the look on your face it doesn't sound too good."

"Remember that patient I told you about? The one who was bothering me? It's getting worse."

"Why don't you get a consult on him?"

"I did. Zachary Leitwell. And he said the guy's a Borderline. But he's not like any other Borderline I've seen before. He's slippery. It's like trying to hold mercury in my hand."

"I'm going to a seminar next month on Borderlines. They're covering Kernberg, Kohut, and Masterson. Why don't you come with me? Maybe it will help."

I wrote down the information and decided to attend. I was sure I just needed to look at the case in a new way.

Before we parted Val asked if Humberto and I wanted to go out to dinner with her and Gordon. It was new for her to have a date she could take out in public.

"Why don't we make dinner?" Humberto suggested later.

"I don't know—cooking isn't my best thing. How about if we go out? Maybe Hana Sushi."

"That's like being at the office for me. Why don't I cook at your house, and we can sit around and have a leisurely evening?"

It did sound more intimate, and although I didn't like giving dinners, it was Val, and I knew she wouldn't care if I served bran cereal. We invited her and Gordon to the house for the following Saturday night.

When I saw Nick again, it once more appeared that he was opening up. He said, "I'm very down. Everything seems pointless. I'll probably be alone the rest of my life." His eyes were a dull gray, and he removed his suit jacket and rolled up his shirtsleeves. "I think about sex all the time. It makes me feel alive, and it's the only place my performance is always successful."

"Performance?"

"You know what I mean. It's the thing I'm best at."

"I wonder if you've ever felt you didn't have to perform?"

He rolled his eyes. "Come on, Doc. Every guy has to perform in bed or else you ladies don't like it. I hear your talk."

"What would happen if you didn't perform?"

"Sayonara."

"Has that ever happened?"

He gave an arrogant bark. "Never. Ready as a stick all the time."

"Have you ever felt loved just for being yourself?"

He shook his head. "That's bullshit. Even those people who say they love you for yourself only love you if you keep being the way they like and you keep giving them what they want."

"How do you feel you have to perform here?"

"Haven't you made that crystal clear? Arrive on time. Say whatever comes to mind. Seek insight. Don't send gifts. Of course you want your patients to perform, and if they don't you probably get rid of them."

"So if you don't perform here I'll get rid of you?"

"Yes. And don't deny it. You know it's true."

In the broadest terms, he was right. I wouldn't keep treating someone indefinitely who didn't pay, or didn't show up, or didn't work at it. I said, "You're a lawyer. You understand contracts. You hire me for my time and skills, and I accept the job in good faith that you want to proceed. Within those limits, you are free to be exactly who you are and nothing different."

He glared at me.

"Tell me how you had to perform when you were a boy."

"With my dad there was no way out of anything. If I disobeyed his instructions for my chores or my schoolwork, he would beat me.

When he felt affectionate, he would take me places, but I had to like it or he might fly off the handle. I was always on edge."

"There was never a time when your feelings counted?"

"Whatever I felt was unimportant. In a movie I had to be completely still and not make a sound. If we went swimming and I began to shiver, he'd get mad at me."

"What about your stepmother?"

"She was drinking most of the time, and there was no point in going to her for protection. Once when it was raining, my dad told me before he left for work to remove the leaves from the eaves gutter, but I played outside instead and the water backed up until the roof started leaking. When he came home Ma stood by and watched while he made me pull down my pants and bend over a kitchen chair. He used a metal spaghetti spoon—you know, with the teeth? I had puncture wounds and bruises so bad I could barely sit for weeks. She didn't lift a finger to stop him."

"Did he beat her too?"

"Sometimes. Whenever she left he used to promise he wouldn't do it again, but it never lasted. A couple of times she called the police, but I lied when they asked me questions because I knew what he'd do to me later."

"As you look back on this now, you must feel very angry about being ignored like that."

He stayed silent a few minutes, tapping his foot and holding back his feelings with crossed arms. Then he said, "I can't talk about this anymore. Don't make me. I'll lose my mind."

After he left, I felt angry at his parents on his behalf. I was glad I had decided to go to the workshop on Borderlines.

When I met with Zachary, I told him I thought I had worked through the problem of Nick intruding on me, and I reported what Nick had told me about his childhood.

"This partially explains his internal fragmentation," Zachary said. "Such a child often develops a secret self that he shares with nobody—a self that stays young and isolated, hurt and filled with rage."

"I always have trouble imagining how a parent can be so mean to a small, helpless child, but of course I know those parents have usually been abused themselves."

"Right. So they don't have the tolerance for the ordinary demands and competition any child places on a parent. And their children represent the hated child in themselves, or remind them of what they never had."

"What do you think about his saying he'll lose his mind if he talks about it?"

"He's already lost part of his mind by not talking about it. He *needs* to talk about it. He has to recover his feelings—his outrage, his sense of being used. Those feelings were healthy."

"But he said so clearly he couldn't do it."

"Then allow him the time. This must be all he can bear to recover at the moment. It's a major accomplishment that he trusted you enough to say this much. He'll probably pull back for a while to see if you'll abandon him. But after a while you must bring up the subject again if he doesn't."

19

On Saturday the mantle of my mother's domestic standards settled over my shoulders. I mopped the floors, lit perfumed candles, put guest towels in the bathroom and a vase of orchids on the table. The one thing I didn't worry about was the dinner itself.

Humberto made wild mushroom soup, a salad of mixed baby greens and crab, and poached sea bass over a bed of linguini. I marveled at the perfect combinations of each course and how expertly he handled the food. At six-thirty I said I would set the table, and he pointed to my mother's china and said, "Why don't you use those?"

"I'd rather not."

"Beautiful china makes everything look more elegant."

"I don't want elegant," I snapped. "I want casual. My everyday dishes are just fine."

Humberto raised his eyebrows. "Perhaps another time." He turned back to the soup pot.

I grabbed my stoneware dishes, flatware, and napkins and went into the dining room to set the table. I placed the dishes down slowly to recover from my aggravation. It wasn't his fault that I had a problem with the china.

Outside, a car idled for a minute. Curious, I stepped to the window and looked out. A black Ferrari sped away. Shaken, I closed the drapes and sat down at the table for a moment.

This situation might be much worse than I thought! How much had Nick been watching me, and how dangerous was he? Maybe I was fooling myself thinking I could contain his therapy. Maybe the more attached to me he became, the worse it was going to get!

I tried to stay calm. He wasn't psychotic, wasn't delusional. But he did have a loaded gun in his car. Oh Lord, should I tell Humberto? No, I thought. He'd overreact. I'll tell Val.

To distract myself, I sat up on the kitchen counter and watched Humberto. He peeled away the shell of each crab like a magician doing a card trick. "My mother would sure admire your skill in the kitchen," I said, but my voice cracked slightly, betraying my ambivalence about both her and cooking.

He stirred the soup. "Complementary colors and distinct flavors are the essentials. Today's chefs have gotten too elaborate."

Made anxious by Nick's intrusion and the discussion of the china, I was looking for a fight. "Chefs. I guess that's what irks me. Most chefs are men and people say they're so talented. Women just cook."

He turned to me, soup spoon in hand, and snarled, "There are plenty of women chefs!" He took a step closer to me. "And if talent is learning how to handle people who don't give a damn about their work, if it's staying up until three in the morning experimenting with soufflés, if it's learning how to talk to pampered, vacuous women and arrogant, demanding men, then I've got talent. And it's hard work!"

I held back tears. "Honey, I didn't mean I don't appreciate what you do. I'm just cranky right now."

Voice tight, cheeks flushed, he looked down at the soup spoon in his hand as if he had no idea he'd been holding it the whole time. "Why? What's bothering you?"

"I don't know. I've just been on edge all day."

"It's that damn case, isn't it? I see how much time you've devoted to reading lately."

"No, no, it's not that." I was afraid Humberto wouldn't understand my determination to figure Nick out, yet I was convinced that if I hung in there, I'd break through some barrier and Nick's treatment would move forward.

Humberto dropped his spoon in the sink. "Then don't shut me out. Tell me what's bothering you."

"It's going to sound stupid to you, but I get nervous when I have people over for dinner, because things go wrong. Once I tried to make a fancy meat loaf, and when I pulled it from the oven, it was sitting in a pool of white ooze."

He immediately calmed down. "Some people have a knack for cooking and others don't, but you can learn."

"Maybe you could teach me how to cook."

He brought me a paper towel for my nose. "I think lovers should look after each other any way they can."

"I want to look after you," I said contritely, and from my position on the counter, hugged him with all fours.

It was fun to see Val with a man. So many of her affairs had been clandestine that she'd usually come alone to parties and dinners, but now here she was, holding hands with the adored Gordon, slipping around corners to kiss for a few minutes, and reappearing altogether radiant.

Gordon had thick curly hair and round glasses, and a cuddly manner that was endearing, but the most important thing to me was the way he looked lovingly at Val. I wanted so much for Val to be happy.

Before we sat down to dinner, I pulled her into the bedroom for a minute. I said, "You know that patient I've been worried about? I saw him cruising my house tonight and he keeps a loaded gun in his car."

She clutched me by the shoulders. "Why does he have a gun?"

"For self-protection, he says. And I think I believe him. My theory is that he's longing for me and can't express it, so he's driving by as another way to keep contact. Like we did when we were twelve. You know? I remember taking a snapshot of a guy I was in love with and having ten copies made. That kind of thing."

"Yes, but he's not twelve, and you know what happened to Paula."

That frightened me. Paula, our schoolmate, had nearly died in a house fire set by one of her patients.

I nodded. "Exactly. So I need to figure out how to take charge of this situation."

"You have to confront him directly and forcefully about it. Don't dismiss his behavior lightly! It could be harmless, but you have no way of being sure of that."

"You're right. I'll be very clear with him about it. Thanks, hon. Now we'd better get back to the dining room."

After we had finished our first course, and Val had raved about the soup, she said to Humberto, "Tell us about Nicaragua."

"It's very lush, very green. The colors are more vivid than here, and the air richer. The U.S. smells like a box of cornflakes. Nica is full of animal scents: blood, cows, rotting flesh, cooking food in the streets."

"Do you ever go back?" Val asked.

He shook his head. "I want to remember it the way it was. My grandmother—if she were alive I'd go back. Maybe one day I'll go to visit her grave."

The four of us dawdled over the food and conversation. It was a particular treat for Val and me to be together with our men, and there were a few moments where we caught one another's eyes and smiled special smiles. When we hugged good-bye at the door, she whispered, "Can you believe this? A foursome!" As we watched Val and Gordon walk to their car, I thanked Humberto for his skill as a host and cook.

Later, while making love, we could see the outline of an attentive basset hound, observing every move. Humberto paused and leaned on one elbow. "You've got to do something about him." In a loud, stern tone he said to Frank, "Lie down," and the dog obeyed. Then he turned back to me and asked, "Would you like to make a baby?"

A sudden rush of desire startled me—an overwhelming wish to conceive a child with coal black eyes like the ones looking into my own. "Some day," I said.

"Good. Of course he'd have to be better behaved than you-know-who."

I was grateful for the birth control pills which protected me from impulsivity and allowed me to imagine, without consequences, that the hot fluid he jammed so high into my center was uniting with my waiting egg.

20

When I saw Nick again, I confronted him and he acknowledged he had driven by my house, and apologized for bothering me. "I was just curious to see what your house looked like."

"But I've already discussed how important it is to keep our relationship confined to the office."

"You think my driving by your house and looking at it for two seconds is taking this out of the office?"

"Yes. I do not want you to drive by my house. If you're curious about me, you should ask me questions."

"Fine. How did you get so goddamn rigid? I'm not some fucking stalker! Do you think I'm going to attack you?"

"I don't know." One thing I had learned from hospital work was how often patients relinquished physical threats when they realized they were frightening the very people they were relying upon.

He looked out the window and said, "Jesus Christ." After a few moments, he turned back with the familiar smirk on his face. "I think you're projecting, Doc. I think you want me to stay near you. The truth of the matter is, I have a girlfriend who lives a few blocks up your street."

I didn't know whether to believe him.

The conference on Borderlines turned out to be very valuable. There was considerable discussion about the Borderline's "ability to invade you," and I realized how aptly that described my experience of Nick.

For weeks I had been struggling with a peculiar sense of his constant presence. I knew his schedule. Saturday mornings, basketball; Sunday mornings, a woman; Tuesday and Thursday evenings, racquetball. I thought about the cases he discussed, mulled over his history, and noticed any black sports cars on the street. I was comforted to know this heightened awareness of a patient had been documented by other therapists.

The conference explored the fragmentation of self and "shifting ego states" typical of Borderlines, and the importance of the therapist providing a steady, predictable environment. I came away from the meeting convinced I was handling Nick just as I should, and proud of myself for tolerating the difficulties. Borderlines were treatable. They just required more energy and more time.

As Zachary had predicted, Nick withdrew from me in the following weeks. Whenever I tried to raise the subject of his early experiences, he became sullen and silent. Respecting his reticence and feeling renewed conviction that I needed to tolerate his variability, I allowed him to ramble on about the women he encountered in his daily life.

He was sure his secretary would go down on him at the first request; a neighbor in his condo was flirting with him; a judge had come on to him in her chambers.

I suspected this sudden perception of being so desired was a defense, but I waited for the right moment to confront him and finally it came.

"I have a new divorce client," he said. "A pouty chick married to a studio exec. We met at her house to review her financial records, and man, was she *dressed*—filmy blouse, short skirt. I could have had her on the dining table."

"You seem to have had an unusual run of opportunities lately, and I'm wondering what all this activity is protecting you from."

"What did you have in mind?"

"If you fill up your therapy hours with talk of women, we don't discuss more painful things. I'm wondering if my questions about your father bothered you."

His face darkened in anger and he leapt up from the sofa so quickly I was afraid he was going to hit me. I tried to look calm even though my heart was racing.

"Don't push me," he said fiercely. He turned away and began pacing in front of the windows.

"Perhaps discussing your father brought you into contact with feeling used."

"You just can't leave it alone, can you?!"

"No, because ultimately, *it* won't leave *you* alone."

He paced back and forth a while longer. When he sat down, he leaned over, put his head in his hands, and spoke through his fingers. "I tried to run away from home a bunch of times. I wanted to find my mother. I couldn't believe she was dead. Then he started locking me in the closet. He made fun of me. That was worse than the beatings. I had to cater to his whims or he ignored me. He never remembered my birthday, he forgot his promises, he acted like I had no feelings, he made me feel like I existed only to serve him."

"Can you give me an example?"

Nick sat up, leaned back into the sofa, and sighed deeply to let out his tension. "He had this ritual every Sunday morning. I had to fill a plastic bowl with warm sudsy water, and wait for him at the kitchen table. After he read the paper, he would join me at the table and put his hands in the bowl. He would soak a while, then I had to scrub his nails with a toothbrush.

"He thought my ma was repulsed by his hands and he wanted me to fix them. He was ashamed of looking like a car mechanic. If I missed any oil in his cuticles, he would smack me across the face with his wet hand, so I was very diligent. Then I had to file his nails, and massage his hands with hand lotion. If he was satisfied with the job, he'd let me play outside for an hour before church. If not, he made me do his feet too. I can still remember the salty smell of his feet, and how thick and cracked the skin on his heels was. His toes were gnarled and disgusting. It made me want to throw up.

"When I was older he stopped beating me because I told him if he didn't, I'd kill him when he was sleeping. After Ma left, he locked his bedroom door at night."

"Suppose he was sitting in that chair right now. What would you say to him?"

Nick stared at the empty chair opposite the sofa for a long time. Then the anguished voice of a young boy yelled, "What you did to me was wrong! You selfish bastard! I was your own flesh and blood and you treated me like a—like a slave. A goddamn slave!"

He sat hunched over, head in hands for a long time. He said, "I can't take this."

After he left I remembered his penchant for a "love slave" and wondered whether it was an unconscious attempt to reverse the trauma of the past.

My other patients were no less distressed. One showed up in a neck-brace, having herniated a cervical disc in a car accident. Luness was still stinging from Nick's rejection, and Joy Romaine was so angry at May's occasional disappearances that she was plotting to hire a detective.

Even William's heart was breaking as he encountered little signs of Elizabeth's infidelity. One morning he'd taken the garbage to the curb, and found in it the *Encyclopedia of Western Garden Flowers* he'd given Elizabeth for her birthday last year. On another afternoon, thinking he would please her by helping with the laundry, he opened the washing machine, stuck his hand into the wet clothes, and pulled out a black lace teddy he'd never seen before.

Hearing this triggered a memory of my mother crying, her doughy frame hunched over her laundry basket, holding in her hand a pink garter belt discovered in my dad's pocket.

I knew there were two sides to this kind of story, and the betrayed one often plays a part in the betrayal, but it was a painful reminder, and left a sour feeling inside me toward Elizabeth and a fleeting fear about Humberto.

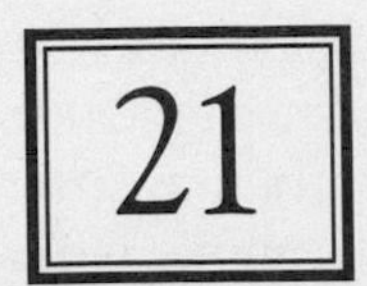

My days were a blur of sex, dictation, and therapy sessions. A few times, Humberto raced over at lunch and we made love in my office during my half-hour break.

One afternoon I was afraid Nick would notice the extra Kleenex in the wastebasket or the way my hair had fallen flat from the heat and sweat. If he could sense I needed a good fuck, could he also tell when I'd had one?

But Nick arrived looking grim, and he wasn't in a mood to notice anything. The skin around his eyes was pinched and dark, his shirtsleeves were rolled up, and there were sweat stains under his arms.

He stretched out on the sofa and looked at the ceiling to tell me these were becoming the two most important hours in the week to him. He often wondered what I was thinking at any given moment. Where was I? Who was I with? What did I look like naked? How did I look from behind when I bent over? What did I sound like at the moment of orgasm?

Although these rhetorical questions were exceedingly personal, it was not uncommon for patients to wonder such things, and if three hours earlier I hadn't been naked on the carpet, I wouldn't have felt so self-conscious.

"Tell me what you imagine," I said.

He expressed intense curiosity about my breasts and genitals, particularly wanting to know what I looked like on all fours. "I like it the way animals do it," he said. "Have you ever seen horses? Those stallions are on top, man! I want to be in control of a woman like that—to hold her under me, squeeze her ass, dominate her."

"I think you're having these fantasies because you want to control me. My becoming important to you is frightening, but if you can control me, it's less frightening."

"That probably explains the dreams I had last night. In one I was a sheet of Plexiglas—cold and hard. In the second, I was the captain of an oil tanker stuck in shallow water. Oil leaked out and ruined everything."

I said, "It seems to me the dreams are about therapy. You started out like a piece of Plexiglas—flat and devoid of feelings. Now that you've been in this therapy harbor a while, you realize how much you have inside, but you're afraid it will leak out and ruin everything."

A surge of material confirming my interpretation came from Nick. He was frightened of what feelings would emerge if he kept seeing me. When he felt this way with a woman he always left, but he was in trouble now, he said. He was tired of running. He sat up and turned to me, his eyebrows knitted together. "This is so depressing."

I felt sympathy for him as he realized how much emotional work was ahead, but there was no way out of it other than through it. I said, "The alternative is staying locked in your fortress."

Toward the end of the session he forced himself to lighten up by talking about Halloween. "I'm going to a party wearing a doctor's white coat, and my date is dressing like a hooker. We're going as Trick or Treat."

I laughed. "That's very clever, but I wonder if you're also trying to stay in control by becoming me—a doctor."

"You're probably right. I even thought you might be at this party. It's at a UCLA professor's house in your neighborhood."

I felt immediately queasy. Was he getting to know my friends? My colleagues? "Whose party is it?"

"Tom Brennan's. Dean of the law school."

I breathed a little easier. "No, I won't be there."

"So am I going to be depressed like this for a long time?" he asked before the end of the hour.

"I don't know. But as bad as it feels, it's a positive sign of real growth and change."

"Like an excruciating bone-marrow transplant is good for leukemia."

When he left, I looked out my window and saw him walk to his car, hands in his pockets, head down. I was encouraged by his sticking with the therapy now that it was getting painful. He locked himself inside his black Ferrari, lit up a cigarette which I knew was marijuana, and drove away.

I was grateful the next afternoon for my radio show, which was a refreshing change of pace. I made it into KPXQ two minutes before airtime and began with a taped three-minute lecture on anxiety disorders. After I caught my breath, I opened the phone lines.

I was enjoying the radio show because I liked to do what I called kamikaze therapy—crash in, bomb the defenses, and get out—and lately the stories had been surprising and interesting. That day a woman caller said her father had killed her infant sister and buried her in the backyard. The more I questioned her the less crazy she sounded, so I referred her not only to a psychiatric clinic, but also to the police.

Before I left the station, I called my service for messages and left with a fistful. One message was from my mother, and I knew she was going to ask me to come up for Christmas. I felt guilty about not wanting to go, but I was imagining some wonderful holiday with Humberto instead.

In my V.A. Hospital interns' group that day, we discussed how to handle Halloween, which was the following evening. Some of the psychotic patients were agitated, their fantasy lives already so terrifying that the specter of dead souls returning served only to heighten their panic. All patients were to be on pass restriction Halloween night.

The next evening, I hurried home early so I could open my door to the young children and see them in their costumes. It was a clear, cold night and some of them were shivering in their crepe paper hats and ghostly sheets.

Humberto joined me for an hour, and during a lull in the doorbell ringing, we lay on the bed, kissing. I thought for a moment I heard a thump, but then nothing, so we went on caressing each other. After another ten minutes I realized it was too quiet in the living room and I went to investigate. Frank had knocked over the basket of miniature chocolate bars near the front door. Torn and partially chewed candy papers were strewn everywhere, and in the middle sat Frank, his muzzle brown and goopy.

When he heard me yell his name, he headed for the doggy door, with me in hot pursuit to give him a whack. Humberto said "This dog is impossible," and left to cater a party.

I cleaned up the mess and gave out dimes, since I had no candy left. At eight-thirty I shut off the porch lights and sat in the dark, thinking of my mother. Halloween always reminded me of her.

It wasn't until I was six that the brilliant image of my mother's perfection cracked.

It was Halloween night. Mom had sewn our costumes—I was a queen in royal robes and rhinestone tiara, she a chunky ballerina. Her costume was as delicate as cotton candy, the tulle skirt tucked at the waist and floating around her to mid-calf. She wore an old pair of toe shoes restored with pink fabric dye.

We first canvassed the row of houses on our street. The air was cool and a light mist was falling. I was cozy under my queenly robes and took care to avoid the small puddles forming from the rain. My mother, oblivious to the temperature and the wetness, led me gaily from one house to the next, occasionally attempting a jeté on the sidewalk.

At one house Mom gave a command performance. She raised her arms over her head in a graceful oval, stood *en pointe,* and slowly completed one revolution, her gauzy figure full from the breeze that held her skirt aloft like a handmaiden. I loved her beyond words.

We walked many blocks, until I began to lag behind, my mouth smeared with chocolate, and the weight of my sack wearing on me until I allowed it to trail along the ground.

After we rounded one corner, Mom called out, "Don't drag your bag of candy. Would you like me to carry it?"

She turned her head around to check on me just as I saw a large crack in the sidewalk ahead of her. Before I could utter a sound, her satin toe-shoe caught on the crack and she tumbled to the cement.

She landed face forward in a big puddle. Dark blotches of muddy water sprayed across her skirt. Her silky hair was partially thrown out of its clasp and splattered with mud. When she turned over I saw a large stain soaking into her leotard.

"Oh, Mommy!" I cried. "There was a big crack there!"

Her face crunched into angry pleats. "You should have told me it was there!" she shouted. "You should have stopped me!"

I breathed quick shallow gasps, not quite able to cry from the shock. When I reached out to touch her hair she pulled her head away abruptly, and a sick feeling curdled my stomach. I stood by helplessly watching blood ooze from her knees, while she lay on the sidewalk like a broken doll, weeping and holding her right elbow.

Gradually she calmed herself and sat up. A sweet smile broke through the pained lines in her face. "I'm so stupid, my pumpkin. It was just an accident. Please forgive me. Mommy loves you." She held out her arms to me.

I hung my head and my tiara crashed to the sidewalk, where several rhinestones sprang out and scattered. The tears which I had been holding back began to well. I turned away from her and groped around frantically in the dimming light for my treasured rhinestones.

I tried to put my tiara back on my head but it wouldn't stay. Finally, I gave up and sat down in my mother's lap to cry. I had glimpsed the future, and I was heartbroken.

At eleven o'clock, I turned on the porch light again for Humberto. At that moment a car drove by, and although I only saw it for a second, I was sure it was a sports car, with a flash of white inside.

Shit, I thought. Was that Nick?

I waited up for Humberto until one o'clock, taking the opportunity to catch up on my dictation. He brought back a half-full bottle of velvety French wine and we finished it before getting into bed.

I was tired and tipsy from the wine, and when Humberto crawled in between my legs, I closed my eyes and felt my head spinning. I moved rhythmically against him, melting into his body, and I sunk my fingers into his hair. And then suddenly it was Nick's thick hair, and his iridescent eyes staring into mine, and I gasped and pulled away.

"What's wrong?" Humberto asked. "Did I hurt you?"

I opened my eyes and focused directly on his face in the dim light. "No, I just had a sudden shooting pain. It's gone."

I pushed the image of Nick out of my mind and melted into Humberto again, but afterward I lay wide awake, worrying about my feelings for Nick. Somehow, some way, I was on a collision course with him.

22

The morning after Halloween, the magnolia tree in my front yard stood wrapped in toilet paper. I laughed when I came out and saw this. I remembered doing the same thing on Halloween years ago in Bandon.

I took a tour of the yard to see if anything else was amiss, and found one thing that upset me. All of my red roses, and only the red ones, had been cut at the base of their long stems and removed. I wondered if this was Halloween mischief or Nick's work, but I had no particular reason to suspect him and I concluded it was probably just an adolescent prank.

When I saw Zachary, I said, "Nick drove by my house again, and I'm worried that he can't control himself. What if he tries to break in?"

Zachary looked up gravely. "Let's review his history."

I went through the checklist of factors used to predict violence—prior assaults on people, paranoid hypervigilance, episodes of explosive behavior, weapons used in physical fights, cruelty to animals. Nick's history contained none of these.

Zachary chewed on a pencil while I talked, and tossed it on his sidetable when I was done. "Certainly he doesn't have the usual warning signs, but that doesn't mean he's incapable of losing control."

"There was one thing—but I don't know if he did it." I described the wallpaper being slashed in my waiting room.

Zachary paused to take an emergency call from the hospital. After prescribing some medication, he turned back to me. "I've had patients carve up plants in my waiting room, send me hate mail and even voodoo dolls. This guy sounds more sneaky to me than anything else, but if you feel uneasy, now is the time to extricate yourself before he becomes any more attached to you."

"But I hate the idea of giving up! And I don't really believe he would hurt me."

"I think he's alexithymic—can't put his feelings into words. So he acts out his feelings or he creates in you the feelings he has and can't express. You feel frightened, intruded upon, and loved in the wrong way, and this is his life experience. You have to translate it into words for him so he can integrate it, instead of denying it."

"What do you suggest?"

"Force him to comply with your conditions. Tell him you won't keep treating him if he cruises your house. He's sneaking contact with you, and once he openly acknowledges his feelings for you, he won't need to do that."

I paused and picked at a hangnail. "I'm embarrassed to admit I'm still having sexual fantasies about him."

Zachary looked at me kindly. "Every therapist who's been in business long enough has experienced this. The important thing is what you make of the feelings and how you handle the situation. Any theories about why him?"

I nodded. "My dad. Nick is a caricature of him—a forbidden man, a sports fan, a ladies' man. Dad never did anything blatant with me, but he was inappropriate. Like we'd drive past a woman in tight pants and he'd say, 'Look at the muffin on that chick. It's enough to bring a man to his knees.' I desperately wanted his love."

Zachary studied my face. "I wonder whether you're so worried about Nick getting out of control because you don't trust your own control."

"I absolutely trust my self-control!" I said emphatically. "I would never have any sexual contact with a patient! But I want to figure out the best way to handle these feelings Nick stirs up."

"You recognize the feelings are probably displaced from your father, so you probably need to explore those feelings in further depth. Are you in therapy yourself?"

"No. But I've worked hard on these issues in my previous therapy."

"I suggest going back into therapy. You apparently have unfinished business you should take care of."

"You're right. I will." But I had no idea when, with Humberto already complaining about my schedule.

It rained more that November than it had in fourteen years. The waterlogged hills of Southern California began to slip everywhere, filling swimming pools with mud and leaving people homeless. Water flowed relentlessly along the curbs of even gently sloped roads, washing away motorcycles and garbage cans. In the valleys, streets were covered by three feet of brown swirl, and several children were swept into storm drains.

My house stood the stress fairly well, but by the last week of the month it developed a leak in the laundry room. On the evening I discovered it, I grabbed a plastic bucket and placed it under the offending spot, because Humberto was arriving in ten minutes with dinner from Paradise. He had one hour to spare.

Later I studied his silhouette in the darkened bedroom. He stood naked from the shower, back to me, impatiently giving orders into the phone. His damp hair curled softly around his ears. A shadow from the door fell across his shoulders, highlighting the graceful curve to his small waist and high buttocks.

That night he had suggested we go to Florida for Christmas, to meet his mother in Miami and then spend a lazy week on the Keys. I wanted to go, but the last two weeks of the year were often the most difficult for patients, and I was a little uneasy about meeting his family. I had said, "I think I can do it."

"Don't want to leave your favorite patient?" Humberto had said peevishly, before calling the restaurant.

He hung up the phone. "Tables are double booked, half the customers want to see me personally, and three waiters have called in sick. Damn! I'm sure they've just gone to the pre-Thanksgiving sales. If I find out any one of them was lying, I'll fire him!"

"Come here, baby," I said, holding my arms open. He lay down in bed and rolled over to me. "I'm sorry I upset you. I'd love to go away with you at Christmas time."

Humberto softened, and began stroking my arm. "Tell me about Nick."

"I can't."

"Why not? His privacy is protected. I don't know his last name or what he looks like."

"You might accidentally find that out."

Humberto continued to stroke my arm, but there was a stubborn silence.

"I can tell you this: what you're worried about is completely unfounded. My interest in him is strictly professional."

Humberto smiled and wrapped his leg around mine. That irresistible gleam of white teeth moved toward my mouth and enclosed it.

The next morning, I sat at the white wooden table on my back patio and sipped coffee while reading the *L.A. Times*. The patio was deep enough that I was sheltered from the steady downpour and received only occasional small sprays from the overflowing eaves gutter. The leaves on the gardenia bush glistened and bent under the weight of the rain. I leaned over and held a creamy white blossom to my nose to breathe in the rich perfume before I left for the office. I was imagining the smell of tropical flowers in Florida.

Nick walked in that afternoon wearing a red cashmere scarf, his dark hair gleaming from the rain. In the middle of the session, he stretched out on the sofa and said to the ceiling, "I have a confession to make. Sometimes on the mornings of my appointments with you, I jack off. It seems like the sort of thing you'd want to know."

I was not surprised by his admission. Intensive psychotherapy usually resulted in a broad range of feelings toward the therapist, including sexual fantasies. If he could talk about it with me, his need to maintain contact with me through indirect means would diminish. I said, "Perhaps your masturbation on those days is an attempt to limit what you feel in my presence."

"I don't know. Maybe. It does make me less nervous."

"What are you nervous about feeling with me?"

He sat up and shrugged. "I think I want too much from you. Two hours a week is not enough."

It was a terrible time to raise the subject of my vacation, but I had to do it. When patients become emotionally attached to their doctor, even a weekend break can prompt depression, anger, or withdrawal. Preparations for longer vacations must be made well in advance, because whatever past difficulty a person may have had with separation is likely to resurface at these times.

Nick was particularly vulnerable in this area, since both of his mothers had disappeared without warning. I said, "Let's talk about increasing your hours here after the Christmas break."

"What Christmas break?"

"I'll be out of town next month from December twentieth to January fourth."

"Why are you telling me so far in advance?"

"So we have time to discuss your reactions to it. I wouldn't want to spring it on you at the last minute."

Never had I seen a patient withdraw so quickly and completely. "I'm sure I'll be fine while you're gone," he said immediately. "Christmas is party time, if you know what I mean." He winked and licked his lips.

It was like watching a spider killed instantly by a quick swat, and in that moment I saw that as he began allowing himself to care for me, my responsibility was increasing geometrically.

My other patients handled the news of my impending absence more gracefully. William increased his exercise schedule because it helped his depression. Luness consented to see Val twice a week during my absence, because we both agreed she couldn't go through the holidays without the support. Some patients were going away themselves; others were relieved to have extra time during the busy season.

Two weeks before I left, Joy Romaine caught May talking to a Safeway produce man, and beat her up. The two of them came for an emergency session, bruised and repentant. May's face was swollen and blue around the left eye, and Joy was missing a chunk of hair over one ear. "It's-*your*-fault-this-happened! Comes-from-trying-to-split-us-apart. *No-more*-divided-sessions-Dr.-Rinsley! *No-more*-do-you-hear?"

"I can see you're right," I conceded. "Full joint sessions from now on."

Grateful that therapy would no longer be a threat to their union, the sisters dealt with my vacation by shopping for me. They knew I would not accept anything costly, so they searched for inexpensive items suited to my personality and interests. For our last session before the break, they brought a green-and-red wicker basket, holding three small silver spoons, a 1910 *Textbook of Psychiatry,* a lapel button of Bugs Bunny's face ("so-you-keep-smiling"), and a packet of bubble-gum baseball cards.

I decided I had been going about their treatment the wrong way. They didn't need money, they had plenty of time, and all they did each day was get on each other's nerves, except, I discovered, when they were shopping for me.

I suggested they consider volunteer work, perhaps with elderly women, who I thought might fill the hole left by their mother, and enjoy their echoing attention. They were unsure about the suggestion, but said they would try calling on the senior citizen's service center near their home.

As for Nick, by December 20 he had scheduled a frenzy of parties and dates, which he said he was sure would keep him so busy he wouldn't miss me at all. I didn't believe him, but since I wasn't going to be around to respond to his needs, I chose not to challenge him.

Before I left, Morry called to wish me a Merry Christmas, and I gave him an optimistic progress report on Nick. "He's opening up," I said. "And his physical symptoms are diminishing." Morry said he was impressed with my work.

Yet I left for Miami feeling apprehensive. Nick's smile during our last session had been too bright, his voice too cheery, and for all his bravado, I was afraid the next few weeks would prove difficult for him. He was the sort of man women played with in their spare time, not the sort they took home for Christmas.

23

The Saturday before Christmas, we arrived at Miami International Airport in the afternoon, amid hordes of vacationers. I was happy to be free of my responsibilities for a few weeks, and curious to meet Humberto's family. "Relax," he said. "I promise they'll like you."

The family chauffeur was waiting outside in a Mercedes-Benz limousine. Such luxury was unusual for me, but Humberto slipped into it like a comfortable sweater, chatting with the man in Spanish, and allowing him to load our luggage into the trunk. It was eighty degrees outside, twenty degrees warmer than L.A., and the sun was shining brightly through scattered puffs of cloud.

Holiday traffic was so heavy we inched along the interstate through the city. Humberto talked about how powerful the Cubans were here, and how many hot new restaurants had opened in the last year. We passed the main business district, a cluster of tall glass buildings jammed together near the water's edge.

As we left downtown Miami, I looked back at it from the causeway that led to Key Biscayne. The skyscrapers sparkled in the afternoon light, a promise to the thousands of new immigrants streaming in every year. "It's actually quite pretty," I said, wondering where Marisombra's office was.

Key Biscayne was a small island, fronted by a long narrow park, a luxuriant golf course, and a tennis stadium. The color of green was as bright as emeralds under a jeweler's lamp.

Just before we reached our destination, Humberto showed me the large white house where Richard Nixon had lived during his presidency. An abandoned helicopter pad was the only remaining evidence of a president once in residence.

Isabella Maria Arias de Cortazar owned both sides of a fingerlet peninsula of Key Biscayne. A broad red brick driveway connected her house on one side of the peninsula to the other side where the family yacht was docked. The money it cost to hand-brick that much road could have fed several immigrant families for a year.

Isabella opened the door to greet us. She was an elegant, fine-boned woman with dyed-black hair swept up from her high forehead and coiled into a French twist. Her strong, straight teeth and full lips accounted for the captivating family smile.

"*Encanta,*" she said, extending her right hand to me. The hand trembled slightly and the blue veins were clearly visible through her thin skin. "You must be tired."

I smiled. "A little, but I'm delighted to be here."

When she embraced Humberto, she closed her eyes and murmured "Tito," and hung on too long. Her manicured nails were painted seashell pink and on her left hand she wore a single, half-inch rectangular-cut diamond. He peeled her arms from him like the sticky tendrils of a blackberry bush.

"Please come in and sit down," she said. Her English was as correct and careful as Humberto's, and as she lowered herself onto her huge sofa in her yellow Chanel suit, she looked like a canary alighting on a branch.

Humberto left me with her when his brother phoned, and Isabella chatted amiably about the length of skirts, the crime rate in Miami, and her racehorses. I asked questions about the family, and her health.

Beneath the smooth skating of our conversation, I sensed in Isabella the shards of ice upon which I might be impaled: a snobbery bred to the bone, an expectation of filial reverence and duty, and a proprietary love of Humberto. She reminded me of Grandma Covey, and the image of Isabella and my father in the same room flitted through my mind: Isabella in crisp linen, Dad in a tomato sauce–stained T-shirt. I better understood Humberto's desire to be messy.

A maid appeared and set a silver service tray on the coffee table. Her sympathetic eyes locked with mine, and she said, "Light or dark?"

"Black, please." Think of Isabella as a patient, I told myself. Do an interview.

When Humberto returned, he picked up my coffee cup and emptied it in one gulp. "Let's go for a drive," he said.

I hurried upstairs to put on some casual clothes. The guest bedroom was enormous, with its own living room, fireplace, and balcony overlooking the water. Our luggage had been neatly assembled in the dressing area.

I changed quickly, started back, and then stopped when I heard Isabella and Humberto below, arguing quietly and intensely in Spanish. The maid began ascending the staircase with an armful of freshly washed towels. She smiled kindly and when she reached the top I whispered, "What are they saying?"

She hesitated a moment and then said very quietly, "The Señora—she invite a friend of the Señor to the Christmas fiesta. He say he is angry about this."

I thanked her and clattered down the stairs noisily to warn them. When I rounded the corner into the living room they had both reassembled their social faces.

Humberto said to Isabella, "Don't wait up for us."

She immediately looked down at her hands. "I prepared dinner."

"In that case, I'll show Sarah a bit of Miami and we'll be back by six," he said abruptly.

We drove through the quiet streets of Coral Gable Estates, where one Spanish estate after the next sat well back from the road. He showed me the neighborhood where most of the Nicaraguans had settled, and then the south end of Miami Beach. There we strolled the streets hand in hand, examining the art deco hotels restored to boutique glitter with fresh sherbet hues, elaborate curves, and layered, angular lighting fixtures.

At a sidewalk table of the News Cafe, we ordered espresso and Humberto insisted I use milk in it. "Otherwise it'll burn a hole in your stomach."

I did have a stomachache. "Is your mother that cool toward everyone you date or just me?"

"She would prefer I marry someone whose background is similar to mine."

"Marry?" A queasy ooze of anxiety intensified my stomach pain, and I had a sudden impulse to call my service.

"You're the first woman I've brought into her house since Marisombra."

I should call the service, but I'll wait till Wednesday. "And she's still hoping for Marisombra?"

"Yes." He reached out and curled his hand around my neck. "She had the nerve to invite her to the Christmas party, even though you were coming. But as far as I'm concerned, Marisombra is history. Believe me. It's over."

That Wednesday I picked up two messages from Nick. The first said to cancel our January 4 appointment. The second said to cancel the first message, he would be there. These messages left me with a heavy sense of foreboding. I worried for a while and then forced myself to forget it, because there was nothing I could do except call him, and that would have been inappropriate.

Whatever Isabella's private thoughts were about me, she contained them and remained coolly gracious throughout the rest of our stay. On Christmas day she held an open house for almost a hundred people, most of them wealthy and politically powerful. It was easy to see where Humberto had learned his social graces.

Marisombra made a brief appearance, squired around affectionately by Isabella. Humberto introduced me and asked her about Isabella's heart condition. I could think of nothing to say to Marisombra and was relieved when she left. She was, as Humberto had described, spectacularly beautiful.

I enjoyed Humberto's family. His brothers were shorter than he, less gregarious, and they all spoke with more of an accent. His sister, Regina, was lovely, and looked almost exactly like Isabella. I felt most at ease with her, and clung to her when Humberto wasn't around, asking questions about her law practice and the family. The one thing I learned from her was how attached Humberto had been to his paternal grandmother, and how terribly upset he was when she had been hit and killed by a sniper's bullet in Nicaragua.

The talk of grandmothers, and Isabella's domineering presence, reminded me so strongly of Grandma Covey that I told Humberto about her on our drive through the Keys.

"She used to pound a bony finger into my chest and say, 'Go to college! Get a profession! Don't leave your fate to someone else's hand!' The awful thing was that after all my mother did for her, Grandma left her nothing."

We stopped at a roadside cafe, and sat down at a Formica table with yellow blowfish salt-and-pepper shakers. Humberto looked cute in khaki shorts and a white gauze shirt, but he was listening with great concentration.

"She left trust funds for me and my cousins—forty thousand dollars each for college tuition and expenses—but after her strokes she signed her house and the rest of her assets to the Episcopalian church. The new rectory was built with Grandma's money, and not a cent was left for my mother or her brother."

Humberto shook his head in sympathy. "How sad."

"The guilt I felt!" I said, slapping my open hand on the tabletop. "And I had no say in the matter! I either used the money as the will instructed or it went to the church too. How could Mom not resent me for getting what she thought was hers?"

Even before Grandma died, Mom and I fought incessantly: I was going to break my neck with that horseback riding! Couldn't I learn to bake lasagna instead of windsailing on rough seas? My standard answer was "I'll be *just fine!*" The more overprotective she became, the more recklessly I behaved, while my father, seeing both sides, said nothing.

But the inheritance, and its blatant unfairness, widened the rift between us into a giant canyon.

The soft, humid air and the talking left me thirsty and sticky, and I gulped down three glasses of iced tea. Back in the car, Humberto said, "No wonder there's so much tension between you and your mother."

I nodded sadly. "The first four years after I graduated, I sent her a thousand dollars a month and it made us both feel better. Now she has her dress shop, and at least I feel we're even."

He took my hand and held it the rest of the drive.

I was relieved when we arrived on Sugar Loaf Key. Unlike Isabella's mansion, her island house was modest and homey, with inviting wicker furniture that withstood the humidity. It was a two-story pink cement structure, with eight-yard-wide screened-in balconies on both the lower and upper levels. The master bedroom and both balconies faced the sea. Outside, a winding path landscaped with tropical flowers and towering shade trees led to a fifty-foot swimming pool with cabana. For occasions when most of the family was there, a smaller house for the servants stood beyond the pool area.

The first few days we did nothing but sunbathe and make love, and I could not believe how much I slept. Humberto said, "You see how tired you are? You need to work less."

I did not tell him something that threatened to ruin my tranquillity: I kept thinking about Nick's messages and wondering how he was getting through the holidays. On one of my walks alone, I found a phone booth and called Nick's home. His voice said, "Ho, ho, ho, tweedle-dee-dum. If you can't leave a message, send rum." He's perfectly fine, I thought, smiling. But look at me. Three thousand miles away and I'm worrying.

One day after I returned from a walk, Humberto asked, "Want to go for a swim?"

We took off our bathing suits and sank into the cool blue of the pool, curving around each other like dolphins at play. Tall vine-covered pink walls surrounded the road side of the property, within which were huge bushes of white and fuchsia bougainvillea, Japanese magnolia, and coconut palms.

For a few minutes I floated on my back, feeling the water flowing over my body. Humberto leaned against the edge of the pool near me and steered me toward him until he could bend and kiss my nose. "Are you hungry?" he asked.

I stood up in front of him and smoothed back his wet hair. My hands lingered on his head and I took his upper lip between my teeth and nipped it gently. "Yes, but I'm not sure for what."

"Let me surprise you. Stretch out on the grass in the herb garden and I'll be back in a little while."

I took my towel and crossed the lawn to a patchwork blanket of greens, protected from the wind by a horseshoe-shaped hedge. It was so fragrant, the spicy smells of dill, basil, thyme, and earth mixed together with the sweet of anise, lavender, and sage. I stretched out on my towel, feeling the grass uneven and prickly beneath the towel. Everything seemed alive—bees sipping from blossoms, small insects, worms, snails, birds, the air itself.

Humberto appeared shortly with a silver tray containing scones and sweet butter, tall glasses of iced tea, and a bowl of fruit with a small paring knife. "I'm going to feed you," he said.

He settled himself next to me and began peeling a peach, letting the juice run through his tanned fingers. I admired the symmetry of his hands, the oval white nails and the grace of even his smallest movements. He slid his knife through the orange flesh, broke off a thin slice and brought it to my lips, scattering three drops of juice, one on the hollow between my breasts, one at the base of my throat, and the last on my chin.

Had I ever tasted anything so sweet, so fresh? The cool sliver of ripeness slid over my tongue and down my throat, and I said nothing, waiting for more. He swallowed a slice himself, then licked the drops of juice from my warm skin, one at a time, finishing with the drop on my chin.

My hands enclosed his face and through his open lips I moved my tongue against his front teeth, upper and lower, the way a blind woman might explore a face with her fingers.

He pulled away from me and sliced the rest of the peach, laying the cool pieces over my breasts and belly. Some of the pieces he ate, licking my skin beneath them. The others he fed me one at a time, kissing me after each slice so the flavor of his mouth and the peach mingled.

Then, slices of mango, papaya, and cherimoya covered me, the juices running down the side of my waist, rivulets gathering in my pubic hair. "I feel like a big dish of fruit salad," I laughed.

The tart flesh of the kiwi he crushed against my nipples and then sucked, causing a jolt of excitement. He rubbed black papaya seeds into my toes and the soles of my feet. I was only dimly aware of a bee humming near my thigh, investigating the possibility I was a giant flower.

Humberto reached for the sweet butter and squeezed it in the palm of his hand until the melting grease slid through the sides of his fist and down his arm. This hand he placed between my legs, spreading the butter against the warm inner skin.

He dragged his first two fingers slowly upward, enclosing the small hard knot, but not quite touching it. In a rhythmic motion he continued this, until my whole being was his, living on the end of his fingers.

"Please," I whispered, "I want you."

He did not yield to my request, but instead kept touching me, and as I became harder, more swollen, he refused to move faster, forcing me to hang on his every stroke, speechless, barely breathing. My eyelids were hot, the muscles in my legs shook involuntarily. I raised my hips off the ground, begging faster, more.

Just as I was about to reach orgasm, he changed the rhythm, moving in a circular motion, then again as I was about to finish, changing to a sideways stroke. I knew he could feel the exact moment when I reached the edge, yet he continued to tease me, and the pleasure was so intense I was mute, unable to force him to satisfy me.

When I thought I couldn't stand it another minute, he withdrew his hand, knelt down between my legs and sucked on me strongly until I came, the intense waves of spasm rolling through my insides and up my belly, while involuntary tears streamed from my tightly closed eyes into my hair.

I rolled onto my stomach and wept with a mixture of joy and terror. This man had me, controlled me, and could make me do anything.

At first he thought I wept only with pleasure, but when he saw the sobbing, he sat me up and held me to him, rocking me like a small child. "Sarita," he said softly, "I love you."

"I love you too," I cried back, clinging to him now, sticky and uncomfortable from drying fruit juice. "But I'm going to become a love slave."

"*Mi corazon,*" he said, tenderly brushing away a strand of hair from my cheek. "Some women like to be teased like that. It heightens their pleasure. But I won't do that again if you don't want me to."

My eyes burned, my face felt full and hot, my body still flush from excitement. "I was hanging on your fingertips, at your mercy."

He rocked me quietly until my tears slowed to a sniffle. Then he drew away from me and asked curiously, "What is this love slave?"

"I have a patient who says that. He likes a woman to do anything. Be totally in his power."

"Listen," he said, continuing to stroke my hair. "If you want it like today, then I'll do it again, but only if you ask. That way you can send your love slave fears back to your patient."

My body relaxed and I smiled at him.

"And I suppose that patient is Nick?"

I nodded and looked away, hoping this afternoon wasn't going to be ruined.

Humberto put his hand under my chin and turned my face back to his. "Sweetie, I'm not going to fight with you about him. I believe what you told me. But don't you see how he eats into your mind?"

"Yes. But that's the nature of my work."

It had become too hot, pieces of fruit strewn across the little enclosure, our bodies sticky and attracting insects. We left for the cool air of the house, where we bathed in a huge oval tub that looked out over the wide expanse of turquoise sea.

On New Year's Eve, Humberto made a dinner of charbroiled grouper and baked potatoes, and from the lower balcony we watched the moon rise. At midnight, he lit candles and we drank Remy Martin, the sharp, warm sensation in the back of the throat a perfect beginning to January.

I didn't know what the real idea was behind the Russian tradition of throwing glasses into the fireplace, but that night I thought I understood. Toasting each other, looking at the slender fronds of the coconut palms playing in the wind, I wanted to freeze the perfect moment in time forever. "After this drink," I said, "these glasses should hold no other liquid. The mold for this moment should be broken."

Humberto swirled the last of his brandy in his snifter, swallowed it in one motion, and stood. He picked up the brandy bottle and the glass, and beckoned me to follow him with mine.

The bright moon lit our stroll along the garden path. When we reached the little servants' house, he unlocked it, lit a few candles, and displayed for me the only fireplace on the property. And after one final toast, we smashed both brandy snifters into the fireplace, and the entire remaining bottle of brandy as well.

PART III

25

Back in Los Angeles, at one in the morning of the Monday I was returning to work, the phone jangled us out of sleep.

"Sorry, Dr. Rinsley," the operator at my exchange said. "I have UCLA Hospital on the line. Nick Arnholt's been in a car accident and they need to talk to you."

A catalogue of horrible images woke me fully—Nick's handsome face mangled, a leg crushed, maybe even a death. When they patched me through to the nurse, I said, "What condition is he in?"

"He's had a concussion and is showing some confusion. He's asking for you. Minor cuts and bruises other than that. You're listed as the person to call for emergencies."

Why was *I* listed as the person to call? What about his boss, or his neighbor, or all those women he was so proud of? In an instant I realized I had become his only family.

As his therapist I did not want to be placed in this position. I couldn't be a social intimate with him and continue our work. But where did professional distance end and sheer human decency begin? "I'll be over in half an hour," I replied.

"It's Nick, isn't it?" Humberto mumbled.

I sat up in bed and turned the light on. "I have to go to UCLA. Be back in an hour."

"I'll come with you."

"You can't."

"I'm not going to let you go over there alone at one in the morning."

What had been endearing concern only a few hours ago seemed like irritating protectiveness now. I stood up jerkily and searched for my underwear. "It would be a violation of his privacy for you to know anything more."

"How about the violation of our sleep?" he said. He stood up and pulled on his pants.

Humberto would never understand professional ethics. "How can you talk like that? I have a patient who's been seriously injured. It's *important.*"

Angry, I stepped into my closet for a dress. If he thought I was going to let my work slide to please him, he had the wrong woman.

He followed me into my closet. "Let me drive you there and wait for you. I won't come in the building, I'll just leave you at the front entrance and sit in the parking lot. That way you can keep his precious privacy and I can make sure you're not assaulted."

How did he think I had managed before knowing him? I could look after myself and would go on doing so. He reminded me of my mother, always fretting over my safety, always calling out "Be careful!" when I left the house.

He put his hands on my shoulders and looked at me tenderly, his bare feet touching mine. "Marisombra used to get up in the middle of the night to go to the hospital. The closer she got to leaving me, the more often she went."

"Well, I'm not Marisombra." And I thought, relenting, he's not my mother. "Okay," I said, pulling him out of the closet, "but I don't know how long I'll be. Are you sure you want to?"

"Yes."

Nick was in a curtained-off bed in the Emergency Room. I stepped up to him and instinctively took his hand.

"Hi, Doc," he said, managing a half smile. "You think this scar will spoil my good looks?"

The right side of his forehead was raised and blue, a deep gash in it neatly stitched. His shirt was covered with dried blood and I could smell stale alcohol on his breath.

"What happened?" I asked, wondering how long I should hold his hand. He was clammy and cold, probably in shock.

He drew his hand away, pulled the sheet up to his chin, and closed his eyes. "I hate you," he managed to squeeze out of his throat before tears rolled down his cheeks.

This was a Nick I had never seen before. I pulled up a chair and sat down next to his bed.

He covered his eyes with one hand. "I missed you. I had a shitty

Christmas. I wanted to quit therapy. Then I changed my mind. Today I started thinking how glad I was to see you this week, and I hated it! I was fine before I met you, and now I'm fucked up!

"I started drinking straight gin. After a while I had to get out of the apartment. I drove around. I wound up in the hills on those curvy roads, and slammed into a tree. I don't know how I got here." He took his hand away from his contorted face and looked at me. "How did you get here?"

"You asked for me."

"You see? Even when I'm trying to get rid of you I'm asking for you."

"I'm sorry you're hurt. I think you hate needing me and missing me."

He raised his head off the pillow. "I love you. That's why I hate you."

Being the object of his love and hatred did not seem a pleasant prospect at this point. "I understand," I said.

I stayed another fifteen minutes, until he was calm and sleepy. At the nurse's desk I made a few notes in his chart and glanced through it. Nick had been treated there four times for various accidents, including a recent hand injury from slamming his fist into a locker. So much for nonviolent behavior, I thought. And no one was listed under next of kin until October, when he had given my name. Even as he was vigorously denying my importance to him, he had begun relying on me.

It was two-thirty when I walked down the outer steps of the hospital. Humberto must have been watching for me continuously, because he pulled the car up within moments of my exit. "Are you tired?" he asked, and when I shook my head, he said he wanted to take me somewhere, and I agreed, not caring where.

He pulled my hand into his and we drove in silence, me thinking of my mother, him thinking of God knows what.

I couldn't be in an Emergency Room without remembering our accident. Mom and I had gone to Eugene for some last-minute shopping because I was leaving for college the next day. Laden with packages, we sat down at a seafood restaurant and ordered lobster and white wine to celebrate my launching. It was hard for both of us to eat because she kept crying, but she put away two glasses of wine and I took a few swigs to calm my nerves.

During dinner we decided I needed one last thing, a suitcase she had seen in Bandon. It was dusk when we started the drive back home, and we were in a great hurry to make it to that store before nine.

The headlight on the train seemed a long way off, and my mother looked impatiently at the red lights just starting to flash. "We can make it," she said.

"You'd better not try," I said.

But she had already pressed her foot to the floor, and the last thing I remember was the deafening screech of steel wheels on steel tracks.

I was thrown clear of the car because I'd forgotten to put on my seat belt. My only injury was three broken ribs. My mother nearly lost her life. Her left leg was severely crushed; she was knocked unconscious and almost bled to death. I sat in the Emergency Room for six hours while she was in surgery. My father, alternately weepy and overly confident, kept saying, "She'll make it. I know she'll make it. She's a tough broad."

When she finally regained consciousness in the recovery room, she squeezed my hand tightly and whispered, "Can you ever forgive me?"

"Oh, Mom," I said through tears, "just get well."

When I said good-bye to her in her hospital bed, her face contorted by swollen bruises, she wept. "I didn't mean to hurt us," she said. I knew it was true, in spite of the terrible damage done. Aching with guilt over leaving her in that condition, I had my first allergic skin rash.

I arrived to begin college two weeks late, and it took her almost a year to recover, but by the time I returned home the following summer she was pretty much her old self. She still walks with a slight limp on her left side.

The image of Nick's pained face returned and stayed with me until Humberto stopped the car and came around to my side. We were in downtown L.A., and dark, forlorn figures wandered by, while others lay motionless in doorways.

He took my hand and we walked quickly into a huge building. Suddenly we were surrounded by a sea of fresh flowers, a dazzling mixture of colors and shapes, piled high, standing in huge bunches, moving on dollies, lying in boxes. I had heard of the wholesale flower market, but had never seen it.

The finest Parisian laboratory could not have invented a smell so intoxicating: the mingling of jasmine, freesias, roses, gardenias, rare tropical flowers, and ornamental eucalyptus. The air was a sweet drug that surrounded us.

It was here that retail florists came in the middle of the night to buy their allotment for the day; where the hotels obtained truckloads full of flowers for their grand six-foot bouquets. Wholesalers yelled to each other, trucks backed up to the doors, more flowers came and went. The place was full of action and incredibly cheerful.

I turned to Humberto and sank my face into his sweater. "Thank you for bringing me here. And I'm sorry about tonight. It was a lousy ending to a wonderful vacation."

He kissed my forehead, my nose, and then my mouth. The florists working nearby ignored us as we stood in an embrace, the fragrance of flowers caressing us.

We wandered among the vendors until I stopped and pointed excitedly. "Lilacs in January! Where did they find them?!"

"If it's spring somewhere in the world, it can be spring in L.A.," Humberto said. He bought me a bunch and I buried my nose in them.

"My favorite," I said, remembering my mother's lilac bushes dripping with a spring rain, and one blossom pressed between the pages of my junior high school scrapbook.

We admired the scene until the wee hours caught up with us, then we left to get breakfast at the Pacific Dining Car, a twenty-four-hour restaurant in downtown L.A. It was here, in a red leather booth, over eggs and toast, that he took my hand and said, "I want to marry you."

My eyes burned and I squeezed his hand. "I love you," I said, "but this is too much for one night. Let's talk about it another time, and just be close for now. Okay?"

"Okay," he said, but I could feel him stiffen slightly, and I knew I would have to face this again soon.

I spoke with Morry Helman several times over the next few days to get updates on Nick's condition. By Thursday it appeared Nick had sustained no permanent injuries from his accident, but he was suffering from frontal headaches which were expected to disappear within a few weeks, and he was being treated for soft tissue injuries to his neck and right knee. Although he continued to have amnesia for the events immediately following his accident, his memory appeared normal otherwise.

As our work resumed, it became clear that Nick's brush with death and the tearful admission of his feelings for me had finally brought him in contact with aspects of himself he had shut away.

A painful rush of earlier memories surfaced, and I scheduled extra sessions to cope with the outpouring, taking time afterward to make notes.

Each memory left him feeling a little more depressed over the childhood he'd wanted and never had. One traumatic revelation was that after his birth mother died, his father regularly locked him in the closet on the mornings when a babysitter wasn't available.

Nick was no more than four, and he lay in the closet long hours in silent darkness. At first he cried and pounded on the door, but when this brought no help, he devised ways to count out time so he would have some boundary to his nightmare. He sang the same nursery rhymes each time, in the same order, and he invented an imaginary friend, with whom he went on adventures. His engulfment in fantasy adventure was so complete that sometimes when the closet door swung open, he was shocked by the sudden reality of his life.

Nick spent several sessions pulling up memories of his "closet days." He returned to work to prepare for an important personal injury trial, but the troublesome memories sometimes interfered with his concentration. One night, after studying statutes into the wee hours, he dreamed he was rabbit hunting with his father. "I shot a rabbit, and when I ran up to it, it was my mother. I knelt down and took her in my arms, but she was dead. I cried and cried, saying 'Mommy, Mommy,' and I woke up like that."

The memories he recovered through the dream were so sad I thought about them all evening. Nick's mother, Victoria, had disappeared Easter Sunday. He was three years old, and had gladly taken off the stiff brown shoes she'd made him wear to church. She sent him to his cousin's house for the rest of the day, and that night his father called and told him to stay there till next evening.

When Nick returned, there was no trace of her. All her clothes were gone, her makeup in the bathroom, even the aprons out of her favorite kitchen drawer. In the bedroom he found a light sprinkling of powder that someone had missed in the clean-up effort. He ran his fingers through it, and put it on his own tiny face. It was the color of sand, and left a mark until his father made him wash it off.

"Your mother had to go away" was all his father would tell him. To his frantic questions about her return, his father said it was just the two of them now.

A soft, white stuffed rabbit—his Easter present—was the last thing his mother had given him, and he had taken it to his cousin's. When he returned home holding his precious rabbit, it was the only toy left. His father had not only removed every last vestige of anything belonging to his mother, but also had taken every toy she'd ever given Nick. His trucks, his beloved fire engine, his toy trains, his bears, all were gone, and his father said, "We're starting a new life, Nicky, and I'll buy you anything you want."

He threw himself on the bed, clutching the rabbit, screaming, and his father left him there to get used to their new life. The only shred of her left was the rabbit, and he clung to it with such ferocity even his father didn't have the heart to take it away. He cried himself to sleep for months.

When Candy came to live with them, she urged Nicholas Senior to stop locking up Nick, but by then Nick began hiding in the closet on his own. Instinctively he was afraid for Candy to see his old rabbit and he hid it from her. It was raggedy by then, filthy and untouched by anyone except him.

One rainy afternoon when she'd stayed home and built a fire, she opened the closet and found him sleeping in there, hugging the disintegrating rabbit to his chest. Before he was awake she ripped it from him. "Where the hell have you been keeping this? It's filthy! It's full of bugs!" She stomped off to the living room and threw it in the fireplace. He ran after her and stuck his hand in the fire to rescue the last physical link to his mother.

Candy tried to soothe him while they bandaged his hand in the doctor's office. It wasn't a bad burn, just enough to leave a small scar later, but the rabbit was burned beyond saving, and to make it up to him she took him from the doctor's office to a toy store and bought him a new stuffed rabbit. He accepted it in silence.

At home, one leg of the old rabbit still lay on the hearth where he had dropped it in pain. He picked up the gray, charred piece, wrapped it carefully in tissue, and put it in the toe of one of his good brown shoes. If Candy knew about it, she said nothing. The next day on the way to the playground little Nick dropped the new rabbit in a neighbor's garbage can, and never thought about stuffed rabbits again.

• • •

Hearing about Nick's early life made me appreciate my parents more. I had called on Christmas day, but had spoken to them only briefly, and I knew my mother in particular would want to hear more about my trip.

"Darling!" she said as usual, "How *are* you? Daddy's out crabbing and he'll be so sorry he missed you."

I smiled, picturing my Dad on the dock, drinking beer, playing crib with the other fishermen, hauling in the crabs every hour. "I'll call him tomorrow."

Mom wanted to know what Isabella had served on Christmas day, what she wore, and what I thought of her.

"She's very formal. Trained to be graceful. But I think she felt threatened by me."

"Yes, of course, because of your profession."

"No, because I'm competition, and I'm not Latin."

"Oh, I see," she said, her voice dipping. Then she brightened. "But the important thing is you and Humberto. How is it with him?"

She would overreact if I told her we had discussed marriage, so all I said was, "I think I'm in love with him."

"How exciting! Is he good to you?"

"He's great. Takes my clothes to the dry cleaners, cooks for me, and confides in me." What point was there in mentioning our conflicts over my work or the trail of debris he left in the bathroom?

"Darling, I'm so pleased. I worry about you being all alone down there. Can you bring him up to meet us?"

"Maybe. It's hard for him to get away from the restaurant." There was a slight pause at the other end, and I added, "But *I'll* come up for sure. Weekend after next."

Later when I told Humberto, he said "I want to meet your parents," and I reluctantly made plans to include him. I knew the four of us together would be an emotional mine field for me.

Although none of my other patients responded as extremely to my absence as Nick, they all had their reactions. In a flat voice, Luness said she'd binged and purged every day since I'd last seen her. William reported that over the Christmas holiday, Elizabeth had packed up and moved in with her boyfriend, and he was coping with the loss by exercising, and working on his stamps.

William also confessed that sometimes he indulged in the fantasy of being a beautiful woman. When I asked him what about this he found appealing, he said, "I don't really want to be a woman. It's the *privilege* I covet. Beautiful women seem to walk around in a protective bubble."

"And what would the bubble protect you from?"

"Responsibility. Risk. Rejection. The three dreaded Rs."

"And yet, here you are facing those dreaded Rs and surviving."

He nodded slowly. "I guess that's true," he said, and I was pleased at his progress.

Most of my other patients had endured my absence fairly well. The Romaine sisters had gone Christmas shopping for a few elderly women who were housebound, and had enjoyed it so much they were planning more trips. A patient who'd terminated therapy in October sent me a card to let me know how well she was doing. Even my supervision group at the V.A. was finally feeling more confident, and it was gratifying to see how much they'd learned.

After having been so relaxed on vacation, I felt overwhelmed by work. Dictation, bills, and reports were stacking up; I had lectures to prepare; the radio show was generating new referrals, and I was finally negotiating with my publisher to write a book on eating disorders.

Pleased as I was about the work, I had to refuse many dinners and parties with Humberto in order to keep up, and I felt torn, because I loved him and missed being with him.

One night he came home from a dinner without me and found me on my stationary bike. He said irritably, "This is what you do instead of going out with me?"

"I dictated all evening. I needed to get the cobwebs out of my brain."

"You're going to develop arthritic joints. And probably stop ovulating. That's what happens when a woman's body fat gets too low."

I turned up the volume on my Walkman and cycled faster. Maybe he would never understand how much I valued my work or how much satisfaction it gave me.

27

I considered it progress that Nick was recovering his memories, but they were wretched memories, and the more he talked, the angrier he became. As he paced around the office, red-faced and yelling, I saw not only how volatile he was, but how fragile. Underneath his rage was despair.

He ranted about what a bastard his father had been, how insensitive and mean. When his father came home drunk, Candy had to be there, and if she wasn't, he beat her up the second she walked in the door. One time Nick threw himself between them. His father tossed Nick across the kitchen table and broke his arm. By all accounts his father had been a brutal, self-centered baby who needed constant reassurance, and the more Nick thought about it the more vengeful he became. "If he wasn't dead I'd kill him," he said.

One day while Candy was out, Nick Senior locked up his son to punish him for bedwetting. When she returned, Candy opened the door and found Nick naked, breathing heavily, eyes closed. He and his friend were riding a camel in the desert, just like in his favorite storybook. He was in fact suffocating in the heat, had taken his clothes off and imagined that the sun was beating down on them. He began to sweat as he rode the camel, his arms around his friend.

"So that's what you do in the closet!" she said.

"It was hot in there," he said in a small voice.

She got down on her knees next to him, her sour whiskey breath warm on his face, and she ran her hands over his shoulders and down his chest. He was so frightened he peed. "Don't be afraid," she said.

"How old were you?" I asked.

"About seven."

"Did you have some sexual contact with her then?"

He hesitated. "I'm sure my penchant for hot tubs comes from my ma. She used to take long baths in the afternoon. At first I thought she was crying or sick, and I'd go up to the door and ask her if she was okay. 'Go and play outside,' she'd say. 'I'm fine.' Later I used to watch through the keyhole." He shook his head and stared up at the ceiling as I envisioned this raven-haired siren, caressing herself in the steam and heat of the bath.

"When my dad didn't come home, she would finish off a bottle and then let me sleep with her. She had big, soft tits. Getting my head between a broad's tits still turns me on. Sometimes when I jack-off—I hold a pillow over my face."

He turned away from me and lay down on the couch. "I hated her after she left. If she really loved me she wouldn't have gone."

"Maybe there was more to it than that. Did you ever hear her side of the story?"

"No. By the time she tried to get in touch with me, it was way too late. I didn't want anything to do with her."

He lay curled quietly on his side. After some minutes he said, "She did one thing for me, though. She taught me how to satisfy a woman."

I was appalled.

During the next session, Nick asked if I kept notes on him. When I acknowledged that I did, he said, "I hate the idea of such personal stuff being recorded."

Remembering his computer searches, I understood why. "I'll try to keep it to the bare minimum."

"Sure," he said, and then returned to the bitter recounting of his childhood.

Whatever was difficult in my own childhood seemed mild compared to Nick's. That week, Humberto and I arrived in Bandon late on Friday evening, and during the three-hour drive from the Medford Airport, I gave Humberto a brief tour of my past—a glimpse of the icy Rogue River where Dad and I used to fish; the railroad crossing where my mom and I had crashed into the train; my high school; and the playground where Dad had pitched the ball to me until I was dizzy from swinging.

I could still see my palms, blistered and red from gripping the bat. I said to Humberto, "I was a failure by my dad's standards—I cried easily, I was a lousy baseball player, and I was afraid of the dark."

"But isn't he proud of you now?"

"I don't know. Maybe." How bad was that, compared to a father who beat you and locked you up?

Still, I found it upsetting that the only time my father had really acknowledged me was when I was in graduate school. His own parents thought he had failed out of high school because he was stupid, which was why baseball was so important to him, but he always seemed smart to me. When I began studying cognitive functions, I suddenly suspected he might have a reading disability, and at spring break I brought home tests to evaluate him.

The pattern of his responses confirmed my diagnosis. Red-faced, he stumbled over eighth-grade spelling and reading, yet when I read words aloud to him, his vocabulary was at college level.

Together we obtained a library card for him from the National

Federation for the Blind, and the world suddenly opened up to him. That week alone he listened to a condensed version of Darwin's *Origin of Species, Great American Political Speeches,* and Zane Grey's *The Shortstop.*

The night before I went back to school, he came into my room and sat down on the undersized chair that still stands next to my old student's desk. The golden hair on his arms shimmered in the light of my chipped desk lamp. There were a few faded spots of gravy on the front of his T-shirt.

"Sarah—" he started, and couldn't finish. He hung his head, the sandy hair then mixed with gray, and silently choked back sobs into his hands. The only other time I'd seen him cry like that was in the emergency room, waiting for news of my mother.

"Thank you," he finally said. That was it.

By the time we reached my parents' small, neat house I was apprehensive. I knew they would be impressed with Humberto's business and his affection for me, but I didn't know whether they'd feel comfortable with him, and it had been a long time since I'd seen them myself.

My mother had polished the kitchen floor, waxed the oak dining table, and bought fresh bedsheets and towels for our room. She greeted us with hugs and kisses. My father looked ridiculously unlike himself in polished leather shoes and polyester slacks, his unruly hair slicked down, his handshake too vigorous.

We fussed over preparations for tea and decaf coffee, my mother commenting on how thin I looked and me thinking how fat she looked. Before our late-night snack, Humberto and I crowded into my old room and unpacked. Gone were his silks, gabardines, and soft leather shoes. He had brought jeans and hiking boots, cotton and corduroy. "You are the cutest," I said, hugging him.

Mom gave him a tour of my photos and awards, which she still kept on the wall in the den. She said, "Sarah was quite the student. Always had to be first in her class."

And what else could I count on? I thought angrily. You were making a doormat of yourself. Dad was at some woman's trailer. I had to invent myself.

Humberto was impressed with the awards. "She never told me about all these! And how pretty she looked in her dresses!"

"I made them," Mom said with pride. "Of course now she shops at those Beverly Hills stores. Nothing but the best for my Sarah."

I tried to ignore her tone. "Mom is incredibly talented at designing and making clothes. If I have good taste, it's because she taught me what to look for."

She served a rich chocolate cake, of which Humberto ate two pieces even though he had sworn off chocolate for the new year. He won her heart by asking for the recipe.

Mom blushed with pleasure. "It's just a homemade cake. I'm sure your pastry chefs could match it any day."

"On the contrary," he said. "You never get quite the same quality in a commercial kitchen as you do at home."

My mother wrote out her recipe and explained her exact mixing technique. Humberto listened attentively, asking questions about nuts and kinds of chocolate, even though he knew much more about it than she. As I watched their heads bent over her recipe, I realized with surprise that they were similar in some ways. How foolish of me to miss it, I thought, and how easily I would have seen it if I were my own patient.

Humberto knew just how to talk to Dad too. Out of nowhere he pulled baseball names, football scores, and predictions for the Superbowl. He had Dad laughing and drinking beer and happily belching out loud by midnight. The ultimate compliment was Dad hauling out his worn baseball glove. Always, when he was enjoying himself, he wore his glove and tossed the ball into it, accompanying the conversation with a *pock* sound at five-second intervals.

Later, as Humberto and I lay mashed together in my old double bed, I said, "Where did you learn to talk like that? You never watch football."

He chuckled quietly. "I have to know how to talk to everybody. We get plenty of ball players in the restaurant. Yesterday one of them gave me the stats on the favorites for the play-offs. I figured your dad would be interested."

"What did you think of my mother?"

"I liked her, but she's a little mean under the surface."

"She feels cheated, but she doesn't take into account how hard I work for what I have."

"Envy never takes that into account."

I kissed him. Quietly, moving so slowly he made no sound, he entered me from the side and stroked me with his fingers at the same time. I came hard and fast, clinging to him afterward like a baby monkey.

When Humberto and my father went crabbing the next day, my

mother and I grocery-shopped and she bore down on me right in the supermarket. "He's so charming, Sare. So gracious. How about the bedroom?"

"Really good, Mom. A little too good." I picked through the tomatoes, looking for the firm ones.

"How can a man be too good?"

"I don't know—too much experience."

She caught my jacket and pulled me to her. "Now don't you go ruining this one! You appreciate him! You're always making problems where there are none."

I jerked my arm away. "You mean instead of putting my head in the sand like you?"

Her face fell, and she turned away and began stuffing apples in the cart. Why did I let her suck me into a fight?

"I'm sorry, Mom. Let's just be patient with each other. I don't know how things are going to turn out with Humberto. I think I'm in love with him. I think he loves me. That's all I know right now, okay?"

My mother was not easily soothed. She said, "Okay," but her mood was dull and she talked less than usual.

Humberto and my dad returned mid-afternoon, reeking of fish, cheeks red from the cold wind. Humberto staggered into the kitchen carrying their heavy ice chest and deposited it on the counter, opening it briefly to reveal eleven beautiful Dungeness crabs crawling over each other. He announced he was going to make a fresh crab soufflé and went upstairs to shower, while my dad cleaned out his truck.

"Helluva guy!" Dad said when he blustered in. "Knows almost as much about tide pools as me." He lowered his voice. "But I think he needs a bit more stamina. Couldn't walk a mile to the crab pot. Said he wanted to bring 'em home raw to cook 'em here, but I think he just needed the rest."

Puzzled, I excused myself. Humberto was in fine shape from swimming in his pool every day.

Upstairs in my old bedroom, I found Humberto fresh from the shower, hobbling across the floor. "What happened?" I asked.

"Shhh. Your father dropped the ice chest on my toe. I think it's broken."

I looked down and saw the little toe on his right foot was blue and puffy. "Oh, honey, I think you do have a broken toe!"

"There's nothing to do for it except wrap it together with the next one. I've broken it before."

"Why didn't you tell Dad?"

"I knew it would make him feel clumsy and ruin his good time."

"Oh, sweetie." I hugged him and went out to the bathroom in search of adhesive tape. He was right. My dad would have been embarrassed, and I was deeply touched that Humberto wanted to spare him.

Taping his toes together helped, and he wore his loosest pair of tennis shoes the rest of the weekend. When I showed him my old high school, he chuckled and said, "Even being the valedictorian of a small school is impressive." I punched him affectionately in the arm, and he took a picture of me at the school entrance, flexing my right bicep. Later he took photographs of me and my parents in front of our house. Never once did he make me feel self-conscious of the discrepancy between our financial backgrounds.

When the weekend was over I felt we'd made it through some treacherous waters, and I told Val all about it.

Gaining access to his emotions and memories changed Nick's physical appearance. He began wearing softer colors and fabrics; he let his hair grow longer; he left his collars open. Short-sleeved shirts revealed smooth tanned skin, well-defined muscles, even proportions. Always he had a fresh smell, like soap and toothpaste and baby powder.

As I had hoped, some of his anger toward his father lost its force. He admitted the man had worked hard to support him; he recounted terrible stories of his father's own childhood; he said by the time his father died he had become a sentimental, lonely man.

Gradually Nick began to talk more about Candy. He alluded to the sexual contact by mentioning that he often fell asleep in her arms. One day he related an incident that revealed just how extensive the contact had been.

He was nine years old, and his father was working the nightshift. Anxious about a math test the next day, Nick wet his bed again and Candy helped him wash the sheets. She wiped away his tears and gave him a few sips of her Jim Beam. "Come and sleep with me," she said.

She was wearing only a thin nightie, and as she swayed toward the bedroom he could see her naked form through the filmy fabric. He wanted to touch her. He wanted to be locked together like the two dogs next door, until someone had to throw water on them.

In bed she let him suckle her breasts. Later that night her hand closed around his penis and he had his first climax. Ever after that his most intense orgasms occurred in total darkness, when a woman masturbated him while he held a pillow over his face. Guilt, suffocation, and excitement were joined in an erotic imprint on his psyche.

Two mornings after Nick told me about Candy, I arrived at work to find my office door unlocked. I went to the manager's office, and together we returned to investigate.

Nothing was disturbed. My paintings were intact, my hand-held tape recorder sitting where I had left it, my little cut-glass elephant untouched. The manager shrugged and said, "Probably the janitor forgot to lock the door."

Later when I went to retrieve a patient's chart from my file cabinet, I discovered that it too was unlocked. Instinctively I reached for Nick's chart. All the pages detailing his personal history were in reverse order.

"Damn him!" I said aloud.

I scheduled another appointment with Zachary to discuss the situation. He said, "The guy is so shrewd! He knows you're legally responsible for the safety of your files, so if you accuse him of breaking in and altering the file, he can act outraged about your failure to protect his privacy."

"I'm glad you see what I'm dealing with. I've had plenty of experience, but nothing like this before. Do you think I should confront him directly about it?"

"No. I'd document what has happened, and keep his chart at home or in your safe if you have one."

"And what if he comes looking for it?"

"What did he find in the chart this time?"

"Mostly insurance information, and notes about his behavior, but not very much personal history."

"Then I don't think he'll come looking for it again."

That day Zachary told me he would be leaving in mid-March for a month's vacation in Asia. I congratulated him, and hoped that by then I could handle Nick on my own.

• • •

In the process of churning up and sharing so much emotion, Nick began to feel not only that he loved me, but that he was *in love* with me, and that to have me physically would remedy whatever was wrong with him. This was not uncommon in therapy—many patients, both male and female, had expressed sexual feelings toward me—but coming so soon on the heels of his revelations about his stepmother, I thought this new infatuation was a compulsion to repeat and repair what had happened with her. It was an easy leap from a real incestuous experience to the physical desire for me—a mother figure who listened to him so attentively.

For Valentine's Day Humberto gave me six pairs of lace panties with my initials embroidered across the front panel. Nick brought me a jade heart.

At first I refused to accept Nick's gift, but he put it on my desk before he left, and said, "Would you take this, please? It only cost fifteen dollars and I'm going to feel like a fool if you give it back." I didn't want to risk shutting him down by being intractable about this small gift. I left it on my desk.

Later, I told Zachary that Nick had gone from being one of the most resistant patients I had had to feeling he was in love with me. I said, "I think it's another form of resistance."

He said, "I agree. Thinking of you fills up his mind, keeps other thoughts out, and wards off depression and loneliness. Basically he wants to abandon the work and possess you instead. You've got to explore it so you can get beyond it."

With Zachary's words fresh in my mind, I said to Nick, "Tell me whatever comes to your mind about loving me. Let's understand it as best we can."

"I've never been in love like this," he replied. "If we could make love, even once, it would change me forever."

Each time he said this I'd ask, "What would our making love do for you?" and on different days, the answers varied.

During one session he replied, "I imagine being held inside your warmth and soothed by your touch. If we made love I'd feel nothing inside me was missing anymore."

"What's missing?" I asked, and he wouldn't look at this, couldn't talk about it, but only of the solution, a cure by immersion in my body.

On another day, he said, "I would feel incredibly powerful if I could make love to you; I'd feel like I could do anything after that."

"Why powerful?"

"Because you don't sleep with your patients, so if you did with me, I'd be very special."

He reported having gotten drunk with a colleague named Billy Checkers, who was newly engaged to be married. "I imagined being married to you," he said.

There were many more of his fantasies we explored. He wanted my mind and my insight, and he thought through physical union he would acquire my psychological characteristics. Sometimes it seemed to me he'd acquired them anyway, and was now talking like me.

Another belief haunted him: for me to take him into my bed would make him feel totally accepted, and having had this absolution, he would ever after feel himself to be valuable. For me to deny him this salvation was cruel, he said, and he ranted at me, frightening me with the force of his feelings.

All my patients were important to me, but the hours with Nick were riveting, and I became even more preoccupied with his treatment. I read everything I could find on erotic transference and countertransference. During sessions with other patients I had to force away fragments of conversation with him that crowded my mind, and while jogging, swimming, or driving I repeatedly mulled over the solution to this Gordian knot of how to get through this new phase of his obsession with me.

There were even several mornings when I arrived at my office and thought he had been there. Nothing was missing, nothing broken, but little things seemed different—the way the pillows on the sofa were arranged or the order of papers on my desk. I concluded I was imagining things, especially when the office seemed to smell faintly of baby powder. You're having an olfactory hallucination, I told myself.

My study of the literature, my consultations with Zachary, and my own thinking led to the same conclusion. Nick's desire to possess me was a makeshift solution to repairing inner problems, which he felt unable to change any other way. To reach the deeper layer, I had to ask him to tell me more; I had to understand what he loved about me, why, and when he felt it most. Only in this manner could we uncover his underlying assumptions and needs. The therapy provided a permanent and possible solution, while his method—possessing me—was a dead end.

The work was very difficult. Nick was mercilessly seductive—fervent, explicit in his language—and in spite of my passion for Humberto, there were moments when I felt a powerful urge to tear off my clothes and succumb to Nick there on the office floor.

I scoured my personal history to understand why I was tempted by a forbidden man, when I was already in love with an available one. I concluded that old anger and unrequited love for my father accounted for my feelings. I was also experiencing an occupational hazard—the temptation to believe the patient's idealized image of me—and I reminded myself over and over that his love was induced by the therapeutic situation itself, based solely on his fantasy of me, and not on the real Sarah whom he barely knew. Yet sometimes I felt I loved him back, not in the way he wanted, but for his struggle, for his pain, and for the intelligence and sensitivity that had unfolded in my presence.

After some consideration, he complied with my request that he regularly lie on the couch, facing away from me. I thought it would be easier for him to discuss embarrassing things. I didn't mention what a great relief it was for me. I often felt with him as if my clothing were transparent, and when his gaze rested on any part of my body, he was seeing it naked, touching it and breathing on it.

29

In bed, needing the release from so much stimulation and tension with Nick, I surrendered completely to Humberto, my orgasms becoming so intense I often felt faint. Out of bed, I could not help holding something in reserve. I didn't like Humberto's resentment of my work or the way he became petty and sarcastic when he didn't get his way. And there were those women at Paradise, who embraced him and invited him over to cater their parties.

One point of open conflict was my dog. Weeknights, when Humberto's maid remained in his house, he slept at my place so I could look after Frank. Weekends, I spent at his home, bringing the dog with me.

The first time he had been honest about Frank, Humberto studied him and said, "I know you love this dog, but he looks ridiculous."

Frank responded by pointing his long muzzle at the ceiling and baying, in true basset hound fashion.

I said, "I think he's irresistible. His face is so full of character with that mournful expression."

The problem wasn't only how Frank looked. He would pull Humberto's pants off the bedroom chair and arrange them into a nice sleeping blanket for himself. If Humberto brought a plate of food home, Frank would gobble it up if it was within reach. He sniffed and poked his cold nose at us while we were making love, and if we locked him out, he howled incessantly. He smelled of salt, and dirt, and often something piney from the yard.

"Why don't you bathe him?" Humberto asked.

"He hates water. I usually let the vet do it once a month."

Frank didn't like being uprooted from familiar surroundings, either, and the first few times he had arrived at Humberto's house, he had shown his displeasure by rushing upstairs and peeing on Humberto's side of the bed. This infuriated Humberto, who yelled, "No! Bad dog!" each time he saw my obstinate pet disappearing up the stairs. After we were forced to sleep in the guest bedroom a third time, Frank was banished from the upper floor altogether.

Unfortunately, Humberto's house was not set up for a rambunctious dog, and although we installed a kiddy gate to confine Frank to the kitchen in our absence, upon our return, we'd sometimes find one velvet sofa cushion on the floor, and a saliva spot in its middle. Each time, Humberto banged more nails into the kiddy gate to secure it better, and I hung back, patting Frank and apologizing.

Then there was the matter of the parrot. It was her house and she didn't like a new animal in it. The first few weekends Frank was there she shrieked "Call my lawyer!" constantly and refused to come out of her cage. Frank, who'd never been close to a bird like her, sat directly below her cage and barked.

Humberto forced Esperanza to acquaint herself with my dog by holding her on his wrist, next to a leashed and seated Frank. When the Amazon grew confident she was in no danger, she began shouting commands to Frank, who sometimes obeyed her since she could imitate my voice perfectly. For his own sanity, Humberto started giving Frank a shot of Jack Daniels on Saturday nights. Frank mellowed right out.

Often awakened by Humberto's snoring, I slept poorly. I kept dreaming of small enclosed houses and beautiful country cottages with bars on the windows. Sometimes I was on a tropical island with no way to get off, or in my office, locked from the outside.

I wanted to talk to Val about all this, and I'd called her three or four times and left messages, but she hadn't returned my calls. Concerned about her, I finally phoned her at home very late one evening. She answered sleepily.

"Sorry I woke you, hon. I haven't heard from you and I was starting to worry."

"I'm great. It's my fault for not calling back sooner," she whispered. "Gordon has moved in."

"Oh my God, Val, maybe this will work out." I started whispering too, even though at my end there was no need.

"What about you and Humberto?"

I told her my dreams, and she said, "You're afraid of being trapped."

"Because he's jealous of my patients! Although I can't totally blame him. At the last minute he had to go by himself to two dinners this week. But what if I marry him and he really makes an issue of it?"

"Maybe if you cut back a little it will help."

"I've been refusing referrals left and right. The problem is more that I'm still preoccupied with that one patient, and Humberto knows it."

"Maybe there's more to all this than meets the eye. Have you considered going back into therapy?"

"Yes."

But I didn't have time for therapy yet, and after I hung up the phone I tried to do the work myself by sifting through all my previous relationships, looking for patterns.

Next time I saw Nick, he confessed to masturbating in the men's restroom just prior to his sessions, in hopes of diminishing the intense yearning he felt. This worried me because I felt his ability to contain his feelings for me was eroding. I told him I thought a temporary stint on medication might lower his anxiety and help him tolerate his frustration, and at my insistence he agreed to see a physician, whom I considered most expert on psychotropic medication. The doctor prescribed both an antidepressant and an anxiolytic, and Nick said he would take them.

This did not really ease my own anxiety. I started imagining Nick was going to lose control of himself and come back to my office when he knew my last patient had left. I wondered if he would try to force himself on me. Rape me, even. And what if he became enraged when he finally believed he couldn't have me? Was he capable of shooting me? Choking me to death? I didn't think so, but I didn't know anymore. Most of us save our cruelty and craziness for those we love, and he was no different.

Although I hadn't seen Nick near my house again, I closed my drapes every night on the assumption that even though I couldn't see him, he was there.

When Humberto noticed, he said, "If you're really worried, you should do something about it."

"I'm not too worried, but I'm having a security system installed because I should have one anyway. I close the drapes mainly to ensure our privacy."

"Why don't you move in with me? I'd like that anyway."

I kissed him. "I'm not quite ready. Maybe soon."

"I hate what this guy is doing to your life. Why don't you see it?"

I turned away and said nothing.

Over the next few weeks I was successful in confining our relationship to the office, until Nick started making emergency phone calls through the service in the early hours of the morning. Even though I got out of bed and took the calls in another room, Humberto knew who it was, and said on several occasions, "You should get rid of that guy." I considered it a triumph that Nick was calling through the service.

The phone calls were desperate outpourings from Nick, usually after he'd downed half a bottle of gin, or come home from another empty evening with a woman. His depression and loneliness were very real, but I resented that he chose those times to call and I knew whatever his stated reason, he was getting satisfaction out of knowing he was rousing me out of bed. On more than one occasion, I cut him off abruptly, saying, "We can talk about this tomorrow."

After these late-night calls, I was always grateful for the respite of the radio show. The one-time contact with my callers was a welcome contrast to months and months of therapy with the same people.

One program began with a compulsive eater. She'd bought two dozen donuts, gorged until she was ill, and yet couldn't throw the rest away because it was a sin to waste food. There were two more calls from compulsive eaters, one from a woman hiding food in her garage, another from a college student addicted to Wheat Thins. My final call was from a man who said he was in love with his therapist.

"It's very common to feel love for a person who listens to you more attentively than anyone else ever has."

"But I feel she loves me too and she can't say it."

I suddenly felt ill. How had I not recognized the voice immediately? I launched into a speech about concern being misinterpreted as love, disconnected the call, and cut to commercial.

The control room jock looked at me and asked what was wrong. "I might be getting the flu again," I said. "My face feels really hot."

The next day when I saw Nick I told him not to call my show again.

"I wanted to see if you'd say something different than you tell me in person," he explained.

"I think you're fighting me with every indirect means you have. How can I be more clear? This therapy must be a direct dialogue between you and me here in the office."

As he was leaving, he studied my face. "You like me, but you don't let yourself like me too much, do you? You even want me sometimes. I sense it."

I was exquisitely careful. "You put me in a position where any response I give would hurt you: if I were to say I do want you sometimes, it might frighten the young you that wants to be protected from his own impulses; if I were to say I don't want you, the adult you might feel rejected or insulted. If I say nothing, you might infer either one."

"You're slick. You're really smart, aren't you? Well, don't answer. I know I'm right and that's enough for me."

I wrung my hands in frustration after he left.

30

That week, Zachary invited me to meet with him at his Bel Air home. His house was a handsome wood-and-stone Tudor, with a timeless, established feel. Oriental rugs, dark walnut floors, and heavy, soft furniture added to the sense of safety and warmth. As he escorted me into his study I felt like a child taken into a mother's arms.

"Would you like some coffee?" he asked.

I nodded and he disappeared for a few minutes, then returned with a tray holding two steaming blue mugs, a sugar bowl, and a creamer.

"I'm burned out," I said. "I'm doing everything I possibly can to contain this guy and it's barely working. He's damaging my relationship with my boyfriend, he's sapping my time, and he's scaring me."

After listening to the details, Zachary said, "He's splitting. He's projected everything good into you, and wants a physical union with you as a way of becoming whole. The boundaries between the two of you are blurred in his mind. He may think *you* feel what *he* feels. He may assume that his needs are your needs."

"But you're making him sound psychotic, which I don't think he is."

"I don't think he's psychotic. But he's regressed in relation to you."

I nodded miserably, loaded two teaspoons of sugar into my mug, and took a sip. "What would you do?"

"More of the same. I would keep firm boundaries. Limit the number of phone calls he makes to you outside his hours. If he needs more contact, schedule extra appointments. You have to ride it out by keeping tight control of the therapy."

Zachary set his mug on a sidetable and leaned back in his chair until it squeaked into a semi-reclining position. "Are you still having sexual feelings toward him?"

"No. His incessant seductiveness makes me angry now. I'm sure he calls late at night because he knows I'm in bed with another man."

"This is not good for you."

I looked across the room at a book-lined wall. "No. It's interfering with my personal life."

Zachary sat up. "Perhaps you're trying to protect yourself from something."

I examined the deep lines that ran from Zachary's nose down to his jowls. He'd been through some pain. I didn't know all the details, but there'd been a child with cerebral palsy, a death, a remarriage. I respected his courage, and his opinion.

"Perhaps," I said.

After our meeting, I was glad to see Humberto's car in my driveway. I opened the door and yelled hello, but didn't hear anything. A tour of the house uncovered the sound of water running in the bathtub, muffled by the closed door. I smiled, picturing Humberto stretched out in the tub.

His clothes were thrown across the bed. I hastily laid my own clothes beside his and tiptoed to the bathroom door, stark naked.

I opened the door and whirled in quickly so as not to let out the heat, but the sound that greeted me was a long, mournful howl, and as I turned I saw the signs of a hairy struggle that involved soap, leashes, dog hair, and terror.

Humberto was in his undershorts, soaking wet, kneeling on his knees next to the tub. Inside the tub was Frank, standing in two inches of water on a rubber mat, a high hat of bubbles sliding down one ear.

I burst out laughing, and at the sight of me, Frank broke into loud barking and tried to climb out of the tub. Humberto grabbed him and forced him down, getting covered with foamy bubbles and dog hair in the process.

"We were almost done. I was going to surprise you." His eyes were level with my hips. "I guess you were going to surprise me too."

"Later." I wrapped a towel around myself and sat down on the toilet lid to watch them.

I didn't know which of them looked more absurd: Frank, with his wet plastered fur, red lower eyelids, and moronic grin, or Humberto, with his long shins splayed out behind him and his feet mashed against the floor and pointed outward. I laughed until my sides ached, while Humberto finished soaping and rinsing the dog. He toweled him dry and then let him shake himself until the whole bathroom was covered in little tiny drops of water.

"I couldn't stand his smell anymore," Humberto explained. "If you don't mind, I'm going to bathe him once a week."

"Be my guest." At least he wasn't totally rejecting Frank.

Suddenly I was touched by this man's patience, and his willingness to accommodate himself to an animal he disliked. I looked at him in his dripping shorts, with dog hair stuck to his skinny calves, and was seized with desire for him. I covered his face with kisses, and as the relieved Frank retreated to the kitchen, I pulled Humberto to the bed and straddled him, pinning his shoulders to the mattress.

That weekend, I took Humberto to Linda Morrison's house. For Jeremy's fifth birthday, she was giving a party in her backyard. It was a clear March day, and I slathered my face with sunscreen before putting on makeup, because Linda had told me sun would make my skin worse.

I smiled, thinking about her as I applied the lotion. Even though she was a nurse, if she read in some magazine that dahlia-tuber syrup strengthened fingernails, she'd scour the herb stores to find it and then use it for a few months until the next thing came along. She had some weird remedy for everything: gel-filled shoe liners for sore feet, frozen neck wraps for headaches, pepper pastes for sinus pain. I teased her about it, but she claimed it all worked.

I felt a pang of jealousy when Linda extended her hand to Humberto. Her dewy skin was flawless. He kissed the back of her hand and I could see she liked him right away.

There were twelve children, confused and excited by the games and live donkey rides. A man in a cheap tuxedo did a lame puppet show. A few of the youngest children cried when he made the sound of a witch's cackle. After the show, the children lined up together on a picnic bench for milk and jelly beans and white cake with red frosting.

Humberto and I stood with a few of the parents, talking about the cost of private pre-schools and the dismal state of public education. We sang "Happy Birthday" to Jeremy, who was over-excited and unable to focus on the gifts in front of him. The kids put on silver paper hats, blew party whistles, and poked their fingers in each other's cake.

It was a chaotic party, inexpensive and full of hassles, but Linda's laugh was joyful, and the adoration of Jeremy plain on her face. Would I ever have a home with Play-Doh mashed to the floor and a sticky-fingered child to tuck in bed?

I watched Humberto smiling affectionately at the children. Linda obviously liked him, and pulled me aside to say, "Go for it, Sare. You've got a real catch there." I hugged her and said, "I think you're right," and thought, I shouldn't feel jealous of Linda.

After we left the party, Humberto and I held hands and strolled along the Venice canal bank. A family of ducks paddled by, four babies following the proud mother.

Our walk led us to Washington Boulevard, where we window-shopped for a few blocks until I became aware that we were rapidly approaching the Marina Towers where Nick lived. "Let's go home," I said abruptly, and turned around.

Humberto practically had to run to keep up with me.

31

William failed to appear for his next appointment. That afternoon his daughter called to say he had suffered a heart attack and was in the CCU at St. John's Hospital, very depressed. "Could you visit him?" she asked.

"Of course," I said. "I'll be there this evening. And please let William know." Momentary guilt over having to arrive late for yet another social engagement with Humberto plagued me, but what could I do? This was more important.

William looked withered and gray against the white sheets. He smiled wanly. "I've done it now, haven't I?" For a half hour he shared his morbid thoughts, while I listened sympathetically. He would be dependent now, he said dully. He wouldn't be able to jog. His life was over and he'd never really lived it.

"What have the doctors told you?" I asked.

"They don't know yet. Time will tell."

"Remember your pessimism," I said gently. "Time might tell something good."

He mustered a small smile. "Perhaps. Anyway, I feel better for having talked. Thank you. And I'm sorry for the inconvenience." It was becoming a strain for him to speak.

I squeezed his hand. "Please call me when you're ready for another visit. I'll be happy to come by again."

He nodded, closed his eyes, and I left, thinking how different it was to visit him than it had been to visit Nick.

Later in the week, Nick continued to plead for my touch. He said he was a dying plant, and my body was life-giving water. I recited the old Zen wisdom: you can't catch the ball if you watch the thrower's arm, emphasizing that he couldn't take what I had to offer if he was fixated on me. We argued this one whole hour.

At the beginning of another session, after I'd closed the door and turned toward my chair, I found him right behind me, and before I could step back he encircled me with his arms and buried his face in my hair, breathing in short warm bursts.

I stiffened, leaving my arms frozen at my sides, and with open eyes staring beyond him, said evenly, "Let me go." I was as panicked as if he was holding a loaded gun to my neck. In as firm a voice as I could manage, I forced the words out again. "Let me go." Red-faced and ashamed, he released me and retreated to the couch.

His desire for me began to feel like the squeezing tentacles of an octopus, and the arousal I used to feel with him was replaced by the horrible inability to catch my breath in his presence. I began having sudden coughing fits during the sessions with him.

Away from him I often felt as if my throat was closing up, and I developed a fear of choking on food. I ate in very small bites, and slowed my eating pace so I wouldn't laugh at some remark and inhale a piece of potato or a mouthful of wine.

Stubbornly I refused to give up and refer him to someone else. Hoping my perseverance would be rewarded, I said to Nick, "I am split into pieces in your mind. Sometimes you hate me. Sometimes you love me. You don't experience me as a mixture of good and bad. And you also experience yourself in pieces. Sometimes you feel as if everything good about yourself is inside me and you have to possess me to get it back."

Stretched out on the couch, arms crossed over his chest, he obstinately said nothing.

In an effort to ease his frustrated desire for me, Nick began dating a new woman, Maggie McCutcheon, the daughter of a senior partner in his firm. He said she was classy, different than his usual choice of women, intelligent, and conservative in her dress. I could have substituted my own name in the description and no adjectives would have changed.

The one odd thing was that Nick didn't mention any sexual activity with Maggie, and focused instead on her wit and charm. Not wishing to evoke any sexual material unnecessarily, I mulled over this omission in silence.

Then one session, he came in angry, and paced back and forth in front of me, slamming one fist into the other palm. "I can't believe this! I'm afraid of you!" he hissed. Then he began walking around the confines of the room like a caged panther. "I think you'll be jealous of my making love to Maggie! I feel like I'm being unfaithful to you!"

"Then you must feel that your being faithful to me is something I want."

"Oh, brother." His arms dropped down to his sides as if I had punched him. He turned, stepped to the window, and gazed outside. "You have no idea how humiliating this is for me. I feel like such an ass. I'm having a one-sided love affair with you and you're probably laughing inside."

"Why would I laugh?"

He turned back angry again. "Because it's so ridiculous! I'm your patient and you're never going to love me back!" He strode out and slammed the door so hard the framed degrees on the wall shifted askew.

After he left, my throat tightened up and I drank several glasses of water to calm myself.

The following session, he returned as if nothing had happened. He lay down on the couch calmly and said, "I had a great time with Maggie this weekend. Her parents are starting to treat me like family. Her mother is beautiful and she *likes* me. I played golf with Mr. Mac on Saturday, and Sunday we spent the day at their ranch. It's a huge estate. Five-car garage, a hilltop view of the whole city." Then he added quietly, "I stole something from the ranch."

Finally he admitted he had stolen something! I would hear him out and then nail him about the thefts from me.

"I couldn't help myself," he continued in this hushed tone. "We were having a barbecue by the pool, and Mrs. Mac asked me to go back and get a jar of pickles from the kitchen. I hurried across the lawn to the house, turned on the pantry light, and stepped inside."

He began to speak haltingly, with many pauses between his words. "I can't tell you . . . how strange . . . an experience it was. There were . . . rows and rows of beautiful glass canning jars with preserves in them. Nectarines, pears, apples, jams, little onions—and such an abundance of everything! Dried pasta, cereals, canned vegetables, cookies, chocolate, juices. There were herbs tied with string and hanging upside down. It smelled so spicy and sweet."

One gulping sob tore through the room. I sat in silence and watched him reach up to his face as if to push it all back inside. He ran his fingers through his hair, breaking the smooth surface of it and leaving one piece at the crown sticking straight up.

"I would have given anything to be a little boy again and have that be my pantry, where my mother had sent me to get something for her cooking. Why didn't I ever have that? Maggie grew up with it. Probably you did too! Why was I destined to miss out?!"

He folded his arms across his waist and turned first on his left side and then on his right. His voice had temporarily hardened with anger, but it softened again quickly. "I stayed there touching the jars, reading labels, and smelling things until I was afraid someone would come looking for me. And then I had to take something. Oh, I'm sure she'd have gladly given me anything I asked for, but I didn't want her to know I wanted it."

He drew his knees up toward his chest until he was in a fetal position. "I chose a silly thing. A bag of dried beans. They were pretty—different kinds and colors mixed together in a cellophane package for gourmet bean soup. It probably didn't cost more than two dollars, but it seemed so homey. So I grabbed the pickles, and stowed the beans in my sports bag before going back outside."

"Why would her knowing you wanted it be uncomfortable?"

"I want so much it scares me and embarrasses me. I figure it would scare anyone else who saw it in me."

He was right. It even scared me. "Nick—have you ever taken anything from this office?"

"Yes. Little things. Even trash sometimes."

Oh my God. What had I thrown in the trash? Used-up lipstick? Rough drafts of other patients' test reports? I was a fool for not using a shredder! "What did you do with the things you took?"

"I kept them as mementos of you."

I imagined an ugly little shrine at his apartment, with the troll dolls and my used lipstick case. I pushed the creepy image out of my mind. "Do you still feel a need to do that here?"

"No," he said. "I don't want to steal from you anymore. I want you to give yourself to me."

This was worse. And how far would he go to achieve that? I wondered grimly.

32

One night Humberto came home late from yet another dinner party I had missed to keep up with my dictation. Spending so much extra time focused on Nick, I had fallen behind in my other work.

Humberto put his hands on his hips and shook his head. "Still at it?" Then he loosened his tie, draped his jacket over a dining room chair, and flopped down on the sofa, disturbing my orderly piles of paper.

"Be careful!" I snapped.

"Sorry."

I sighed loudly and quickly rearranged my papers in neat piles on the floor.

He clucked his tongue. "Why do you drive yourself so much?"

I continued straightening papers. What would Humberto understand about being trapped in a job like my father was until he finally scraped together enough money to buy his store? "I want financial security and independence. And I don't want to have to answer to anyone else."

"But you have to answer to fifty patients!" He went into the bedroom to change, while I fumed over my dictation. He returned in five minutes still wearing the same clothes. "I was embarrassed to be at another dinner party alone. People call you my phantom girlfriend."

"Why should I give up working for what I want? You wouldn't!!"

He shook his head. "You don't see it, do you?"

"Try me." I was getting angry.

"You can't work as much as you do, and exercise, and look after your house and your dog and your friends, and still have time for me. Maybe other men in your life have been willing to take your scraps, but I'm not one of them!"

My self-righteousness crumbled. I wasn't sure of my motivation for working so hard, and I didn't want to ruin my chances for marriage and a family. I pictured myself as an old woman, dictating late into the evening with nobody there beside me. Tears spilled down my cheeks. "I love you and it scares me," I confessed.

Humberto sat down next to me, reached his hand over, and pulled up my chin. "But don't you see how you shut me out?"

I abandoned my papers. "Don't let me do that to you." I wept, feeling very young.

The heat of his lovemaking that night overwhelmed me. He jammed his fingers into my mouth, held my entire throat in his hands, clutched my hips and rammed them against him. He inhaled me, buried himself in my body. I felt as if he was escaping something and running toward it at the same time. He left me breathless and light-headed, disoriented. Who was he that he could possess me like that?

For days afterward I could feel the pressure of his hands on my neck, his teeth biting my earlobe, his hands squeezing my buttocks. Sometimes on my lunch breaks all I could think of was his hand on my breast, and the palm rubbing my nipple in ever smaller concentric circles. I felt as if I was slipping off the edge of a precipice.

One day later that week, when I opened my front door with hands full, Frank rushed past me and headed across the street. I dropped my things and ran after him to Mr. Slewicki's yard.

Mr. Slewicki was standing on his front sidewalk patting Frank by the time I crossed the street. "You like something to drink?" he said in a thick accent.

He looked ridiculous in a pair of women's bedroom slippers and a pink chenille bathrobe. The robe barely stretched over his potbelly, and the lace collar scratched gently against several days' stubble on his neck.

He must be harmless, I thought, and smiled. "Thanks. But I can only stay a few minutes."

He led me along the side of the house and around to the back door. A well-tended vegetable garden stretched the length of the yard to a high fence fronted by blooming rhododendron bushes, daisies, and chrysanthemums.

"Please to wait one minute," he said, glancing at Frank rooting through his flowers.

"Frank!" I called sharply, and the dog reluctantly picked up his head for a moment.

Mr. Slewicki emerged from his back door with a soup bone in his hand. "It's okay?"

"If you don't mind him rushing over here to pester you again."

"Here, boy," he called, holding out his hand. The dog backed out of the flowers quickly and trotted toward his benefactor. "Dogs have good life here, no?" he chuckled.

I smiled at his kindness and followed him inside, leaving Frank to gnaw on his bone.

The kitchen and living room were spotless. A partially finished needlepoint project lay on an arm chair in front of the TV, and a recipe for carrot cake was tacked to the refrigerator with a plastic duck magnet.

Mr. Slewicki made fresh lemonade and we settled ourselves at the kitchen table. He was from the old country, he said, looking at me with big sad eyes. Poland. He and his wife had come over only ten years ago.

"Your wife?"

"Yah," he said. "I was bricklayer. In old country I learn at age eleven. My wife, she sewed. Here we worked for wealthy couple. They buy us this house. Then," he said, his eyes watering and blinking, "my wife she got breast cancer. A year and three months ago she die." He tugged on the lapel of his robe. "These things are all I have left of her."

"I'm so sorry," I said, saddened by his loss.

He shook his head slowly. "You never know what life bring. We could have died ten times over in my country, sometimes just from no heat in apartment. Who knows, maybe that weakened her?" He attempted a smile. "You look so young and full of energy. Are you happy?"

Only a stranger would ask such a thing. "I think so."

"You get married to your gentleman friend?"

"I don't know." I felt my cheeks color.

"Don't wait," he urged. "Grasp it quickly. Things change and there's no turning back."

I finished my lemonade and rose to leave. "Thank you," I said softly, and put out my hand.

He held my hand in both of his and pumped. "You think I look stupid in this robe, no?"

"You certainly look distinctive," I said, smiling.

"What is distinctive?"

"Unique. Different from the others."

"Good. I like this. Distinctive. Your dog. He's distinctive, no?"

I nodded and laughed. "If you've got carrots in your vegetable garden, watch out for him. He might dig them up."

"No, no, I give him one."

"You will have made a friend for life."

"I need friend."

He went out the back door and I followed him, watching the hem of his pink robe sway. When he reached the patch of cultivated rows, he bent over and pulled up a carrot, and Frank, who'd been lying on the sidewalk lazily gnawing on the soup bone, looked up, panted, and focused his eyes on the right hand of Mr. Slewicki. When he accurately perceived what was in it, he abandoned the bone, and trotted toward the dangling carrot. If he escaped from the yard again, I knew where I would find him.

For the rest of that evening, Mr. Slewicki's urgent plea rang in my ears. *Don't wait. Grasp it quickly.*

I'm in love with Humberto, but I need more time, I thought. I have to straighten out this thing with Nick first. But how long will Humberto wait for me?

A wave of melancholy practically brought me to my knees.

33

It was at that time that I realized how much I relied on my other patients. Tension and worries about my personal life melted away when I reached the office. My patients' stories engrossed me. Their courage and hope cheered me. If my love for Humberto failed, I would have success with them. If my own family dynamics were indecipherable, I could figure out theirs. Except for Nick, the relationships were manageable and predictable, divided into neat fifty-minute segments, defined by rules of therapy etiquette, limited in scope. While my personal life and the therapy with Nick became more turbulent, my other patients became my orderly, safe place.

The Romaine sisters increased their volunteer work at the retirement home to the point where they were busy every day of the week. I could see how bedridden people would enjoy their peculiar charm.

I was relieved to learn William's condition was better than expected. His other arteries were fairly clear, his surgeon treated the narrowed vessel by balloon angioplasty, and William was discharged to an out-patient cardiac rehabilitation program.

Ironically, having this focus to his daily life served to alleviate some of William's depression. He had his medications and pulse rate to monitor, a clinic to attend five days a week, and other cardiac patients with whom to compare notes. Fearful of another infarction, he slowly built up his physical endurance, devoting a great deal of time to his rehab program, and he announced urgently, "I have to live whatever is left of my life as you said—in concert with my private self."

When I heard this I felt the small intense pleasure of my profession: the joy of assisting in growth, and watching something old and constricting break apart, to be replaced by a new flexibility that brings so many more possibilities.

Sometimes even my sessions with Nick were gratifying.

"I did it again," he said one day. "This time it was a photograph. Mrs. Mac showed me the family album, with pictures of Maggie and her two brothers when they were little. She was so warm, so proud of her children. That same jealousy came over me of wishing this was *my* family album and *my* mother who remembered me so fondly."

Memories of my own mother came bubbling up—of warm summer nights lying on the swinging outdoor loveseat, with my head in Mom's lap, and the fragrance of body lotion and detergent mingled with the sound of her voice, soft and low, singing a church hymn.

"I waited until we were all out at the car saying good night, and then I said I had to run to the john before we left so I could go into the house and take the picture."

Nick got up and wandered around the room, touching things. He dusted one of the shutters, ran his fingers over some book spines, picked a few brown leaves off the palm tree and threw them in the trash. Then he sat down, opened his briefcase, and pulled out the photograph. For a moment, he cradled it in his hand like a rare opal, and then he rose, handed it to me, and retreated to the couch.

Did he want me to divine, from looking at the photo, what it was he needed?

I studied the cracked picture and the smiling faces. Maggie and her two little brothers were piled on a huge draft horse, each one with arms wrapped around the one in front. Holding the reins was the father, a dark, short man with a wide grin. The mother, taller than him and very blond, stood next to him in front of the horse. Her hair trailed out in the wind, and she had one arm raised to hold it. Little Maggie had her mother's blond hair, and her two front teeth were missing.

"What does this picture mean to you, Nick?"

"I guess it's what I imagine our family could have been if my mother hadn't died. Maybe she would have had a couple more kids, maybe we would have done stuff together as a family, maybe my dad wouldn't have been such a prick."

"And you feel the only way you can have that kind of closeness now is to steal it? You could never create it for yourself?"

Those remarkable azure eyes searched my face. "Do you think I could?" he said in a tone so low it was almost a whisper.

"Yes," I replied, feeling the ache of his longing as if it were my own.

That night I woke suddenly, with Humberto shaking my shoulder. "Sarah—what's wrong? You were moaning. And you're covered with goose bumps."

The clock said twelve-thirty and I knew we hadn't been asleep more than a few minutes. "I was having an old dream that sometimes scares me. I'm sorry if I woke you up."

"What was the dream?"

"Oh, it's a strange thing that happens to me sometimes when I'm falling asleep. I'll tell you in the morning."

I was disturbed that this experience had suddenly returned and I brooded over it after Humberto resumed his quiet snoring.

It had started in early childhood. Sometimes as I was falling asleep, a huge round mass loomed larger in my vision until it obliterated me. Fuzzy at the edges, darker at the center than the periphery, it was silent and surrounded by a blank background. Always it was in shades of gray without color. As it got closer to my face I usually jerked involuntarily into waking, but sometimes I let the thing envelop me and absorb me into sleep.

When I first saw this, I would run the short distance to my parents' room, my hands and feet cold with fear. My father was often gone—to a poker game or bar—but my mother would be lying in bed, her orange terrycloth robe wrapped around her ample body, while she knitted and watched TV. After I climbed onto her bed, she'd cluck her tongue and cuddle me up to her side, where I would surreptitiously pull out little loops of string in her robe until I drifted off.

By the time I was eight, I had toughened up, and I insisted on sleeping in my little league uniform, my fielder's mitt by my head. I was determined to catch the thing before it hit my face. My father knelt down so his bloodshot eyes were level with mine and said, "That's it, sport! Pretty soon you'll be sittin' in the catbird seat." He always talked as if he was standing at first base, waiting for an infield roller.

Years later, my pre-dream experience faded away and I assumed it was gone for good. Now I was distressed to see it again and did not understand why it had returned after all this time. I was certain of only one thing: it was related to Nick.

34

Saturday night, Humberto and I were scheduled to attend a black-tie fund-raiser. Many of his best customers had urged him to attend, since the proceeds would go to a favorite charity of theirs.

Humberto took me shopping at Neiman-Marcus and bought me a lovely full-length gown in royal blue. The neckline dipped gracefully to a low-cut center, and we bought a single strand of fresh-water pearls to complete the look.

He wore his new tuxedo with the blue silk cummerbund and matching pants stripe. It cost four thousand dollars to have it made by the exclusive tailor he favored, and I thought privately he should have sent the money directly to the charity instead of attending the dinner.

The food was forgettable, and the orchestra old and boring, but we drank wine, danced until midnight, and enjoyed ourselves in spite of the crowd.

After a nightcap at Paradise, we drove home singing Broadway show tunes and laughing about our lousy voices. It was 2 A.M. by the time Humberto unlocked his front door.

A peculiar sound greeted us—a raspy, wheezing sound, like a child with asthma trying to sleep.

I knew instinctively the noise had something to do with Frank, and I rushed to the kitchen to check on him. The kiddy gate was hanging limply from one nail. Frank was lying on the kitchen floor, semi-comatose, having left a trail of bloody, brown liquid across the floor.

"Frank!" I cried, and bent to see if his airway was clear. He half-opened one eye and allowed me to shove my hand toward the back of his throat, which made him gag. At least he could breathe. "Quick!" I yelled. "Bring a towel! We need to carry him to the car and get him to the vet!"

Humberto stood rooted to the spot, staring at me. "You're going to ruin your dress. Let's change before we take him."

Frantic, I pulled off my dress so fast I ripped one seam. Leaving the garment in a heap on the kitchen counter, I ran up to the bedroom, changed quickly, and ran back to cradle Frank's bloody head in my arms. "Let's go!"

Humberto changed, came to the kitchen entrance, and said, "I'll be right back. I have to find my sneakers." The next sound I heard was a wail from the living room. "This dog is impossible!" Humberto yelled. "Why don't you let him die, for Chrissakes!"

I tried to gather Frank up in my arms to attempt carrying him to the car myself. "Hurry up!" I cried. "He's too heavy for me!"

Humberto raced back to the kitchen, clutching some scraps of navy velvet. "Look what he did! He tore open two of my pillows and ate the stuffing! I'll never be able to replace these cushions!" He shook the fabric pieces at my face. "That animal's ruined a ten-thousand-dollar sofa!"

I stood up, livid. "I don't give a shit! Are you going to help me or will I have to drag him to the car?"

"He's a bloody mess!" Humberto's beautiful mouth was twisted into a spitting hole.

Frank weighed close to fifty pounds and I couldn't carry him myself. My voice rose to a hysterical pitch. "Are you going to help me or not?"

"Oh, for Chrissakes!" Humberto grabbed a towel from the laundry room, wrapped the dog in it, picked him up, and carried him to the car.

The vet was a matter-of-fact woman with waist-length brown hair. "The kapok and foam rubber he chewed expanded in his stomach. If he can't pass it within the next few hours, we'll have to remove it surgically."

Humberto and I barely spoke two words to each other during the four hours we sat on the flimsy plastic chairs. At one point he said he was going for a walk and when he returned, he smelled of cigarettes.

"I didn't know you smoked," I said.

"I don't, except when I'm very upset." The fluorescent lights cast gray shadows on his dour face.

To my tremendous relief, Frank didn't need surgery—intravenous fluids and emetics did the job. We left him there for another day of treatment, and drove home slowly, the silence in the car compressing my chest.

In the house, I saw for the first time how much damage Frank had done. Scattered across the living room carpet were the remnants of two perfect pillows, the stuffing torn out of them and half eaten. A bloody path from the kitchen to the front door completed the disaster.

I collapsed into a dining room chair. "I know he's ruined your sofa. I'll pay you for it. I promise."

He retrieved a garbage bag from the kitchen and silently retraced Frank's path, stuffing the remains of the pillows in the bag.

I said, "I know how much you loved that couch. I'll repay you within four months."

Humberto's face darkened. He dropped the bag and paced over to the table. "It's not the money! Fuck the money! It's us! You care more about that moronic dog than you do about me!"

"That's not true!"

"Not true?" He banged the tabletop with his hand. "Will you marry me? Apparently not. Will you limit your work to spend time with me? Heaven forbid. Will you even take off an expensive dress I bought without tearing it? Forget it! You think about nothing but yourself and what you need. Well I'm sick of it! And I'm sick of mattering less to you than everything else, including your dog. I deserve better!"

I laid my head across my arms on the table and wept, and after a few minutes he left for the upstairs bedroom.

I suddenly remembered my mother in this very position at her own dining room table, crying over my father's infidelities. Hiding under the stairway, I had vowed never to let a man reduce me to such abject helplessness.

If it was over, I was going to go in a dignified manner, I decided. I went to the kitchen to clean up.

My head throbbed and my mouth was swollen and warm. Leaning over the shiny porcelain sink, I splashed cool water on my face, and filled up my hand several times to suck water from my palm. I didn't want to dirty anything else in Humberto's house, not even a glass. I decided to wash the kitchen floor, vacuum the carpet, and leave.

After locating a mop in the pantry, I filled the sink with warm sudsy water. Esperanza was making purring noises under her cover and shaking the cage. It was time for her breakfast. I removed the cage cover and said good morning.

"Fuck the money!" the bird yelled loudly as soon as her cover was removed. "Fuck the money!"

In spite of my misery I burst out laughing, and stuck two fingers through the cage to scratch the bird's neck. By the time the kitchen was almost restored, Humberto walked in, wearing a clean pair of warm-ups and carrying the garbage bag filled with rubble.

"Oh, for Chrissakes!" Esperanza shrieked. "Call my lawyer!"

We both looked at the bird and each other, and giggled.

"Fuuuuuucck the money! Hurry up!" Esperanza shouted.

This time we doubled over.

"Will you marry me? Will you marry me?" the bird called.

I set the mop handle carefully against the sink edge and stepped closer to Humberto. "I love you very much," I said. "Please don't give up on me."

"Come here," he said, and turned and walked back to the dining table and sat down. "If you and I are going to stay together, some things are going to have to change."

I sat down across from him and nodded.

"Are you willing to spend more time with me in the evenings?"

"Yes." I wasn't sure how I'd manage it, but I didn't want to lose him.

"What about that special patient of yours? Are you ever going to be rid of him?"

A good question, I thought. "I'd like to refer him to someone else, but I have to wait for the right time or all the gains we've made will be lost."

"Okay, I can respect that. I'm just tired of it."

"Honey—I'm sorry. I'm going to do my best to spend more time with you. I don't blame you for being mad."

He raised his hand and made a narrow space between his thumb and forefinger. "I'm this close to leaving you."

My eyes filled again. "I hope you won't. The only thing is you have to understand when I have emergencies, I have to drop everything. That won't change."

"If we're really close, I can handle that. But something has to be done about Frank, too."

"There's a guy I went to school with who's an animal psychologist. I'll call him today."

The animal psychologist arrived at Humberto's house promptly at nine the following Saturday morning. Jared looked older than I remembered him, and slightly rounder, with a small gut sticking out over his khaki Bermuda shorts. Seated in the living room, he listened attentively to our story, nodding and patting Frank, whose nose was locked against his socks.

"There are two causes for the problem. First, Frank is jealous of you," Jared said, pointing to Humberto. "He's used to being the man of the house and you've moved in on his territory. Second, he's not adapting well to his weekend environment."

"No kidding," Humberto said.

"Dogs are creatures of habit. They function best when the routine is the same."

I confessed guiltily that I'd never properly obedience-trained Frank.

Jared smiled confidently. "No problem. We can start now, but here's the kicker: it has to be Humberto doing it."

Humberto shook his head in disgust. "I knew this was coming."

Frank had to wear a choke chain at all times. For training sessions Humberto was to use a strong six-foot leash and begin with the simple obedience commands.

Jared added, "And don't hit him anymore. Get a can of peanuts, empty it, and refill it half with coins. The next time he moves toward the sofa, give the can a sharp shake. The noise will startle him and he'll learn to avoid the behaviors that elicit it."

"I didn't know there was so much to this," Humberto mumbled.

"Also, it can't be all business. Take ten minutes a day to play Frank's favorite game."

"That would be pissing on my side of the bed," Humberto offered.

Jared laughed and patted Frank's ears. "Try tossing a ball to him, or rough-and-tumble with him on the floor."

"I'll try the ball." Humberto brushed imaginary hairs off his shirt.

They moved to the backyard, and I hid my enormous amusement as Jared instructed Humberto on the proper way to lead Frank around by the leash and use the choke collar for training. Frank looked bored by it all, sitting when he was supposed to stand, lying down when he was supposed to sit.

"Look at him," I called. "It's useless!"

"No. It takes time and consistency," Jared said. "But I guarantee it'll work."

35

Every time Nick visited the McCutcheon ranch, he took something else symbolic of the family life for which he longed: Maggie's baby dish with painted puppies, her dad's golf trophy, a videotape of an anniversary party. Each week we discussed the meaning of these items in the hope that doing so would lessen his need to steal. Privately I worried that he had somehow made a key to my office and might steal something more from me or eventually harm me.

In the ensuing weeks, Nick's relationship to Maggie became increasingly stormy, with him alternating between intense lovemaking and verbal attacks. He began hating her cool self-control. Several times I pointed out that he was repeating with Maggie the same feelings he'd had with me, but he would reply "It's different," and refuse to consider it further.

Final preparations for his upcoming trial were exhausting him. He was representing a man who had sustained brain damage from exposure to toxic chemicals, and the firm was "taking on the big guys" by suing the prominent corporations that manufactured the products. The case was a critical one for Nick's career, with the partners of his firm relying on him to spearhead the strategy. They had invested hundreds of thousands of dollars in pretrial expenses, knowing if he won, it would bring an immediate profit, as well as future business.

After the trial began, each of our sessions started with a recounting of the day's testimony and his assessment of how it came across to the jury. One day in the second week of the trial, he said, "I might have blown the whole case today. I froze on cross. Couldn't challenge the guy. Couldn't concentrate. I asked for a ten-minute recess just to pull my head together. I'm lucky he was the last witness of the day."

"What do you think happened?"

"Don't know. As I listened to his direct testimony I thought, 'This is the critical one. If I can shoot him down, I'm home free.' Then I blew it."

"So the extra pressure of thinking how important he was made you too anxious?"

"Yes, but I usually love to move in for the kill."

"Maybe this case is different."

"Yeah. I could lose my job."

I hoped that wasn't true. His equilibrium was fragile at best.

"You know what's funny? I used to do great in court, but have to run to the bathroom all the time. Now I'm doing terrible in court and my stomach feels fine."

"Maybe the final stage will be both doing well in court and feeling well physically." I was fervently clinging to hope.

When I saw Val she took one look at me and said, "You're so thin! What's wrong?"

"I'm working too hard. No time to eat."

"Is it still that same patient?"

"Partly. I think I'm making slow progress with him, but it's a high-wire act. Sometimes it looks like he's on the verge of getting out of control, but he's not dangerous enough to hospitalize. I swear I'm never taking a case like this one again."

"What else is going on?"

"Hassling with Humberto. Worrying about all the women around him. Not getting enough sleep."

"You'll work it out. Why don't you go away together? Soak up some sun and lie around for a few weeks."

"That's a great idea. I promised my mother I'd come home for Easter, but maybe we could go somewhere in June. How are you?"

"Mixed. Gordon's driving me crazy with his hypochondriasis. Every day he develops a different kind of cancer. And now he's getting into homeopathic remedies."

"He should talk to Linda. She knows all that shit."

"The last thing I want to do is encourage him!"

We laughed, imagining an orgy of potions and salves. Before we parted, Val caught my arm. "Listen. I know you can manage almost any professional situation. But everyone has some patient they can't handle. Even Harold Searles said one guy nearly made him psychotic."

"I can do it, Val. I can. I'm almost through it."

That week in my interns' group I discussed hypochondriasis and psychosomatic illness, and I brought them a copy of a lecture I'd done on the subject.

I looked forward to meeting with the group. I felt respected and relaxed there. The radio show also gave me an opportunity to be an authority on many topics, but it took two full afternoons of my time, and I started paying a post-doc fellow to read and answer the mail my show generated.

As the close of his trial drew near, Nick said, "I don't know what I'm going to do if I lose. Oberdorf asks me how it's going every day."

"What's the worst thing that could happen?"

"I'd be fired. I'd have trouble getting a good position at a new firm. I'd feel totally useless."

"But in every trial one side loses."

"Yes. It's part of the game and you tell yourself it doesn't matter because you did a good job. But that doesn't hold much satisfaction for me. For me, winning is everything. I'm not very interested in the law."

"How did you choose it?"

"I wanted money and clean hands. Other people in law school had dreams of becoming senators and fighting for justice. I was dreaming of a great car."

"Is there something else you were genuinely interested in?"

He sighed and scratched his head. "This is going to sound stupid—but I've always wanted to play the piano. I loved the way the organ music filled our church. After school I used to sneak into a nearby music store and try to play. I can still remember the store's smell of furniture polish and old linoleum. One of the salesmen taught me how to play 'Amazing Grace.' Sometimes when I'm at other people's houses, I sneak over to their piano and play that piece."

"You never took music lessons?"

"Nah. We couldn't afford a piano. I brought home a list of rental prices once, but my dad just said 'Maybe later,' and later never came. The salesman let me play a Melodica and I fell in love with that too."

"What's that?"

"It looks like a miniature piano keyboard. You blow into it and press the keys at the same time. The good ones come from Germany, and they were only about fifty bucks then. I begged Ma to buy me one for Christmas and she promised she would. I even went and picked out the one I wanted in case she came into the store. How pathetic. She left that November. I never went back to the store."

"You haven't talked much about what her disappearance was like for you."

He fell silent, struggling with his feelings, and when he spoke again, his voice was thin and plaintive. "It was the worst. No trace. Not a phone call, not a letter. It convinced me of the futility of loving. Dad called her The Bitch after that, and so did I."

"Couldn't you find her now to talk to her?"

"That would be pointless. And I already told you—as far as I'm concerned, she's dead."

"Perhaps you might learn to play the piano now."

"It would make me too sad for the life I never had."

"That life must be mourned so the present one can be lived."

"Not this week. This week I have to concentrate on winning."

I met with Zachary again, apprehensive about the fact that he was leaving for Asia the next day on vacation. He said, "Sarah, you're doing a marvelous job in spite of how your patient affects you. He's stopped having stomach symptoms and nightmares, he's much more in contact with his feelings, he's developed a relationship with a woman, and he's handling the pressure of a trial. I think it's an enormous accomplishment."

"At enormous cost to me."

Zachary smiled kindly. "It has taken a lot of courage on your part to sweat this one out."

I relaxed a little, thinking maybe my hard work had in fact paid off. "He does seem to be handling things now, but I don't know how he'll react if he's fired."

Zachary leaned back in his chair to think. A book on learning

Japanese lay open next to him. "My most salient advice to you is this: don't hesitate to hospitalize him if you have any reason to doubt your own safety or his."

"I'll keep your recommendation in mind. Hopefully it won't come to that."

Zachary walked me to the door of his office. I wished him the best, but felt uneasy about him being gone. I said, "Have a good trip. Maybe by the time you get back, the treatment will have moved to a new phase."

The following Monday, Nick left me a message. "Lost the case. Can't come in. See you Wednesday." His voice was deeper, his words slurred. I considered calling him, but I had tried so much to discourage him from phoning me outside sessions that I felt it set a bad example. Besides, I thought it would imply he didn't have the strength to handle his crisis without me, and I didn't want to communicate that. I was already seeing him three times a week.

36

On Wednesday Nick showed up fifteen minutes late. In the waiting room he stood in the middle of the floor, his suit jacket over his arm, his loosened tie hanging from his neck. As he strode past me I smelled the kind of old sweat that comes from three days without a shower.

He was agitated and restless, unable to sit, sniffing and pacing. "That fucking jury! They saw how brain-damaged this guy was but they didn't have the balls to find those big corporations liable!" He slammed one fist into the other palm repeatedly. "I swear someone got to the jury. Man, I'd like to get something on those companies! I'd fuckin' ram it up their corporate assholes."

He ran his hands through his hair, blew his nose, and excused himself to run to the bathroom. When he returned I asked, "Are you using cocaine right now?"

He laughed hysterically. "Good, Doc! Very good! Done a little blow yourself?"

More laughter, while I considered how to handle him.

He threw himself on the sofa and stretched out his arms above his head, leaving one foot on the floor. His blue dress shirt stuck to his skin where it was wet. "I am one hundred percent fucked. Does that answer your question?"

"What does that mean?"

"As many meanings as you can think of. Blow. Weed. Gin. Out of a job. Out to lunch. Out of luck."

I felt downhearted watching him flail around on the sofa. "How has your firm reacted?"

"Oberdorf was verrrrry gracious. You know. Give the guy a steak before the hanging. They're just waiting till the end of the month to give me notice."

"Maybe that's not the case."

"Ha! What planet have you been on?"

"A lawyer isn't fired everytime he loses a case."

"They didn't like my attitude, anyway. I told you McCutcheon caught me tossing something in the round file."

"No."

"Some old school records on another case. I figured no one but me knew about them and it was better that way. Maggie intervened on my behalf."

"Won't your alliance with her help you now?"

"Who knows? It's pretty much on the rocks anyway." He sat up and composed himself some. "This is serious shit. I'll probably be out of a job in a few weeks."

"Perhaps you're tired of not doing what you really want anyway."

He held his hands to his temples. "I'm tired beyond belief. So tired it practically takes a crane to get me out of bed in the morning."

"I think it would help you to spend a few weeks in the hospital."

"*What??!!!*" He sprang from the sofa, grabbed my little glass elephant, and started pacing.

"You're depressed. I'm thinking of your safety."

"Motherfucker!" he yelled, and threw the elephant against the wall, where it shattered and fell to the carpet.

I stood up quickly and backed toward the door.

He patted the air with open hands. "Relax, it's just the coke. I won't hurt you. Come back and sit down." He plopped onto the sofa. "I'll clean it up."

I returned to my chair. "Doesn't this make clear to you how close you are to losing control? You need the safety of a hospital right now."

He picked up his briefcase and put it on the coffee table. "No way I can go to the hospital this week. I'm going to show you my schedule."

Before I could protest, he swung open the briefcase to reach for his calendar and a loose razor blade fell out and clattered to the table. It was obviously for cocaine use, but what else? Would he draw long cuts up his arm as I had seen other patients do? Sever a vein?

"Whoops," he said sheepishly, picked up the razor, and put it back in the briefcase.

"You're proving my point. Let me call Westwood and see if they have a bed."

"Doc, you know what that's for."

"That's not the only thing you could do with it."

"Oh." He sat back and rubbed his hands down the length of his thighs. "But you don't put someone in the hospital for cutting up wallpaper, do you?"

My mouth fell open. "You mean—"

His eyes widened in surprise. "I thought that's what you were talking about! I assumed you knew."

I was incredulous. "Why would you slash my wallpaper?"

His eyes watered and he sniffed a few times. "Your life was too perfect. I just wanted to mess it up a little. But I was sure you knew and just decided to let it go."

I felt helpless and furious. He wasn't dangerous enough to hospitalize against his will. It didn't seem I could get rid of him, and I didn't have any proof that he would hurt me. "It cost me three hundred dollars to repair that wall!" I blurted out.

He pulled a roll of cash out of his pocket and laid five one hundred dollar bills on the coffee table. "That should take care of it and the elephant too."

I blamed myself for not investigating that vandalism more thoroughly. Now I was plagued with the worry of what he would do if I reacted too strongly to his admission. "Nick, I'm going to take the money, because I think you owe it to me, and at some future time we'll discuss the whole thing in detail. But right now, I'm still concerned that you might injure yourself."

The energy seemed to have left him. "I'll be okay. You want to keep the blade?"

"What good would that do? You could easily buy another one." Although just having the therapist keep a weapon often engendered a feeling of safety in the patient.

"This is what I'm going to do." He withdrew from his briefcase a piece of folded yellow paper, secured with a paper clip. "This is all the blow I have. I'm going to flush it down your toilet right now, and throw the razor away. And I promise I won't buy any more. The stuff makes me too weird."

Together we watched the lumpy powder disappear under water, and I said I'd see him in two days.

That night Humberto noticed I was tense and tried to cajole me out of it. "Another bad day at the funny farm?"

I smiled. "It was action-packed. But I'm going to put it aside now. *Casablanca* is on TV at nine. Let's make popcorn and watch it."

"Great," he said, and I felt relieved I was able to camouflage my anxiety about Nick. He added, "There's a new restaurant in Santa Monica I should see. Food's supposed to be spectacular. The chef invited us to come Friday night."

"Sure," I said, and in my appointment book I wrote, "Mustard, 8:15." I was determined to make time for us.

In the following days, the apprehension I was containing began to interfere with my ability to respond properly to my other patients. Luness called to cancel a session, and I assumed she was backing off from the intensity of the therapy because it was going well—a common pattern in treatment. When she did show up, I said, "Let's begin by discussing the cancellation."

"It was the only time I could get a ticket for the opera I wanted to see. *La Traviata*. My favorite."

"Perhaps you chose that afternoon because you felt uncomfortable about coming here that day."

Luness shook her head and looked blank. "No. It was the only ticket I could get and I really wanted to go."

I kept pressing my point, and as the session progressed, Luness began talking about food, and how she wanted to eat at that moment, and how she was getting so sleepy she could hardly stay awake.

I suggested Luness didn't want to take in what I was trying to give her. She collected her purse and hat, and left early. Two hours later I received a message from her: "Please cancel all my future sessions. I need a break from therapy. Thanks for everything."

I knew immediately I'd made a grave error with Luness and I called to apologize. She squeaked her explanation and tearfully agreed to come in at least once more.

When I saw her, she reported a dream. "I was in a darkened house. It was snowy outside and I finally felt relaxed and safe. I had no food in the house and I didn't need any. Then I could hear a horde of people coming and I began boarding up the windows and bolting the doors, but they knocked and shouted and banged until they made little holes in the house and shoved handfuls of snow through the holes. I felt violated, I felt I was disappearing. Then the snow turned into rice."

I said, "The dream tells us that I tried to force-feed you in our last session by insisting you should have chosen to be with me. I was violating your boundary. Now we can see how you defend yourself against such an attack. You shrink away and then take over the attack and force-feed yourself, just to control the process."

Through my almost disastrous mistake, a huge leap forward in her therapy was accomplished, and I praised Luness for having the courage to risk losing me.

However, the incident alarmed me. This was not the only instance recently in which I had overreacted to other patients or misinterpreted their behavior. I was losing control of my reliable professional judgment.

Friday, Nick returned looking quite sober. On his way to the sofa he glanced at my open datebook, and said, "Mustard, huh? Supposed to be great." I was angry with myself for holding the book so he could read it, and furious with him for intruding on me again.

He was, however, very apologetic, and seemed to be much more self-contained. "I hope you can forgive me for my outburst. I just can't handle blow anymore. Must be getting old. Are you still mad?"

"You've damaged my property and intruded on me repeatedly. Don't you think there's a limit to my patience?"

"Ah, c'mon. I'm sorry. *I'm sorry!!* Okay?"

"If I find you've damaged any more of my property, I will terminate this therapy immediately."

"Fair enough." He lay quietly for a while. He said both McCutcheon and Oberdorf had been friendly and he began to think perhaps his job was still secure. "But I've been thinking about selling my condo and finding a funky little house in Venice. I could just read and walk on the beach for a while."

I wondered if he had seen me at Linda's.

"Only thing is, what if I can't afford to see you?"

That would be a blessing, I thought.

He sat up and gazed at me intently until I could barely stand it. "I *have* to see you. No matter what. You're my lifeline. I couldn't go on without you."

I felt a dreadful weight descend on me.

37

That evening I drove home to change before dinner. As I closed the front drapes I saw Mr. Slewicki hauling his garbage cans out to the street. "Oh, that's nice," I said to Frank. "His blue apron is complemented by bright red lipstick tonight in an early spring fashion statement."

"Brew," Frank answered.

I put on a black silk dress and higher heels while I waited for Humberto. On the drive to Mustard, he chattered about food storage problems and rising wholesale prices, and I listened, comforted by his presence and his buoyant mood. Some people don't spend all day in intense conversations about misery, I thought. Must be nice.

The restaurant was a one-story glass-and-cement building facing the ocean. Humberto took my hand and insisted we stroll to the end of the parking lot to get the last glimpse of sun over the water. We stood at the edge of the sand and he put his arms around me to protect me from the chilly evening air.

I rested my head on his shoulder for a moment, hoping his warmth would pull me back to him. "I'm so burned out."

"It would be okay with me if you quit work entirely."

"You know I couldn't do that."

"Maybe at least you could schedule one weekday off so we could enjoy ourselves when things aren't so crowded. Museums, bicycle rides, movies. It would be good for both of us."

I forced a smile. "Maybe soon."

I saw Humberto shrink back. He closed his mouth tightly and avoided my eyes. We walked to the entrance without holding hands or touching, and I felt unhappy. As soon as things lightened up with Nick, I would take a few weeks off as Val had suggested.

At the reservation desk, I turned momentarily to glance at the people near us, and saw Nick, standing with three other people who, I assumed, were Maggie and her parents.

My heart raced and my hands turned cold in seconds. I realized he had come there purposely to see me and from the restless way he was pacing he was extremely nervous, and was now joking uncomfortably to cover it.

I dreaded the thought of where this was leading. For the first time I thought I might have to terminate the therapy and get a restraining order. But our classmate Paula had filed a restraining order, and her patient had still set her house on fire. Was there any real protection?

For one agonizing moment Nick's eyes met mine, and from the immobility of his face I knew he didn't want me to speak to him. I turned away quickly, just as Humberto took my elbow to guide me to our table. It would have been a violation of confidentiality to acknowledge Nick first. It was the patient's choice to make public our relationship, not mine, and I didn't need a lawsuit.

I ordered a drink immediately and belted it down. Disgusted as Humberto was about Nick already, I didn't know how he'd react to the news that Nick was there, and I decided not to risk telling him. I concentrated on Humberto instead, thinking I could rescue our relationship and shut Nick out at the same time.

I made it through the hors d'oeuvres without looking into the room. The chef came out briefly to sit with us, offering fresh ahi tuna with diced tomatoes and tiny wild-rice pancakes.

Humberto ordered an excellent Sauvignon Blanc that I drank so quickly my skin turned numb. He said, "I like this place, but nothing good stays small in L.A. for very long. It will be discovered, and expand like dough in the sun."

I smiled and drank more wine. Humberto relaxed with the attention and his interest in new food. "I'm sorry for being in such a shitty mood," I said. "Forget it," was all he offered. I joined in his animated gossip about the chef, who'd been stolen away from one of the other restaurants in town. Dessert was a marvelous Tarte Tatin—a glossy, caramelized pile of fresh apples on a flaky, crunchy crust.

When Humberto left for the bathroom, I glanced around and found Nick two tables away, watching me. I avoided his gaze and examined the faces of his companions.

Maggie's profile revealed a long sharp nose and a receding chin, but there was a confidence to her manner that was attractive. Her mother was prettier, with fine features, fair skin, and hair curved neatly into a short cut. Whatever Nick had said was amusing and she laughed and clasped his arm. Her husband, whose back was turned to me, was a dark contrast to the women. Nick probably reminds Maggie of her father, I thought.

When Humberto returned, I took another sip of wine and tried to focus my attention on him. I said I loved him, and although I was going home alone for Easter the following weekend, we could plan a vacation together in June.

Some of his coolness melted. He took my hand, and at one point kissed me lightly on the mouth. When Nick's party rose to leave, I saw how red Nick's face was, and I thought, oh Lord, there's going to be hell to pay on Monday.

The rest of the weekend I was so jittery I couldn't concentrate on anything. I was afraid that after seeing me with Humberto, Nick would deteriorate into a jealous rage. I imagined him lurking around every corner, and except for a jog I took to burn off some anxiety, I insisted on staying indoors.

Saturday night the heat of Humberto's desire felt like a blanket that threatened to snuff out my very life. I wanted to slip out of his grasp and be alone; to run to my beach in Bandon and think things through. But then images of my parents crowded in on me. I was trapped everywhere.

I turned onto my side and Humberto caressed me until I felt like a worm in the hands of a giant fisherman, struggling and squirming, wanting to slip back into the private dark earth and live my own life. When I fell asleep, I let the gray thing envelop me.

On Sunday, Humberto showed me his obedience progress with Frank, which consisted of Frank sitting on command. That was easy for Frank, who preferred to be lounging at any given moment. Getting him to walk on cue was yet to be accomplished.

Sunday night Humberto tucked me in and said, "You're drinking more than usual. Want to talk about it?"

"Just trying to relax!" I said brightly.

"You wore one black and one brown sock all day."

I said, "Let it go."

"What happened to those days when we told each other everything?"

"They'll come back. But you can't force it."

To my relief we didn't make love that night. I already felt like Luness in her dark house dream. People were bashing holes in my exterior and shoving snow inside. More and more I felt thin and naked and unable to keep warm. I was shrinking away from everything.

38

During the Monday four o'clock hour, while the Romaine sisters sputtered happily about their volunteer work, my eyes kept wandering to the tiny red light that beamed Nick's presence in the waiting room. He was a half-hour early.

When I finally opened the door to him, I was jarred by the sight: disheveled hair, bloodshot eyes, chin darkened by several days' growth, an old sweatshirt, torn jeans. The rancid smell of stale liquor and sweat hit me as he walked by.

He sat down facing me on the couch and put his hands on his forehead. "Splitting headache."

"What happened?"

"After dinner Friday night the four of us went to a comedy club and we bumped into an old boyfriend of Maggie's. A hot-shot tax attorney. Mr. Mac pumped his hand like he was Jesus H. Christ. He sent us all drinks, which pissed me off. I started getting real paranoid. Like they wanted Maggie to marry that guy and they were just putting up with me. Then Maggie went to the powder room and didn't come back for fifteen minutes. I was sure she was in the lobby talking to him, but I didn't have the guts to follow her.

"And—oh, man—what a fucking fool I was. We got back to her place, and there was a message from some other guy on her machine. She said it was a neighbor she sometimes jogs with, but I just exploded! I could hear my old man's words coming out of my mouth. You whore. You bitch. You belong to me and if you can't get that straight you better pray.

"She'd never seen me like that before. She was crying and defending herself, and the more she tried to explain the madder I got until I just hauled off and smacked her hard across the face.

"That was it, man. She got real quiet and I got down on the fucking carpet and begged her to forgive me. I pleaded and crawled and she lay there and said nothing, until I shook her by the shoulders to make her talk. And then she said 'Get out,' very quietly, and when I said no, I wanted her to forgive me, she started screaming at the top of her lungs that she never wanted to see me again, and if I didn't get out she'd call the police and call her dad, and call the fucking fire department.

"That's all. I've lost her. And I don't know what the fuck came over me. I acted like a goddamn animal. Like my dad, for God's sake. I vowed I would never hit a woman in my entire life, and bam, out it came."

I knew instantly what had come over Nick: it was seeing me with Humberto. Nick had wanted me, had been compelled to place himself in a public situation where he knew I would be, and then could not handle it.

"You haven't mentioned seeing me Friday night," I said.

"With all that went on, I forgot about it."

While I had been imagining him around every corner, he had forgotten seeing me! "I think the reverse is true: because you forgot about it, all that went on."

"What the hell do you mean?" he gasped.

"I'm saying you acted on your feelings for me with Maggie, instead of containing them so we could talk about them here. Your jealousy was meant for me."

Incredulous at first, his face gradually darkened into despondency as the veracity of my explanation took hold. "Oh my God," he said. "It's true. I insisted we go to Mustard. I had to see you. And when I did, I was crazy. I wanted to rip you away from that table. Later, after I flew into a rage at Maggie, I stopped thinking of you."

I began coughing, and left the room abruptly to get a glass of water. I had a pounding headache that started at the base of my neck and covered the top of my head.

When I returned, Nick was sitting on the edge of the sofa, elbows on his knees, head in his hands. There were large circles of sweat around his armpits, and he smelled like a caged animal.

"How can I go on?" he said into his hands. "How can I face Maggie at work? And her father? I couldn't bear the thought of seeing them today so I stayed home and drank. I tried to call her a hundred times over the weekend but she won't even talk to me."

"Perhaps now that you understand what happened you could explain it to her."

He drew his hands away from his face and sat up. "Are you crazy? What am I going to say? Oh, Maggie, forgive me because I'm really in love with my shrink and since I couldn't have her, I got insanely possessive of you?"

That was a stupid idea, I concluded, but said nothing.

"No. It's finished. The real reason I did it sounds sicker than any reason she could imagine. I've lost her."

He stood up, wrapped his arms around his chest, and began pacing. "So what! She was just a substitute for you anyway. It's you I'm in love with and can never have, so what is the point? What is the point of anything? Life is meaningless!"

I couldn't possibly have felt worse myself. How could I continue this man's treatment? I had said and done everything I knew how to do, and he was hopelessly stuck. I tried to make my face immobile because I was afraid I was going to cry. I left my hands resting on the arms of my chair, even though my fingers were icy and my palms clammy. "Please. Sit down," I said. I could barely breathe.

Nick took a close look at me, saw how distressed I was, and retreated to the couch.

I said, "The way you're talking gives me the impression you might hurt yourself. If you're having thoughts like that, or thoughts of hurting someone else, please tell me."

He sat in silence and rolled his thumb over his first two fingers in fast, tight circles. Finally, he said, "Look, I'll handle this somehow. I'm not going to kill myself or hurt anyone else. But you've got to know one thing. I love you. I want you. And you're not going to get rid of me. When you close your eyes at night you'll see me. You're stuck with me. I am inside of you as much as you're inside of me. And I won't let go."

He got up abruptly and left. It was one half-hour since we'd begun. I sat shaking. Then I put my face in my hands and wept.

39

On Good Friday, Nick arrived fifteen minutes late. If I was seeing him for the first time I could not have imagined the confident, well-groomed man of the old days. His suit jacket was wrinkled, his shoes were mud-splattered, and he was thin and pale. "It's over," he said. "I'm out."

"You're fired?"

"Yup," he replied listlessly. "I've got the weekend to collect my things."

"What about McCutcheon? Didn't he defend you?"

"Sure. I lost the firm over a million dollars, and beat up his daughter. He'd really be in my corner."

I felt stupid.

Nick stretched out on the couch and lay motionless. He barely spoke for the whole hour.

"What are your plans?" I asked before our time was up.

"I don't know. I don't feel like seeing anybody. Man, what a shitty year. You're the only thing I have left."

I prayed for the session to end. I couldn't stand being the only thing he had left. I could hardly wait to get home and pack my bags for the long Easter weekend. Nine-thirty that night I was flying out.

"You're going to be gone Monday, right?" he asked when he got up to leave.

"Yes, I'll see you Tuesday instead, at five o'clock."

The sun was still bright when I left the office that day and the temperature a pleasant seventy-six degrees. At home I dumped my business suit and underwear in a pile on the bed and pulled on a pair of jogging shorts and a tank-top. I wanted to sweat off tension.

I put on a Rolling Stones CD and danced in the living room, dissolving into mind-numbing motion and sound. Frank watched my legs like a spectator at a tennis match. I didn't care about anything other than the sensation of moving. Free, for three whole days. Free.

Then Frank turned to the door and barked.

I stopped dancing and turned off the CD. A loud knock on the door sent Frank into a new frenzy of barking, and I tried to quiet him before opening the brass peephole to see who was there. Two intent blue eyes gazed back at me.

Into my stunned silence, Nick said, "Please. I need to see you."

I swung the door open and Frank rushed past me, heading for the street. I yelled at him, but he kept going. "Have a seat, I'll be back in a minute," I said, and ran after the dog. This was one occasion when I was grateful for Frank's disobedience because it gave me a few minutes to think.

Nick looked even worse than he had in my office. His shirt was rumpled and half out of his pants. He was sweating. His hair was unkempt and he smelled of liquor.

Frank made a beeline for Mr. Slewicki's yard and I followed him, conscious of how brief my shorts were, and of my nipples showing through my tank top. In response to Frank's baying, Mr. Slewicki emerged from his house, wearing a frilly pink apron over his pants. I apologized for the intrusion, and he said, "No, no. He reminds me of wife. Short and loud. Would he like soup bone?"

"Thanks." A bone would keep Frank busy for an hour. And then hesitantly, I said, "Could I ask a favor?"

Mr. Slewicki's heavy eyebrows rose. "Sure."

"If that black car in my driveway isn't gone in fifteen minutes, would you come over and ring my doorbell?"

"You have problem?"

"Hopefully not, but just in case."

"Okay. Fifteen minutes."

I thanked him and pulled Frank back by the collar, soup bone held tightly in his teeth. After locking him in the backyard, I returned through the front door and found Nick in the living room, studying my tapes and CDs.

"Sorry I caused so much trouble." He seemed calmer.

"Give me another minute," I replied and left for the bedroom. In spite of the warm air my hands were icy, and I pulled on an old sweatshirt and jeans. Back in the living room, I asked, "Would you like some tea or instant coffee?"

He laid down the CD case in his hand and nodded, running his fingers through his hair to try to straighten it. "Tea. Any kind. No sugar. Thanks."

I put the kettle on the stove and came back.

"I know I shouldn't be here." He had seated himself on the edge of a chair.

I sat awkwardly on the sofa opposite him. "Why didn't you call if you needed to see me?"

He raised up his palms in a gesture of ignorance. "I've been driving around since I left your office. I thought I'd pass by your house a few times to be near you, but when I saw your car in the driveway and I didn't see anyone else's, I had to come to the door." He sat back into the chair and shook his head. "I just *had* to."

The kettle whistled shrilly.

I got up immediately and disappeared into the kitchen, where I fumbled through the box of tea for two bags, and nearly dropped them on the floor as I pulled the dunking strings free.

"Why don't you come to the table," I called as I stepped through the kitchen doorway with the cups. The austere dining table and chairs were more formal.

He seated himself at the table end closest to the kitchen, and I sat along the side, near him.

We sipped our tea in silence a little while. Nick ran his forefinger around the rim of his cup. His mouth was puffy, his eyelids red. "I feel like I'm at the bottom of black quicksand. And I'm begging you to grab me and pull me back to life, and you won't. You're watching me die."

"I'm doing everything I can to help you." Surreptitiously I glanced at my watch. Six-fifty. Mr. Slewicki should be at the door in a few minutes.

Nick hunched over his teacup and held it with both hands. His face was no more than two feet from mine. "I'm desperate for you and I'm disgusted by my desperation. So hear me this one last time, and if the answer is still no, I'll never ask again."

I too hunched over and cradled my cup in both hands, leaning my forearms against the table.

His tone was hypnotic and low. "We're right for each other. I understand you as well as you understand me. If you let me love you I can release you. There's never been anyone else like me in your life and there never will be."

I felt myself sinking into the light and energy pouring from those piercing blue eyes. My limbs grew heavy, and I was only dimly aware of the sharp edge of the table pressing against my forearms. The sound of my breathing was loud enough that he could hear it.

"Just once," he said. "Tonight. Now. And then you decide."

I must have moved my head slightly from side to side in a tiny "no" gesture, because he pressed on, more urgent than before. "Don't say no. I'm yours. Be mine. I can make you feel things you've never felt."

I tore my gaze away from him abruptly and fixated on the fading light of day. "The answer is no."

"I know you want me," he said, his voice cracking.

I turned back to him. "It's not a question of whether I want you or not! The question is, what have I become to you that you feel you will die if you don't touch me? Am I your connection to life itself? Am I the only reality? Is there not a separate living you that continues to exist in my absence?"

"Your wanting me is like one half of a magnet. I'm the other half and you know it."

I was frantic to get away from him. He said he would die if he didn't touch me, and I felt I would die if he did.

The doorbell chimed loudly, startling both of us. I excused myself and slipped around the corner to the hallway. Through the peephole I could see Mr. Slewicki's faded gray eyes with tiny red veins and yellow fat deposits on the whites. I opened the door, stepped outside, and quietly thanked him for his kindness. I said everything was fine.

He gave me a thumbs up sign and shuffled back down the sidewalk. His thumbnail was painted iridescent pink.

I paused a moment before going back in. The interruption had helped. I knew what to do.

When I returned to the dining room Nick was standing by the window, watching Mr. Slewicki cross the street. "Did you tell him to come over here?" he asked, turning to me.

Feeling fairly safe, I nodded.

"Were you afraid I was going to hurt you?"

"I didn't know what to expect."

His chin quivered and when he opened his mouth to speak, his lower lip moved around erratically. "I would never hurt you."

"Sit down," I said, seating myself again.

Nick pulled back the chair at the end of the dining table nearest the window and sat down.

Any hope I had of successfully treating him was gone. All I wanted was out. I said, "Nick, I have to protect you from your feelings. I have to protect myself. This treatment is at an impasse and we can't get beyond it. I think you should start intensive treatment with another doctor, and the best place to do that is in the hospital."

He folded his arms on the table and laid his head on them for a few minutes. When he raised his head, he said, "Jesus. I feel like such an ass."

"I'm sorry. You knew you shouldn't have come here. But it just demonstrates the problem we have. We can't go on like this. Please, let me refer you to someone else, who can try to make sense of all this for you."

He put his elbows on his knees, leaned over, head in his hands, and wept. "I can't believe it. A lunatic asylum."

"Nick! You're imagining some state hospital from the forties! I'm talking about UCLA. It's just a safe place for a few weeks."

He shook his head. "No, no, I don't need that. I can look after myself."

I sat with him until his crying subsided. When he regained his composure, he looked up and said in a matter-of-fact tone, "So it's all over between us."

"Yes." I prayed, please let it be all over.

He stood up and shook my hand. "Okay, Doc. You win. But no hospital. I'll just call you on Tuesday so we can discuss other therapists."

"All right," I said, reassured that he was able to handle it. And it was so easy! I thought, after he left. Why didn't I do this months ago?

I called Humberto to tell him the good news, knowing this was really the beginning of our path back to each other. I briefed Val, who was covering for me that weekend. An hour later I dropped Frank off at the canine hotel and flew to Oregon, feeling like a two-hundred-pound weight had been lifted from my shoulders.

40

The raw stretches of beach in Bandon were a soothing and healing balm for the failure I felt. I went for long walks alone on the sand and, Saturday evening, sat in my old grotto to watch the moon rise.

Before dawn Sunday, my dad and I borrowed our neighbor's horses and trotted along the surf, bundled up against the stiff wind that always blows across that portion of the coast. Out there my dad was the dashing figure of my childhood, his hair whipped straight back, his heavy-set body still graceful as he skillfully directed his mare around the rocks. On a horse was where I liked him best—strong and sure, the critical voice silenced for a time.

When we turned around a shimmer of sunlight tipped over the edge of the bluffs, lighting up the vast surge of waves. I remembered another morning long ago when my Uncle Silky was in the lead, Dad behind him on a bay stallion, me on my pony. Silky had whipped his horse into a gallop, and after Dad had shouted to me to stay behind, he followed, crouching low over his horse's neck, racing him for all he was worth.

I had watched for a minute as the hoof prints cut deep into the sand and began to fill with saltwater. I knew I belonged on that wild ride with them. I wasn't going to be left behind. I yelled giyup! to my pony, dug my little heels into his sides, and set out full gallop after them, the wind reaching into my chest and grabbing my breath away. When Silky and Dad reached their marker and slowed to turn, they saw me thundering toward them, jacket flapping wildly behind me, little hands pumping the reins, racing toward love, racing toward laughter. We were the "fiercesome threesome," and the world was whole.

When Dad and I unsaddled the horses and rubbed them down, I said, "Do you ever hear from Silky?"

My father's face shut down as if I'd flipped a power breaker. "Postcards. He married some young thing from New Orleans. Makes his livin' as a fishin' guide down there."

"Do you ever write or call?"

"Nope. Don't have the address or number."

I knew not to tread any further. And I knew Silky would have sent his address and number many times.

He was my dad's younger brother by nine years, and when I was young he lived with us to help pay the rent. His real name was Evert, but they called him Silky because his pitching arm was so smooth. He could throw a trick ball so straight you had no idea it would curve at the last minute.

The year I was eight, Silky did so well in his AAA team he was catapulted into the National League and signed with Kansas City. I guess my father, having failed to make the majors, never believed his younger brother would surpass him like that. They parted on bad terms and Dad started drinking more and staying out late to play poker. Laughter drained away from our house like spring runoff.

Saturday night I dreamed of being in the car with my mother as the train approached. She smiled a wide, sinister smile, and said, "We can make it," and as that black steel filled the window, my mother's face turned into Nick's and I gasped awake, sweating.

Easter Sunday dinner was the toughest spot of the weekend. Mom had been preparing food for a week, and had invited my father's sister, husband, and children. Aunt Lydia and Uncle Harold had two daughters, twenty-four and twenty-eight, both married, one with a son. The older daughter, Carol, came with her husband and little boy.

Mom liked Lydia but always felt competitive with her. Uncle Harold had done well in the lumber business, they lived in an expensive house in Medford, and Lydia's daughters called and visited Lydia very often.

In the afternoon, I listened to Lydia and Carol whispering and laughing together. I didn't whisper and laugh with my mother like that. Later Lydia cooed over her little grandson and I saw my mother watching, her mouth smiling, her eyes sad. I knew she was fighting her envy.

I tried to avoid my mother's needs by working on her jigsaw puzzle. This one was a massive Hawaiian landscape, with waterfalls, tropical foliage, and big clumps of orchids in the foreground. The pieces were laid out on a three-by-five-foot plywood board, which my mother had temporarily placed on the living room floor.

Right before dinner, Humberto called and I was happy to hear his voice. For the first time in months I actually felt close to him. He said his restaurant was heavily booked for Easter Sunday meals and he was swamped with work. Since my car was at the airport, I said I'd see him Tuesday night.

Mom outdid herself with the dinner. Roast turkey, cornbread-sausage stuffing, broccoli, yams, coconut cream pie. I thought briefly of Nick and how sad Easters must always be for him, but I quickly dismissed that thought.

After dinner, as I stood at the kitchen sink drying pots, Mom said, "Honey, tell me about Humberto. How are things going with him?"

"A little rough. Both of us are working so hard we haven't had enough time for each other."

"So," Carol said, strolling in with her little boy's pajamas in hand. "Are you getting married?"

Is that all that mattered to my family? "I don't know," I said. I started wiping the pans vigorously and stacking them up noisily.

"Oooo, touchy, isn't she!" my cousin said.

"Why don't you just back off?" I said, dropping the dishtowel and walking out. I joined the men, determined to stay in control of myself. Don't let them do this to you, I thought. Just because they have to act that way doesn't mean you have to react the same old way.

Later, Mom came into my bedroom. I was lying on the bed, fully dressed, remembering how sweet Humberto had been when we were there together. He had even asked the names of my old stuffed bears still crowded on the rocking chair.

Because she was tired, Mom's limp was more pronounced than usual. "I'm sorry Carol upset you," she said.

"It's okay. I'm just tired and stressed. I overreacted."

"Why don't you stay the rest of the week and just relax here? I'd love to baby you a little."

I smiled. "I know you would. But I'm up to my armpits in work."

"Sweetheart, you have to take better care of yourself. You have dark circles under your eyes and you're too thin. I don't want you to get sick."

My mother fussed over me and insisted on taking my temperature. A storm blew up and rain pelted the window. I was thirteen again, stuck in my room, needing to escape. After my mother tucked me in, she brushed her hand across my forehead, and whispered, "Sare—I love you more than life itself." I broke into a fit of coughing.

After everyone was in bed, I snuck downstairs, put on my dad's rain slicker, and ran into the cold darkness of the back alley. Once I was running I felt nothing, and out of old habit my body turned down the path to the beach and kept running. The wind tore at me but I found it soothing and numbing, and I ran faster.

By the time I reached the sand, the rain had let up and I walked the broad width of beach to the shoreline more slowly. The whole pattern of my life was clear—my mother's intense longings, my thick determination to be strong and separate and self-reliant. Running was the only way I knew to find relief.

Navy-black clouds and thinning gray ones floated past the moon as the storm moved on. I lay down on the sand and counted stars in the bright patches of night sky. The words from a Pablo Neruda poem Humberto had quoted came back to me: "*La noche llega: faltan tus estrellas* . . ." Night arrives, but your stars are missing.

Monday morning, my mother and I took Carol and her son to an indoor skating rink. While my cousin struggled around the rink with her little boy, my mother and I stood at the railing, watching. Three young skaters whirled by, moving gracefully, a trail of their wind touching our attentive faces. They reached the other end of the rink quickly and whooshed back again, lifting their legs up to waist height, backs arched, blades gleaming.

"I never had that experience of feeling so free and moving so quickly," my mother said wistfully.

I was sad for her. Even before the accident, fear had kept her from the ordinary physical freedom of movement—horseback riding, skiing, skating. Now, with her one leg permanently impaired, it was even more unlikely. "You could try swimming," I suggested.

"Yes, I could," she said, but I knew she wouldn't. She had lost the will to loosen her internal chains, and once again, out of love for her, I felt intolerable frustration.

I left Oregon feeling somewhat restored in spite of the emotions stirred up by my mother. I had the strength to go forward with my plan for Nick the next day.

My fragile new calm was shattered in seconds by a phone call that same Monday night. I was snuggled in bed at eleven-thirty to watch the news, having already touched base with Val and Humberto, and called my parents to say I'd arrived home safely. The call could have been any one of my patients, but I *knew* it was Nick, and I dreaded answering.

On the third ring I forced myself to pick up the receiver. An unfamiliar male voice said, "This is the Los Angeles Police Department, Sergeant Darville speaking. Is this Dr. Sarah Rinsley?"

"Yes."

"Do you have a patient named Nicholas Arnholt, Junior?"

Alarmed, I verified that Nick was indeed a patient of mine.

"Doctor, your patient made what appears to be a suicide attempt tonight."

The room immediately began to spin like a whirligig. Over the spinning motion, I heard the officer say Nick had taken a combination of liquor and pills and was now in a coma at Daniel Freeman Hospital. Could they come to my home to ask me some questions?

"Yes," I said. I hung up the phone, sprang out of bed, and frantically tore through my closet looking for a pair of black slacks. Black slacks and a black sweater. Black slacks and a black sweater and black shoes. Black slacks and a black sweater and black shoes, and brush your hair and turn on the porch lights and lock up Frank and put on lipstick and put on another sweater to stop this shaking, and oh no oh no oh no oh no.

Then, get ahold of yourself. Maybe he'll be okay. Calm down. It's not your fault. Maybe he's better. Call the hospital.

The hospital nurse said they were working on him. They would let me know.

Sick to my stomach, too shocked to cry, I paced around my house waiting for the police, while the ugly reality crept into the very center of my being and froze it.

How could I have missed so many cues? This was Easter weekend—the anniversary of his mother's suicide! And he had lost Maggie, and lost his case, and lost his job! And he had said he would *never* ask me to touch him again. And I had turned him away. And he had said, "It's all over."

I paced and chanted, "Don't die don't die don't die." When the two officers arrived, I took them to the dining table and tried to look calm.

They were formal and respectful. "How long have you been treating him? Has he ever made a suicide attempt before? Do you have any reason to believe this is not a suicide attempt?"

I answered as quickly and honestly as I could, explaining that most information about Nick was privileged, assuming he survived. Could they tell me what happened?

They said before Nick had slipped into a coma, he had called 911. When they arrived at his apartment they found him naked on the bed, the sheets and blankets on the floor. The bedroom was in total disarray, with papers strewn all over. A full-length mirror was shattered from the impact of a briefcase hurled at it. A half-finished bottle of gin sat on the bedside table next to an empty pill vial. At the foot of the bed was a Pyrex dish with a few chocolate crumbs in it. His dog was roaming the apartment, whining.

One officer opened a plastic bag he was holding, pulled out two photographs, and handed them to me. One was the picture of Maggie and her brothers on the horse. The other was a photograph of my house. I explained both and handed them back.

He gave me another thing for inspection—a small brass cardholder and a pile of my business cards. "Yes," I said. "These came from my office."

Finally, the officer placed something in my right hand, and said, "Do you have any idea what this is? He was clutching it in his hand when we found him."

I raised my right hand to chest level, and stared at the object in my palm. It was about three inches long, gray, furry except where areas of it had been burned to the fabric underneath. It was the charred remains of a rabbit foot, the only piece of a stuffed toy rescued long ago from the fire by a desperate little boy.

Don't die. Like a prayer I repeated the words throughout the night while I roamed from room to room. I cried. I put on two sweaters because I was so cold.

At seven in the morning the attending psychiatrist, Abner Van Handle, phoned to say Nick had made it through the worst. I knew

Abner—a competent middle-aged physician with a blustery manner. He estimated they had evacuated the contents of Nick's stomach within three hours of drug ingestion, and the likelihood of brain damage was slight. Nick was still sleeping it off.

"I know how you must feel," Abner added. "I've only had one patient suicide, but that was too much. I'll call back late this afternoon to give you an update." I was calmed by his positive report and thanked him.

When he called later, the doctor was brief. "All mental status signs are normal. Mr. Arnholt appears to have survived intact."

Enormously relieved, I asked when I could see him. My desire to run away from Nick was gone. I was just glad he was alive.

Abner paused for a moment, and then said, "Mr. Arnholt does not wish to see you."

"But we've been dealing with some very difficult issues in his treatment. He *needs* to see me."

"I think your seeing him now would be disruptive to him and not in his best interests." Abner's tone had changed since that morning. He sounded strained and distant.

"What is it? Did he say why?"

There was a pause and then I heard him take a breath. "I suppose I wouldn't be violating any confidentiality. You have been his treating doctor. He says he made the suicide attempt because you had sex with him, and then tried to refer him to another therapist."

I was aghast. "Abner, I would never have sex with a patient!"

"There are no signs of psychosis. Reality testing is intact. Even if he's delusional, I have to respect his wishes. I've written orders to that effect in his chart."

"Either he's lying or he *is* delusional!"

"My suggestion to you, Dr. Rinsley, is to get yourself an attorney. It would be unwise of you to continue this discussion with me."

I hung up the phone in a cold panic. I knew Nick wasn't delusional. He was angry. But surely this could be ironed out. Surely Nick wouldn't do this to me! Was he going to take out all of his misery on me? Make me pay for others who had let him down?

A flood of hatred passed over me. That obsessive monster. He was going to ruin me. Proven sexual contact with a patient was grounds for immediate loss of my psychology license, and the accusation itself was as damaging as an accusation of incest against a parent.

I canceled the rest of my day and called Humberto. "I am in big, big trouble. Please come home."

At home Humberto flew into a tirade. "I knew it! That bastard! Him and his love-slave bullshit! You should have gotten rid of him when I told you!"

"You're right. Okay? You're right. Are you here to help me or to make me feel worse?" I sank down on the sofa.

"Sarita," he said, and sat down beside me. "If something comes of this, you'll fight it, that's all."

He held me for hours.

PART IV

Nick's suicide attempt carved away my self-confidence like a butcher trimming a bone. I no longer trusted myself with other patients, and I believed that something I was ignoring in myself had contributed to this disaster.

I began watching for danger signs in even my most stable patients. When they expressed anger, it frightened me and they knew it. Even Luness, a person totally preoccupied with herself, asked me if something was wrong, and I covered by feigning illness.

My anxiety was often overwhelming. I was jumpy when I heard unexpected noises, and fearful of shadows. Afraid Nick would come to my office unannounced and try to hurt me, I changed all the locks and added dead bolts. I insisted Humberto sleep with me every night, and then, since I felt safer at his house, I virtually moved in.

Although Humberto was tolerant of my demands and my distress, I felt my needs were driving him away. I was poor company, morose and quiet, and I slept very restlessly. Sometimes when he appeared distracted, I became outright paranoid. "Do you love me?" I asked over and over. "Of course," he replied each time, but it didn't reassure me.

I did not try to contact Nick. I prayed he would disappear from my life, yet I feared he was around every corner. At a crosswalk in Westwood, my heart raced when I saw him on the opposite curb. Then as the man walked toward me I realized it wasn't Nick. I heard footsteps in my office hallway, and when I opened the door there was no one there. I leafed through my mail, searching for his return address.

After a few weeks I received a notice from Leona Hale Atwater, a media-hungry attorney known for winning huge personal-injury settlements in controversial cases. Nick was suing me for all I was worth, claiming not only that I had had sex with him, a crime in California, but that throughout his treatment with me I had done him substantial mental, emotional, and financial harm.

I was livid. How could he fabricate a sex claim against me after the hundreds of hours I had devoted to him? He was going to destroy my carefully cultivated reputation.

Television images of Atwater flipped through my mind—straight auburn hair; long acrylic fingernails; a hawknose; small, searching eyes; and a diamond-hard smile. When the roof of a clothing factory collapsed, she held a press conference at the site within five hours. When an Olympic skier slipped in the shower, Atwater was there to condemn the facility on behalf of the skier. Mine was going to be a publicized case or she wouldn't have taken it.

I was forced to accept an unknown attorney provided by my malpractice insurance company. Humberto offered to pay for an additional attorney—a celebrity who would be an equal match to Atwater—but he would have had to borrow too much money and I couldn't let him do it. Instead I resigned myself to Clifford Underbruck, the insurance company's choice. I felt I was already at a huge disadvantage.

For my first visit to Underbruck, I wore a black wool Armani suit with a white cotton shirt and a cameo at the base of the collar. It reassured me to look as conservative and professional as possible.

On the top floor of a Century City high-rise, the firm of Westhold, Underbruck, and Isadell was at the end of a long series of identical corridors punctuated by tall mahogany doors. The sameness of the doors and the absence of any noise or movement made me dizzy, and I leaned against the wall, trying to remember some biofeedback technique that would restore my equilibrium.

Inside the firm were more corridors, with identical internal doors, and several enormous conference rooms with tables accommodating twenty or more chairs.

Clifford Underbruck's office was a prestigious corner suite, with north- and east-facing glass walls that displayed an expanse of Beverly Hills and the mountains. He wore a lightweight, cordless headphone that allowed him to walk around and use both hands while he talked. Before settling himself behind his desk, he shook my hand firmly and called me "Doctor." I heard Nick's voice echoing Doc, Doc, Doc.

Underbruck was average in height, stocky, with a deep and loud voice, and a mouth that moved around like a hand puppet's when he talked. Grateful to be off my feet, I sat down in one of his upholstered chairs, and nervously watched him take a few brief calls.

While in conversation, he stroked his full beard and mustache. His unruly head of reddish-brown hair flopped from one side to the other as he tilted his head. Even his arms were covered in hair. Hulking over his monstrous glass-topped desk, with a panorama of the city behind him from floor to ceiling, he looked like a big bear suspended in space.

"Why don't you tell me your side of the story?" he asked after he disconnected his last call.

I told him Nick had developed an erotic obsession with me. I said I had sought consultation. As I described in detail my last evening with Nick, I emphasized that no inappropriate physical contact had ever occurred.

"Atwater has named a neighbor of yours as a witness."

"Mr. Slewicki?"

"That's the guy."

Stunned, I explained what I knew of Mr. Slewicki and how he had come to my door that night. In my new state of paranoia, I wondered if Mr. Slewicki had disapproved of me in some way.

"What about Nick's claim that he's now worse than when he came to see you?"

"I know a suicide attempt looks bad, and it's a serious thing, but his underlying emotional problems were always there. Therapy just brought them to the foreground. He was actually getting better. His physical symptoms disappeared; he was becoming more flexible, more in touch with his feelings and more insightful."

Underbruck rocked back in his chair and put his feet up on the desk. "You know Atwater, of course. Ms. Show Business. Ten-thousand-dollar designer suits and high heels, except when she goes to court. Then it's a simple off-the-rack beige outfit and comfortable shoes. Juries love her."

"I can't believe he picked a woman! He has so little respect for women."

"That may be. But he's smart enough to know a jury might be sympathetic toward you if a bunch of men gang up on you."

The calculating son of a bitch.

Underbruck reclined in his chair and steepled his fingers. "You understand that the question of your innocence may have little to do with whether we win."

"Why?" My voice sounded too loud.

Underbruck angled his head toward his shoulder and his hair flopped over to that side. "Strategy and psychology in selecting the right jury, and managing their opinion, is everything. And of course there's luck."

He slammed himself forward in his chair and leaned over the desk toward me. "Tell me exactly how you felt about him and anything you did that could have been interpreted as sexual contact."

The last thing I wanted was to expose myself to this oaf, but I told him everything, including the fact that I had initially had sexual dreams and fantasies about Nick.

"Did you keep any private notes about your sexual feelings towards Nick?"

"No."

"Probably best. But you know since you consulted with Leitwell on Nick's case, he'll have to testify?"

"But nobody knows I consulted with him!"

Underbruck was buzzed by a secretary and he held up his hand in a stop sign as he took a call that couldn't wait.

I tried to control my panic. Zachary on the stand, talking about our private meetings. The worst. Reporters scribbling the lurid details. Screaming headlines. My professional reputation damaged beyond repair. How would I ever face anybody again?

Underbruck walked the length of his office while he gestured animatedly. His belly hung over the top of his eelskin belt and the shirt button over the buckle had come undone, allowing tufts of stomach hair to stick out of the small opening. When he removed his headset and laid it on his desk, he explained, "In the interrogatory, they're going to ask if you consulted with anyone else on the case. It's perjury to lie."

"Oh my God. Could they sue Zachary too?"

"That's why 'Does one to one hundred' are named with you as defendants—for anyone else uncovered in discovery who can be held liable."

My throat got so dry I started coughing and Underbruck called his secretary, who brought me a glass of water.

"Did Leitwell ever know who Nick was?"

"No. I kept his identity confidential."

"That was smart, Doctor. If he were your supervisor in a clinic, they'd sue him too, but as a consultant who discussed the case anonymously, he probably had no legal duty toward the client, so most likely they'll pass."

I breathed easier. "Does Zachary have to tell them everything I said to him?"

"No. You hold the privilege to those confidential meetings and you can refuse to waive it if you want. But it's better to admit you had sexual thoughts and were responsible in seeking consultation, so we can use him to back up your treatment plan. It's to your advantage to have him testify, although I admit it'll be embarrassing."

Driving home that day, I felt life was empty and pointless. My career was going to be over. The financial security I had worked so hard to build would be destroyed. Who even knew what would happen with Humberto? Something was wrong that he wasn't telling me. I thought maybe my needing him so much scared him.

Too depressed to eat, I crawled into bed at seven in the evening and stayed there till dawn. When Humberto came to bed at two in the morning, I pretended to be asleep.

Underbruck tried several legal maneuvers to have the suit dismissed, all of which failed. His next strategy was to take Nick's deposition as soon as possible, because the longer we waited, the more likely Nick could adjust his testimony to accommodate new information uncovered in the discovery process.

Nick's deposition was scheduled for the second week in June at Leona Hale Atwater's office. In preparation, Underbruck subpoenaed all of Nick's military, school, and medical records, as well as his personnel records.

I typed out an extensive account of the course of Nick's therapy, using my chart notes as a base. Forced to defend on paper my decisions in the case, I became as preoccupied with the development of a defense as I had been with the treatment of Nick himself. Nothing staved off my overwhelming sense of failure.

Every intervention I'd made seemed different in the light of what was now happening. I should have administered a psychological test battery to Nick. I should have referred him to someone else after the evaluation. It was a mistake to wait as long as I did to see Zachary. I should have gone into therapy myself, as Zachary had recommended.

I should have never let Nick into my house. I should have kept Mr. Slewicki with me the whole time.

My skin grew worse and I developed a rash on my face. It was hard for me to force down food, and I ate only tiny amounts at any one time—a quarter of a bagel, a half-cup of soup. Mushy food made me nauseous. Like a pregnant woman, I nibbled on crackers.

Humberto complained that I looked emaciated, and I knew he was getting tired of my constant state of crisis. He was staying at the restaurant later and leaving home earlier. Our relationship consisted mostly of notes left in the kitchen: "Home after midnight. Don't wait up." "Your mother called." "Going to Seattle Thursday to meet a chef. Can you come?" "Can't go. Meeting with Underbruck."

The notes were always signed with love and kisses, but we were clinging to an empty relationship like an old married couple too scared to change. It made me feel more lonely than if I had been living by myself.

I tried to fill the hours left empty by Nick, but every week at those times I thought of him, and clenched my fists in impotent rage. He seemed close enough to reach out and touch, so much in the habit was I of opening the door to him. I wondered if he thought of me then too, and that old sense of being able to smell his fragrance returned. I left the office during those hours to get away from it.

The work with my other patients was the only thing that helped me. William came in with pleasant news—a budding friendship with a woman.

"Her name is Ruth," he said. "I met her in my rehab program. We schedule our treadmill walks together and I've had her over for dinner a few times."

One Sunday evening, after he had cooked skinless chicken and steamed vegetables for her, she moved past him to clear the dishes, and accidentally brushed against his hip with her sturdy little body. Instinctively he reached out to her receding figure, and as she disappeared into the kitchen, he looked at his hand poised in mid-air and realized for the first time he wanted her.

"Dr. Rinsley, I was as awkward as a fourteen-year-old boy. But she made it easy until I thought about my heart. Then I was afraid to do anything. I don't want to die yet."

I was glad to see this surprising change in him. At least some of my work had been helpful.

Luness too was improving. She reported a dream in which she was playing in a huge, snowy field, and formed the body of a small child out of snow. For hours she worked, patting the limbs into place, scratching out hair, creating eyes. While she worked, she sensed the presence of someone with her, cheering her work. Then the snow-child came alive and smiled. I told Luness she had turned snow/rice into her own existence, and I was the presence, cheering her on.

"You are my real mother," she said to me.

Feeling such a failure with Nick, I was pleased.

My worst task was calling my parents to tell them the news. My father said, "Tough break, kid. But you gotta roll up your sleeves and fight." That was how my father liked to deal with things. Frontal attack or disappear. Negotiations were out of the question.

In the same hushed tone my mother reserved for town gossip, she said, "This is awful. Do you think you'll lose your license?"

With a confidence I didn't feel, I said, "Don't worry. Everything will work out. I'm innocent."

"Just remember, if you need me, I'll come down any time."

"Thanks, Mom, but I'm okay. Humberto's been very supportive. And my friend Val has called every day. Just keep a good thought for me."

She actually did say one thing that gave me courage. "Sarah—you'll handle it. You always have."

It was true I had always handled things, even when I was ten. Back then I had a constant ache in my chest from holding everything in, but I handled it. I didn't tell my secrets to any of my friends because I thought they might make fun of me, or tell on me like my father did. I hated what was happening to my mother, but I just worked harder in school. When Mom talked about running away with me, and leaving Dad and Grandma behind, I was afraid, but I kept it to myself and tried to soothe her instead.

That old ache resettled in my chest and pressed against me like a hot iron. Maybe all my accomplishments would come to nothing. Maybe I would be lonely my whole life. Maybe I had finally come up against something I couldn't handle.

But my dad was right. At least I had to fight.

As Nick's deposition grew near, I became more agitated. The depo was to be held at Atwater's office in the presence of a court reporter and all attorneys. I dreaded attending, but Underbruck insisted it was best. He said Nick would be less able to lie to my face.

I jogged every day to keep calm, but that only served to take more weight off me, and I had to wear loose warm-ups and bulky sweaters at home so Humberto wasn't constantly reminded of how thin I was.

Humberto stopped asking me if I was interested in attending dinners or parties with him. He simply made his plans without me and told me when he'd be home. So as not to disturb me, he sometimes slept in the guest bedroom. I didn't mind, because I felt guilty about waking him with the groaning and talking I was doing in my sleep.

On the morning of the depo, I met Underbruck at seven-thirty and we drove to Atwater's Beverly Hills office. I wore the same black Armani suit with the white shirt, black mid-height pumps, and small pearl earrings. I spent an inordinate amount of time applying makeup.

I dreaded seeing Nick. I was afraid I would cry or faint or do something horribly embarrassing, and I told Underbruck if I felt I was losing control I would leave.

The reception area of Atwater's office had a large wraparound desk in gray plastic laminate, which blended nicely with the lavender chairs and carpet. One corner was occupied by a life-sized sculpture of Lady Justice.

Atwater's staff escorted us to a large conference room supplied with coffee, breakfast rolls, and legal pads. She came in ahead of time to introduce herself to me, and she and Underbruck joked and laughed together for a few minutes. Old comrades, I thought. What do they care that my life is hanging in the balance? It's just a day's work to them.

We seated ourselves along one side of a long table, each place set with a water glass and napkin. When we were settled and ready to begin, Atwater left the room and returned with Nick.

All attempts to desensitize myself to seeing him failed. I trembled. My elbows itched. I clenched my teeth so hard my jaw hurt. As he entered the room, I stared at him woodenly, hoping that the mere sight of my face would make him break down, announce this was all a terrible mistake, and beg for my apology.

Our eyes locked for a moment, and except for a slight flicker of recognition, his face remained impassive. He had lost at least ten pounds and he looked tense and uncomfortable in a pin-striped suit and a starched shirt.

There was some scrambling to rearrange the seating when it appeared the only chair for Nick was directly across from me. Nick looked at me and said, "I can sit in front of her. She can't hurt me now."

I was so enraged all color bleached out of my field of vision and my left ear started ringing. I dropped a pen so I could put my head down to the floor to prevent myself from fainting.

Underbruck said quickly, "Let's keep this as pleasant and businesslike as we can, Mr. Arnholt."

Nick nodded and remained circumspect after that.

Underbruck began his questioning slowly, focusing first on neutral territory—how Nick came to choose me for a doctor, why he thought he needed therapy, how things went in the beginning.

A sickening realization occurred to me as I listened to Nick describing his life—the exercising, the moving from one woman to the next, the ambition, the pride in his possessions. We were more alike than I'd ever admitted. He had said so and I had denied it. Why hadn't I seen it?

At the mid-morning break, Underbruck pulled me into the outer hallway and walked me to the other end of the building. "Jesus Christ!" he whispered heatedly, "Why didn't you tell me the guy was so good-looking?"

I became panicky. "I said he had unusual eyes. Why are you so upset?!!"

"Jesus Christ. He's too good-looking, that's all. I'm sorry, Doctor. Are you okay? Do you want some water?"

I shoved my fists into my suit pockets. "No. Just tell me how it's going and explain why you're reacting to his looks."

"I'll explain later. It's too soon to tell right now how it's going. I'm just on a fishing expedition."

"How long do you think it'll take?"

"Probably all of today and tomorrow."

I called my service and picked up my messages, grateful for two new referrals. Aside from the trauma of the moment, I was worried about money.

The insurance company had already filed a declaratory relief action, stating that if I was found guilty of sexual misconduct, they would not pay more than twenty-five thousand dollars total for legal fees and damages. The way juries were awarding huge settlements these days, that could be a fraction of what I would owe.

When we resumed, Underbruck explored the details of Nick's childhood with him. The idea was to note any discrepancies between Nick's current story and my notes of what he had told me originally.

Nick spoke quietly, knowing enough to answer no more than exactly what was asked. Although he did not deny any of the details of his past, he downplayed their importance. His father was "stern," but not mean; his stepmother had gone "a little over the line," but was "decent."

Nick looked at Underbruck the whole time, and never at me. He was articulate, cogent, and consistent. Perhaps my session notes could be used to contradict him, but they were too sparse, and it was going to be primarily my word against his. I thought about Candy, and wondered if she was still out there somewhere, and what she would say if we could find her.

The second day of the depo, Underbruck grilled Nick for hours about his sexual claim against me. I thought as I watched Nick relate the story that I was staring into the face of a psychopath. The man could lie better than anyone I'd ever heard:

"What happened after she sat holding your hand?"

"She led me to the bedroom and laid me down on the bed. Then she opened the drawer of her bedside table and pulled out a condom. I rolled it on and she straddled me."

"At what point did each of you take off your clothes?"

"After we went into the bedroom, I took off all my clothes, but she only took off her jeans and panties. She left her top on."

"What happened next?"

"She—took me inside her until she had a climax. I was still erect when she rolled off me, so I asked her to bring me to orgasm with her hand."

"What about the condom?"

"I removed it, wrapped it in a tissue, and threw it in the wastebasket near her bed. Then we dressed and returned to the dining room."

I watched his face and shook my head as he continued.

"After that I started feeling very bad—embarrassed and apprehensive. I wondered why she didn't stop me and what would she do now. We sat down at the dining room table and drank some tea. That's when Slewicki came to the door."

"Did Slewicki see you at that time?"

"No. I stayed at the dining table around the corner from the front hallway. I heard her tell him everything was okay, and then she shut the door. I got up from the table and looked out the window to watch him leave."

"Why did you do that?"

"I was curious as to who it was."

"So you could identify him later?"

"No. I always wanted to know anything about Dr. Rinsley. Even which neighbor she liked."

"But you watched him until you saw which yard he went into?"

"It was right across the street so I couldn't help but see where he was heading. The main thing was I realized she'd asked him to come over and check on her. That made me feel small and cheap, like she was afraid of me."

"Did she tell you she was afraid of you?"

"No. But I asked her why she'd had him check on her, and she said she didn't know what would happen."

"And how did you interpret that?"

"That she was afraid I would hurt her. And that insulted me."

"What happened after that?"

"We sat at the table and talked a bit longer. When I said I felt awful, she told me she couldn't keep treating me and she would have to refer me to someone else. I didn't think there was any point in living after that. I felt used by her and discarded."

That was just the beginning. Underbruck challenged him in every way possible, but for each question, Nick had an answer. To requests for further factual information about my bedroom, my body, or the specifics of what happened, he said he couldn't remember, or it had happened so fast, and he'd been so upset, he didn't notice everything.

He could have won an Academy Award for the performance: just the right amount of anger and despair, the right number of odd little details that make a story sound credible. In fact, Nick's account of what happened was such a strange mixture of truth and fiction I began to wonder if rather than being a psychopathic liar, he had actually willed it into reality in his mind and believed what he was saying. Maybe he *was* delusional.

Atwater objected every time Underbruck came close to punching a hole in the story. If this was the way it went in court, I was doomed. Who wouldn't believe Nick?

By the end of the day I felt as if Nick had sliced up my internal organs and strewn them around the room. When we stood up to adjourn, my abdomen was a sheet of pain.

45

That night Humberto came home early to be with me, knowing it was a rough day. He found me in bed at ten in the evening, holding my stomach, tears streaming down my face.

"Sarita," he said, and immediately joined me in bed. "Tell me what happened." He listened intently while I blubbered the story—how skillfully Nick had told lies, so many lies. Humberto said very little as he listened, but I felt comforted by his presence and I fell into an exhausted sleep.

The deposition ended late the next afternoon. During the morning break, Underbruck steered me out of Atwater's office and strolled down the hall with me again. He asked if Mr. Slewicki might have looked in my windows or seen anything I hadn't mentioned.

Taken aback, I said, "Don't you believe I've told you the truth?"

He stopped, grabbed my arm and shook it slightly. "I do believe you, but I don't know if anyone else will. Nick's very convincing. And again, I ask you, is there any physical feature you have on your body that's unusual? A mole? Trimmed pubic hair? A scar?"

I shook my head, muted by helpless rage.

"I covered it all," Underbruck said wearily at eight o'clock that evening, back in his office. The rest of his staff was gone. "I think so far we've laid a good foundation."

I breathed a little sigh. I didn't care how offensive I found Underbruck if he could defend me well. "Cliff. There's one thing I've been thinking about. Nick glossed over his childhood. Lied, basically. The truth is his stepmother sexually abused him, and his father was brutal. Now, Nick hasn't had any contact with his stepmother for years, and he considers her dead, but I think she is out there somewhere, and I wonder whether it might help us to find her. Maybe she could verify the real facts of his childhood, which would show that Nick's a liar."

Underbruck laughed. "You think a woman like that would admit to incest when her son is denying it?"

My spirits flagged. "I guess not."

Seeing my dejection, his voice softened. "Okay, let's pose the best scenario. We find her. She testifies that Nick's childhood was horrible. So what? How does that absolve you of any responsibility?"

"It doesn't. Many people in a therapist's office have terrible childhood stories. But if we can show that his problems didn't start with me, doesn't that help?"

"Not really. Everyone assumes he had problems in the first place or he wouldn't have come to see you."

I was grasping at straws. "But at minimum it would show he lied, wouldn't it?"

Underbruck stood and lumbered over to the window, where he gazed at the expanse of twinkling lights and stroked his beard. When he turned back to me, he said, "If we can find her, and if by some miracle she contradicts him, then it would show he was at least downplaying his past. Whether that would be of any value to you with the jury, I don't know. But it can't hurt to try. Tell me whatever you know about her and I'll put a trace on her."

A stinging memory flitted through my mind, of Nick laughing, and saying, "Don't you know we can find anyone in this country?" What's good for the goose is good for the gander, I thought.

Underbruck returned to his desk. "Look. There's one more thing I've got to discuss with you," he said, sounding cautious. "I don't have a nice way of saying this, so try not to take it too personally."

I pushed my glasses up the bridge of my nose. "What?"

"We have to assume this case is going to trial. It may settle, but we have to proceed as if it won't."

"So?"

"So you've got to spruce up your appearance."

"What do you mean?"

"Sarah, a jury's going to take one look at you and Nick, and believe that you went to bed with him. He's a handsome shit, and you—well, you need a little work. They're going to think you couldn't resist him."

"You are kidding, I assume."

He shook his head. "I'm dead serious. I don't mean to offend or insult you, and under ordinary circumstances you're certainly attractive enough, but Atwater will exaggerate the differences between you and Nick. She'll imply you're a plain woman who was flattered by this handsome lawyer's attention, and she'll get away with it because she's a woman herself. So our best defense is to nullify that before the trial."

"What did you have in mind, a face transplant?"

"Look, I told you not to take this personally. I just want to polish you up a bit. I can send you to a dermatologist to help you with your complexion. I have a dentist who can whiten and straighten your front teeth—"

I was livid, and I stood up and began packing my briefcase to leave.

"I'm not finished," he boomed. "Sit down!"

"You are finished!" I cried. "I'm not some poodle at a kennel show! I don't have to be physically perfect to prove I'm a competent professional! This is outrageous!"

"Sit down!" he thundered again, and out of fear for the outcome of my case, I obeyed.

He resumed stroking his beard. "The jury doesn't have time to get to know you personally. All they're going to hear is a tiny slice of your life that's blown up so it's the whole picture. Surely you know the research on physical attractiveness—even in a courtroom, good-looking people are more likely to be presumed innocent than others. You can either use it to your best advantage or ignore it and suffer the consequences."

He came around to my side of his desk and sat on the edge, with one leg dangling. "I'm sorry."

I took my glasses off and covered my face. Awful feelings of ugliness came rushing to the surface. For a moment I felt a huge hand on my left shoulder, and then it was gone. When I thought I could control myself, I took my hands away from my face and said evenly, "Tell me what you think I should do, and I'll consider it. That's all."

Looking relieved, he sat down in the client's chair next to me and used his fingers to count off the list. "I mentioned a dermatologist and a dentist. I would also like to send you to the Xavier salon for hair and makeup. Then I have this woman who dresses people; she's great. And you need to start wearing contact lenses."

"You want me to look like a model?" I asked, outraged.

"No. I want you to look like the most attractive, professional, competent woman those jurors have ever seen."

"You know it's people like you who keep women starving themselves to look beautiful."

"No. It's people like me who win trials."

I knew Humberto was behaving differently toward me, but I assumed it was because I was so miserable, until I began to notice his questions. Several times he asked me to repeat what Nick had said at his deposition. Once he asked, "Why don't you just settle the case and be done with it, instead of going through all this?"

Sometimes he hugged me and said everything would be all right, and I felt temporarily safe again, but I couldn't shake the feeling that something deep was terribly wrong.

One Saturday night, while we were getting ready for bed, I realized we hadn't made love for three weeks. I put my arms around his neck and said, "I'm sorry I've been so preoccupied." He kissed me peremptorily and turned away.

"What is it?" I asked, focusing full attention on him.

He avoided my gaze, made some excuse about being tired, and lay down on the bed, TV remote control in hand. I shut off the TV abruptly and sat down in front of him at the foot of the bed. "We'd better talk," I said. "Is it the lawsuit? Are you angry with me?"

He sat still, tight-lipped, unwilling to explain.

"I don't blame you for being mad. I know I've been busy and very upset and unavailable. But you know how awful this is for me."

He nodded.

"Please. Talk to me!" I pleaded. "I can't stand the silent treatment."

"I don't know if you can deal with what I have to say."

"What is it? Is there someone else? Are you not in love with me anymore?"

Shaking his head in apparent amazement, he asked, "You have the nerve to ask me if *I* have someone else?"

I sputtered, "Well, I've always been afraid that—"

"Yes, yes, poor little Sarah with her Latin gigolo."

Thrown off balance by his sarcasm, I became combative. "What do you mean, do I have the nerve to ask you? Do you have someone else or not?"

"No. But *you've* always had someone else."

"He's the one who's ruining my life! You know what I mean by someone else."

He looked at me sharply. "And hasn't he been your someone else for a long time?"

My head reeled from the ugly understanding of what had been bothering him. In a voice small with the wish for denial, I said, "You don't believe the accusation, do you?"

After some minutes of silence—answer enough—he said, "I don't know."

I jerked up involuntarily to a standing position and yelled, "How could you think that of me? Do you think this whole process I'm going through is a masquerade? That I'm lying?" In his bedroom, facing a closetful of clothes that were mine, I calculated how long it would take to remove my possessions from his house and pile them in the car.

"Who in my position wouldn't wonder?" Humberto asked.

I sank to the floor, and Humberto, perhaps thinking I was about to confess, came to my side and touched my shoulder. "Get away from me," I shouted. "You're the one person I thought I could count on!" He stepped back and I remained sitting on the floor, shivering in the center of the room, arms wrapped around my knees.

Then, TV remote still in hand, Humberto said harshly, "Look how much time you spent thinking about this guy and answering his calls and worrying about him. Maybe you liked his being in love with you? Maybe you encouraged it? Maybe even, just for one night, you gave in to him?"

I stood up and faced him. "That's the only way you could understand this? It would have to be sex with him?!!" I started hunting for my shoes. Humberto stood in the middle of the room, saying nothing.

I found my shoes and put on one, then dropped the other shoe and turned on him. "My work is your competition and you can't accept that, can you? Don't you realize that's always been your problem? You say I'm smart, you say you admire my work, but the fact is you hate it! What you really want is a subservient little woman whose life revolves around yours! That's the real reason you didn't marry Marisombra, isn't it! She was a fucking doctor and she put her patients ahead of you!"

His face turned deep red and I thought he might hit me. Instead he turned and threw the TV remote against the wall, where it tore off a chunk of plaster and fell apart.

I took the few steps to him and punched him as hard as I could on his right upper arm. "How dare you think I'd have sex with a patient! How dare you!" I shouted.

He grabbed both my wrists and held them so tightly they burned. "Anybody in my position would have thought that!" he hissed. "Anybody except a fool or a lapdog. You want a lapdog? Go back to your old friend Morry!"

With that he let go of me, turned, and strode out, and I threw myself on the bed and cried until my head ached. When I finally calmed down and looked at the clock, it was two in the morning. The house was completely silent, but now this comfortable haven had become enemy territory.

I was too upset to sleep in Humberto's bed. Numbly, I removed the one shoe I had put on, pulled a pillow and blanket into the bathroom, and made a bed for myself in the tub. Then I locked the door, turned out the light and climbed into the tub, where I huddled like a small child and tried to sleep until the first light of day.

I dreaded facing Humberto again and wished I could take my things and leave without seeing him. I even imagined staying in the bathroom all day until he finally left the house and I could depart on my own.

I needn't have worried. He was just as anxious to avoid me as I was to avoid him. In the early morning light I listened to doors opening and closing downstairs, and then the sound of his car driving away.

Grateful, I wandered down and found Frank dozing in the kitchen. Humberto's golf clubs in the hall closet were missing and I remembered he'd planned an early game for this morning, probably another attempt to avoid me.

"He won't have to leave his house to escape from me any more," I said to Frank. In the guest bathroom I looked at myself in the mirror. My eyes were swollen and my face blotchy and red.

It took me less than an hour to collect my things and pile them into the car. I cried when I scratched Esperanza's neck and said good-bye to her. "Good-bye, good-bye," she repeated, imitating the sound of my sniffling.

I pulled out of the driveway slowly and took one last look at the house. As far as I was concerned, it was over between us.

47

Although Humberto and I had drifted so far apart, the final break from him made me feel like a jigsaw puzzle fallen into pieces. I couldn't remember anything without writing it down in my appointment book, and one afternoon I was frantic over losing the book until a restaurant called to say I had left it there.

My house sounded hollow when I walked across the hardwood floors. What I had enjoyed as a spare look now seemed downright barren, and I couldn't keep warm no matter how high I turned up the heat or how many layers of clothing I wore.

In the evenings I turned off the lights and lit a dozen votive candles in the bathroom before sinking into the tub to soothe myself. I tried to clear my mind of everything as I watched the little flames dance. I'll get through this, I said. I ate brown sugar for dinner every night.

Two weeks later, when I thought I might manage to come out of this zombie state, I received a warning call from Underbruck. Leona Atwater had called a press conference to announce the lawsuit. That night on the local evening news, I watched her hold forth from a book-lined room. Hair perfectly in place, glib and quick-speaking, she said there was so much sexual abuse between therapist and client these days, that "we have no idea how many victims there are in this country. The problem could be bigger than child abuse." She finished by saying how important it was "for victims to come forward so the abuse can be put to a stop."

My phone rang continually that night until I shut off the ringer and unplugged the answering machine. Then, instead of shivering and shrinking into the tub, I began to clean with a frenzy.

By the light of my porch lamp I washed my car and chamoised it dry. After wiping the dashboard and shampooing the seats and carpet, I detailed the panel with leather polish. In the house, I separated my blouses into cold wash and warm, threw the cold items in the machine, and put the dry cleaning in the car. At two in the morning, I ironed my blouses, when they were just damp.

The next day three new patients canceled their first appointments, and by the following week every one of my current patients knew and was talking about the charges against me. By then I had reorganized the garage, bathed Frank, washed the dining room chandelier with a vinegar-and-water rinse, trimmed the roses, shampooed my area rug, and scrubbed the bathroom tiles with Ajax.

Humberto left a message on my home machine during business hours, when he knew I wouldn't be home. "Sorry your name is being dragged through the mud. Just wanted you to know I'm thinking of you." It enraged me to hear his voice.

I called my parents so they would find out the whole thing from me, rather than a nosy reporter. Naturally, my mother said, "You can always come back here."

"Yes, thanks, but I wouldn't dream of running away."

"And what does Humberto say about all this?"

"We—broke up. Mom, I know you want to talk about it, but I can't right now. Okay?"

"Of course, honey. You tell me when you're ready." That was a miracle right there.

Even my father cheered me some. "Looks like you're takin' it on the meat, sport. But be tough. Let 'em know you're out there."

It was no great surprise that Luness was the first of my long-term patients to go. The week after the TV news conference, she came in and said, "You've helped me a lot, Dr. Rinsley, but I couldn't go on with you, wondering if you slept with Nick. After all, I was in love with him. And maybe you were too. For all I know, you ruined my chances with him because you wanted him."

This galled me, but what point was there in protesting my innocence to her? She was going to believe what she wanted anyway. I spent the rest of the hour reviewing the progress she had made during our work together. I gave her the names of several other therapists, she thanked me and said good-bye.

I felt unfairly dismissed and profoundly hurt by the assumption of my guilt, which only magnified what I was already feeling toward Humberto. After she left, I walked into the waiting room and tore a fan palm to shreds.

The following week what remained of my privacy was completely eradicated by a series of articles in the *Los Angeles Times* about "therapist-patient sex syndrome," in which the charges of my upcoming lawsuit were described. An old photograph of me from a conference brochure was printed with the articles.

I had only two choices: either disintegrate completely or fight. Out of some ancient loyalty to my father, I fought.

When reporters showed up at my office, I obtained a court order to ban them from the building as an invasion of my other patients' privacy. After they camped on my home doorstep, I kenneled Frank and stayed with Val until they stopped hanging around. I forced myself to function with my patients—to pay attention to their needs, to listen to their stories. I forced myself to eat peanut butter and ice cream to gain weight. I even tried to figure out how I might benefit from the publicity.

Although spending nights with Val and Gordon was comforting, it also heightened my loneliness. I hated Humberto. How could he abandon me in such a crisis? Be such a traitor, and have so little faith in me? As soon as possible, I returned to my own house, because seeing Val and Gordon holding hands was torture.

People magazine contacted me, offering to publish my side of the story; cable and network TV development people started calling to make offers. Militant anti-psychology groups picketed my office building. I saw my patients in the evenings at Val's office, which was disconcerting for all of us.

News of my predicament reached Bandon through articles about patient-therapist sex in *Newsweek* and *Time,* and although my parents didn't tell me until much later, their customers and friends talked about it. My parents, who hated answering machines, were finally forced to invest in one. Reporters were hounding them too.

My father sent me a *Bandon Herald* article after the paper interviewed them at home. "It's a crime that one false accusation can ruin a brilliant career," he was quoted as saying. I wept when I read it. He had never told me he thought so highly of my work.

The necessity of having to respond to the constant onslaught kept me going. If I had been forced to face the still, quiet center of my being, I might have crumbled.

As I expected, the program director of my radio station phoned and said, "Sorry, Sarah. You know we love you, but we can't afford to be associated with this. We'll have to replace you."

"I understand," I said coldly.

"Good luck, babe," he said. "Call me when it's over and we'll see what we can do."

None of my other patients were quite as abrupt as Luness. I tried to get each of them to discuss their thoughts and feelings about the charges against me, but even after we'd exhausted that and gone on to usual topics, it was an elephant in the room we were pretending to ignore.

William was the most supportive. "I know you're innocent of this charge and it's a damn shame you have to go through it," he said emphatically. So touched was I by his confidence in me that I broke down and cried.

"There, there," he said, bringing me a box of Kleenex and patting me on the arm. I felt comfortable enough with him to talk a little about how disrupted my life was. "I won't charge you for this session," I said before he left.

"Of course you must," he replied, and pulled out his checkbook. "I'm very saddened by how badly this has affected you, but in a peculiar way, it was good for me."

"Why?"

"Because it reminds me that no one is immune from misery, and that my life isn't so bad."

I smiled. "I'm glad my misery did somebody some good."

48

One morning, Underbruck called me at home before eight o'clock. "I've got some news for you. We found Candy Arnholt. She's Candy Lanehurst now. Married to a Pasadena businessman."

"Have you contacted her?"

"Yes, and she wants nothing to do with this."

"So what did you say?"

"I told her we would like to come out and interview her. That if she wouldn't at least give us an hour of her time we'd subpoena her. It's set for Thursday afternoon."

"Good work, Cliff! Maybe this will help us!"

"Don't get your hopes up. This is just a stab in the dark."

But I couldn't help feeling excited. For some reason I was convinced that Candy would shed some light on this situation.

She lived in a large Victorian house in old Pasadena, with white-blossomed azalea bushes lining the path to the front door. By the time Underbruck rang the doorbell, I was bursting with curiosity.

She was of average height, with a voluptuous figure and narrow, sculpted ankles. She wore an oversized red V-neck sweater, matching bright red nail polish, charcoal gray leggings, and thong sandals. Framing her features was a coif of wavy black hair, loose to the shoulders.

Candy offered a cold, sweaty handshake and took us into her living room, where we sat on floral-patterned chairs. I studied her, imagining how beautiful she must have been at eighteen, and how unbearable to lose her.

"What can I do for you?" she asked. Her big green eyes looked coldly at each of us.

Underbruck explained the lawsuit, mentioning that Nick was falsely accusing me, and asking if she might be willing to testify about the particulars of his childhood.

She said, "I'm sure he's already told you all about his childhood, so I don't see why you need me."

He said, "But your version of things might be different than his. So if you would answer a few questions now, we might have a better idea of whether your testimony could shed some light on the situation."

She waved her hands away from her body in a gesture of dismissal. "I don't want to be involved in this business in any way. The last thing I would do is dredge up the very things from my past I've worked so hard to forget."

"But a grave injustice is being done here," Underbruck said gruffly. "Perhaps you would do it out of fairness."

"Fairness! You think it's fair of you to come here? To ask a man's own mother to testify against him? Why would I want to help you under any circumstances? Why would I want to harm my son's case?"

"Have you talked to Nick about it?"

She shook her head.

"Do you ever talk to Nick?"

"That's none of your business."

"What difference would it make if you helped me?" I blurted out. "Nick's lying! And I know you don't have a relationship with him anyway!"

A shadow of pain crossed her features and then was gone. "How do I know he's lying? Maybe you're the one lying. But no matter. My husband says even if you subpoena me, you can't force me to say anything. And you're right, I don't have a relationship with Nicky, so why would I step into that spotlight? I have my husband's business to think about."

I felt as frustrated as if I were talking to my own mother. "Please, Mrs. Lanehurst. If you would just be honest with us, maybe the truth would come out. Couldn't we ask you a few questions about him?"

She stood abruptly. "I owe you nothing. Don't involve me in Nick's life. He's shut me out and that's the way he wants it."

She walked briskly to the front door, her sandals slapping against her heels. We stood reluctantly, unable to prolong the discussion. Underbruck handed her his card. "If you change your mind, please call me."

Her red nail polish glittered as she took the card and scanned it quickly. "Don't call me again," she said, and opened the door. There was nothing to do but leave, and I was keenly disappointed.

"Forget about her," Underbruck said on the drive back. "It probably wouldn't have helped anyway."

But I couldn't forget about her, and I thought of her often after that, wondering what she might say if she were willing to reveal herself.

Atwater filed a complaint with the psychology board, initiating a separate investigation which would require a defense lawyer not covered by my malpractice insurance. Cosmetic work wasn't covered by medical insurance, and as my patients gradually quit treatment with me, my bills started piling up.

This, more than anything else, made me desperate. I loved my house and the fear of losing it kept me awake at night. I still remembered my father begging for time to pay the rent, and my mother's constant fear of being evicted.

I called the Chief of Psychology at the V.A. and asked if he could increase my hours, but he said they were bound by a federal freeze on salaries at the moment. I asked Kevin Utley if he had any room for me at his clinic and he said he would see what he could do. My car phone, my membership at the Sports Club, my cleaning lady, even my restaurant meals were fast becoming a drain on the only remaining money I had, and I decided to give up all of it.

I discussed a loan with my bank manager, but he was forced to deny it because there was no guarantee I'd have a decent future income. I hated the idea of asking my friends for money because I didn't know when I would be able to pay them back, and I didn't want to impose.

My parents sent me all the money they could spare—fifteen thousand dollars—and I will always be grateful for their support. I guess my mother quietly wrote a note to Silky, because he sent me a check for two thousand dollars, and a note inviting me to visit him any time. I ran my finger over his return address on the envelope, the memory of distant merriment tugging at me.

These gifts didn't last long. My mortgage payment alone was twenty-eight hundred dollars a month. More than once I thought of how helpful Humberto's money would have been, but I was too proud and too angry to call. Finally I bowed to the inevitable, and called a realtor. The only way to survive was to sell my house.

Don't fall apart, I told myself. It's a possession. When this is over, you can buy another one. But it felt like amputating a limb to save my life.

Once I put the house on the market, I obtained a small second mortgage to pay off my credit card bills and start saving for legal fees. After the media attention died down I still had six private patients, which gave me enough to manage my office overhead and keep my car. The consulting position at the V.A. and the eating-disorders clinic at UCLA were still secure. I hadn't yet heard from Kevin.

Unexpected kindness from friends evoked my deepest gratitude. Val gave me ten thousand dollars. Gave, not loaned. She said it was small payment for the thousands of therapy hours I'd given her, and although I said the therapy had been mutual, I accepted her gift. "If the tables were turned, I know you'd do the same for me in a second," she said.

Linda lent me three thousand dollars, and said I could take up to ten years to pay it back, although she was sure I would win the case and be in good shape again soon. For her, three thousand dollars was a sacrifice.

Even Pallen called me after the publicity and offered to help. I didn't take anything from him, but I was touched by his generosity, and wondered if I had made a mistake in walking away from him so quickly.

Humberto sent me a letter offering assistance. I wrote a thank-you note, politely refusing. I felt so hurt by him I couldn't bear the thought of accepting his help, but I thought regretfully of how often he had pleaded with me to get closer to him, and how I had pushed him away and kept running. Those thoughts nagged at me, because although I saw what I had done, I didn't understand the reason.

William remained my most reliable patient. I took pleasure in learning that his relationship with Ruth had turned into a full-blown love affair. One day he said, "If I can't have sex the usual way, we do other things and it works out quite well. I have you to thank. I never would have been capable of this without you."

Feeling so maligned, I enjoyed his gratitude.

"I'm still the same old me," he hastened to add. "I'm sure either she or I will die next week. I dwell on those mean phone calls from Elizabeth. But I'm not as bad as I was. Do you see it?"

"Yes. You're taking the chance of having a good time."

"But why is having a good time taking a chance?!"

"To reach for pleasure is to be willing to bear the loss of it."

He nodded. "You've been telling me this for a long time, but it took a heart attack for me to get the point."

"Some people never get it," I replied, feeling the loss of my own pleasures so acutely. I could see William was almost finished therapy, and although I was happy for him, it would mean another reduction in my income.

I was amazed at how much I had taken for granted financially. Suddenly everything was exorbitantly expensive and I felt sympathy for the homeless people who wandered the streets near my house.

Through random assignment our case was put on an accelerated schedule, and Underbruck said as soon as the discovery was completed we would hit the courtroom. I don't know how I would have survived if we had been forced to wait years.

Naturally he referred me to a Beverly Hills dentist where it cost ten dollars just to park for two hours. The dentist estimated putting plastic laminates on my front teeth would cost about three thousand dollars, and he wanted half the money up front. Resenting it on principle alone, I reluctantly paid out the first fifteen hundred dollars of the money Linda had loaned me. Enduring novocaine injections under my upper lip left me feeling wounded, but the finished results were remarkable. Within four weeks I had white, even front teeth for the first time in my life.

The hairdresser, dermatologist, makeup artist, and clothing buyer were also outrageous. I spent seven hundred dollars at the Xavier salon and another five thousand dollars on clothes, but when Underbruck saw a practice run, he yelled, "Yes! Looking good, Doctor!"

Chauvinist pig asshole, I thought. Chauvinist pig jury and judge. But the image I saw in the mirror was prettier, and I grudgingly admitted I liked it.

My house sold in four months. The day I signed the escrow papers I walked out of the bank onto San Vicente Boulevard and wandered down the street aimlessly. Strong Santa Ana winds were blowing, and clouds of dust swirled around my feet and soiled my dress. I had no home, no lover, no future. While people around me scurried to get out of the wind, I let it beat my hair against my face. Ahead of me a woman's skirt blew up over her head and I couldn't even muster a smile.

I roamed up and down the residential streets off San Vicente for hours, looking at the snug houses—a child's bike left on the lawn, a basketball hoop over a garage, a gardener hauling out garbage cans. There were expensive cars—Mercedes, BMWs, Jaguars—maids and nannies leaving for the day, husbands arriving home. Wasn't I supposed to be living in one of those homes? With a husband and a child and tickets to the symphony for Friday night? And if not that, wasn't I at least supposed to have my success?

When I was finally tired enough to notice, I couldn't remember where I'd parked my car. I tried to retrace my steps, but nothing looked familiar. Confused, I sat down under a tree and took off my shoe. A sore spot had turned red on my right heel, and I rubbed it gently while I tried to orient myself.

I knew how to get back to San Vicente, but it took me a few minutes to recall that my car was parked at the bank. I limped back. Then I drove to Pacific Palisades, turned down Humberto's street, and passed his house quickly to see if he was home. It was Monday, a night he rarely went to the restaurant, and from the dark street I saw him clearly in the lighted kitchen window. I turned around and parked one house away to watch him.

He was cooking. I could tell by the quick motions between the sink and the stove. Did he have someone else with him? Was he gone for good? I had been so angry with him I had been able to put him out of my mind for months, and I had discarded the few tentative cards he had sent, but now I longed to see his smile and feel his arms around me. He had tried to fill me up with love and I had offered him a leaky glass that dribbled away everything he gave. I reminded myself of

Nick, sitting in my parked car, watching. I broke down in the car and cried, and finally drove home at nine o'clock, cold and depressed.

I tried to stop feeling sorry for myself. At least I had friends; I had parents; I would have the money from the house; I was healthy. I lectured myself constantly, and it did help a bit.

Valerie helped me scour the apartment buildings in West L.A., searching for one that wasn't too dismal. I rented a small one-bedroom on the second floor of a fifteen-unit building on Barry Avenue. The living room balcony faced another apartment building across the walkway, but the bedroom looked out on a private backyard with a beautiful sycamore tree. The apartment smelled of insecticide, so there were roaches in the building, but other than that the place looked clean and adequate, and the price was right.

Because I couldn't afford professional packers and my friends were too busy, I hesitantly accepted my mother's offer to come down and help me move. It was difficult for me, because I sensed some undercurrent of secret satisfaction she felt in seeing my demise—proof that I could never really leave her, never not need her. Her presence grated on me like chalk on a blackboard.

I don't remember my mother being sad when I was small. I remember the trilling sound of her laugh, cheerful as a mockingbird, and the excited way she'd announce "Daddy's home!" She bustled in those days—designing dresses, relining the closets, canning green beans and salmon and corn and jelly. It was only later in my childhood, when Dad's comings and goings became erratic and her own mother got so sick, that the energy left my mother's face, leaving a tired discouraged look.

The greatest joy of my mother's life was having me. She treasured even the tiniest things about me—my baby shoes scuffed down to bare leather, the hair ribbons I'd tossed carelessly under the kitchen table. Later, she told me that to be adored by your own child is a temporary paradise. "As wonderful as it is," she said, "you know the serpent is in the garden, waiting, because eventually your child will learn judgment, and she will pass judgment on you." This was said with a dark bitterness I could never have imagined in those early days.

She lumbered through my front door, suitcase in hand, filling up the hallway with her large frame. Frank immediately barked at her, but after she knelt down and scratched his ears, he accepted her, and I liked that she didn't mind getting dog hair on her raincoat.

I insisted she sleep in my bed the first night, and I used the sofa bed in the guest room. Frank was confused by my being in the wrong room and couldn't decide where to sleep. All night he kept switching rooms and waking us. In the morning Mom's asthma had kicked up and we decided it was best if she slept in the little room with the door shut.

When I came home from work that night, the smell of pot roast filled the house. I didn't feel much like eating or talking, but I was trapped by my mother's presence and my need for her. I sat up on the kitchen counter, watching her wash lettuce leaves.

"Have you heard from Humberto?" she asked casually.

"He's left me a few messages."

"Maybe you could patch things up."

"I doubt it. We hurt each other pretty badly. Anyway, I don't understand why you're so hell-bent for me to get married. Marriages are falling apart constantly. And your marriage hasn't been so hot either."

She tore little pieces of lettuce into my wooden salad bowl. "Your father is my rock."

It sounded so peculiar to hear my father described that way. In my mind he was like those random reinforcement machines used to train rats. You never knew when he was going to pay off, so you just kept trying endlessly to please him. "I thought he would walk out on you any time."

She shook her head. "He would never leave me. He needs me as much as I need him."

"So why did you put up with that crap?"

"I accepted I couldn't be everything to him, that's all. It's something you don't understand. That's why you keep looking and looking and never find. You have to love a man long enough and hard enough to forgive him for who he is."

"Why should I have to forgive a man for who he is?"

"For the same reason he has to forgive you for who you are—because we're all so flawed. And having forgiven each other, we can be partners, and that, sweetheart, is God's greatest blessing."

I turned away, suddenly sad, and went to wash my hands.

To my embarrassment, she served dinner on the china plates. The pot roast was good and for the first time in months I actually tasted what I was eating. When she asked how I'd enjoyed the dishes, I said, "I haven't found the right occasion for them."

"You've never used them?" She was obviously hurt.

I shook my head.

"You never did have a knack for cooking. I suppose you didn't want to serve Domino's pizza on china."

I let that one pass. It was just her way of getting back at me and I understood her anger.

I remembered there was some point in my childhood when I didn't want to be like her anymore. She was afraid to fight openly, and because of it I lost respect for her. I turned to my father and knocked myself out trying to please him.

When she took a third helping of roast, I said, "You don't have to swallow your anger. Just say it! You're pissed off!"

She shook her head. "They're your dishes now. You can do whatever you want with them."

"But I hurt your feelings! Don't you think it's better to tell me, instead of stuffing it down with more food?"

She put her fork down and left the rest of her food untouched.

"I'm sorry," I said, and I got up from the table to clear the dishes. I reminded myself that the mark of adulthood is not having to change your parents, and I had proved myself still a child.

The demands of the task ahead pulled us back together. Systematically we went through each room and I showed her what I wanted to pack and what I planned to give away or put in storage. I left her to work in the den, while I waded through the closet in my bedroom.

Late in the evening, still buried in my closet, I heard my mother walk into the bedroom and call my name brokenly, as if a bone were caught in her throat.

"What?" I said, coming out.

The room was lit only by my bedside lamp, and my mother stood outside the pool of light, holding something in her hands.

"What?" I repeated.

My mother moved to the bed, sat down heavily, and showed me my old pink dress, the tiny white pearls now yellowed with age, the skirt flat and rumpled, the satin ribbons wrinkled. "Oh, Sarah, sweetheart. You still have this."

The ache in my chest threatened to close my throat.

"Ever since you refused to wear this you've moved farther and farther away from me."

I sat down next to her and picked up an edge of ribbon. I stroked it, felt its velvety smoothness. "Not as far away as you think, Mom. You see? I couldn't bear to wear this dress, but I couldn't bear to give it up either."

Later in bed, I thought I heard my mother crying, but I could not go to her.

51

By Thursday of that week my house was a jumble of packing boxes, disassembled furniture, and garbage. I brought home Chinese food, and Mom and I sat down in front of the TV for a quick meal.

"Were you lonesome here by yourself all day?" I asked.

A peculiar look came over her face. "Actually you had a visitor."

"Oh no! Who?" A catalogue of danger went through my mind: Nick, a bill collector, another subpoena.

"Humberto."

"He *came* here? Why didn't he call?"

"He said you haven't answered his calls. He came by to leave a note, but when he saw movement inside he thought I was you and rang the doorbell."

"What else did he say?"

"He said he was concerned about you and wanted to know how the lawsuit was going."

"I'll bet. What did you tell him?"

"We sat down and talked for a while. No one knows how it's going, I said, but I told him I was worried about you."

"Oh, Mom!" I wailed. "You told him you were worried about me?" Still angry at him and insulted, I didn't want my soft spots exposed. I put down my fork.

"What was so bad about that?"

"You don't understand!" It was just like her to meddle in my personal life.

Fuming, I got up and went into the kitchen to pack the china. I'd purchased a special box with internal dividers and a mound of blank newspaper for padding. I stepped up on a chair, placed a pile of dinner plates on the counter, and climbed back down to wrap.

From my position in the kitchen I could see my mother still eating, looking like a scolded child, and I resented feeling I had to take care of her, when *I* needed looking after.

When she brought the leftovers into the kitchen, I asked, "How long was he here?"

"About an hour."

"What the hell did you talk about?" I put a plate back on the counter and turned to face her.

She looked guilty. "About your running all the time, about how you're never going to be satisfied with anything. He said he's still in love with you, but he doesn't think it'll work out."

"And what did you say?"

She folded her arms over her chest. "I told him I didn't know if you'd ever be able to settle down with any man. That you're a ship with no anchor."

My whole being filled with rage. "How could you talk behind my back to a man who believes I'm guilty?!!" I yelled.

Her face closed into a tight shield. "Because I love you and I'm worried about you. Because he loves you too."

"How can a man love a woman he doesn't believe??!!"

My mother, arms folded, leaned against the counter, and said, "Sarah, I hate Nick Arnholt for what he's done to you. You have achieved so much and this public attack is a tragedy. But wasn't it also a tragedy for that smart young lawyer to nearly kill himself? For an outsider, it's hard to know what to think."

Bursting into sobs, I ran from her. Even my own mother doubted my innocence! I found my purse on the living room floor, grabbed my keys, and headed out the front door toward my car. She ran after me, calling to me from the sidewalk, "Be careful!!" as she had every day of my childhood. I backed out of the driveway and sped away, glancing once in the rearview mirror to see her, distraught and immobile, holding a wet dishtowel.

I drove my car at eighty miles an hour up the winding curves of Pacific Coast Highway. When I reached Zuma Beach, I slowed down and turned into the parking lot.

It was a clear, soft night. Dangerous though it was to walk on the beach at that hour, I left the car and headed across a wide stretch of sand.

I was Nick's victim. Wasn't that obvious? He had taunted and embarrassed me, invaded my personal life, my mind, my dreams. He had pulled me down with him toward death, and having escaped it, had begun to ruin my life.

But I was haunted by the apparition of Nick's tortured face on our last evening together. What really *did* happen between us? Did I lead him on? Was there some hateful part of me I was trying to ignore?

The horizon looked bent like a rainbow and I lost all sense of direction. Frightened, I ran to the water's edge, lay face down on the wet sand, and pressed my cheek into the cold grit. I closed my eyes, pretending I was on my Bandon beach. I hugged the ground for a long time.

Finally my vision cleared and I began shivering, so I stood up to walk along the sand. Near the cement wall of a storm drain I saw a dark figure enclosed in a blanket. I turned and walked in the other direction.

I focused on the lights marking the curve of the bay down to the Palos Verdes peninsula. I could make out the Marina high-rises—Nick's neighborhood. Be honest, I said.

Maybe when I dressed so carefully to avoid Nick's criticism, I was also trying to look appealing. Maybe while I was analyzing his love for me, I was secretly enjoying it. Wasn't there some part of me that *wanted* Nick to dream of me at night, wake up in a sweat, gulping for air, his hard-on a lead weight, hurting? Wasn't it payback for those skinny, stuck-up boys who never asked me to dance? For Pallen? For my dad, who let me down again and again, raved about other women, and never even told me I was pretty?

Now I reeled at the possibilities. Maybe I *allowed* Nick to see the name Mustard in my appointment book? Hadn't I, knowing he might be there, gone anyway? Maybe I *ignored* the warning signs of his desire for death. Didn't I know the idea of death as a beautiful woman was a suicidal fantasy? And worst of all, didn't I try to get rid of him on the anniversary of his mother's death?

And now that I was at it, what else was I hiding from myself? What was all that coughing and choking about?

One thing was sure: I needed psychotherapy. Badly. My life, founded on the principle of self-knowledge, was a sham.

Relieved to admit this to myself, my senses returned. As I headed toward my car, I saw the figure, still wrapped in a blanket, coming my way. I walked straight back up the sand to the parking lot. As I quickened my step, I glanced behind me to see the person speed up to follow me. I broke into a run, made it to the car, and locked myself in before he knocked on the window. Shaking, I started the car and backed up. The man stood in the beam of my headlights, one filthy hand outstretched. His hair was stringy. He was wearing three coats. From my purse below the seat I grabbed a five-dollar bill and tossed it out the window before driving away. He ran after it.

When I returned, the house was quiet. Frank greeted me at the door with a whine, and I knew he hadn't had his dinner yet. I filled his bowl, removed a half-empty bottle of Chablis from the refrigerator, and went to sit on the sofa in the dark.

My mother turned on the hall light and came out in her nightgown. "Are you okay?" she asked softly.

I turned on a lamp in the living room and nodded. "Want to sit down and talk to me?"

"Let me get my robe."

When she returned, she settled herself in the chair opposite me.

I looked into my mother's face, every square inch imprinted on my brain, so that sometimes before I went to sleep I could see perfectly the soft eyes, the crooked mouth, the mole over her left eyebrow, the bags under her eyes. "I'm sorry." I took a swig out of the bottle.

"I'm sorry, too."

"I'm really scared, Mom. Of a thousand things. But worst of all, I'm afraid of what might come out at the trial."

Her eyes were serious and dark. "Honey, did you sleep with that man?"

"Honest on a stack of Bibles, I didn't."

"Then what are you afraid might come out?"

"That I drove him to suicide."

"Did you?"

"Maybe. Partly." I pressed my clenched fist against my mouth.

She looked down at her stubby fingers. "I don't know anything about your business, but I think you'd better try to understand why you would do that."

I nodded and began crying. "I'm going to go back into therapy."

Mom joined me on the sofa and held my hand. "I know one thing. You're going to be harder on yourself than any judge or jury out there. Once you get through the trial you're putting yourself through, you'll be able to handle the public one."

I smiled a little through my tears, raised her hand to my lips and kissed it lightly. "You're probably right. When did you get so wise?"

"I've been convicted in a few trials of my own."

52

Moving day was so hectic it didn't seem as awful as I'd anticipated. Val and Gordon rented a big van and the three of us did the heavy lifting, while Mom stacked the smaller boxes. After they left for the apartment, I stayed to lock up, and was alone for the last time in my empty house.

The final reality hit me—my lovely house, my monument to self-sufficiency—was irrevocably gone.

I wandered through the empty rooms. I touched walls, noticed a spot that needed paint here, a tile coming loose there. Glancing through the kitchen window to the backyard, I thought of the party where Frank had gorged himself. In the dining room I saw Nick standing at the window, holding the curtain aside. In the bedroom, the memory of my first night with Humberto tormented me. I crouched down on the floor and ran my hand over the painted floral pattern that I had loved so much. "Good-bye," I said.

The house was my real lover—the one I trusted and cared for and counted on. Back in the dining room, I lay face down, spread-eagle on the hardwood floor as if I could reach out my limbs wide enough to hug it. My tears made little white spots in the waxed surface.

Finally, I rose and turned away from it. As I stood on the front stair locking the door for the last time, Mr. Slewicki saw me and came over. On Underbruck's advice, I said nothing to him about the trial. "Would you check on the roses once in a while?" I asked. "Just for me?"

"Sure, sure. Sorry to see you go," he said, gruffly. "You were good neighbor. Frank too. Any time, you come by for soup bone. Any time."

I shook his hand and headed for my car.

"Doctor—"

I turned back.

"Your case—even if you don't win, you're a winner."

"Thanks." I smiled sadly.

The apartment was a shock after my pretty little house. I had sold most of my furniture, and all that remained was a sofa bed, the dining-table set, coffee table, bed, and exercycle. The new place was so small it was cluttered by even those few things.

That night, after my mother had retired to my bedroom to sleep, I lay on the sofa bed wide awake, depressed, staring at shadows on the ceiling. It was dark in this little space, shabby and noisy. Loud music from the apartment below vibrated the floor. Voices leaked through the cracks of the door and the windows. It was like being back in college, except it wasn't fun anymore, I wasn't nineteen, and poverty was no longer an adventure.

In the morning before my mother left, I thanked her for working so hard, and admitted I would be lonely without her. "I don't even want to have anybody over here," I said.

"The people who love you don't care where you live." She hugged me tightly.

I did not feel lovable. That night, alone for the first time in my apartment, I cried into my pillow so my new neighbors wouldn't hear me.

For my therapist I chose Dr. Beryl Dandelone, a psychoanalyst who was chief of clinical services at the Family Institute of L.A. She was a plain woman in her mid-fifties who wore low-heeled shoes, no makeup, and dark suits that covered her full figure. I had seen her at a couple of conferences, read both her books, and heard only good things about her from my colleagues. I knew she smoked cigars, and it was rumored she cracked walnuts with her teeth, but she was a singularly clear-thinking analyst, and that's what I needed.

On my first appointment, she escorted me through the Institute to her private office. It was crammed with furniture—a desk, a couch, and three comfortable chairs—and cluttered with books, manuscripts, journals, and small statues of primitive South American art. She said she never smoked except when alone in the office, but the masculine scent of cigars permeated the room.

It was easy to talk to her. I spoke almost nonstop for forty minutes, pouring out the pent-up anguish I'd been struggling to contain so long. When I reached the subject of Nick's therapy, I said, "I've got to understand what happened. Why I was so drawn to him, and why I later felt I was going to choke to death in his presence."

Dandelone said it would take time to uncover the answers to those questions.

I began weeping. "I feel like such a failure."

She looked at me thoughtfully, not deterred by my tears. "It sounds like you define yourself solely by your achievements."

"That's exactly right," I blubbered. "I started by knocking myself out to please my father, but then I never stopped."

"Why don't we try to find out what's underneath that?"

Continuing to cry, I nodded. I was in the hands of a brilliant clinician, and now that I was made vulnerable by the cracked shell of my life, I was prepared for the first time since adolescence to ask all questions of myself.

"See you Wednesday at seven," she said, and I was comforted by the familiar rhythm of therapy, even though, this time, I was on the other side.

I saw her three times a week after that, lying on the couch, where I gradually began to feel safe. The cost was beyond what I could afford, but I sacrificed everything else because I needed it so much.

I knew how to be a good patient. I analyzed my own dreams, I free-associated, I even explored my feelings for her—my envy of her position, my longing for the wise and strong mother I never had.

Some part of each session I devoted to talking about Humberto, because I was lonely and still unable to call him or respond to his overtures.

One session she said, "You were afraid if you got too close to Humberto, you would disappear."

"But it wasn't just him. I've left every man I've been involved with."

"Yes. And even with me you're afraid if you get too close, you will disappear."

After that session I called Humberto. Our conversation was awkward and stilted.

"I'm sorry you're going through such an ordeal," he offered.

"I guess this whole year's been hard for you too."

There was a long silence at the other end, and then, "Yes."

"My mother still likes you."

"She understands you better than you do."

My temper flared. "I don't think so."

He changed to less volatile subjects and we caught up on some of what had transpired over the last seven months, each of us trying to avoid any subject that would provoke the other. Finally he suggested we get together for dinner.

"Would lunch be okay?" I asked. A time-limited meeting during the day seemed more manageable.

"Sure. The Seaview in Malibu?"

"Fine." I didn't know how it would go, or how I would feel, but I missed him too much not to test the waters.

Our lunch was amiable. I told him he looked thin, and he told me my new hairdo was pretty. It was strange to sit so formally across the table from him, as if our shoes hadn't been scrambled together in the same closet, as if he didn't know every square inch of my body.

When he asked about my case, I said, "I don't think we should talk about it. Maybe when the trial's over." I knew he still wasn't sure whether I'd slept with Nick and I couldn't bear that mistrust.

He placed his hand over mine. "I'm sorry for doubting you."

"Hey—even my mother's not sure. It's just something I live with. Anyway, I'm in analysis—there's a lot I have to figure out."

"I'd like to hear about it." He stroked my fingers a few moments, and then said, "I actually went to see somebody myself."

It was the last thing I expected from him. "Who?"

He mentioned the name of a prominent Beverly Hills psychiatrist. "And one of the things I've talked about is my problem of wanting such accomplished women—Marisombra and you—and having trouble living with them."

"So you don't blame me for everything that went wrong between us?"

He smiled. "Not entirely."

We agreed to keep in touch. In the parking lot he gave me a peck on the cheek.

53

Despite the grave self-doubts about my professional competence, I forced myself to continue working to the best of my ability, but my work consisted mostly of good-byes.

William announced that he and Ruth were going on vacation to England. "I've arranged a tour of our former estate," he said. "I'm hoping if I hang onto Ruth she'll protect me from the ghosts."

"Good luck," I replied. "I hope it goes well."

"And good luck with your lawsuit. Maybe the whole thing will be settled out of court."

I smiled and said I would see him upon his return. I knew Nick wouldn't settle—even for the million-dollar limit of my insurance policy.

I was also getting to the end of my time with the interns' group. After they finished their stint at the V.A., we met once a week in my office to discuss cases and work on their preparation for the psychology licensing exam. It was ironic that just as they might be receiving their licenses, I might be losing mine.

I met with them in August for the last time. The licensing exam was in October and they would gear up for the final push by taking an intensive two-week review course in September. With my impending trial, I was sorry to lose even their small fee.

They brought a chocolate torte, a thermos full of coffee, paper plates, forks, and napkins. The computer whiz, having been elected spokesman, said, "There's no way we can tell you how much you've done for us."

I said, "It's been a privilege to watch you blossom into real professionals. Thank you for allowing me to participate."

The women were moist-eyed, and I could hardly swallow my cake. I felt that every part of my life was built on earthquake faults, and the ground was shifting frequently.

In the waiting room I wished them luck on their exams and told them I knew they would all pass. As they stood at the door, one of the women said, "We know you're going to be vindicated, but it's a shame you have to go through this lawsuit." The spokesman capped off the good-bye by saying, "Personally, I'd like to rearrange the guy's face."

We all laughed.

After they left I had a strange pang of missing Nick. It was ridiculous under the circumstances, but I couldn't shake it. I sat down in my chair and closed my eyes. I could see his face, hear his voice, smell his fragrance as subtle and sweet as a baby after a bath.

I had hurt him. I didn't deserve the lawsuit, but I had done something wrong, and I still didn't know why. This private guilt gnawed at my insides like a sewer rat. If I couldn't unlock the reason, I couldn't trust myself with other patients in the future—if I had a professional future.

The Romaine sisters finally succumbed to the publicity about me. "We're-so-busy-shopping-you-know. Personal-shoppers-uh-huh-uh-huh." They nodded emphatically.

For their daily rounds they were now wearing lavender sharkskin suits with rhinestone buttons, black pillbox hats, and black cotton gloves. "Our-customers-clamor-for-more-time, isn't-that-right, May," said Joy. "Right-right-right," said Joy. "*No*-time-for-therapy."

I relinquished their treatment with relief, actually surprised at how well they had done. They had a fledgling business, and May had shown an ability to sound normal on the phone, by which she made all the customer arrangements. I'm sure their clients were taken aback by their appearance and mannerisms at first sight, but the Romaines must have been providing a good service, because their business was burgeoning.

For their last session, they brought me one of their white baskets, with a *Fodor's Travel Guide to the Caribbean* and a sun hat. "Good-luck, good-luck," they echoed down the hall. I waved to them affectionately.

William returned from England flushed with happiness. The visit to his former home had been difficult but productive. In his father's old bedchamber, he examined one wall until he found the configuration in the stone that had always looked like an elf's face to him. He remembered fixing his eyes on that spot while his father lectured him.

Talking to his sister about their father's plight, seeing at once how much of his own cowardice had led to the sequence of events, William was able to forgive his father to some extent, and to forgive himself.

"Dr. Rinsley, I'm very grateful to you," he said. "The straitjacket which has constrained me my whole life has been removed." He blinked rapidly and looked away from me.

William was winding up his therapy and he was one of the few patients whose termination from treatment was not motivated by my situation. Our work together and his life circumstances had resulted in remarkable growth and change.

I was sad to think of him leaving. He meant a great deal to me. Yet I was preparing myself for a battle that required my full attention, and I planned to finish with every patient before my trial. I had no idea if I would be free to practice afterward, or if I would even want to. Under the circumstances, my office landlord agreed to let me out of my lease before the trial.

I still had four patient hours a week, and with the salaries from my consulting jobs I was able to make ends meet if I gave up all luxuries. To save money, I shopped and cooked for myself, and even learned how to make one of those beautiful Tarte Tatins, although I had to call the chef at Mustard for some advice on how to caramelize the apples.

One morning, I fought depression and loneliness by making the two-hour trip down to Del Mar to watch the horse races. I sat in the bleacher seats, amid college kids, welfare mothers, and migrant workers, and bet two-dollar tickets on horses with fast-sounding names. I even won twenty dollars.

I did continue to follow the dermatologist's regimen, and I saw significant improvement in my skin problems, for which I was grateful to Underbruck. I was most surprised by the acquisition of contact lenses. For the first time, I was fitted with a pair that didn't hurt, I had peripheral vision, and I didn't have that thing on my face, separating me from other people.

Later that month Humberto called me, mentioning he'd heard I was baking apple tarts. I said how absurd that must have seemed after everything that had happened. He offered to come over and help.

"No. My feelings are so jumbled I need time to think. I don't know who I am anymore. Could we just talk on the phone once in a while?"

After that he called me every Sunday morning. Maybe it was to see if I had someone else in my bed after a Saturday night, but I was always there alone. He mentioned dinners and parties he was attending, and although he tactfully skirted the subject, I knew he was dating. I wasn't prepared for anything more than a friendship with him at that time, so I swallowed my feelings.

Although I talked to Val every day and she remained my mainstay of support, the one friend I actually spent the most time with was Linda Morrison. She was the only person I knew who was free during the day, because she worked the evening shift, and many mornings I went over to her house for a walk along the canals.

One day, when we'd strolled along the Venice boardwalk and sat down at a beachside cafe, I told her, "I hate my apartment. It's so ugly and dark, and that green shag rug looks like a roomful of vomit."

"You can't get rid of the shag, but you can change the color. It's a trick I learned from a carpet layer I dated last year. Get one of those do-it-yourself rug shampooers, and instead of using the solutions they sell, use bleach, diluted half with water. It won't damage the shampoo equipment, but it'll bleach the rug. The only thing is you'll have to leave for a day because it stinks."

"Are you serious?"

"Absolutely! I'll help you do it."

The following Sunday, Linda and I bleached the carpet and I took Frank to her house and spent the night. I slept soundly in a sleeping bag, although I was sore and stiff in the morning. It was nice to be in a house again. Around noon, she dropped off Frank and me outside my apartment building.

I got quite a shock when I walked across the newly bleached carpet. It looked a wonderful color, a pale cucumber, but with each step I took, the fibers of shag rug disintegrated, leaving footprints of bare weave. Frank ran around, stirring up small clouds of the pale dust and getting covered in the stuff.

I called Linda and left a message on her machine. "What am I going to do? It looks like the rug has mange!" The absurdity of it all made me burst into a gale of laughter—the best laugh I'd had in many months.

"Gosh, sweetie," Linda giggled when she called back. "We must have used the wrong proportions. It was probably a cup of bleach for the whole thing. Try vacuuming."

I vacuumed for hours until my neighbor finally banged on the wall.

The shag hairs had disintegrated unevenly, leaving a swirling pattern of short and long fibers, like a sculptured carpet. When I was done, it looked like those haircuts where men shave initials into the side of their head. I sat down and laughed, but really I didn't care, because that revolting color was gone, and in its place was something clean and restful-looking, albeit rather odd. The place smelled like bleach for weeks.

For his last session, William arrived with a gift—a first edition of Freud's *Interpretation of Dreams*.

"What a beautiful present," I said, touched at his thoughtfulness. "Thank you so much."

We talked about the past and the future, and reminisced about his early months of treatment when he lay on the couch in tongue-tied silence. He added, "Ruth says what matters most about love is having a person next to you in bed, who pats you when you're having a bad dream."

My eyes filled with tears and I looked down to conceal them. I was living a bad dream. I wanted someone in bed next to me, patting me.

"She calls me her swan song, because she's planning to go out by my side."

"And you?"

"As soon as the divorce is final, I'm going to propose to her. I'm already planning how I'll do it."

I smiled, and reminded William of how far he had come from the days of his three dreaded Rs—responsibility, risk, and rejection.

He said, "I've faced death and had a temporary reprieve. At the end, you realize that what you thought protected you actually robbed you of your life."

I embraced him before he left and thanked him again for the book. "But seeing you like this is the best thanks of all," I said, and meant it most sincerely.

After he closed the door behind him, I wept. It was like being at a child's graduation from college, and I wept for the passing of time, and for our accomplishment together, and for death, and for all the good-byes I would say throughout my life.

At the end of September, I vacated my office and put the furniture in storage.

Part V

55

A week before the trial there was a new surge of media attention to "patient-therapist sex syndrome." Uncle Silky must have seen something back in Louisiana, because he sent me his favorite baseball glove for luck. I stopped reading the paper and watching TV, but even in the supermarket, people whispered and pointed at me. The trial was scheduled for Court TV.

My mother insisted on coming to stay with me during the trial. When I told Humberto, he said, "Last time your mom visited, didn't Frank make her asthma worse?"

"Yes. I'm going to have to kennel him."

"Why don't I keep him at my house while she's here?"

I was touched by his offer, and even though I had been reticent to impose on him in any way, I accepted. I hated to put Frank in a kennel for four or five weeks.

The night of my mother's arrival, Humberto took us to Paradise for dinner. Although we had talked on the phone, it was the first time he had seen me since my cosmetic work had been completed. He took both my hands in his and said, "You look truly lovely, Sarah." My mother beamed.

At dinner, Humberto and Mom treated each other as if they were on a first date. He poured her wine, discussed the menu, and made sure there were no interruptions. At the end of the evening when he came in to pick up Frank, he said, "I don't believe I've ever seen a carpet quite like this." I laughed and told him the story.

Before he left, Humberto gave me a quick kiss on the mouth, and said, "I'll be thinking about you." Frank marched off with him dutifully, yanking on the choke chain to smell something just out of leash range. I closed the door and sagged back into the fear of facing the next day.

Beginning with the preliminary proceedings of the trial, I arrived at Underbruck's office early each morning so we could drive to court together. We went back to his office at the end of each day, to review it and prepare for the next. Sometimes I didn't get home until midnight.

The most critical part of the preliminary proceedings was selection of the jury. Underbruck tried to eliminate all potential jurors who'd had a bad experience in therapy, and Atwater tried to eliminate all those who'd had a good experience in therapy. The result was that anyone who'd been in therapy at all was eliminated.

Fourteen jurors were selected in case some had to drop out during the trial. Several seemed friendly, including an aging surfer with a sunburned face, and a salesclerk from The Gap. The rest seemed fairly impartial—a number of retired men, a Japanese art dealer, a Mexican-American dog groomer, two housewives, a construction worker, and a weathered-looking cab driver.

There were one hundred and eighty-two exhibits, which included a pair of panties Nick had stolen from my bedroom, photographs of my office and home, a state pamphlet describing the laws relating to the practice of psychology, videotapes of pretrial depositions, and a stack of medical records.

The judge was Samuel Grabbe, a lean, sallow man with a face like a dried apple. He had a thin mustache, a few strips of long hair that were combed over his bald skull, and he spoke in sharp, irritable bursts. He seemed like a man who would turn away Girl Scouts selling cookies.

The first day of the actual trial, I dried my hair the way Xavier had shown me, applied my new makeup carefully, and finished by putting in my contact lenses. I wore a powder blue suit, a peach silk blouse with a short strand of pearls, gray pantyhose, and navy pumps. My mother said I looked perfect, but by six-thirty in the morning, my mouth was dry and my hands were trembling. Nick was going to be there, and I had not seen him since his deposition.

I stopped for one last examination of myself in the mirror, and tried to imagine how I would look to him. Before I turned away I knew that without realizing it consciously, I had agreed to cosmetic changes to defy Nick. I tested a smile. It was prettier than I'd ever remembered.

When I met Underbruck at his office, he said, "You look terrific, kid—even though you resisted it." He seemed both relaxed and excited, with the taste of battle in his mouth. "Occasionally look directly at the jury and smile slightly," he advised. "Don't fidget. Keep your hands in your lap. Don't look at Nick, it'll throw you off. Keep your notebook handy and if anything comes to mind, write it down. And Sarah, Atwater's a pistol, so prepare yourself for her opening argument. Just keep in mind the jury has to go on the evidence, and we've got plenty of ammunition."

I was surprised by how protected I felt.

Although he spirited me into the courthouse via the side entrance, a swarm of ambitious reporters converged on us, frightening me with their pushing and questions. I clung to Underbruck's arm as he steered me up the escalator to the third floor where our courtroom was located.

The Sheriff's Department had provided a press table at the far end of the long hallway, and demanded that the reporters line up against the wall in preparation for admission to the courtroom. No cameras or tape recorders were allowed inside except the official ones set up for Court TV.

In front of our locked courtroom a crowd was already gathered around Atwater and Nick. I was probably as surprised by Nick's appearance as he was by mine. He was handsome and fit again, the weight back on his face, and a healthy sheen to his skin.

When he looked at me, he smiled the old I've-got-you smile. I felt sick to my stomach and turned away quickly. New curls and contact lenses couldn't cover up how vulnerable I still felt in his presence.

Reporters continued to pester us. "I'm confident my client will be found innocent," Underbruck said firmly, and I said, "No comment." I could barely see for a few minutes because of the flashbulbs.

As the bailiff unlocked the courtroom, Underbruck's junior attorneys arrived, hauling five large boxes full of documents loaded onto portable luggage racks.

The courtroom was a drab melange of browns made duller by fluorescent ceiling panels covered in a wooden grid. The only permanent color came from the two flags—the California on the right, behind the jury box, and the American on the left near the entrance to the judge's chambers. Two cameras for Court TV were in place.

The seats behind the bar quickly filled with spectators and reporters, most of whom were there to hear Atwater. I was glad the plaintiff's and defendant's tables were in a long straight line, because once we were all seated, I couldn't see Nick without making a special effort to do so.

I was surprised by how much contact everyone had with each other—jurors, plaintiffs, and defendants milling around together in the hallways, spectators shopping one courtroom to the next for an interesting trial. Only artificial walls were erected—the silent glances of opponents, whispered communications between clients and attorneys, protocol and decorum.

Before we began, Judge Grabbe threw out every spectator who didn't have a seat, and warned the reporters he'd evict them if they asked questions of any of us inside the courtroom. Then the jurors silently filed in.

During the proceedings Judge Grabbe's long bony fingers riffled through stacks of paper, and seemed never to be still. He looked at me occasionally with a piercing stare, and on those occasions I smiled slightly and tried to meet his gaze.

To calm myself, I focused on the bailiff, a trim black woman who looked quite shapely in her khaki uniform. Her eyebrows had been plucked out and replaced with a thin pencil-line that slanted upwards, her hair was straightened and combed into a pageboy, and she wore gold hoop earrings. Her nametag read "Violet Knight." In the same way I'd watched the pores on my dentist's nose to distract me from his procedures, I concentrated on this woman's earrings and eyebrows, and tried to imagine what she was saying as she chatted comfortably with the court clerk.

For her opening argument, Leona Hale Atwater stepped to the podium, a look of sincere concern on her predatory features. As Underbruck had predicted, her designer suits and high heels were gone. With her clear French manicure, rose-colored lips, and conservative suit, she looked decent and unpretentious.

"Ladies and gentlemen," she began. "When Mr. Arnholt was referred to Dr. Rinsley, he had a good job at a prestigious law firm, he was dating women regularly, and he had never made a suicide attempt or been seriously depressed. Now he's a ruined man, unable to work, unable to think clearly, and unable to have a relationship with a woman. And we believe the evidence you are about to hear will prove that the treatment he received by Dr. Rinsley is directly responsible for his ruin.

"Why do we believe this? Because this man grew to love his therapist and desire her physically, and unfortunately the feeling was mutual. But instead of referring him to another therapist as she should have, Dr. Rinsley did the unthinkable! She had sex with Mr. Arnholt, and *then* tried to refer him elsewhere!"

There were exchanged looks and raised eyebrows among the jury.

I was furious that Atwater had begun by stating Nick's lie as simple fact. Underbruck leaned over and whispered in my ear, "Stop shaking your head. Keep your face neutral." I tried.

Atwater stepped from behind the podium and began pacing in front of the jury box. Her gaze was direct, her words clear and steady. She looked as confident and masterful as an Olympic diver teaching a group of new swimmers.

"Ladies and gentlemen, you might ask, what would be so harmful in a patient having a love affair with his doctor? Suffice it to say at this point that in many ways the patient feels toward the therapist the way a small child feels toward a parent. Therapist-patient sex is very much like incest, and the consequences are equally harmful."

As Atwater continued, I inched back my chair so I had an unobstructed view of Nick. Unaware of my gaze, he watched Atwater, and I took the opportunity to study his thick, dark hair, his perfectly tailored suit, his argyle socks in those expensive loafers. How much of his pain had been real? How much of all this was a Machiavellian plot to improve his life?

"Now Dr. Rinsley contests Mr. Arnholt's claim of sexual contact, but the evidence will also show that Dr. Rinsley did Mr. Arnholt substantial harm aside from the sexual issue. She misdiagnosed him, failed to provide the proper treatment for him, and mismanaged the therapy, allowing her work to fall below the recognized standard of care."

She held up an APA brochure and stabbed it with her manicured finger. "That's why the code of ethics of the American Psychological Association is so important!" she spouted loudly. "Because in psychotherapy, it's so difficult for you to know whether you're getting the proper treatment, and you have to rely on the conscience and good judgment of your psychotherapist. And what do the ethical principles say? Don't keep treating someone who isn't getting better! Don't use the patient to gratify your personal needs, particularly sexual needs!"

The phone on Violet Knight's desk rang, and she picked it up and spoke so quietly no one could hear her. A learned skill, I thought.

"And let me address another issue," Atwater said. "You are going to hear the doctor's attorney talk about how sick Mr. Arnholt was even before Dr. Rinsley saw him. But the law on this issue is clear: a doctor takes her patients the way she finds them."

Atwater left the podium, walked quickly to her table, and from a large cardboard box retrieved a two-foot-high, shiny black vase. Carrying the vase, she walked back past her podium and set the vase on the court clerk's desk, in front of the jury. "Let's say there's a ceramic vase on a table, and someone comes by and knocks it off the table. Let's suppose it falls on the floor, and doesn't shatter, but only gets a crack in it. It can still hold water; it can still hold flowers. Now, someone else comes along and knocks that vase off the table again, and *because it already had a crack in it,* this time it shatters."

She waited for this to sink in, and then said, "Well, before Dr. Rinsley saw Mr. Arnholt, he was a cracked vase. He admits he had some problems or he wouldn't have sought help in the first place. But he was functioning. And functioning well! When he came to see Dr. Rinsley, his life was holding water. His flowers were blooming. And then he began treatment with her and the vase shattered, and look at him now—unable to function, perhaps ever again."

Atwater walked over to her section of the counsel table, picked up the empty packing box, returned and placed it on the carpet in front of the jury. Then suddenly, she grabbed her black vase, squeezed it around the middle with both hands, and it fell apart into a pile of rubble in the box at her feet. The entire courtroom was as silent as a field of new fallen snow.

Atwater said, "That's what happened in this case when Dr. Rinsley committed the malpractice she did, and the intentional infliction of emotional distress on Mr. Arnholt!" The shocked silence was broken by sudden, uncontrolled conversation, until Judge Grabbe pounded his gavel repeatedly and called, "Order!"

I realized Atwater must have had someone painstakingly glue that vase back together and paint a thin glaze on it so it looked normal until she squeezed it. I turned to look at Nick, who sat with a grave expression on his face—the perfect portrait of a broken man.

When the courtroom was quiet again, and Atwater had returned her box of rubble to her table, she resumed her position at the podium and said to the judge, "I apologize for that disruption, Your Honor. I felt there was no other way to state clearly how strongly I think Mr. Arnholt has been damaged."

The judge looked at her coldly and snapped back, "One more performance like that and you'll see how strongly I can think about cutting your argument short."

"Thank you, Your Honor," Atwater said contritely, and stayed at the podium to wrap up. She finished with this: "Ladies and gentlemen, I am satisfied that when you have reviewed the evidence about to be presented, you will find the defendant liable for sexual misconduct, gross negligence, and intentional infliction of emotional harm, and you will award both compensatory and punitive damages to my client." She left the podium and returned to her counsel table, the cheap satin lining of her skirt rustling as she passed.

It took every ounce of my will to keep my face immobile. What proof was there that I hadn't slept with Nick? What evidence of how sick he was when he came to see me? No previous psychiatric records, no history of poor school performance, or drug charges, or gross violations in the military. I prayed for strength, and for eloquence from Underbruck, even though I didn't believe in God or even very much in Underbruck.

After a tortuous lunch break, in which Underbruck couldn't sit still and I couldn't eat, he gave his opening argument. His unbuttoned suit jacket barely reached across his belly, and his pant legs were so long they crumpled over the top of his shoes. I could tell by the slightly higher tone of his voice that he was nervous. He gripped the podium with both hands to steady himself.

"Weren't we all dazzled by Ms. Atwater's demonstration? Couldn't we feel Mr. Arnholt breaking into a million pieces from the pressure of Dr. Rinsley's heavy-handed work? But as dramatic as that demonstration was, it *does not represent the truth.*" He pounded the podium with each word for emphasis. Then he pointed at Nick. "When Dr. Rinsley saw this man for the first time, he was *more* than a cracked vase; he was a *broken* vase, no more well-glued together than the one Ms. Atwater so kindly showed us today. *But* he was broken in a particular way. You are going to hear evidence that Mr. Arnholt *lied* when it was convenient; he *manipulated* women; he *stole* from those close to him. His illness—his ability to lie and manipulate—is what brought us here today, *not* Dr. Rinsley's treatment of him.

"Now how am I going to clear the name of a competent, reputable psychologist whose patient lies? The answer is that I am going to need your help. I will have to rely on you to sort through the complex and technical testimony of experts. But I am confident that when you do, you will conclude that Mr. Arnholt is a slick, smart attorney who's savvy about the law and wants to pull the wool over your eyes in accusing his therapist!"

He reached up and scratched his head, smoothed his hair, and adjusted his reading glasses. Then he let go of the podium and approached the jury to look at them directly.

"You are going to hear evidence from respected experts that Dr. Rinsley provided psychological treatment to Mr. Arnholt that was *above* community standards. Dr. Rinsley showed extreme tolerance with Mr. Arnholt. She explained to him ahead of time the therapy might be painful. She stuck by him through many crises. She made herself available to him for his emergencies, and she sought consultation on his treatment to make sure she was handling it properly."

Underbruck paced back and forth in front of the jurors, but he had no cracked vase to crush, just words, diminished slightly by the large ketchup stain he had acquired on his white shirt during lunch.

"Given his problems and his history, it was inevitable Mr. Arnholt's therapy would be difficult. Now you might say, the man made a suicide attempt and that proves he sustained damage. But I say, not necessarily! Mr. Arnholt called 911. He wanted to live. And perhaps this suicide attempt was a calculated act, thought out ahead of time, to destroy his doctor."

There was a commotion at the plaintiff's table as Nick shoved back his chair in disgust and blurted out, "I can't believe this!" Atwater immediately leaned over to him and calmed him. The judge issued a warning about any further outbursts and Atwater apologized on Nick's behalf.

Underbruck ran his hand through his hair, stepped over to our table and took a sip of water, then continued. His belt was now well below his belly, which was forcing a gap between buttons.

"And what about Mr. Arnholt's role in all this? If he felt he was being so inadequately treated, why didn't he speak up? Why didn't he leave the therapy? Why didn't he seek consultation himself?" Underbruck threw up his arms and bellowed, "I ask you, who better than an attorney would know his rights? The answer is that Mr. Arnholt *knew* he was getting the right treatment, and that's why he stayed!"

After he paused for a minute to let that sink in, Underbruck moved to the jury box for his final big point. "Ladies and gentlemen, I want to propose to you what I think really happened in this case. Mr. Arnholt was a vain man. He was a womanizer and he enjoyed the conquests. But Dr. Rinsley was a woman he couldn't have, and the fact that she did not want to abandon the therapy and have a love affair with him was something Mr. Arnholt *could not stomach*. The truth is that Mr. Arnholt, in a rage over his failure to seduce Dr. Rinsley, made a manipulative and safe suicide attempt, and fabricated this sex story to seek his revenge—the most damaging revenge he could wreak upon a professional woman—and in the process gain himself some money."

Again there was a commotion at the plaintiff's table, but this time Atwater yelled, "Objection!" as she sprang to her feet. "Your Honor,

I have sat here patiently listening to counsel's argument, but this is unconscionable. It is an inflammatory and derogatory picture of my client which has no relation to the available evidence!"

Judge Grabbe said quietly into his microphone, "We've tolerated plenty of antics from you, Counsel. And may I remind you, this is argument. Overruled."

Underbruck finished up. "After all the expert testimony is presented, you will have to decide whose version of the story is the truth, and in some areas none of us may ever know. But one thing will become crystal clear to you: when Mr. Arnholt first arrived at Dr. Rinsley's door, he was a much sicker man than Ms. Atwater would like you to think. And sometimes a doctor can do everything right and still lose the patient."

Underbruck sat down, pink-cheeked and fragrant with sweat. He'd done well and I felt we were at least on even ground.

56

That week I admitted to Dandelone that I had enjoyed sparring with Nick at the beginning of his treatment. "He was such a tough nut to crack. I was determined not to let him get the best of me."

"And what constitutes getting the best of you?"

"Defeating me. Making me give up. My father always thought that was the worst thing you could do—probably because he walked away from baseball."

"And even though your father allowed himself the luxury of giving up, he insisted you keep trying endlessly?"

"I guess so. He always excused himself the same way: 'I had a major-league arm, Sare. Just had a bum season. And I was damned if I'd play the coffee-and-cakes route the rest of my life.' " I could see his eyes avoiding my face every time he said it. "Are there some patients *you* give up treating in the middle?"

"Some therapist-patient relationships are wrong from the start, like a bad marriage. If you're sharp enough you see it in the consultation. If not, you have to extricate yourself as soon as you know."

By the time I knew it with Nick, it was far too late.

• • •

Kevin Utley finally called to tell me he might have a job for me. "It would be a position created specially for you, assuming your name is cleared."

"Big assumption." I was irritated. Did I need a job dangled in front of me that might be forever out of reach?

"Come on, Sarah! You're one of the most ethical and responsible psychologists I've ever met! I'm sure a jury will see that."

"Who knows? Lawyers can slant the truth to make it look like lies."

Kevin said firmly, "I believe the truth will out. And when this is over, we'll have fun! I'll be sole administrator and you'll be chief of clinical services."

"Thanks. I appreciate your vote of confidence. But if I lose the case, do me one favor, okay? Don't call me for a few months, because I won't feel like talking to anyone."

"If you lose the case, it will be a grave injustice."

My irritation vanished in response to his faith in me and I thanked him again. After we said good-bye, I allowed myself to imagine that job—patients again, colleagues around, students to supervise, staff meetings in which to sit and drink coffee and share stupid jokes. It was a distant dream.

Atwater's first witness was Richard Oppenheimer, Chief Psychologist of the Stanford University Medical Center. An impressive figure, he was about sixty, comfortably solid in build, with clear blue eyes and a broad, warm smile. He joked casually with Atwater before taking the stand, obviously comfortable in the courtroom.

The meat of his testimony was this: that early in the treatment I had misdiagnosed Nick as a Narcissistic Personality Disorder, a fact documented in my notes; that I was remiss in not administering a test battery to him, and that if I had done so, it would have taken me much less time to figure out that he was Borderline; that I'd then failed to manage the treatment properly, failed to refer him to someone else as soon as sexual feelings between us became an issue, and failed to see the impending signs of suicide. For all of these reasons, my conduct had fallen below the accepted standard of care. As far as the sexual contact, he stated that "if it occurred, it was a flagrant violation of good clinical care by any competent therapist." His testimony was convincing, well thought out, and intelligent.

Atwater had her junior assistants haul in a huge white cardboard chart on which they had diagrammed the major events in Nick's therapy, plotting a graph that showed his progress. They placed this exhibit on an easel, facing the jury. The graph showed an erratic up-and-down course until it plunged sharply downward. As far as I was concerned the chart was fit for firewood, but it was dangerous, because such images are stronger than words.

Oppenheimer took the jury through the points on the graph, explaining every peak and valley, and emphasizing the terminal plunge. He was convincing in his low-key style, crisp dialogue, and apparent calm. He said as the result of treatment with me, Nick was now suffering from a severe depression, and prognosis for the future was "guarded."

Underbruck had hired an expert forensic psychologist to refute the man's claims later, but still, by four o'clock I had such an intense headache, I felt disoriented when I stood up. If Atwater's whole presentation was going to be this convincing, I was sure I had no chance.

At Underbruck's office later, I changed into warm-ups, and we ate sandwiches, Danish, and coffee from the deli downstairs, while we went over the day's testimony in detail, picking out the holes and weaknesses for tomorrow's cross-examination. When I arrived home at midnight, a few tenacious reporters were camped on my doorstep, but I told them I had nothing to say and slammed the door on them.

My mother was waiting up for me as usual, crocheting so fast her hands looked like moving wheels. Per my instructions she had neither answered the door or the phone, and I felt sorry for her, trapped in my dingy apartment. "Would you like to come to court with me tomorrow, Mom?"

"Oh, I'd just be in the way, honey. Don't worry about me. Just tell me how it's going." My cable TV service did not carry the Court TV channel.

I filled her in while I drank the glass of wine she poured. I noticed her fingernails were chewed to the quick.

Later I listened to my messages while I removed my clothes. There were two calls from Val, the second one saying I could call late, three from reporters, a couple of crank calls, one from Linda, and one from Humberto. I asked my mother to call Linda and Humberto in the morning to tell them I was okay. Then I phoned Val.

"It's the worst," I said. "Reporters following me, everybody staring. Nick strutting and carrying on."

"How awful. I just hope the truth comes out."

"You don't know how much it means to me knowing you believe me."

"Sisters for life," Val said softly. "And how is it going with your mom?"

"So-so." I knew Val understood that Mom was listening, and I had to be circumspect.

"Why don't you try to take advantage of her being there? Ask her to cook. Or design a dress."

"I can't eat. And what do I need a new dress for?"

"I might need one."

"Great. Why don't you come over?"

"I will. Saturday afternoon, okay?"

"Just a goddamn minute! Is this a *special* kind of dress?!"

"It might be."

"Val! Are you—is it a wedding dress?"

She laughed. "Yes! I wasn't going to tell you until after the trial, but I'd love to have your mom design me something."

We made plans for Saturday, and I felt genuinely thrilled for her. But later on the lumpy sofa bed, envy consumed me. She was finally getting it all together, while my life was falling apart.

The next morning when we resumed, I was disgusted to discover that Nick had developed a fan club. As we approached the courtroom, at least a dozen women were crowded around him, and he was actually signing autographs. When he caught my eye he gave me a sheepish grin. People idealize someone they don't know, I reminded myself.

Underbruck began his cross-examination of Oppenheimer with a barrage of questions: Aren't there patients who might be alienated by psychological testing? Isn't it true that a therapist operates on a "working diagnosis" and that often the diagnosis of the patient changes over time? Didn't a patient sometimes make a suicide attempt impulsively, with no prior warning?

The doctor was forced to acknowledge Underbruck's points, which brought the previous day's testimony back into perspective and balance, but suddenly a woman in the audience yelled, "Save us from doctors!" and as everybody turned to look, Nick raised his fist to her in approval and grinned before she was hauled out. Judge Grabbe banged his gavel to restore order.

Underbruck paced in front of the witness box to try to refocus. "Ladies and gentlemen, I said I was going to need your help, and obviously I do. Let's try to concentrate on the testimony, and ignore the surrounding circus."

Judge Grabbe helped us by adding his own comment: "I would like to emphasize that this is a court of law, not a street corner. No conclusions should be reached until all the evidence has been presented. Any further demonstrations like that will result in arrest."

Underbruck resumed cross-examination by approaching the question of sexual contact between Nick and me.

"Doctor, is it common for therapists to have sexual feelings for their patients?"

"It's common to have fleeting sexual thoughts and feelings. Less common to feel sustained desire."

"But even in some cases where the therapist does feel desire, might it be considered wise to continue the therapy, as long as the therapist can prevent those feelings from interfering?"

"Yes."

"Other than Mr. Arnholt's claim that Dr. Rinsley had sex with him, do you have any reason to believe Dr. Rinsley acted on her sexual feelings toward him?"

"I think the deterioration in his functioning is a sign of possible therapist sexual abuse."

"Might there not be many other factors accounting for that deterioration?"

"There might be."

Satisfied with that admission, Underbruck paused for a minute and searched through his notes. The jurors shifted in their seats, whispered and joked to one another.

Nick pushed his chair away from the table enough that I could see him out of the corner of my eye. He was looking at me, and I could feel his energy as if only the two of us were in the room. He's gloating about my admission of feelings for him, I thought. I turned to catch a quick glimpse of him, and he blew me a kiss. I turned back as if I'd seen nothing, but I could barely contain my fury.

What had ever turned me on about him? I picked at hangnails around my cuticles until one of them bled.

Underbruck continued with the goal of catching Oppenheimer in his own contradiction: if Nick had begun his therapy by being a Borderline, he would already be prone to bouts of depression and suicidal thinking, and therefore those symptoms couldn't be attributed to the therapy itself. He was successful in his goal, and gained considerable ground with that point, which pleased me.

"Doctor," Underbruck then asked, "is it common for Borderlines to lie? To cover up? Manipulate? Seek revenge for imagined hurts?"

Oppenheimer acknowledged that Borderlines, including Nick, were prone to such behaviors.

"And," Underbruck said, moving in for his final thrust, "if a patient fails to tell his therapist about suicidal thoughts, if a patient covers up or lies about his past, isn't it likely the therapist may develop an inaccurate picture of the patient?"

"Objection!" Atwater shouted, jumping to her feet. "Compound and argumentative!"

"Counsel," Judge Grabbe snapped, "in my chambers, please. We'll take a ten-minute recess."

When they emerged ten minutes later, Oppenheimer acknowledged that a therapist was in part dependent on the client's willingness to tell the truth. From the nods and whispers, the jury seemed to have gotten the message: if Nick hadn't told me the whole truth, I could have made innocent mistakes.

During the lunch break Underbruck explained why they had moved into chambers: Judge Grabbe was expecting a call from his stockbroker to see how the morning's selling had gone. I was appalled. My life was hanging in the balance and they were discussing futures.

That night when I arrived home, reporters were still hanging around my apartment building and rooting through the garbage. Ironically they provided some protection along the path to my door, and for that reason I didn't mind them there. It was not a security building and my notoriety made me a target.

Inside, my mother was surrounded by an array of bridal magazines, a sketch pad, and colored pencils. "How was the weasel today?"

"Infuriating, as usual." I made myself a drink and took off my shoes.

"I had to go to the market this afternoon and a couple of those reporters fired questions at me."

"Oh, shit. What did you say?"

"No comment, no comment, no comment."

I thanked her for her good judgment and complimented her on her new sketches of bridal gowns, but it was painful to feel her unspoken wish that she was designing the dress for me. I reminded myself of something Dandelone had said: "You like to please your mother almost as much as she likes to please you. That's why it's so hard for you not to comply with her wishes." I swallowed my feelings, and went to the bedroom to take off my clothes.

Later, I ignored the peeling grouting around the edges of the bathroom tile and sank into a hot bath, where I drank another glass of Chablis and considered what I would do if I lost my license.

Maybe it would be a relief after all this. But what if I owed so much money it would take ten years to pay it off? I could give lectures, or work for a spa catering to overweight women, or sell my story to one of those cable TV people who kept calling. But it all sounded bleak.

I shut my eyes and imagined I was on a raft in the surf of the Caribbean. Warm breezes, hot sun, an unknown man with me speaking a language I didn't understand, and didn't even want to know. Maybe I would drop out and live like that, away from everybody's expectations. If I needed to please as much as my mother did, I was tired of it.

57

That Saturday Val came over to meet my mother and talk about wedding plans. In anticipation of being a bride, Val had stopped overeating, and her cheeks looked more angular. She grabbed the bulk of her hair with both hands and piled it on top of her head. "What do you think? Up or down?"

"Up," I said. "Elegant and formal."

It was hard for me to participate in her planning. I missed Frank, I was dismally depressed about my own personal life, and my mother's enthusiasm was particularly grating, but I worked hard to hide my true mood. For a few hours I was even able to concentrate on dress designs and fabrics, and the debate over which hotel to use. Then the desire to run away and hide overtook me. Never had I felt more alone, and yet there was no place where I had a moment's solitude.

When I walked Val out to her car later, she said, "Would you be my maid of honor?"

"Of course!" There was no one's joy I wanted to share more.

We put our arms around each other and cried, each for our own reasons. Val said, "I feel guilty being happy when you're going through such hell."

"Don't. It wouldn't make me feel any better if you were unhappy too." I admitted later to Dandelone that wasn't true. I would have felt better if we were both on trial, just so I wasn't going through my ordeal alone. I hated myself for feeling that way, but after I said the words out loud, I realized the feeling wasn't as strong as my genuine love for Val, and I had even greater respect for the healing process of acknowledging destructive thoughts.

On Monday, Atwater continued her case with another expert who emphasized the importance of maintaining firm therapy boundaries with Borderlines.

On cross-examination, Underbruck attacked the claim that I had broken the boundary of therapy when I visited Nick in the Emergency Room.

"Doctor, is there any textbook you know that discusses whether a psychologist should visit an injured patient in the hospital?"

"No, not specifically."

"So each situation must be decided by the clinician at the moment, based on the unique circumstances?"

"Yes."

After a half-hour more of counter-attack, Underbruck asked his final question. "Doctor, do you always know six months into the treatment how much self-disclosure is good for a patient?"

"You don't always know anything in my work. That's why it's still considered an art."

That was a good one for us, and we took a ten-minute recess.

For relief, I slipped down the escalator to the floor below and sat on the bench in front of a family court. A man dressed in a black suit and alligator cowboy boots was talking heatedly with his lawyer. A few feet away, a beautiful woman, perhaps thirty-five, pretty enough to have been a model but now fading, argued with her own lawyer. The man and woman seemed as if they belonged together—she with her lovely blond hair and mean mouth, him with his arrogance and spreading middle, and I realized they were divorcing, and haggling over the contents of their home. I watched them for five minutes, imagining their initial romance, how pretty she must have looked to him with those big doll eyes, how promising he must have seemed to her with some big career ahead of him. And all the love and romance came down to disillusioned bickering over lamps and armoires and clocks. I hoped that didn't happen to Val and Gordon, and I felt sick with sadness thinking of the distance that had grown between me and Humberto.

When I returned to our courtroom, most of the reporters were still outside sending faxes and chattering on portable phones. The spectators remained in their seats so as not to lose them. Two young women in leather jackets and nose-rings held up a "We Love Nick" sign. A few budding lawyers were there, fresh-faced and well-dressed, taking notes. A middle-aged woman with short blond hair sat scribbling in a notebook—probably a late-bloomer student.

Our jury filed in, munching on peanuts and potato chips from the snack bar. It was odd for my fate to be in the hands of strangers who appeared so casual. They looked like a movie audience, waiting for the film to start.

Atwater next called to the stand Billy Checkers, an old law school friend of Nick's with whom he sometimes drank.

Billy wore an unstructured teal linen suit, a pink shirt buttoned up to the neck, and no tie. His dark blond hair was long on top and short on the sides.

He described the changes he'd seen in Nick during the time Nick was in treatment with me, how morose Nick had become, and how he didn't want to "party" anymore. The worst moment came when Billy described an evening with Nick a few months before Nick's suicide attempt.

Billy was engaged to be married and they went out to celebrate. "Four or five drinks later, Nick blubbered he was in love with his shrink and it was killing him."

I had a vague recollection of Nick telling me about that evening. My stomach churned and gurgled as I listened to the details. The jury members were entertained by Billy, as opposed to the droning of the experts.

"I'd never seen him like that. He actually had tears in his eyes. Man, that was somethin'. Said he would be with her twenty-four/seven if he could."

Leona Hale Atwater requested permission to approach the witness, walked slowly over to Billy, and said softly, "Can you tell us what twenty-four/seven means?"

"Well, you know," Billy said flatly, "twenty-four hours a day, seven days a week."

Atwater returned to her podium and the courtroom was entirely silent for a moment, comprehending the depth of Nick's obsession with me. I felt light-headed, until I forced myself to breathe slowly.

On Wednesday, they called Abner Van Handle to the stand. I resented Abner for preventing me from seeing Nick right after his suicide attempt. I believed if I'd had a chance to talk to Nick then, this whole disaster might have been averted.

Van Handle was a powerful witness. "Mr. Arnholt cried like a baby over Dr. Rinsley. He was adamant about the sex and I have no reason to disbelieve him. Neither in the Emergency Room nor later did he show any signs of impaired contact with reality."

I felt my case was a hopeless cause upon hearing this testimony. I could still see Nick weeping on my sofa, pleading for me. He was a convincing patient and it was easy to understand how Abner could have been taken in.

Atwater led Van Handle through a description of Nick's suicide attempt in a manner designed to highlight how close he had come to death. Underbruck countered with questions that undercut its importance, showing how little time there was between ingestion of the pills and Nick's call to 911.

It didn't matter how much ground Underbruck gained, a suicide attempt was a suicide attempt, and it stood, an accusation to my competence.

The day was rounded out by the appearance of my former neighbor, Mr. Slewicki. He had dressed very conservatively in a gray polyester suit and black shoes, but he did have a woman's engagement ring on his pinky finger.

He recounted his memory of Nick's visit simply, stating that from his observation, Nick's car was in my driveway a total of about an hour. Mr. Slewicki looked very nervous and his voice shook when he talked, which made it seem like he was trying to hide something.

Underbruck asked, "Did you ever see Mr. Arnholt's car in Dr. Rinsley's driveway before or since that one night?"

"No. But I saw same car drive by on four or five different days." I thought perhaps it might give the older women on the jury a sense of how frightening it was for me to know that Nick had been cruising my house.

Before he stepped down, Mr. Slewicki blurted out to the jury, "Dr. Rinsley is good person." Atwater had that struck from the record.

Later I felt so down that I called Humberto from Underbruck's office and asked, "Could I come over tonight?" I thought if I could be with him a few hours, I could get through the rest of the week.

There was a slight pause at the other end, and then, "Yes, absolutely. I made plans but I'll cancel them."

Did he have to tell me he had plans? I should never have called. Too late. I'd already humiliated myself. I was going to go anyway and try to have a pleasant evening. At home, I changed into jeans and a sweatshirt, and had dinner with Mom before leaving.

She had roast chicken ready, and I forced down a small plate of food so she wouldn't feel her work was wasted. I apologized for leaving her home alone while I went to Humberto's, but she was pleased by the news and didn't mind.

When I walked through Humberto's door, Frank barked and whined and jumped up in the air with excitement. I stooped to the ground and let him lick and sniff me. Humberto laughed as he watched us, but afterward he was tongue-tied, and talked uneasily about how overbooked they were at the restaurant.

"I'm sorry," I said. "I hope this wasn't too inconvenient for you."

"No, no! It's just—I was just—" He flailed his arms, and then dropped them to his side in a gesture of surrender. "I don't know what to say to you. I don't know what's safe to talk about."

"Nothing. Let's not talk."

He raised his eyebrows, and I realized he thought I wanted sex. "I mean, let's just sit by the fire and hold hands and not say anything. Could we do that?"

He seemed relieved. "Sure."

I watched him build a fire, remembering that night on the island when we had smashed our glasses. How I wished I could turn back time. I wanted again that easy closeness—the cuddling, Humberto's off-key singing, the hope and optimism we had shared. But that was before the fall, before the fall. Those words kept running through my head.

We sat in front of the fire for an hour. Humberto held my hand, and slowly stroked my arm. Frank slept contentedly at my feet, and for that brief time, I thought of nothing, and felt soothed.

Before I left, I used the guest bathroom, and saw on the countertop an open package of tampons. I wondered what her name was, and practically ran out the door so Humberto couldn't see my face.

Later, I made the mistake of watching the late CBS news. On a taped piece, a reporter who usually sat right behind me held forth from the courthouse steps:

"The trial does not appear to be going well for Dr. Rinsley. Testimony today from Nick Arnholt's attending psychiatrist was strong and convincing. Of course Mr. Arnholt himself will be the most important witness, and he's scheduled to testify in a few days."

Why did they have to give an opinion every goddamn day? I clicked off the TV and prayed for a time when each detail of my life wasn't being analyzed on the evening news.

They're worse than hyenas and vultures, I thought. They eat people alive.

58

The publicity lured ever larger crowds to the courthouse, some people heckling, some cheering, some making a day of it with picnic baskets and sunscreen.

Atwater produced several more witnesses before calling Nick to the stand. The head of the civil division of his law firm testified to the way Nick's work had gone downhill during the last year before his suicide attempt. An economist analyzed Nick's income to demonstrate how much financial hardship he had suffered and was likely to bear over the next ten years. They even found a psychologist whose specialty was "therapist-patient sex syndrome"—a vague collection of symptoms (depression, anxiety, mistrust) that could have belonged to almost any psychiatric category. She thought the prognosis on Nick was poor and it was unlikely he'd be able to work again for years.

Nobody really knew Nick. His colleagues had bought his professional act—the clever, sexy litigator who felt great about himself until he met me. The professionals had bought his sick act—the innocent, destroyed victim. Nobody saw that he used his cleverness to wound, that he used his pain to destroy. I was the only one in that room who had actually cared about him; the only one who had seen the splits in his character and tried to bind them.

Yet as the psychologist detailed her reasoning, even I, who knew better, believed her. I went home early that night, too miserable even to make small talk with my mother.

Nick's direct testimony was saved for the last day before Atwater rested their side of the case. Because this day was likely to be the most lurid in detail, the courtroom was more jammed than usual with reporters, fans, and spectators, and Judge Grabbe forced some of them to leave. The man in plaid was there early with his wizened wife. The middle-aged blond sat ready with her notebook, staring first at Nick and then at me. I was so nervous I wanted to crash my fist into a window just to feel it shatter.

Nick wore his navy suit, with a sea-green shirt that made his eyes look like two aqua marbles. As he recounted his story, his handsome face was ravaged by grief—his smooth skin wrinkled into a frown, his cheeks mottled, his mouth trembling. The jury sat at rapt attention.

"She became the focal point of my life," he said. "My preoccupation with her overshadowed all the problems I came to therapy to discuss."

Atwater took him through his paces like a master lion tamer, signaling him with a finger or eyebrow to slow down, or emphasize this phrase or that.

When he recounted his story of sex between us, the description was so detailed, so credible, that even I wasn't sure it hadn't happened, and I began to feel that one of us was crazy and it might be me.

"She explained she had some skin irritation and she was using cortisone cream on her arms," he said.

Unconsciously my right hand moved to cover my left elbow through my suit jacket. How had he known? It must have been the sleeveless dresses I'd worn a few times on hot summer days. And the cortisone cream! He must have memorized my bedroom in the few minutes I was gone.

"I was so raw—so vulnerable being with her like that—and she chose *that moment* to reject me. I didn't see the point in living. It convinced me I would *always* be abandoned. If even my own doctor would reject me, what hope did I have that *anybody* I loved would stay with me?"

The jury members cast sidelong glances at each other and wrote in their notebooks. The dog-groomer's eyes grew large and teary, and the construction worker shook his head. I heard sniffling behind me and turned to see the blonde in the audience dabbing her eyes.

As proof of his presence in my bedroom, Nick identified Exhibit 87, a pair of pink panties with my initials on them. "I just had to take them, even though I knew it was wrong," he said.

In my own deposition I had explained that I was unaware he had been in my bedroom at any time, but that he had stolen things from other people's homes and he might easily have stolen something from mine.

The fact of his being a thief seemed of little import when Atwater waved the pink evidence in front of the jury. That Nick had gained entrance to my bedroom at all was a violation of the therapy boundary, even if nothing more had happened.

He completed his testimony with a description of how ruined his career was, and how hopeless his prospects for a decent personal life. "The sad thing is, as much harm as she did me, I still miss her—" He broke off and covered his eyes with his right hand.

I turned my face away so the jury wouldn't see me as I struggled to hold back my own angry, sad tears. The judge called a ten-minute recess and Underbruck whispered to me menacingly, "Don't look at anyone but me. Don't cry."

I focused on the hairs in his beard and counted them as a form of self-hypnosis.

In a voice so low only I could hear him, he said, "It was an act. The man is out to destroy you. Pull yourself together. If the jury sees you react to his performance, they'll think you were in love with him."

I relaxed my facial muscles, and gazed at the curly brown jungle in front of me till every juror had filed out.

When I had regained my composure, Underbruck took me for a walk down the hall, steering me with his hand, demanding that people let us pass. We went two floors down to get some relief, and sat on one of the long wooden benches that lined the corridors.

Out of one courtroom came five sets of parents, holding babies ranging from a year to three years of age. The parents were beaming, kissing their babies' faces, laughing and crying. Underbruck explained they must have all been granted final adoption decrees, and for some reason, that pushed me over the edge. I wept uncontrollably, covering my face with the big handkerchief he handed me.

Underbruck began cross-examination by questioning Nick about the events in his history that revealed long-standing problems. The idea was to emphasize that Nick's current difficulties did not start with me.

Nick acknowledged that his father had beaten him and locked him in the closet, but he said it hadn't done him any permanent damage. His parents had loved him, and whatever anger he felt had been put to rest in their graves. What rubbish, I thought, but a reporter behind me blew her nose with several loud honks, expressing how much sympathy there was in the room for Nick.

My therapy notes were full of Nick's complaints about not feeling anything, which was no help. Feeling nothing sounded a lot better than suicidal depression, and without a year's coursework in psychology it was tough to convince a jury that underneath Nick's numbness, depression had been waiting to surface for years.

During the lunch hour the crowd was voracious, craning to look at me and mumbling opinions. It was that day that I flushed the reporter's microphone down the toilet. Some people even called me a charlatan and a whore.

After lunch Underbruck moved on to another portion of the legal defense—establishing that Nick knew the risks of therapy and knowingly assumed those risks.

"Did Dr. Rinsley tell you at the end of the first three consultation sessions that the work would be difficult and uncomfortable?" he asked.

"Yes."

"And didn't you, as an attorney, know it was your responsibility to exercise reasonable care on your own behalf?"

"Yes, but in this context there was no way for me to know what reasonable care was."

"Isn't it reasonable care for yourself to seek outside consultation if you're in doubt as to the treatment you're receiving?"

"Yes."

"And you never sought such consultation?"

"No."

"And wouldn't you consider it important to tell your doctor any suicidal thoughts you had?"

"Yes."

"Yet you didn't tell Dr. Rinsley that you were thinking of suicide, did you?"

"I didn't have those thoughts until she had sex with me."

Underbruck fell silent and searched through his papers. It was an awful moment, with that lie hanging in the air like a body swinging from a lynching tree.

Underbruck began a new line of questions to further establish Nick's own role in what happened. "At any time, did Dr. Rinsley give you her home address?"

"No."

"How did you know where she lived?"

"I ran a computer search on her to check her credentials. Routine practice in my profession."

Underbruck forced Nick to admit that he had driven by my house at least eight times, had stolen things from my waiting room and vandalized it, and that he had called me often in the middle of the night.

The jury made notes as Nick talked, and the real estate broker smiled at me reassuringly, but I stayed in my seat during the afternoon break. The vehemence of some people in the crowd scared me.

About the suicide attempt, Underbruck leaned on Nick full force. When did you decide to do it? Why didn't you call someone? Where did you get the pills? How many did you take? How long after you took them did you call 911?

Nick became more and more agitated by these questions. After pausing to drink water he said, "How do you know when you decide to commit suicide? Maybe it was the night she rejected me. Maybe it was weeks earlier. And how can I know what made me pick up the phone at the last minute to save myself?" He bit his lip and requested a tissue to stop the bleeding.

I was elated by how well Underbruck was doing, and how nervous Nick looked, until Underbruck's final question: "Mr. Arnholt, isn't the real reason why you attempted suicide that the sexual contact you wanted with Dr. Rinsley never occurred, and you realized it never would?"

"Oh God no," Nick said, and broke down into weeping. Not only was there sympathetic crying from Nick's fans, but even some of the jury members were dabbing their eyes again.

I was disgusted by Nick's lying, and unable to tell how much of his distress was genuine and how much was manufactured. And if I, who had spent so many hours with him, couldn't tell, how could a jury possibly tell?

On that day Atwater rested her side of the case, and Underbruck made a motion for a directed verdict to dismiss the charge. He told me attorneys always did this after the plaintiff rested, because if the judge felt clearly there was insufficient evidence, it saved time and money to avoid an unnecessary defense.

Judge Grabbe denied the motion to dismiss, and my hopes plummeted. If the judge thought there was enough evidence against me to warrant more of his time, I could easily lose.

At home, what I feared would happen between me and my mother did. Cooped up in that little apartment together—her sleeping poorly, me tense to the breaking-point—the old hostilities emerged.

"Have a little more fettucine," she said, the night after Nick had testified.

"I can't. You eat it."

"I suppose you know I'm gaining weight out of nervousness."

"Maybe it's too hard to be here and watch this. Maybe you'd feel better back home."

"Would you rather I didn't stay?"

"Mom, I'm perfectly happy to have you with me, but I'm not much company, and you're here alone all day. I'm just trying to be considerate."

She gathered up the plates too quickly, hurt for what I considered little cause. In the next hour she scrubbed the oven, polished the fading linoleum in my little kitchen, and washed tomato sauce off the wall. Later, we sat across from each other in the living room and drank wine, while she crocheted a cream-colored afghan, intertwining popcorn stitches and cables.

"Your limp looks worse," I said, eager to show my concern. "Are you developing arthritis in that joint?"

"I guess." She wasn't going to accept my overture. "So what do you think the jury will decide?"

"I think they'll find me negligent, because I tried to refer him out when he was very depressed."

"I hope that doesn't happen." The crochet hook moved so fast it was a blur. "They might feel sympathy for him, though. For your leaving him."

How could she do this to me now? "You mean, you understand that, right? Because I left you too?"

Faster crocheting. "Yes. I've never understood how you could leave me when I was so close to death."

I tried to control myself. "I missed the first two weeks of college to stay with you until you were out of danger! I didn't leave till the doctor said you were okay!"

She shook her head with that old look of betrayal I despised.

I leaped up, too angry to stay in the apartment, and went to put on my jogging shoes. She had come to support me, but she was pulling the same old shit. At the door, I said, "You would have liked it if I had never left home, isn't that right? Or if I'd gone to college in Eugene and come home every weekend to hold your hand?"

"The University of Oregon is a perfectly fine school," she said flatly.

"But it wasn't the one I wanted! Was it?!"

She counted stitches swiftly and resumed her crocheting at lightning speed. "No. You had to go away. You had to do whatever you wanted. You didn't care about me." Her lips formed a mean line.

My words bubbled up from a place inside me I didn't even know existed. "You would have rather killed me than let me go!" I shouted. "And you nearly did!!"

She put down her yarn and took in a sharp breath, but to my horror her face did not crumple into pained injustice. Her mouth and eyes opened in a look of shocked recognition.

Practically blind with fright, I said, "I'm going for a run," and left.

Somehow I managed to drive to the UCLA football field, where I parked and started running as fast as I could around the outside lane of the track. But as fast as I ran, my mind raced ahead of me. Why had Mom rushed in front of that train if not ready to kill both of us? It was so reckless! So unlike her! And she had been so thwarted in her efforts to keep me there.

Had she been suicidal? Of course she was suicidal! And homicidal!

How could a daughter live with such an ugly stone in the center of her being? What could be more terrifying than knowing my mother loved me so ravenously she would rather have killed me than let me go? My God! I thought. I have been running from this for years. No wonder I was so driven to succeed. No wonder I was so ambitious. It was the only protection from her. And I thought it was just to please my father and give me financial security. How stupid of me!

I ran until I collapsed, coughing and choking, on the lawn next to the track.

A man in a blue velour sweatsuit bent over me. "Are you all right? Can you breathe?"

I nodded. "Just winded. Fine."

He resumed his jogging, and I got up and started a slow walk around the track, still coughing and choking as I went.

I had been trying to deny this knowledge since the day of our accident. I had wiped the thought clean from my consciousness. But I still had dreams of the crash, and always there was that resistance to her, that fear of getting too close.

I kept gasping for air as I walked, and that suddenly reminded me of Nick. Nick!!! *It was he who threatened to bring all this to the surface!* Nick was my mother all over again! *No wonder* I hated his clinging! No wonder I was determined to stop it, and keep him at bay! Of course I had missed the cues to his suicide, and felt like I was dying in his presence. *It was him or me.* Her or me. Survival.

I walked slowly to my car, and inside, leaned back and shut my eyes. First my mother, and then Nick, had tried to love me to death. I needed to talk to Dandelone, and our next day's five-thirty appointment seemed years away.

I called her from a phone booth and scheduled a 7 A.M. hour for the next morning. Then I forced myself to return and face my mother.

She had been crying, and her nose was so plugged she was breathing through her mouth. The half-finished afghan was stuffed into her crochet basket. She was sitting in a chair, holding her elbows.

"Let's talk," I said.

She began crying in soft whimpers that sucked the anger out of me. "Can you ever forgive me? Will you ever love me again?"

"Mom—I'll always love you. Tell me about it."

She shook her head. "It was such a foolish thing I did, stepping on the gas like that! But the store was closing, and I was hell-bent for you to have the right clothes and the right suitcase. I thought at least if you weren't with me, you'd look beautiful and you'd appreciate what I'd given you."

Tears dribbled down my cheeks. "Did it have to be so perfect because you really wanted to ruin it and you couldn't admit that?"

"I don't know. I was hurt that you turned away from me. And college was the final break." She clawed at the skin on her hands. "But why did you turn away from me?"

"I lost respect for you. And I missed the old, happy you."

Her voice broke into a wail as mournful as the cry of seagulls over their dead young. "You thought I was crazy to look after Grandma! You hated me!"

"I hated that you gave up your life for her. And that you locked your dreams in a box in the attic. You had so much talent, and you gave up on it."

She snapped her fingers angrily. "And what would you have done? Dumped Grandma in a nursing home to eat pudding and play bingo with bored nurses' aides who never knew how smart and beautiful she was?"

"I don't know. Maybe I would have done exactly what you did. But isn't that what made it so hard to let me go?"

"Oh, Sarah, I'm sorry. The summer you were leaving for college I was so unhappy." Her voice wound itself around my heart and squeezed. "The closer it came to your departure, the more down I got. I started saving up my asthma pills."

"That's weird. I remember you wheezing a lot that summer, but I never made the connection."

"I tried to hide it from you. I wanted you to have a bright future. But I thought you could have it and still stay near me. After the accident, I couldn't bear to think about why I pushed my foot down on that pedal. What I thought instead was that if you loved me, you would have changed your plans. And that's the way I've remembered it all these years."

"I must have understood and buried it, because all I knew was I was very angry and I used that anger to wrench myself away."

"I thought I'd failed you as a mother or you would have stayed."

"But don't you see that you succeeded as a mother because I was capable of leaving?"

She shook her head slowly. "I've told myself that many times, but deep down I don't believe it. I was loyal to my mother and I thought a daughter who loved me would be loyal to me."

"But there's more than one kind of loyalty! Wasn't I loyal to your spirit? Wasn't I loyal to your dreams? All these years I've wanted you to be so proud of me, and yet you could never praise me without adding some sarcastic remark. And now I see why. Whatever I accomplish reminds you of what you gave up. And the only way I could have avoided that was by making the same sacrifice you did."

"But Sarah," she said, "I *am* proud of you."

Mom got up and sat down next to me, and we cried in each other's arms. There was much for us to think about.

After a while, she went to bed and I stayed up to watch TV. At midnight she came back into the living room and said, "Why don't you shut that off and try to get some sleep?"

"I'm still wide awake."

"Would you like me to put lotion on your feet like I used to?"

The thought seemed comforting to me and I said yes. I got some hand lotion and a towel from the bathroom, and stretched out the length of the sofa. She sat at the far end, placed my feet in her lap, and began rubbing them. She told me how pretty she always thought my toes were.

I could feel an ancient ache in my chest flow away from me, and for the first time I could admit what it was. I needed my mother, and whatever her flaws, I loved her deeply.

The next morning on Dandelone's couch, I summed up what had happened the night before. The relief of understanding had taken the punch out of my anger and fear. I said, "I felt so *guilty* about taking myself away from her."

"I think," Dandelone said, "that Nick's love for you felt very much like your mother's love. It wasn't until he tried to smother you that the unconscious belief of her attempt to kill you threatened to break into consciousness. And it was that budding knowledge that choked you and left you feeling as if you couldn't breathe."

Like a kaleidoscope turned in a new way, it all made sense now—my missing the signs of Nick's increasing depression, my abhorrence of his clinging, my dread of marriage. The knowledge that Nick had at first reminded me of my dad was nothing compared to this: I was afraid I would never get away again. I believed Nick would kill me rather than let me go.

Dandelone said, "This crisis with Nick has brought to the surface a question that has plagued you for years: Is anybody really capable of loving you without destroying you?"

"That explains why I've often picked men who couldn't really commit to me. As long as they were slightly out of reach I didn't have to worry about them consuming me."

"Exactly. And if a man is willing to commit to you, and is capable of loving you without destroying you, you are faced with another question: Can you allow him to love you, without your fear of being possessed eventually ruining that love?"

I left for court with these questions on my mind.

60

Our first witness was Herb Tannenbaum, a man with blond curly hair, small blue eyes, and the remnants of a Brooklyn accent.

The Chief of Psychology at UC San Diego Hospital, he was an expert on Borderline Personality and had testified in a number of other trials.

Tannenbaum had administered a test battery to Nick, and he used the results to bolster his opinion. He said Nick was suffering from "Don Juan Syndrome," and that not being able to seduce me had sent Nick into a rage, prompting him to stage a suicide attempt and sue me.

When Nick heard this he slammed his hand on the arm of his chair, and several young women behind us hissed. Atwater put a calming hand on his arm and whispered to him.

When she took over for cross, Atwater began punching holes in Tannenbaum's credibility. The scoring system he used for the Rorschach was out of favor, wasn't that true? His post-doctoral fellowship had been a research project on overfed mice, wasn't that the case? And if a patient was mistreated by a therapist, wasn't he entitled to feel rage? Wasn't it in fact normal to feel rage?

"Dr. Tannenbaum," she continued, standing politely at her podium, "I have in my hand the current Diagnostic and Statistical Manual of the American Psychiatric Association. Can you show me where it lists 'Don Juan Syndrome'? "

"It's not listed there."

"So you *invented* this diagnosis?"

"Absolutely not. It's been in the literature for years, and refers only to part of a person's behavior."

"And what basis do you have for using this pejorative term with reference to my client?"

"He's had a long series of brief affairs with women."

"Isn't it true that most men as handsome as Mr. Arnholt have had a long series of relationships with women?" The audience tittered, and Nick's mouth curled into a wry grin.

"I have no research statistics to that effect. I do know that a man who can't make a commitment to one woman often seeks continuous reassurance by endlessly conquering new women."

Atwater's voice became strident. "Might a man appear that way if he's ambitious and hard-driving and hasn't had the time to devote to a committed relationship?"

"Perhaps."

Atwater paused to switch gears. "Doctor, do you acknowledge that Mr. Arnholt is depressed, that his life is worse than it was two years ago, and that he blames Dr. Rinsley for his current problems?"

"Yes."

"Then even without sexual contact, wouldn't it be likely that he would blame Dr. Rinsley for his condition and seek remedy?"

"Sure he might blame her for his condition but that doesn't mean she's responsible for it."

I was thrilled with that point, but for her finale, Atwater used Tannenbaum's own theory against him in a brilliant twist of logic. "Doctor, let's suppose for a moment that Dr. Rinsley's version of events is true—she refused Mr. Arnholt's sexual demands and he became angry and frustrated. Wouldn't there come a point in such a therapy where these two people were stalemated? Him demanding something of her, her refusing, and the therapy immovable?"

"Yes, that's possible."

"And under that hypothetical circumstance, wouldn't it be professionally in order for the doctor to refer this patient to another therapist?"

Tannenbaum had walked right into the trap and now he squirmed there, stammering for time and glancing at Underbruck. "If that were the case, the answer is yes. But in my opinion, that wasn't the case."

Finally he was forced to say on record that Atwater was right—if the therapy were stalemated, I should have referred Nick to another therapist.

On re-direct, Underbruck tried to clean up the damage. "Dr. Tannenbaum, is it your opinion that Mr. Arnholt's treatment with Dr. Rinsley was at a stalemate?"

"No. I think he was in the middle of treatment and if he had been willing to accept the limits of what Dr. Rinsley offered, he might have continued to improve."

From the jurors' nods and murmurs I was sure they believed the therapy was stalemated and I should have referred Nick out. It was in fact true.

The next day was consumed by the testimony of James Rehmer, our expert on depression. He was so tall and gangly he looked like a daddy longlegs in a suit, but Underbruck assured me he was very poised on the stand, and would be helpful in providing an alternate explanation for Nick's depression other than my treatment of him.

Rehmer began by summarizing the current research, which demonstrated that "depressive disorders tend to run in families."

Underbruck took advantage of this with a question: "Given that Mr. Arnholt's biological mother committed suicide, might Mr. Arnholt be prone to developing a depressive disorder by adulthood?"

Rehmer answered well: "It's likely that he would have repeated episodes of depression, not only because of the genetic predisposition, but also because his mother was depressed. Our research shows that depressed mothers often fail to meet the child's early needs, which lays the foundation for later depression in the child."

When Atwater took over for cross-examination, she hammered out her questions coldly. Was Rehmer's opinion about Victoria Arnholt's depression anything other than pure speculation? Did he acknowledge Nick could also have been depressed because his life had changed for the worse? Shouldn't Dr. Rinsley have been on the lookout for suicidal thinking if Nick had a genetic predisposition to depression?

Rehmer stuck tenaciously to his opinions, unintimidated by Atwater, but I grew more despondent with every question.

That night was the lowest point in the trial for me. I chastised myself endlessly. I should have worked even harder than I did to understand my own reactions to Nick; I should have sought a second consultation, or gone back into therapy myself. Barring those steps, I should have referred him to another therapist long before I finally attempted to do so. He had obviously been showing signs of severe depression and I had run away from them. I felt I deserved to be found liable for negligence.

Underbruck proceeded the next day by bringing a neurologist to the stand, who testified that Nick's head injury and chronic drug and alcohol use were a much more likely cause of his memory difficulties than emotional distress. Atwater countered by asking him if depression could interfere with memory function, and he had to say yes. I marveled at how knowledgeable Leona Atwater was, and had to admit a grudging admiration for her.

On my way to Dandelone's office that evening, I heard another brief news report: "Recent evidence at the patient-therapist sex trial suggests that even if Dr. Rinsley is cleared of the sex charge, she may still be found liable of malpractice." I switched to a soft rock station immediately. The whole town was analyzing my behavior and speculating on my future. I felt like a football team before the Superbowl; for all I knew they had a line on me in Las Vegas.

Once I lay down on Dandelone's couch, I relaxed a little. It was a rare privilege these days to feel safe, with someone who would listen to me intently. She absorbed my distress about the trial like a sponge, diffusing some of my anxiety and embarrassment. Finally I was able to talk about a dream I'd had the previous night.

"I was on trial for larceny of the heart. I was in the witness box, and the jury was everybody I knew—my parents, Aunt Lydia, Pallen, Humberto, Kevin, Val, Linda, Morry. When I turned and saw the judge, it was me, dressed in a black robe, looking older, and stern.

"I explained I hadn't stolen Nick's heart; he had given it to me for safekeeping and I had treated it tenderly.

"Then the lawyer pulled out a human heart, walked up to me and showed me this thing, dripping with blood, still beating—a bare heart in his hands—and he said, 'This is what you call safekeeping?'

"I thought as long as I lived I would have to suffer the terrible guilt of this damaged heart. Then my mother stood up and gave the lawyer a dress box, and told him to put the heart in it. After he did, she took it back, and said, 'I can take care of that.' The dress box looked like the one that held her old drawings and papers for Paris."

Dandelone waited for my associations.

"Maybe my mother will finally start to take some responsibility for herself. I hope so. I'm tired of being blamed for her lot in life. I'm tired of feeling guilty."

Dandelone cleared her throat. "You hate weakness in her, and deny it in yourself. You love power in yourself, and deny it in her. That is the true source of your guilt."

I was shocked. Me, splitting? As profoundly as I had told Nick he did? "I can't believe it."

Dandelone waited, while I struggled. "You mean I *deny* her strength? Don't even *see* it? Why doesn't she tell my father off? Why did she make a servant out of herself?"

"There are different kinds of strength, including the strength to endure and the wisdom to forgive."

It was a new thought about my mother. I had never considered her life in that light, and I left Dandelone's office feeling humbled.

61

The next day was to be devoted to Zachary Leitwell's testimony—the most agonizing for me to endure.

When I arrived in court, Nick was already seated next to Atwater, reviewing some papers. As I walked past them, I glanced into his open briefcase and to my surprise saw, lined up in one pocket, a row of red crayons. *My* red crayons, I was sure.

Why only the red ones? I sat down in my chair and racked my brain to remember anything he had ever told me about the color red. Red, red. Red crayons, his red scarf. It was probably he who had cut my roses on Halloween because only the red ones were gone. But why the hell red?

That mystery distracted me only briefly. Underbruck thought it best if Zachary started by recounting my sexual feelings toward Nick. Always take the other side's ammunition and defuse it, Underbruck explained.

It was horrible. As Zachary described the sexual arousal for which I had sought his help, I focused again on Violet Knight, who was rubbing one of her gold-hooped earrings.

I sweated so much that the pink silk shirt I was wearing dried later with stains under the arms. The jurors and reporters ate up the sexual tidbits like love-starved adolescents.

At the lunch break, when I came out of the ladies' room, Nick passed close to me in the hall. "I knew it," he said, and I saw the old flash of bright blue before he turned away. My cheeks burned for half an hour.

The most embarrassing information covered, Zachary moved on to establishing how competent and responsible my work with Nick had been. As he described my diligence, my extra reading, my struggling for insight, I was soothed by his words. I *had* worked hard, I *had* made exceptional efforts to move Nick beyond his stubborn focus on me, I *had* made significant progress in helping him.

"Why, Dr. Leitwell," Underbruck asked, "do you say that Dr. Rinsley's care was *above* the community standard?"

"Because the treatment of a patient like this is so arduous many people just throw up their hands and apply a Band Aid. Dr. Rinsley stuck by him and kept working at it."

Zachary looked directly at the jury to be more persuasive. "Sometimes chemotherapy makes a cancer patient so sick he would rather die. Still it's what the doctor has to offer and it's the patient's choice to go on accepting the treatment. How is it any different in this case? Mr. Arnholt had an emotional cancer—an obsession for his doctor burgeoning out of control. The treatment was to understand it, to get through it and move forward. Not to abandon him, not to send him somewhere else where the same thing might happen again. And when Dr. Rinsley finally reached the point of knowing he could never get beyond this with her, she decided to refer him elsewhere. That's what her ethics demanded and that's what she offered to do."

Zachary then introduced an idea which had barely been touched: Nick's current depression was most likely the result of being unable to move forward in therapy, and of damaging the one person who had cared about him—me. This contradicted Atwater's claim that Nick was depressed because I had failed in my work.

Zachary explained his conclusion. "The middle phase of psychotherapy is difficult and painful—a time when the patient has lost his old way of coping and hasn't yet grown newer, more resilient ways of facing life. Mr. Arnholt was at this delicate juncture in his therapy—something like an immigrant, who arrives in a new country not being able to speak the language, and not understanding the customs. He felt uneasy, inept at the language of emotions, and anxious about whether he would ever feel comfortable in this new place. Instead of sticking with it, he turned and ran back to his old country, where desolate as it was, it was familiar. He tried to convince Dr. Rinsley to have sex with him and abandon the therapy completely."

"And what is your opinion about why Mr. Arnholt chose to do this?" Underbruck asked.

Zachary pulled the microphone closer to his face. "No one can predict who has the courage to go forward. It's an unknown quantity in therapy, and certainly not in the therapist's control."

I heaped silent thanks on Zachary, and felt enormous affection for him as I always had. Listening to him, I relearned something I tended to forget: psychotherapy was only half my responsibility. The other half belonged to the patient.

I noticed that day that Nick had struck up a friendship with Violet Knight. As I packed up my papers and waited for Underbruck, I watched Violet and Nick, certain from the way she laughed that Nick had said something amusing and seductive.

It was just the way he looked at her that made things click. She was laughing, her hand over her mouth to be discreet, and I saw that he was watching her hand, not her eyes, and her nails were painted bright red. As shiny and red as Candy's.

Of course, I thought. He's drawn to women who remind him of Candy. He is like Candy. Seductive and sexually inappropriate. And Candy probably favored red. Why else would he be so drawn to that color?

And then the meaning of it sunk in. He didn't even know it, but after all these years, Nick was still trying to maintain a connection to Candy. He had only a few vague memories of his birth mother. For Nick, Candy was his real mother.

If the denial about my own mother hadn't been stripped away, I'm sure I would not have made the connection for him, but now it practically shouted at me. Nick still loved Candy, and he needed her as much as a car needed a motor. He couldn't move forward in his life without her.

As we left the courthouse, I said to Underbruck, "I want to go back and see Candy Lanehurst. Alone."

We walked quickly to his car. Once inside, away from prying ears, he said, "Things are looking bad enough as it is! She's a hostile witness, and even if she verified your version of Nick's childhood, so what? It doesn't make a goddamn bit of difference!" He started the car and inched into the exit line, obviously annoyed with my misdirected focus.

"I grant you all that. But I can't shake the feeling that getting her to talk to me will help us somehow."

"Discovery is over. The witness list is set. And even if the judge agreed to have her testify, it's not going to help your case. You can go back and see her if you want, but it's a useless exercise. Just make sure you don't tell her anything. For all we know she's talking to her son every goddamn day. Reveal nothing. You got that?"

"Got it."

"And call me later to tell me what happened."

"What if it's late?"

"Then call me at six A.M."

62

After a quick hello to Mom, I called Candy's house. She answered in a breathy, childlike voice.

I introduced myself and asked, "Have you been watching the trial on TV?"

There was a brief pause. "Of course. Every day. My son is very handsome, isn't he?"

I tried to ignore the possible meanings that might have. "I'm sure you must enjoy watching him. But I think he needs your help. And I need your help."

Her tone was much softer than it had been at her house. "I already told you I don't want to be involved."

"I'm not asking you to get involved. I'm just asking you to talk to me about Nick."

"Look. My husband's out of town. Even if I were willing to see you, I wouldn't do it without him present."

There was a chink in the armor. *Even if I were willing.* And I understood something new about her from my own mother. In spite of what she had done, she was the one who felt hurt and wronged, and she was aching for contact with Nick.

I talked urgently, in a fast rush. "Mrs. Lanehurst, maybe if we talk about it, you'll find some way to build a bridge to him. I need to understand what happened between the two of you, and I think you do too."

"But you just want to strengthen your case."

"At this point I doubt you can help my case."

"Then why would you care?"

I faltered a little before finding the truth. "Because his false accusation has hurt me deeply, and I need to understand it better."

Maybe that touched her. Maybe she knew what it was to be falsely accused. There was a long pause at the other end, and then, "Just you? No lawyer? No tape recorder?"

"Just me. You can search me when I come in."

I was at her door an hour later, having stopped first at the Westside Mall to ditch a reporter following me.

I opened my purse for Candy in her hallway, and allowed her to pat my body from shoulder to knee to check for hidden microphones. Satisfied that I was being honest, she led me into her living room again, and offered me tea.

I waited, remembering that Nick had requested tea at my house. She returned holding two full mugs and carefully put one down in front of me. This time she wore black leggings and a long white sweater, her red toenails sparkling as they peeked through her sandals.

I smiled. I had been too combative with her before. "Nick told me all about his early years with you. Please don't feel that I would judge you. I'm sure you did the best you could at the time."

She sat down and twirled her wedding ring. "What did he tell you?"

I looked directly at her. "Everything. The sexual contact with you included."

"I was a good mother to him!" she said vehemently.

"I believe you." I backed up into more neutral territory. "Tell me how it all started. How did you meet Nick's father?"

She took a sip of tea. "I was eighteen. I had run away from home and was living in a one-room apartment, working as a hostess in a restaurant/bar. Nicholas used to come into the bar. Late at night we would sit and drink together till closing. He was sad over his first wife's death, and I felt sorry for him."

"What did he say about his first wife?"

"That she committed suicide. He said she was always depressed; couldn't do the housework or take care of Nicky. He felt guilty about her suicide. Blamed himself. That's why he was drinking so much."

"Do you have any idea why she killed herself?"

"He said she was depressed for a couple of years—but the main thing was he caught her fooling around on him."

This was a surprise. The pristine good mother was not so good after all. "What did he do when he found out?"

"I'm sure he beat her to a pulp, but that's not what he told me. He said they talked it out, but she couldn't get over it and that's why she shot herself. It was a grisly mess. Blood splattered all over the place. He had to throw everything out."

In Nick's memory, the clean-up was an angry elimination of his perfect mother, but Nick's father may have protected him more than Nick realized. "You said you were also drinking?"

"Way too much. Since I was thirteen. When I met Nicholas I thought I'd finally found someone who would look after me. I married him in a few weeks."

"How was the marriage?"

"Great for a month. But little Nicky was mad that I was there. He was still real upset about his mother being gone and he was jealous of the attention his dad was giving me. Nicky tried to hit me once, and Nicholas threw him in the closet and locked the door. I told him I thought that was too hard a punishment, but he told me to stay out of it.

"Then I began seeing the ugly side of Nicholas. I still had my job at the bar, and he was crazy jealous. He always picked me up at closing time. Sometimes he left his gas station early to come over and spy on me. The first time he beat me up, I couldn't believe it. I'd married a guy just like my dad."

I could believe it. I had often seen people choose a mate who appeared on the surface to be different from their parents, but later proved to treat them the same way. "Did you try to leave him?"

"Not at first. I was still in love with him in spite of his meanness. So I quit my job, and tried to get little Nicky to like me. I bought him toys and played with him."

"How long did you remain in the home?"

"Five years. I left when Nicky was ten."

"And what was family life like during that five years?"

Her composed demeanor melted into sadness, and she shook her head as she talked. "I was drunk most of the time. Nicholas beat both of us if we didn't cater to him. Nicky and I became pals. We huddled together to face the ogre."

I tried to be as tactful as I could. "Do you think your drinking interfered with your being able to look after Nicky properly?"

Candy's eyes teared up and she reached over to a sidetable for a Kleenex. "I loved him, but I was a baby myself. Sometimes I had no time for him, and thought if he wasn't there things would be easier. I wasn't an ideal mother, that's for sure."

I prayed she wouldn't cut me off when I asked, "How did it happen that Nicky slept with you in your bed?"

She blew her nose. "Nicholas started working night shifts at the station. I was alone every night, and I was lonely. Nicky was wetting his bed and his dad beat him every time he found the sheets wet in the morning. I felt real sorry for him, and I thought if I cuddled him a bit before he went to sleep, maybe he'd stop wetting."

"And that's why you took him into your bed?"

"I knew he'd be too scared to wet our bed, so I cuddled him there."

So sad, I thought. Two lonely children. "How often did you do this?"

"Maybe three or four times a week. Then after he was asleep, I'd kind of walk him to his own bed and he wouldn't wake up. It helped him. He stopped wetting."

"But being together in bed somehow led to the sexual activity?"

Candy nodded and covered her face with her hands. "You think I'm a sick, terrible person, don't you!"

"No," I said gently. "I think you were lonely, and drinking, and sad."

Candy continued through her tears, wanting now to tell me, wanting this pain exposed to the light. "You have to understand I was drunk all the time! Drunk and lonely and blue. Mostly Nicky and I just cuddled, but sometimes he asked if he could play with my tits, and I let him. Sometimes he wanted to pretend he was a baby and suck them, and once in a while I let him do that too because I thought he needed the comfort."

"But that wasn't the only sexual contact you had with him."

"No." She paused to collect herself and burst out crying. "I think of this so differently now that I'm an adult! I feel so bad about what happened!"

"All of us make foolish mistakes when we're young. It goes with the territory."

She blew her nose again and nodded. "A few times after he'd played with my tits and then fallen asleep, I was turned on, and I—I touched myself real quietly beside him. But one time, he opened his eyes and asked me what I was doing. I explained it a little and told him to go back to sleep. A couple of weeks later, we fell asleep together one night, and I started dreaming a man was making love to me. I had a climax and woke up and found Nicky had his hand between my legs. I pushed him away real hard, and told him that was bad and he should never do it again. And he said he was only doing what he saw me doing. I explained to him he couldn't touch me like that again—that he would do that with other women when he was older. So he promised he wouldn't do it again, but he asked me would I show him what it looked like. I turned on the light and let him see."

"Did you ever teach him anything else about sex?"

She blushed deeply. "I showed him how to get himself off. He had seen me doing it, and he wanted to know how it worked on him. So I showed him. I figured it was better for him to find out from me than from the schoolyard. Of course I realize now it was all wrong!"

No wonder Nick had masturbated so much. And it was easy to see how similar he could have made Candy and me in his mind: how I stood for a woman who let him have a little of herself, but not enough; how I was about to traumatize him in exactly the same way she did—by leaving. So much of his rage toward me was obviously transferred from her.

I asked her more questions. After leaving Nicholas, she had moved to the Bay area, and after her divorce was final, married another alcoholic. A turbulent second marriage followed, punctuated by several miscarriages. Then she reached a crisis point and began to turn her life around. She left her second husband and went to Alcoholics Anonymous. Three sober years later she moved back to L.A., met

Harry Lanehurst, the owner of a software company and a recovering alcoholic himself. This marriage had been different. Harry protected her, and understood her. They had been together for fifteen alcohol-free years. Five years ago she had located Nick and made a number of attempts to reach out to him, all of which had failed.

The final thing she told me was that after she left, she sent many letters to little Nicky, and a Christmas present, all of which were returned, unopened. "I used my brother's business address in San Francisco, because I knew Nicholas wouldn't come after him. And you know what Nicky's pa did? He had his mail rerouted to a post office box, and sent everything back to me. The bastard knew Nicky would think I'd just abandoned him and I had to leave it that way or risk getting killed. There was no way to tell Nicky I loved him."

If only Nick had known! "But couldn't you have contacted his school?"

"I thought of that later, but I was too scared."

Candy stood up shakily. "I kept everything. I hoped that one day I could show Nicky and he'd understand. But he wouldn't have anything to do with me. He wouldn't even give me five minutes to explain. Just said I was dead and I should stay that way."

Tears had made her mascara run, and there were two black rings under her eyes. "I'll show you," she said. She swayed slightly as she disappeared upstairs.

While I had listened to her answers, a powerful conviction had taken hold of me: that if Nick could hear what she had said, it would alter the course of events. He had never known the depth of this woman's love for him.

She returned carrying a cardboard box, which she set at my feet. "There. Look at the postal dates. Twenty-five years ago."

I opened the box and leafed through the letters. They were musty-smelling and yellowed with age, and as she said, postmarked twenty-five years ago. With them was an oblong package.

"And that parcel is a Christmas present I sent him a month after I left. I kept it all this time, thinking maybe one day he'd listen, one day he'd care enough to see me."

I was holding in my hand the key to Nick's life—the key to his personality, to his cure—and I felt a need so strong I couldn't reason with it. "Mrs. Lanehurst—why don't you let me take these to him tonight? Let me be your emissary."

She grabbed the box away from me and sat down with it on her lap. "How could you possibly do that? In the middle of a lawsuit? And how could I trust you? This is the only proof I have for him. I need it in case he ever comes back."

I said softly, "You don't have any other children, do you?"

She clutched the box as if it were a baby. "Harry and I lost a little girl. She was stillborn after thirty-six hours of labor. And I never got pregnant again. Nicky is my only child."

"Then let me go to him. I know it's a risk for you to give me these things, but I'll be taking a much greater risk. And I think he will hear me out."

I saw hope struggling to conquer the fear in her eyes. "He's my only child, Dr. Rinsley. I have AA, and I have my husband, but sometimes at night when I think about taking a drink, it's to fill a hole in my heart that only Nicky can fill."

"Then let me go to him." I stood and reached out my arms, and she gave me the box.

Back in the car, my head swam. What on earth was I thinking? How could I do this? I drove through downtown L.A. and onto the Santa Monica Freeway, hypnotized by the urgency of my impulse. When I reached the interchange with the 405 Freeway, I had my final choice to make: north to my own apartment, or south to his.

At the last moment, I moved into the exit lane south.

63

Fog had crept over the coastal areas that night, and as I exited the freeway, visibility dropped down to a few feet. When I left my car in front of the Marina Towers, moist air curled around me like cigarette smoke. The only sound I heard was the tinkle of wind chimes from a nearby balcony.

I rang the bell at Nick's apartment and heard an explosion of loud barking inside, followed by Nick's voice saying "Quiet!" An instant later Nick swung the door open, his face a portrait of surprise. "Well, if it isn't the good doctor!" His dog was enormous, a black-and-white Great Dane, and he barked a few more times, making me jump.

I held the box to me like a shield. "May I come in?"

Nick was barefoot, in white shorts and a T-shirt, his hair rumpled, a bandage on his left big toe. He hooked his fingers around the dog's collar and made a sweeping arc toward the living room. "Be my guest."

A huge, white wrap-around sofa hugged the bay windows that looked out on the dimmed lights of the Marina. The decor was modern, all polish and chrome, with a sleek ebony entertainment center. On the thick, glass coffee-table was an open bottle of Tanqueray gin, a briefcase, and some trial documents.

Suddenly the enormity of what I was doing hit me. I was insane to be here. Underbruck would be livid.

I sat down gingerly on the corner edge of the sofa, and Nick strolled past me and plopped down in the middle, with that old look of triumph on his face. "I see you've taken complete leave of your senses."

"Almost."

"I always knew one of us was crazy."

His dog trotted up and sniffed my knees.

"Floyd! Down!" The dog edged away and sank into the white wool area-rug.

"Floyd?"

"From Pink Floyd, *The Wall*. Perfect, don't you think?"

I nodded, thinking, I *have* taken leave of my senses. But it was too late to turn back. I put the brown box next to me, and said, "I came here because I'm still clinging to some belief in you."

He gave a mean laugh.

I sat back in the sofa and cracked my knuckles. "I've just spent the last two hours with your stepmother."

"What??!!" Eyes narrowed in disgust, he stood up immediately and jabbed a finger in my direction. "Well, isn't it just like you to raise the dead!" He strode to the kitchen, while I tried to hang on to my faith.

The racket of ice falling into a glass broke the silence, and a moment later he walked back and poured himself two inches of gin. He appeared to have recovered some from the news. He sat down, sipped his drink, and said, "So now you're in the resurrection business."

"She's heartbroken about having lost contact with you. She's never stopped loving you."

He laughed uproariously. "Bullshit. *Bullshit*. You ruined your case to come here and tell me that? You really are crazy!"

Trying not to lose what little composure I had left, I said, "She told me the whole story. Things even you don't know. Please hear me out."

He swirled his drink more calmly. "Sure, why not? It'll be good entertainment." He gave a wry smile. "And with this latest stunt of yours, there's no way I can lose."

I repeated what I had learned about Candy's marriage to his father—the beatings, the loneliness, the drunkenness. "Did you know she was an alcoholic?"

"She always kept a bottle of Jim Beam in her underwear drawer."

"She was drunk every day, and it affected her judgment. Like what she did with you in bed."

"Oh, you shrinks make such a big fucking deal out of that shit. So she got me off once. So I played with her. It just doesn't matter any more!"

"But it does matter! She's felt horribly guilty about it all these years."

"She abandoned us! How many ways can I tell you? And why the fuck did you want to come here to drag me through it again?!"

I couldn't fully answer that question. I ran my hands through my hair, looked him straight in the face, and kept going. "Candy left five or six times, usually after your father beat her up. But she says she couldn't bear to leave you alone there, so she always came back. She said after the third year she wanted to adopt you—"

"*Adopt??!!!*" He searched my face intently, the disdain and triumph gone.

I said firmly, "She wanted to adopt you. That's what some of their fights were about. But your father always refused. He knew if she had some legal right to you, she would have taken you away from him."

"I never heard a fucking word about this."

"Of course your father wouldn't tell you, but Candy says they fought more and more about adopting you until she realized it was hopeless. She said she called the police to come out to the house a few times when your father beat her up, but they didn't do anything. And she was sure your dad would kill her if she told him she was leaving, so the only way to escape was to disappear. She called her brother in San Francisco and asked him to come and get her. They met at a cafe near your house and planned her disappearance."

"More bullshit!" Nick yelled. "She was in that cafe with a boyfriend! I saw her!"

"It was her brother. Her *brother.* She says she never fooled around on your dad!"

In response to the commotion, Floyd trotted over and tried to get up on the sofa. "Get down!" Nick said so sternly the big animal cowered.

I knew just how the dog felt, but I continued. "It was your mother, Victoria, who had an affair. And when your father found out, she killed herself. Then he practically kept Candy under surveillance. It was a miracle she got out to see her own brother."

Nick's mouth dropped open. Victoria was his perfect mother, the one who would rescue him on a horse. I saw that I had at least accomplished one thing—his idealization of her was shattered.

I raced on, afraid if I lost momentum his defenses would close him up again. "Candy tried to contact you many times after she left. She sent you cards and letters explaining everything. She sent you birthday presents—"

"She's lying!" shouted Nick, springing up. The dog stood up too, ready for anything. "She sent me nothing! I went to the mail box every day! This is all bullshit! Everything you're saying is bullshit!"

Nick paced back and forth, his eyes ablaze, his voice as spiteful and angry as a young child's. "She could have called my school! She could have waited outside the school! She could have called me on a night when he wasn't home!"

I said quietly, "That's true. And later Candy realized it. But at the time, she was too scared for her own safety. And after a while she married someone else, and got pregnant and thought it was better to turn away and forget everything."

A slight yearning crept into his voice as he came to a standstill. "You mean I have a sister or brother?"

I shook my head. "The baby was stillborn. She says you're her only child, and she's kept these things for years in the hope that one day you'd be reunited and she could prove to you what happened."

Shakily I put the box on the coffee table, and said, "Look through this. There are letters postmarked twenty-five years ago. And a Christmas present sent back unopened."

Nick collapsed onto the sofa in front of the box. Slowly he opened it, picked up a handful of letters and leafed through them, pausing to read the dates. Then he tore open the package. Underneath the brown shipping paper was a layer of Christmas wrapping—green paper with laughing Santa Clauses.

I watched in silence as he tore away the paper. Inside was a black oblong leather case. He opened it and withdrew a musical instrument that looked like a little piano keyboard with a mouthpiece.

Holding it so tightly his knuckles were white, Nick stood up abruptly, walked down the hall into the bedroom, and shut the door.

I heard muffled sobbing and I waited, thinking it best not to intrude. Then I heard the shower running, and the toilet flush, after which Nick returned, his eyes rimmed in red, his new T-shirt and shorts fragrant with soap and baby powder.

He sat down closer to me, the Melodica in his right hand, and I took hope in the thought that he had been through the worst and come out the other side. The shaft of light from a chrome lamp fell across his face. Behind him the lights of the dock wore halos of fog.

"You had to do this, didn't you," he said quietly. "You had to break down the only barrier I had left."

"Yes. Because she's your only family, and she still loves you."

He leaned into my face suddenly, frightening me. "You have destroyed me! You have walked into my fucking home and into my heart and ripped it to shreds."

Astonished, I pulled back and stammered, "But I thought—"

"You thought I wasn't miserable enough! You had to make it worse! Look at me! I don't even know how I'll be able to maintain my sanity tomorrow in court!"

He sprang up and paced in front of me, spouting his words. "Should I beat you up? Should I call the press? Call my lawyer? How many ways would you like to be made a fool of tomorrow? How in the hell did you think you could come in here and work me over again, the way you did so many times before, and have me stand for it? Are you forgetting that you sucked me into your therapy and then let me down when I needed you most?!!"

I stood up. "But don't you see??? You will always think people are letting you down because she did! You turn everyone else into Candy, including me! Because you love her! You steal red things because they remind you of her! You need her. I'm trying to tell you she's been there for you all along! You should go back into therapy with someone else and work it out!"

He pointed toward the door. "Get the fuck out of here!"

I was too stunned at first to move. I hadn't expected this rush of anger and I didn't understand it. I had just given him the thing he wanted most in life.

"What are you waiting for?" he shouted. "Get out of here! *NOW!!!*"

I walked jerkily to the door, stepped out and shut it, and he came up behind the door and locked the dead bolt immediately. The bottom seam of the door went dark.

I sagged back against the wall. Tomorrow was going to be the worst day of my life. Atwater was going to put him on the stand to announce what I had done tonight, Underbruck would concede, and the jury would find me guilty. I sank down to the carpet, too devastated even to cry.

After a little while, I heard one tentative note on the Melodica. Then another few notes.

Grim and exhausted, I stood up, and to the tune of "Amazing Grace," walked slowly to the elevator.

64

I called Underbruck at six the next morning. When he heard what I had done there was an explosion of cussing on the other end of the line. "Did you think the guy would repent? He's going to use this to crucify you! What more proof could there be that you were in love with him than your showing up at his apartment in the middle of this lawsuit? Your goose is cooked, Doctor!"

When we appeared in court three hours later, Atwater and Nick were already there. Atwater looked like a lion after a fresh kill, having already talked to Underbruck about Nick's request to be recalled to the witness stand. Nick looked exhausted, his eyes still red, his features serious. I turned away quickly, not wanting to watch his pleasure in torturing me.

While everyone waited, the lawyers conferred with the judge, who announced that Nick would be taking the stand. Atwater told the jury that Nick had requested additional time to provide new information about my credibility.

I hated Nick. Some things are worse than death, I thought, and what I'm about to go through is one of them.

He began by saying, "Dr. Rinsley came to my apartment last night."

The courtroom broke into loud chattering, and I bowed my head momentarily. Judge Grabbe banged his gavel until the noise quieted down to a restless murmur.

"I can therefore prove with complete confidence everything I've charged."

There were whispers and nods from the jury, and Atwater turned to Underbruck and gave an apologetic shoulder shrug for the winning moment ahead.

"But the truth is that Dr. Rinsley never had sex with me and she never did anything improper with me."

Someone in the audience gasped, and a couple of reporters exited quickly. Atwater, apparently as shocked as everyone else, interrupted Nick and said, "Your Honor, I have not had enough time to confer with my client on the substance of his testimony. May I request a brief recess?"

Before the judge could reply, Nick said, "I don't want to confer, Your Honor. I have just a few more things to say for the record, and I would like permission to do so."

Judge Grabbe, looking fully awake for the first time in weeks, said, "Counsel, if you have no objection, I'll let the plaintiff go ahead."

Atwater opened her hands in a gesture of surrender and said, "No objection."

Nick continued. "Dr. Rinsley's experts were right. I fell in love with her and because I couldn't have her, I wanted to destroy her. But now I know that wanting to own someone isn't really love. Caring about someone else's needs—that's love. And in spite of my actions, Dr. Rinsley still cared enough about me to show me last night that I have a family, a fact I have steadfastly refused to believe.

"I paced the floor for hours after she left, and I have decided I can't go on with this trial. If I destroy the one person who has tried so hard to reach me, my life is hopeless."

Nick turned those beautiful blue eyes directly to me. "I want to publicly apologize to Dr. Rinsley. And to ask forgiveness from the Court and everyone else involved."

I wept with relief, and satisfaction, and something deeper: I believed again I could count on that still, small voice inside me that knew how to put into words what it felt like to be someone else. I could practice my profession again.

Back at Underbruck's office, I put my arms around his neck and kissed his cheek. His suit smelled of dry-cleaning fluid and piney cologne. "Thanks for everything," I said.

He scratched his beard. "If you had told me how this trial was going to end, I would have eaten my hat."

I called my mother first, and then Humberto. I told them quickly what had happened, and I invited Humberto for dinner the evening after next, so he could bring back Frank and we could talk. My mother said she would fly out in the morning because she was homesick, and now she could leave happily.

My face was on every local newscast. At home Mom and I called Dad, and he said, "Gimme some steel, baby." I could picture him, flat palm held upward for a hit from mine. It was his greatest compliment. I was an iron man—a tough player who keeps on pitching. "Thanks for your support, Dad," I said, and turned the phone back to Mom, so he wouldn't hear me sniffling. Iron men don't cry.

That evening, I fielded congratulatory phone calls until I was too tired to talk and had to unplug the line. Reporters milled outside my door, and I was glad Frank wasn't there, because his barking would have driven me crazy.

In the morning, I took Mom to the airport and hugged her tightly. There was so much more to say, so much more work between us to do. "I love you, Mom," I said at the boarding gate. "And you know what? I always had one advantage over Nick. No matter what the jury decided, I knew one thing for certain from the time I was old enough to know anything: I was loved."

I could not have given her any gift that would have meant more to her.

I spent the next day preparing the dinner for Humberto. First I made the appetizer tray, a mixture of patés and cheeses surrounded by crackers. Then I roasted a fresh duckling, tore up greens for a salad, and baked wild rice. I wanted almost everything prepared ahead of time so I wouldn't have to fuss in the kitchen.

In the afternoon, I set the table with my mother's china, two crystal wine goblets I bought for the occasion, white linen napkins, tall white candles in crystal bases, and a small bouquet of white roses.

I wore a flattering, black jersey dress and spent an inordinate amount of time on my face and hair. I couldn't wait to see Frank, but I was unsure of what to expect with Humberto. In the fifteen minutes before their arrival, I flitted around the apartment rechecking everything—the position of the napkins, the temperature of the wine, the lighting in the bedroom, the selection of CDs on the stereo.

When they walked in, Frank barked excitedly and rushed around in circles. I squealed and cooed and hugged him. He was so excited he raced from room to room like a rabid dog, stopping each time to lick me and bark.

Humberto wore a loose beige shirt and full-cut brown slacks, but the fabrics couldn't hide how thin he was. We hugged briefly and I could feel his ribs protruding.

My voice was too bright. I felt awkward with him, as if I barely knew him. I stepped hastily into the kitchen for the wine and he followed, pausing at the dining room table. "Your mother's china," he said softly, tracing his finger around a salad plate.

He watched me fill the goblets half full of wine, and when we clicked glasses, he said, "You look beautiful."

"Thanks," I said, triumphant in my vindication. "The spoils of war."

He sank his hand into my curls and crushed them for a moment, then let go.

I paused uncertainly. "I have a paté and cheese plate, but we'll have to leave it up here on the kitchen counter. You know Frank."

"No, no. I have something to show you. Frank! Come!"

Frank, whose frenzy of motion had diminished to a brisk walking tour of the apartment, turned and trotted obediently to Humberto and lowered his rump to the floor.

"Lie down," Humberto instructed.

Frank lay down.

"Now, we're going to put this appetizer tray on the coffee table and leave the room for five minutes. When we come back the paté and cheese will still be here."

"Sure they'll be here," I laughed, "just relocated to a canine interior." But I put the plate where directed.

"Frank, stay," Humberto commanded, and Frank, mouth drooling, lay down at the base of the coffee table and watched us.

We went into the bedroom, remained standing, and talked about the trial. After the requisite five minutes, I tiptoed to the hall and peered around the corner into the living room.

Frank, bored by having to wait and apparently trained into obedience, lay dozing on the floor next to the coffee table. The plate of food was untouched.

"What a good dog!" I said, and rushed into the living room. "Good dog!" I rubbed his ears and let him lick my hand, and he leapt up again and raced around the apartment.

"My God, Humberto, you've worked a miracle!" I said.

He flushed slightly, and standing in the doorway to the living room, he shoved his hands in his pockets. "I wanted to do something to apologize."

Remembering how Humberto had always found my dog smelly and obnoxious, I was deeply touched.

The food was excellent. Humberto raised his eyebrows in surprise as he tasted the breast of duck with blackberry sauce. "This is terrific," he said.

"Thanks."

Gradually, the tension eased as we talked about our lives during the past year. I told him what I was learning about the problems with my mother. He said the restaurant was doing so well he was thinking of starting another one in Malibu. Earlier in the year he had suffered what he thought at first was indigestion and turned out to be acute appendicitis.

"You mean you had surgery and you didn't tell me?" I asked, taken aback.

"It was before we were speaking again."

"But since then you've never mentioned it!"

He brushed some bread crumbs off his lap. "You had enough on your mind. I didn't want to bother you."

"Oh, Humberto, I would have wanted to know." I put my hand on his arm and squeezed it gently. "Are you okay now?"

"Fine. Just a little scarred up."

After dessert we did the dishes together like casual friends. He did not touch me, and uncertain of who might be in his life or how he was feeling toward me, I did not move toward him either.

My apartment had a fireplace of fake logs lit with gas jets, and I turned it on. The gas made a steady hissing sound, but the little fire was cheery, and I blew out the dining candles and turned off the overhead lights.

I placed a bottle of Courvoisier and two snifters on the coffee table, and we sat down facing each other on the sofa. He gazed at me in silence.

"Have you—are you—dating anybody now?" I finally asked.

He began rubbing his upper lip with his forefinger. "I've been seeing three or four women. How about you?"

"No." I poured the brandy to keep control of myself. Of course he was dating. I already knew that.

He picked up his brandy, swirled it around and took a sip. "When I hold someone else, I imagine it's you."

I had to fight that old voice inside—saying sure, sure—and I watched the fire for a few minutes while I finished my brandy. "Why me, Humberto? What is it about me you want instead of someone else?"

The sound of my neighbor's keys rattling outside provoked Frank into a sudden barking fit. "Frank! Down!" Humberto commanded. I watched, incredulous, as Frank sank to the carpet with no more than a quiet whine.

Humberto rubbed his upper lip with his forefinger again and then turned to me. "All my life I've been loved as someone else's trophy. When I was young, my mother used to take me to church on Sunday to show me off. Then it was women—even women I didn't know—coming on to me in the street or in the supermarket. They'd send me cute cards or little presents and leave their phone numbers. After the restaurant became successful, it was the money or the celebrity or this or that about me, but none of them was interested in the real me, not even Marisombra.

"Then I met you and I knew even from hearing you on the radio that you would be different. You really understood me. You took my interest in birds seriously. I thought you really cared for me—that's what made it so hard later."

He lowered his head. "I've been lonely since I was a small boy. I lost my grandmother too young. I had to leave my country and be a stranger in a new place. I was waiting to be discovered, and I didn't know it until you found me."

Our knees were touching, and I put my hand on his thigh. He stood up, pulled me to him and held my head. "*Cómo te he extrañado,*" how I've missed you, he murmured.

It had been so long I felt shy with him. In the bedroom when he took off his clothes I saw how painfully thin he was. The scar across his pubic line was still red and raised, and after we lay down I touched it gingerly. "Does it still hurt?"

"It just itches sometimes."

His erection came and went several times as he caressed and kissed me. Even after continuous stimulation I could not climax. I didn't know if we could overcome the distance and mistrust of the past year.

We were quiet for a while. He dozed. Then he turned on his side facing me, his head propped up by his elbow, his dark eyes troubled. "I missed you long before we stopped seeing each other."

I shut my eyes and gathered him to me. At some point we toppled over onto the carpet. I was vaguely aware of the rug burning my knees and then my tail bone. When I finally came, I cried in wracking spasms, and he rocked me and said, "Baby, baby, baby." The carpet, so close up, still smelled like bleach.

Humberto went to the bathroom and returned with a towel. I dried myself and sat partially up, noticing something in the shadows. Then I realized what it was: the whole time we had been in the bedroom, Frank had remained in the corner, shockingly polite.

Humberto helped me up, and we went to the window and looked out at the sky. The moon was new, just a thin smile in the sky, and through the branches of the sycamore tree, I could see one planet shining brightly.

For the first time in many months, the outside world came back into focus.

EPILOGUE

It is November again, a year since I last saw Nick, and a few weeks ago I received a card and photograph from him. The note said simply, "Still in therapy. Think of you often. All the best, Nick."

I studied the photograph a long time. Nick was seated at a piano, hands on the keys, his expression solemn. I wondered if a new girlfriend had taken the picture, or a buddy. Perhaps it was a time-delay photo he had taken himself.

His skin was brown from the sun. Maybe he hadn't found another job yet or he was living by the beach. He was wearing a Hawaiian shirt, a yellow-and-turquoise splash of palm trees. It was a bit wrinkled and loose, suggesting he no longer ironed all his clothes or that he was warm that day. On the piano was a can of Coke, next to a glass with some dark liquid.

I examined the fingers on the keyboard. On his right hand was a glimpse of something shiny, probably a ring. Maybe he had gone on vacation and bought himself a token, or maybe someone had given it to him.

He was looking at the piano keys, and I couldn't see the translucence and color of his eyes, but there was a relaxation to his jawline, a softness around the eyes, maybe even a hint of kindness. I knew he was happier and I imagined he was finally doing the one thing he always wanted to do. I wanted to think so.

Once, in Bandon, there was a nuthatch who nested near our house, and in early April when he was looking for a mate, he flew against our greenhouse window in the kitchen. My mother worried he would hurt himself, so persistent was he at challenging his own reflection. He was fighting off intruders for his lady, she said. We thought if we hung a towel over the window he would stop attacking, but he simply moved to a new spot and continued marking his territory.

As I studied the photograph, Nick reminded me of that nuthatch. If I had raised a towel for him in any location, he would have found another. He had to play out his scenario, as driven by his own needs as that bird was by instinct.

I work now at Kevin's clinic in Santa Monica, but I work no more than forty hours a week. My office window looks out on a private patch of grass, bracketed by wisteria and bird of paradise. Although I am the chief of clinical services, I still allow one day a week for my own private patients.

In my second week at work, I accepted a new patient into therapy—a depressed forty-five-year-old woman with panic attacks. In the middle of the first session, I said to her, "There must be moments when you're so frightened you don't know how to breathe—you don't know how you're going to get through the next hour."

Her eyes brimmed with tears, and she said, "That is exactly how it is." And then she looked at me oddly, head cocked to one side, and said, "Did you—do you have panic attacks or depression?"

I thought she might be the one person in Los Angeles who hadn't heard about my trial. Trying not to hide, I said, "I've been through hell and back, and I hope what I've learned will be helpful to you."

"There is so much to tell," she said, and we began the delicate process of unraveling it.

Three days a week now, I lie on Dandelone's couch and sift through my own experience. I take comfort from the rich smell of tobacco that permeates her office, the rows of books, the dim light, the soft timbre of her voice.

I finally told her about the big, gray thing I sometimes see looming toward my face when I fall asleep.

"How do you react?" she asked.

"Sometimes I jerk awake, frightened. Sometimes I'm fascinated by it or I keep my eyes closed and let it engulf me."

"What you're describing is called the Isakower Phenomenon. The large shadowy mass is thought to be a primitive memory of the breast, and its looming toward your face, the onset of breastfeeding."

"I've never heard of that before!"

"It's considered to be a momentary psychological fusion again with the mother, sometimes welcomed, sometimes accompanied by the dread of annihilation."

"So it's the earliest ambivalence?"

"That's the theory."

"In my case, it was followed by plenty more ambivalence."

"Yes." She put her feet up on the footstool behind me. "On that Halloween night when your mother fell, you saw clearly that she had her shortcomings. And although you've come a long way, you have yet to fully make peace with who she is."

"It's easier for me when I'm not actually with her."

"And perhaps it always will be. But we'll work on that together."

"You're talking about a solid sense of separate self. Without that you don't feel fully alive, do you?"

"No."

"Zachary used to say Nick needed me to feel his feelings so he could come alive. I guess on a smaller scale, that applies to all of us."

"Oh yes," she said softly. "In the reflected light of a loving face who sees you and knows you and loves you as you are, you are truly born."

In August, I was the maid of honor at Val and Gordon's wedding. My parents came down for the weekend, and stayed with us at Humberto's house. My mother looked slimmer and prettier than I had seen her in years, and I knew that what had changed me had also changed her.

The ceremony was held at the Bel Air Hotel, in the garden, where two swans floated lazily on the stream near us. Valerie looked breathtaking in her lace gown, with the rhinestones and pearls my mother had sewn on by hand. I walked down the aisle on Humberto's arm, and when I caught sight of my mother with tears in her eyes, I wasn't angry.

After the dinner, Humberto and I danced. The room was hot and the band was loud, and as he twirled me, it felt like one of those summer nights before Uncle Silky left, when I would race to greet my father coming home, and he would grab me and pull me up in the air and swing me around until I was dizzy.

Whirling around the dance floor with Humberto, my parents watching from a nearby table, I saved the images in my mind: Humberto smiling, beads of sweat on his forehead, working to breach the gulf between us; me, bound too tightly into the periwinkle satin dress, feet hurting in my high heels, trying to reach across my fears and embrace him; my mother, misty-eyed as she watched, a half-eaten piece of wedding cake in front of her; my father in his first rented tuxedo, his arm resting on the back of my mother's chair.

And one more image as the song finished: my father leaning to my mother tenderly to wipe from her cheek a small spot of icing.

When the band started its next waltz, I asked my father to dance.

ACKNOWLEDGMENTS

I would like to express my profound gratitude to Sandra Scofield, who took my writing seriously and gave so generously of her time, wisdom, and encouragement. I am grateful to Tony Gardner and Frank Wuliger for being willing to represent me with a manuscript that needed work. Many thanks to my editor, Laurie Bernstein, for her excellent suggestions, her patience and persistence.

Both Joan Sanger and Joan Kalvelage contributed invaluable ideas to this book and I appreciate the time they devoted to it. Thanks also to Betsy Beers, Dori Appel, Jan Gregory, and Leah Ireland for their time and opinions, and to Pamela Thatcher and Michele Licht for their legal advice.

I reserve my deepest gratitude for my husband, Bob Comfort, who saw something in me I didn't know was there, and gave me the opportunity to discover it.